Happy Reading!

M. Reed McCall

3/2015

Moose Tracks on the Road to Heaven

M. Reed McCall

ISBN-13 (Trade Paperback): 978-0-9862467-0-8
ISBN-13 (eBook): 978-0-9862467-1-5

"Red Trillium" photo credit: Robert Johnstone

Cover and interior design by Bri Bruce Productions

Cover image courtesy of Getty Images

Published by Teabury Books

Visit mreedmccall.com for more information.

For the real Pa and Ma, who taught me the
true meaning of love generously given.
Death is a transition and life is a gift meant to be *lived*.
I will remember.

You are always in my heart. . . .

Acknowledgements

The work of this book happened over many years, and I had a great deal of help and inspiration along the way. In particular I'd like to thank:

My husband John and daughters Megan and Rebecca, for their love, support, and patience over the past few years, even those times when I got so carried away with writing that I burned the green beans or broccoli to the bottom of the pan (more than once, I'm sorry to say . . . one pan had to be tossed after it had happened too often). I love you more than I can say.

Samantha Malagré, friend, journalist, teacher, and author of the upcoming book, *Brandon Lee: A Life Worth Remembering*, for countless lengthy emails and discussions about the nature of grief and its context in the wake of the sudden loss of a loved one. Your insights helped me to create some of the emotional resonance of this novel.

Dr. Melinda McMinn, Palliative Care Team Medical Director, whose unfailing care, understanding, and support of my father in his final illness were true gifts. I and our entire family will always be grateful to you. Your kindness, insight, and consummate professionalism will never be forgotten.

All six of my "real life" sisters and two "Fresh Air" sisters, for the drama, humor, hijinks, and, above all, love as we were growing up and beyond to adulthood. You have each added something special to the fabric of my life. This novel is indeed a work of fiction, but so many of the beautiful and meaningful moments and emotions in it are very real, thanks to all of you.

My parents, for the wisdom, humor, sense of home and family, wonderful memories, and the unconditional love you gave me, not only as a child, but always. You provided the bones of this story and encouraged me to flesh it out and share it with the world. I could never put into words what you mean to me, so I will just have to settle for a simple "thank you." I appreciate and love you both beyond measure.

My generous beta readers, who gave of their time and energies to not only read parts or all of this book in various stages, but also to provide invaluable feedback along the way: my sisters Linda Grahame and

Deborah Stanton, my mother, Marion C. Reed, my father, David L. Reed (who before he died was able to read and give me feedback on about fifty pages of the book—scenes that ended up in the middle third of the novel), and kind friends and colleagues Michelle Boylan, Dr. Christine Dawson, Kathie DeKalb, Cyndra Flanagin, Theresa Kovian, Kat Simmons, and Lisa Trembley.

And Bri Bruce, of Bri Bruce Productions, for all your help in creating the cover, editing, formatting, and getting this book ready to go out into the world.

I thank you all.

"TO LIVE IN HEARTS WE LEAVE BEHIND IS NOT TO DIE."

- Inscription on Pa and Ma's Headstone
Peaceful Glen Cemetery
Adirondack Mountains, New York

The Wright Family Tree

David (Pa) Wright	~	born 1929
Elizabeth (Ma) Wright	~	born 1932

The Girls

Anne Cecelia	~	born 1955
Melanie Lynne (Mel)	~	born 1957
Katherine Margaret (Kat)	~	born 1960
Lisa Marie	~	born 1961
Jennifer Josephine (Jen)	~	born 1965
Patricia Dawn (Trish)	~	born 1966
Alexandra Wallis (Alex aka "Zippy")	~	born 1968
Elena Elizabeth (El/Ellie)	~	born 1969

The Good Neighbors

Hank ("Pops") Steiner	~	born 1928
Gladys Steiner	~	born 1930, died 2004
James (Jim) Steiner	~	born 1955, died 1973

The Bad Neighbor

Joe Durbowecz	~	born 1934

WGRR FM 103.9, THE BEAR

"Give a Growl for the Adirondacks'
Most Trusted Radio Station"
January 16, 1969

Welcome back, Adirondack listeners. It's Willard T. Boggs here with you on another frigid Thursday evening in the North Country. Reports have come in that the ice is now twenty-one inches thick on Seventh Lake. It looks like most of the hearty souls who venture out this week in hopes of catching a few trout or whitefish will be spending their time in ice shanties, sipping from flasks more often than checking their lines. Sorry about that, ladies, but at least if your mister comes home empty-handed, you'll know why.

In entertainment news, actress Ethel Merman, whose powerful singing voice is the delight of stage and film audiences, was born on this date in 1908 in Queens, New York.

And last, but certainly not least, a three-quarter moon last Friday signaled the arrival of a baby at North Country General as Dave and Elizabeth Wright of Moose Junction added a new bundle of sugar and spice to their brood. Yes, it's another girl, bringing the total in the family to eight. Watch out, Adirondack softball enthusiasts. One more and there'll be enough Wright girls to field a fast-pitch team all by themselves!

Of course a boy would throw a monkey wrench into that prospect, so for now we'll hold off and just send out a WGRRRReat big congratulations to the whole family. Look for the new arrival being wheeled around the Super Duper, where Mrs. Wright will surely be spending a lot of time getting groceries. . . .

Prologue

Eternity is not something that begins after you are dead.
It is going on all the time.

- Charlotte Perkins Gilman

Until she was five years old, Elena Elizabeth Wright Maguire believed she was an ordinary girl.

Then she went to kindergarten and realized other kids didn't think it was normal to salvage mummified squirrels and bird skeletons, search the woods for ghosts of Adirondack hermits, or look forward to cemetery visits. Of course some of them went to the cemetery when they *had* to, just not for the reasons Elena and her family did: to experience the peacefulness, examine interesting headstones, or maybe leave some leftover Easter candy for the invisible residents to enjoy later.

It never occurred to Elena to keep her ideas about such things to herself, and so it was that after a few conversations with startled classmates over midmorning snack and cartons of faintly sour-smelling milk, she'd been forced to entertain a troubling possibility that she was, in fact, *different*.

It had been a tough pill to swallow.

What had made her this way? She remembered someone once telling her that people were born with the seeds of their own finished personalities inside them, waiting to sprout and seek out the light. That no matter what you did or didn't do, you couldn't change your basic nature.

She didn't know how she felt about that. Truth be told, she almost didn't get the chance to find out. Even before the dodgy reception by her pint-sized peers, Elena had lived through two personal and unexpected encounters with the Grim Reaper (more details on that in a bit). However, many considered her surviving to adulthood at all an even greater accomplishment, since being born dead-last into a large family of girls came with its own special set of challenges.

Yes, except for her beloved father, Pa, every member of Elena's household had double “X” chromosomes (even the dog), and she learned early on that underestimating a houseful of females in various stages of hormonal crisis could be lethal. Bringing up the rear of this estrogen-laced version of running the gauntlet helped her blossom into what her maternal grandma had called a “singular” young lady, but most people didn’t notice anything just by looking at her. It took a while and a few conversations to realize what was different about the way she thought and felt.

Let’s go back, for instance, to the subject of death.

Elena’s two youthful run-ins with the Reaper hadn’t caused any permanent emotional scars (though there were a couple of physical ones); instead, she’d carried with her a bone-deep awareness of life’s impermanence, along with a tendency at moments of deep fear or distress to murmur a phrase that broke her father’s heart and earned teasing from certain sisters each time she uttered it: “Am I going to die, Pa?”

The first brush with eternity happened the summer after she’d turned four, at the bustling Adirondack theme park called Fairytale Adventure. She’d been bucked off the live pony-ride—an attraction where children rode tethered ponies round and round in a circle for a pre-set length of time. Unbeknownst to anyone, Elena’s pony had been in the harness for too long. A sore had developed near the edge of his saddle. An insect might have landed on the raw place, or perhaps Elena had accidentally touched it. She couldn’t remember.

Whatever it was, a jumble of sights, sounds, and not very nice feelings had followed that instant as she’d sailed through the air and landed with a crunching thud a dozen feet away. She’d later learned that her skull had narrowly missed a rock when she’d finally reconnected with Earth. She didn’t know any of that at the time, though. She only knew that her shoulder ached something fierce, her collarbone having snapped upon impact.

However, if all else was muddled, the memory of looking up and seeing the worry in Pa’s handsome face had stuck with her, vivid as blood upon snow. He’d scooped her up and carried her tucked against his chest all the way to the park entrance, where they would find their van and go on to the hospital.

As he moved her swiftly through the crowd, that desperate question had slipped out in a whisper. Pa had met her gaze, his striking blue eyes filled with such love for her, and he’d answered in a calm and reassuring voice that, no, she wasn’t going to die. And so Elena had nodded in grave acceptance, blinking away any lingering tears. He was her Pa—the best Pa in the whole world—and he always told her the truth.

But the anxiety of the experience still lingered in the back of her mind when the second brush with eternity swooped down about ten months later. This time it came in the form of a very large Saint Bernard dog suffering from a hidden brain ailment. One minute Elena had been standing in the driveway of a large house up the road, right next to her oldest sister, Anne (who happened to be friends with the teenaged girl whose family owned the dog), and the next thing she knew she was dangling head-first out of the massive canine's jaws.

One of the animal's incisor teeth had sunk into Elena's right eye socket; once her sister and the friend had managed to subdue the dog and pry its mouth open to free her, blood had poured from that and a few other puncture wounds on her scalp. It had prevented her from seeing much of anything except a reddish blur as she was rushed into the neighbor's house and a wet cloth was pressed to her head until Pa could race up the road (in the van this time) and spirit her away to the hospital yet again.

She'd struggled mightily to recall Pa's words of comfort to her whispered query on this occasion after seeing a mirrored glimpse of her face covered in blood. She was certain that this time he couldn't possibly be right. This time she *was* going to die.

But she didn't.

The nurse wrapped her in some kind of restraining device so the doctor could stitch her wounds. Then she'd been bandaged and sent home to recuperate. She hadn't lost her eye, though it had been scratched by the dog's fang. She'd forever bear a one-inch scar beneath her eyebrow from the stitches, but the worst of that damage had healed by the time she entered kindergarten that autumn.

And so perhaps it was in part because of these two experiences that Elena was pretty matter-of-fact about what others liked to call "passing over" when she was little. She was used to thinking about it. And that kind of acceptance, especially for one so young, tended to make people nervous.

Still, it wasn't something she could take the *full* blame for. As mentioned earlier, her family's unusual way of handling many things, including the subject of mortality, added to her outlook, too. In the end she was thankful for it, but there were times, especially in those years after she'd entered school, when even she didn't quite know what to make of it.

Here's an example: The general consensus in Moose Junction was that her parents had been a bit odd in opting to purchase their own headstone and cemetery plot when Elena was seven. Neither Ma nor Pa had had any reason to believe death was imminent. Both were in their forties, in fact. But they'd decided it was wise to be ready.

In keeping with that philosophy, a few times a year they'd bundled the family into the old Volkswagen van, making a pilgrimage to visit their plot and wander around the cemetery. Sometimes they'd even bring a picnic lunch.

Once Pa had gone there by himself to take double exposure pictures of the headstone and then of him sitting near it in various poses with a blanket draped over half of his head. In the finished product, he and the blanket had looked transparent against the headstone, thereby producing a creative representation of himself as a "ghost," sitting at his own graveside.

They'd all laughed when they saw the prints, but no one in the family considered it morbid. Ma and Pa used humor and whatever else they could to ensure none of their daughters felt anxious about death. It was just another phase in the cycle of life, and it should be accepted as such, rather than denied or avoided until it smacked them in the face.

Of course Elena was also the only person she'd ever known whose mother played hide and seek in coffins as a child with a neighbor boy whose family owned a funeral parlor, while Pa in his teen years (long before he met Ma) had been in the habit of taking all the pretty girls one at a time to the cemetery so they could do a little passionate necking behind the gravestones.

With that kind of combined DNA, she'd reasoned, what kind of chance did she have?

(After-Easter visit)

The Homestead
Moose Junction, Upstate New York
May 25, 1975
Elena is six years old

Every goodbye is the birth of a memory. . . .

The mood was solemn as they completed the ritual, interrupted only by seven-year-old Zippy's occasional hiccup. She and her little sister, Elena, stood on one side of the small hole Pa had dug near the Wright family's one-room camp in the woods behind the garage; both girls clutched handfuls of freshly picked, blood-dark trillium (a.k.a. *stinkpots*, for the wet-dog fragrance of the flowers). The shovel Pa had used lay nearby, cradling a newspaper-wrapped bundle in its square-edged scoop.

Jen, who at almost ten years old was considered mature enough to handle the duty, held a homemade cross of tied-together sticks. Kat, Lisa, and Patricia stood a little behind Pa along with Anne and Melanie, who were home from college for the summer. Kat looked ready to roll her eyes at any moment, but managed to keep her opinions to herself, thanks to a pointed look from Ma, who stood behind Zippy and Elena, one hand resting on each of their shoulders.

"Who wants to say a few words?" Pa looked from Jen to Zippy, and then to Elena, since they were all standing nearest to the grave. All three gazed back at him, and Elena's eyes welled with tears.

"Rest in peace," Jen murmured.

"I hope you find a friend to play with in heaven," Zippy added.

Kat snickered at that, hiding the sound behind a cough at the last minute when Ma raised her eyebrow. Elena was too preoccupied with the task at hand to really notice. Then it was her turn to speak.

"I can't think of anything good, Pa. You do it. You always know the right words."

Pa nodded in all seriousness and looked up for a moment at the blue sky with wispy white clouds just visible through the treetops, before dropping his gaze again to the newly dug burial spot as he spoke. "Now he can be happy without any worries. Have a good journey. Amen."

"Amen," everyone intoned after him. Then they all waited in silence as Pa lifted the shovel and gently placed into the hole the newspaper-wrapped body of the "road kill" woodchuck that Jen, Elena, Patricia, and Zippy had found on their walk along the road past the Steiner's house and up the hill yesterday.

After filling in the hole with dirt and patting it down, Pa nodded to Jen. She placed the cross, adding it to the dozen or so other markers that had been pushed into the dirt nearby to identify the sometimes mummified corpses they'd find on the road or in the woods and ask Pa to retrieve and bury (because animals had rights, too) in their "Animal Graveyard."

Elena let out a sigh of relief after placing her stinkpots on the new grave, feeling better already about the lost little creature at least having been treated with more respect in death than it had been given in life.

Shortly thereafter, Zippy broke off a dead branch from a nearby tree and swatted at Elena with it, chanting, "Slow poke, slow poke!" before running off shrieking, followed in close pursuit by Elena, who screamed, "I hate you, you big meanie!" while she scowled and clenched her fists. Jen, who was always up for a friendly challenge (not to mention that, as an older sister, it was her unspoken job to make sure nothing got out of hand) brought up the rear and kept any blood from spilling. Pa picked up the shovel to return it to the shed before rejoining the rest of family as they made their way back toward the house to eat the lunch of hotdogs and beans Ma was keeping warm for them on the stove.

Chapter One

Maple Creek, Upstate New York
October 30, 2007

As might be expected, Elena evolved from the quirky girl she'd been to the (mostly reasonable) woman she became by her thirties, the transition joyful in some parts and devastating in others as happens for anyone who inhabits this world long enough. Eventually, however, her life settled into a comfortable rhythm and stayed that way . . . until about ten weeks before her thirty-ninth birthday when trouble crashed both literally and figuratively into her routine existence.

We'll get to the event itself in a bit. For now, suffice it to say that it was important in a lasting way, a catalyst in helping transform the way Elena viewed herself, people she loved, and even the universe at large. But at the onset, it all kind of snuck up on her (as momentous changes sometimes do).

The actual date commencing all this was apropos for its unexpected nature, since long before Halloween cornered the market for autumn holidays, Mischief Night, which was the prank-filled night *before* All Hallow's Eve, was more the rage. However, like most people, Elena didn't know that history, and she certainly had no inkling of the great upheaval about to be unleashed on her life.

In fact, October 30th began for her just like any other, with little Violet waking her before six and Max rolling over with a snore until his alarm went off half an hour later. Their two older girls, Claire and Jillian, weren't up yet, but when they came downstairs, they'd be muttering at having to get up for school when it was still dark and rainy outside. Not that they really had anything to complain about. It had been a sunny autumn, but now it was just two days shy of November, and anyone in the North Country of New York State could tell you that meant the unofficial start of winter.

Elena buried her head deeper into her pillow as she listened to the babble of sing-song phrases coming through the monitor they still used to hear the baby (who couldn't really be classified as such any longer, since she was going on three years old now, but like Max always said, you couldn't spell the word "smother" without "mother" so the monitor stayed for now). Violet had just learned the words to a few lines of her new favorite nursery song, "All Through the Night," and was giving it a try as she waited for her mama to come get her.

"Are you getting up?" Max mumbled from under the blankets.

Elena thought about answering him with something smart like, "No, I'm going to go back to sleep and let you take over for once," but she restrained herself and instead rolled over (in the process managing to dig her elbow into Max with the stealth of a ninja) to squint at the clock.

Almost on cue with the minute display changing, Violet shifted to a warbling cadence of "Mama-up, Vi-awake!" and Elena rolled out of bed, wishing as always for another hour, or ten, of sleep. She knew she should count her blessings. At least she wasn't being roused to the sounds of crying, like she'd been when fourteen-year-old Claire was a baby. Jillian, who was now ten, had been a mixed bag depending on whether or not she was getting another ear infection. Since Violet's first day home, she was almost always happy in the morning.

Pulling on her robe, Elena peered out the side of the shades. It was just as she'd suspected: more rain. She closed her eyes for a second, imagining sun and blue skies. Violet started singing again, a little louder, and she let the shade fall, making a quick dash to the bathroom before she went to get her youngest. Tomorrow was another day and another chance for sunny weather. No use wishing (or worrying) your life away, Ma had always said. There was plenty of time if you wanted to feel lousy down the road.

Pushing her sleeves up to wash her hands, she glanced down at the outside of her left arm where distinct, threading scars trailed upward, disappearing into the bunched up fabric above her elbow. The marks glowed white in the fluorescent glare. *Nothing new there*. Her face was another story. As she washed her hands, she squinted at herself in the mirror. Not good. She'd need some major help this morning. A nighttime visit from the no-wrinkles-or-gray-hair fairy would have been nice. Maybe she *should* have gone to that Botox party last Christmas like Zippy had suggested, but the thought of needles poking her in the face still made her shudder, wrinkles or not.

Grimacing, she turned off the water hard enough to make the pipes squeal and dried her hands. In a perfect world, she wouldn't have had to go to work (even though she liked her part-time job as a research specialist at the local library well enough), but she'd long ago accepted that perfection rarely existed on Earth. Luck was another matter. To that end she played the lottery once a week. Only three more days until the next drawing, called out on the news by Yolanda Vega. . . .

A few minutes later she was in Violet's room, wrapped in a morning hug as she carried her downstairs for some Rice Krispies with sliced bananas, and then poured herself her first cup of coffee. Soon enough Max would be up to keep an eye on Violet so Elena could hop in the shower and get ready for work.

Not long after Elena came back downstairs, dressed and set to go, the cat threw up on the living room rug, Claire scowled and stomped into her room to pretend to wash her face and (actually) change her clothes when informed that she had on too much makeup and her jeans were too tight, Jillian spilled half a gallon of milk on the floor trying to be a big girl by getting her own breakfast, and Max needed help finding his cell phone.

In other words, the day rolled on pretty much as usual with none of them the wiser about what was coming.

WGRR FM 103.9, THE BEAR

"Give a Growl for the Adirondacks'
Most Trusted Radio Station"
October 31, 1974

Welcome back, Adirondack listeners. It's Willard T. Boggs here with you on a cold North Country All Hallow's Eve. The temperature is already down to forty degrees. If you haven't harvested your pumpkins for jack-o-lanterns and such, get 'em in soon. The frost that wilted the vines a week ago is strong enough now to hard-freeze the fruit. No one likes a rotted pumpkin, which is just what you'll have when you bring a frozen one indoors and it thaws.

This Day in History is handpicked for you poetry lovers out there. On this day in 1795, John Keats was born. He penned "When I Have Fears That I May Cease to Be," a title that is fitting in light of the catastrophe last evening.

As almost everyone knows by now, Don Luftkin's barn burned down last night in a Mischief Night prank turned deadly. Young Elmer Jones and Travis Davies made a tunnel in the hay bales and accidentally started the inferno with a candle they lit to play cards. Moose Junction next-door neighbors and longtime friends Dave Wright and Hank Steiner were passing by late on their way home from work at the military base when they spotted the flames. The boys were saved, but the barn collapsed with more than a hundred milkers trapped inside.

A spaghetti dinner is in the works to try to raise funds to help the Luftkins rebuild. Anyone wishing to donate should contact the station. And of course a "WGRReat!" job goes out to Dave and Hank for helping to prevent an even greater tragedy and loss of life by their keen attention and quick actions.

(Carved pumpkins on the porch before and after snow)

Chapter Two

Maple Creek, Upstate New York
October 30, 2007

At four o'clock on the afternoon that changed everything, Claire was still tied up at volleyball practice, but Elena was on her way to pick up Violet from the sitter and Jillian from her after-school program. Even more annoying for a catalyzing event, it happened in the blink of an eye. Glowering rain clouds made the afternoon seem more like night than day, and it was clear that Mother Nature was brewing something big.

The wind was blowing to beat the band, tossing leaves all over the road and adding to the general wildness of the afternoon. It was the kind of afternoon Elena had always loved, as long as she was indoors with a cup of tea, cozy as she watched the world through the safety of their big picture window.

Today she was out in the thick of it, when the heavens opened up in a lightning-cracked downpour. She'd just turned off Sleepy Hollow Road onto Jasper when it happened. There was a blur of metallic blue and a blinding light. A surge of adrenaline swept through her, and she managed to draw in a single breath before the impact of metal crunching against metal rocked her senses—along with the stinging collision of the air bag striking her face and upraised hands.

Car accident.

She hadn't been in one since . . .

Her mind blocked out the details as it always did when something jarred her into thinking about it. Still, she felt the rumble of those long-suppressed memories tipping her backward to that day. Fear rose up before she could stop it, kept at bay only by the realization that she was alone in the car this time. That it was different in so many ways. . . .

Then everything was still.

Vaguely she heard the staccato rhythm of the rain on the car roof, accompanied by the sound of steam hissing, and a fainter echo of music playing. Chemical dust from the airbag swirled through the interior, smelling like gunpowder, and she knew her skin should be burning from where the bag made impact, but strangely there was no pain. She was in shock, she supposed. Her head felt heavy and she was disoriented.

She tried to open her eyes, but she was having trouble overcoming the urge to surrender to the darkness that seemed to siphon away her thoughts as swiftly as Violet's bath bubbles gurgling down the tub drain. She felt sleepy. A nap couldn't hurt. Help was sure to come soon. It had better, because she needed to frost the pumpkin cupcakes for Jillian's class party tomorrow.

Elena decided to make one more attempt to regain her concentration before allowing herself to drift into the black void beckoning her. Focusing all her energy, she tried to look around, but everything was blurry and dim. She wasn't even sure her eyes were open.

And then suddenly Jesse was there, and Elena gave a little gasp.

The logical part of her mind knew it wasn't possible, but she couldn't help wanting to hold on to the image of him as long as she could. He smiled at her, looking exactly as he had more than twenty years ago, his blue eyes crinkling at the corners and his handsome face illuminated like some kind of light was shining on it. The glow even lit his hair, making strands of it gold.

She saw the shadow of another figure behind him, but she couldn't make out any detail. Jesse nodded, and the words "It's going to be fine, stay calm, don't move" filled her mind even though no one spoke. She tried to smile back at him, feeling tears sting her eyes as bittersweet memories spilled through her.

But before she had time to understand what she was experiencing, the feelings multiplied tenfold, overwhelming her with a rush of love and longing—and then the switch flipped at last, dropping her into the darkness.

WGRR FM 103.9, THE BEAR

"Give a Growl for the Adirondacks'
Most Trusted Radio Station"
July 5, 1968

Welcome back, Adirondack listeners. It's Willard T. Boggs here with you on a sweltering Friday afternoon. The famous dog days of summer don't usually arrive until August, but you'd never know it by the weather today. Business is booming at Lake Pines Park, especially Stan's Ice Cream. Stop by for a Sno-Cone and tell Stan that Willard sent you. He'll give you a dime off your choice. You can thank me by calling the station and casting a vote with the manager for an air conditioner in the broadcast room. Don't come in person, though, or you'll be treated to an eyeful of the Hawaiian shorts I'm wearing to stay cool.

During this heat wave, make sure to thank any French people you know. Yes, folks, it was on This Day in History that the bikini made its debut in Paris in 1946. Oooh, la, la, those Parisians sure know how to keep fashion interesting.

On a tamer note, in news from downstate, we're told that former local resident Janie Simms and her husband, NFL great Jim Wilder, are the proud parents of a new baby boy. Grandma Simms, who still lives in Moose Junction, reports that the baby has been named Jesse James Wilder. All of us at WGRR send our congratulations, along with the hope that young Jesse will follow in his father's career footsteps as opposed to those of his other namesake.

And now stay tuned for a word from our sponsor, Wild Root Cream Oil, for taming the most unruly hair. . . .

Chapter Three

Maple Creek, Upstate New York
October 30, 2007

Looking back on the accident with the buffer of a little time to cushion it, some came to see it as providential. A tune-up for things to come. Whatever you want to call it, it set into motion events and realizations that would change Elena forever, even if she had to be dragged to them kicking and screaming.

Before continuing, however, something should be made clear: she didn't die in the crash (the proliferation of "dead person" narrators in modern fiction notwithstanding). There was no "crossing over" or even what some people might term a near-death experience, wherein the soul leaves the body only to come zooming back in once the person is revived. What, exactly, did she experience in the moments after the accident? Well, that remained to be determined. She'd felt Jesse's presence at a bone-deep level, that much was certain. She'd seen him sitting next to her, there in the car.

Jesse.

Even acknowledging his name sent something strange, dark, and dangerous spiraling through her insides. She could feel herself teetering on the edge of memories she wasn't ready to take out and examine. So she pushed back, blocking them out, and forcing them under the veil of conscious thought as best as she could. It was like slapping a piece of duct tape over a crack on the big dam near Lake Pines, but it was enough for now.

She remembered sitting there in the soupy dark of her damaged car, smelling burnt chemicals from the airbag, her head pounding. A lot of other parts didn't feel so great, either, but her head was the worst. She was conscious when the emergency vehicles arrived, but so groggy that the medics opted to place her on a backboard with her neck immobilized before they hauled her to the hospital, sirens blaring.

Max rushed there as soon as someone called him about the accident. Because Elena was awake, they let him see her even though she was still in the emergency room. He told her the sitter had brought Violet home while he'd picked up Jillian, and Claire was keeping an eye on both her sisters until he got home from the hospital (she'd earned her babysitting certificate from Red Cross when she was twelve).

Max had never been a huge talker in public, but he placed his big, warm hand on Elena's arm and sat with her while she waited on the gurney in the hallway for the next in the series of x-rays, CT scans, and examinations they'd lined up for her. By then they'd given her some kind of pain medication and applied salve to the minor burns she'd sustained from the airbag, so she was feeling physically a little better. All the big tests seemed to turn out all right, but the doctors told her she'd need to stay the night for observation and rest.

Because of that, Max ended up bringing all three kids to visit at the hospital after supper to give her kisses and hugs goodnight. Seeing them made Elena's throat ache, even though she had wanted more than anything to see them and reassure them that Mama was all right.

Long before visiting hours ended, Ma and Pa arrived, too, their worry helping them make the thirty-five-minute drive in record time with Ma at the wheel. They both might have been in the latter half of their 70s, but they looked and acted at least a decade younger. Good genes, maybe, but a lifetime of hard work, homemade food, and the occasional highball of Black Velvet mixed with ginger ale didn't hurt, either.

Pa kept his cool during the entire visit, but Elena could see how unsettled he was. Of course, even when she was a little kid, Pa had always hated seeing her hurt. He'd scoop her up and call for the Mercurochrome if she so much as skinned a knee.

Ma got teary as soon as she walked into Elena's hospital room, and then she got to work, adjusting her pillows and making sure she had plenty of ice in her water in between giving her hugs. After that she just sat there and held Elena's hand like she used to when Elena was little and had to stay home from school with a bug or something. In quintessential "Ma" style, before she left the hospital she assured her youngest daughter that she'd stop by her house in Maple Creek and make certain the cupcakes for Jillian's class were frosted before she and Pa headed home.

Seeing Pa and Ma calmed Elena's jostled emotions. It had always been like this for her (Zippy used to make fun of her for admitting that, even to herself). But as much as Elena soaked up every second of seeing her parents, she convinced them to tell her sisters within driving distance not to fuss by trying to come by the hospital tonight, reminding them that she'd be released and home by the following morning.

It wasn't that she didn't love her family. The truth was that, similar to the majority of the adult population, she hated being the center of attention. Many people who knew her found that kind of ironic, since her closest (age-wise) sister, Zippy, was the poster child for being *not* like most of humanity, having graduated high school and then literally become a movie star.

Other people tended to find it funny—or else they wanted to read deep, psychological principles into why one sister was so . . . *public*, while the one born just eleven months later was so intensely private.

All Elena knew was that the only time she didn't mind everyone focusing on her was when she was at work, and that was only because she knew what she was doing and was good at it. It helped that at work she was around books all the time. They were comforting: solid on the outside with magic on the inside. She felt like she was in her element when she was in the library. Being the focus of a medical emergency was an entirely different animal.

The extra uneasiness had started right after she was taken by the medics from her car. Add to it the fact that some of those emotions she'd buried so carefully all those years ago had been stirred up, and she was having a hard time finding her equilibrium again. She couldn't cram everything back into the neat little box she'd kept it in for so long.

This was a problem.

She didn't realize how big of a problem at first. In her usual way, she tried to ignore it. Scarlett "Tomorrow is Another Day" O'Hara had nothing on Elena Wright Maguire and her ability to catalog and to rationalize. She considered this a talent in certain circumstances, but in others it could be a curse. She had no idea which it would turn out to be this time.

Have you ever watched someone decorate a cake with one of those funnel-shaped bags full of icing? If you cram too much in, it oozes out the top when you squeeze it to do the decorating. An odd choice of metaphor, perhaps, but the cake of Elena's life was only partially trimmed, and her stirred up emotions were like that frosting, packed to overflowing inside the little white piping bag.

She continued on, determined to maintain control and to keep squeezing the amount *she* wanted through the tip, as slowly as possible.

You've probably noticed that what we intend in life isn't always what we get. The best laid plans and all that, courtesy of Robert Burns and adopted by John Steinbeck as a title for one of his novels, later. All it takes is too much icing in the bag, some extra pressure, and a little time before, odds are, you're going to end up with a colorful mess on your hands.

(The Halloween cupcakes)

The Homestead
Moose Junction, Upstate New York
November 15, 1982
Elena is thirteen years old

Families are like fudge—mostly sweet with a few nuts. . . .

The Wright family's "Bad Neighbor," Joe Durbowecz, was watching them.

Again.

Lurking in his usual spot behind the woodpile on his side of the ditch, he was spying on Elena and Jen while they took down the badminton net for the winter. Ma was in the house cooking up a pot of her famous hamburger and vegetable soup with a side of cornbread muffins. Not long ago, Pa had been out in the red shed, cleaning the lawn mower to put it away for the season, but he'd been forced to take a break and go into town to get some more of the grease he needed to lubricate the fittings.

Zippy, the only other person home at the moment, was holed up in her room poring over the latest *Tiger Beat Magazine*, featuring a pullout centerfold of drool-worthy Michael Damian (who she considered the hunkiest celebrity under twenty-five, even though she wasn't allowed to watch *The Young and The Restless*).

Only Jen and Elena were aware of Joe's covert presence . . . and they were getting ready to do something about it.

A crackle of dry twigs told them what end of the fifteen-foot stacked pile of split wood concealed him. Over the course of the past dozen or so years, the older Wright sisters had passed down information about Joe to their younger siblings: He was nosey and a little creepy, but mostly harmless.

Still, it was no fun having a neighbor like him. He kept his survey map handy to make sure you didn't "cross his property line" when you were out in the woods playing, and threw rocks and shouted at the deer that sometimes wandered out into his yard looking for food when the seasons changed and edibles got scarce. You could often see him skulking around his yard, setting out poison to kill the rabbits and other small animals that dared to nibble at his garden, and scowling (even though he wasn't that old and shouldn't have been cranky).

He was creepy because he almost always managed to be outside when any of the Wright girls were sunbathing in the backyard, and you could be sure to find him (and hear him) revving up his lawnmower whenever the family had a cookout or company over in the nice weather. All in all he wasn't a very nice person, and none of the girls could ever remember having a conversation with him about anything, because he simply wouldn't respond if one of them tried even to wave to him from across the yard.

Jen was almost seventeen now, and she'd decided it was time for her—and Elena if she could talk her into it—to take up the torch left to her by her older sisters in college or even beyond, involved in marriages and families of their own. Before she'd left home, Kat especially had offered various bits of advice to her younger siblings for how to best deal with Joe, from outright ignoring him to making direct eye contact, waving, and calling out a loud, "Hello there, Mr. Durbowecz!" Both methods worked temporarily, but the change never lasted. Sooner or later, Joe would be back to his spying and generally being a bad neighbor.

Jen felt it was her moral obligation to concoct a plan for putting Joe off (hopefully) for a long time, if not for good. Once Elena heard the details, she was in. It was extreme, but it played to Elena's sense of justice, not to mention that letting loose a little sounded like a lot of fun.

They'd planned it carefully, knowing they'd have to wait until Pa wasn't home. If he was around, Elena was afraid she couldn't pull off her part of the plan; she was nowhere near as talented as Zippy, but she could be a good actress when she needed to be . . . just not when it came to Pa. One look from him, and she'd feel compelled to spill the beans about whatever she was up to (another quality that had earned Zippy's teasing over the years).

But now the time had come.

Jen gave Elena a sideways glance as she lifted the net-pole on her end and started to wind it vertically toward Elena. Responding to the signal her older sister gave her, Elena carefully slid her gaze toward the woodpile, just in time to see the telltale movement of Joe's red-and-black checked cap as he ducked back out of view again.

Good. He was still there, spying.

She gave one quick nod and Jen stiffened up like she'd been shocked with a thousand volts of electricity, dropping her end of the net and letting her eyes go wide, while her jaw fell slack.

"Oh, no!" she shrieked, her right arm shooting up to lock straight and tight next to her head, her right hand flapping in that upraised position like a flag atop a pole. "Help, Elena. It's happening again!"

As she called out her plea (worthy of an Academy Award, Elena thought with pride), Jen made what appeared to be a desperate effort to drag the offending limb down with her left hand, only to have it pop back up to the extended, above-her-head position as soon as she let go of it. This process repeated twice more as Elena did her best to appear frantic with worry, running in circles around her sister and trying to soothe her with loudly called comments like, "It's okay, keep calm!" and "Do you want me to get Ma?" and "Just try to keep your arm against your side!"

They heard a muffled sound near the woodpile, and Jen took the opportunity to take her acting job one step further, her right hand shooting up this time to just beneath her chin instead of above her head. Her fingers wrapped around her own throat in a pantomime of choking herself, as she kept making the appropriate strangled sounds and staggering around the yard like a drunken sailor, Elena in pursuit.

This time there was no mistaking the noise coming from across the ditch. Several chunks of wood toppled off the stacked pile with a thud, and the red-and-black checked hat went flying as Joe himself fell sideways from behind the woodpile, his eyes bugging out of his head. He scooted backward, crab-like, for a yard or two before scrambling to his feet. Then, without stopping to try to replace the logs that had fallen, he sprinted to his own house as if the hounds of Hell were nipping at his heels.

Jen and Elena barely made it around the far corner of their own house before they both collapsed to the ground in a fit of guffaws, unable to catch their breath and only managing to get control of themselves when Elena got a piece of grass up her nose and started sneezing. When they were no longer gasping so much, they sat back up, helping each other smooth out their mussed up hair and brushing away all the dried grass and leaves that were clinging to their clothes.

When they could breathe again, they made their way into the back yard again to see that there was no sign of Joe. Not even a light on inside his house. Mission accomplished. At least for now.

Grinning, they finished their original task of stowing the rolled up badminton net in the red shed and made their way to the house, linked arm-in-arm. About twenty feet from the kitchen door, Elena tugged at Jen, making her lurch forward a couple steps; a second later Jen returned the favor. That started them up again, and they broke off into snorting giggles, shoving each other as they headed inside to warm up.

Chapter Four

Maple Creek, Upstate New York
November 13, 2007

"I wish you'd stop acting like this."

"Like *what*?" Elena challenged her husband with a look as she added a baggie of potato chips to Jillian's lunch for school. "Do you realize how many kids choke on peanut butter sandwiches every year?"

"Toddlers, maybe. Not kids Jillian's age." Max sounded nonchalant, but his jaw had taken on the rigid line it did when he was being stubborn about something.

He was tall, and thanks to regular workouts he was still in good shape for a guy nearing forty. He had thick, dark hair and brown eyes. Normally, Elena thought his determined expression was handsome, but she never liked it as much when he directed it at her.

He took the tuna sandwich she'd carved up into four perfect sections out of Jillian's lunch bag and put it in the fridge, replacing it with the horizontally sliced-in-half PB on white he'd just finished making.

"*Thank* you," Jillian said dramatically from her perch on the stairs outside the kitchen. "Tuna smells! And Jordan always picks on me when Mom cuts up my food like that." She scrunched her nose. "Yesterday I had to mush it into a big ball and—"

Max cut her off with a pointed look. "Watch it, young lady. You're lucky your mother makes you a nice lunch every day. And peanut butter *is* stickier to swallow than tuna salad. So no talking while you chew, and make sure you drink plenty of milk while you eat this." He jerked his chin toward the hall and added, "Now go and get your shoes and your coat on. It's almost time to leave for school."

"I don't have to wear my winter parka again, do I, Dad? Pleeeeeasse, tell me I don't have to. I'm sweating already!"

"It's warm enough today. You can just wear your hooded sweatshirt."

Elena gave him another glare. Tall, dark, and handsome or not, he was making her more irritated by the second.

"Go on now," he said to Jillian, not yet acknowledging his wife's reaction.

Jillian scampered off, looking relieved.

Elena supposed she should have been thankful that Claire was still upstairs, or else she'd have been angling for her own death-defying freedoms the way Jillian had been lately, thanks to Max and his penchant for being more of a softy than usual.

"If something happens to her, it's your fault," Elena said in a tight voice once Jillian was gone, trying to quell the fear that kept swelling up out of nowhere, eclipsing even her irritation.

"Nothing is going to happen, El. I don't know why you're so worried about everything lately." Max looked at her then, and she felt a jolt as she saw the worry and frustration in his eyes. "Are you sure you're feeling all right?"

"I'm fine." Her voice was tight as she tried to push her anxiety back down to manageable levels. "I just wish you'd stop undermining me with the kids."

"Maybe you ought to have the doctor check you over again."

"There's nothing wrong with me."

"If you say so," he muttered, moving away from her to grab a travel coffee mug from the cupboard.

Elena busied herself with the English muffin she was trying to get inside another baggie, so he wouldn't see that her hands were shaking. *Why were they shaking?*

But less than a minute after venting his opinion, Max set down the spoon he'd used to stir the milk into his coffee, walked over, and put his hands on her shoulders, kneading the tense muscles there in that way that always made her melt. Still without saying anything, he rubbed down to the tops of her arms before turning her around and kissing her forehead, her cheek, and then down just below her ear, sending a little warm shiver up her neck.

He was a master at that: Trying to make up without saying anything. Actions speak louder than words, he'd always said, but sometimes she just needed a little space before getting cozy again. And the option to talk about what was bothering her.

Still, contrary to gender stereotypes, Max wasn't averse to talking things over as needed. He just preferred to be in a quiet, private spot without interruption. And with three Ts (a teenager, a tween, and a toddler) in the house, that was almost impossible. Right now Elena wished they could put the world aside and just retreat somewhere by themselves. At the very least, she wanted to lean into him and have him hold her for a while, but she couldn't seem to release the rigid, anxious energy filling her. She felt like she'd crack into a thousand pieces if she tried.

Feeling her tension, Max pulled back, and the strained look came back into his expression. He let his arms fall back down to his sides.

"Look, I don't want to fight before I leave, ok?" He sighed and jabbed his fingers through his hair. "I just need to know that things will be on an even keel when I'm gone."

"They always are. I've gotten pretty good at holding down the fort while you're away." Elena tipped back against the counter and folded her arms in front of her, daring him with her posture to say just one thing more.

He did, surprising her by being reasonable instead of pigheaded. "I know it puts more of the burden on you, El, but being overnight once in a while is part of my job. I can't get out of it."

That was true enough, though it was also true that he set his own schedule. He didn't have to be away *tonight*. He was choosing to. Big difference. But she was too tired to argue any more. Shrugging, she murmured a neutral "Okay."

His lips quirked in a half smile, and he shook his head a little as he came over to hug her again, brushing the hair back from her face affectionately. "Look, why don't you let me take Violet to the sitter? I have a little extra time before I drop Claire off at the high school, and you're running late."

Elena was the one who pulled back this time, staring at *him*. Max rarely offered to do something extra in the domestic department, especially in the morning. It wasn't his favorite time of day. She felt like asking who he was and what he'd done with her husband, but she decided not to push it. Besides, his bringing Violet to the sitter *would* be a help this morning. So she just agreed and watched his retreating back as he went in the living room to go get Violet and bring her in for a goodbye kiss from Mama.

Then, after giving Elena another peck on the cheek, he carried Violet back into the living room to gather up her daycare knapsack, saying over his shoulder that he'd call and check in tonight to see how her day had gone.

A tingle of wifely worry slipped up her spine as she stood there, alone, in the kitchen (no, not about *that*—Max was as true-blue as they came). It was just that, other than Pa and Ma, Max was the most perceptive about what made her tick most of the time. And he was being really considerate. Even extra sensitive not to set her off, even when she was being prickly (and she knew she was, but she just couldn't seem to stop herself).

That kind of overt thoughtfulness came out most often when she was sick or he thought something was really wrong.

It worried her. A little, anyway. Maybe there *was* something off about her. The uneasiness slipped like a chill up her spine before she could shake it off and reassure herself. There was no problem; he was making a mountain out of a molehill.

It was true that some things had felt a little . . . different since the accident, but at least she hadn't gotten into the car and kept driving for three days without stopping like a few flipped out celebrities she'd read about in *People Magazine*. She'd fantasized about it once or twice, and had even gone as far as to get into the car and drive, but the farthest she'd gone was to the grocery store across town. She'd never come close to heading into the sunset. Max had teased that it was only because she was still using Ma and Pa's second car since hers had been totaled in the accident, and she'd never just up and disappear with something they needed back.

That really frosted her (even if it was mostly true). She'd been tempted to go ahead and do it just to prove him wrong, but so far she'd restrained the impulse. No, how she felt came from the usual stresses and strains of life as a working mother. That was it. She knew how it could be from watching Ma.

Ma had been a stay-at-home mother when all eight kids were living at home, but the fact remained that she'd gone back to work when the youngest three were still in the nest and somehow managed to retain her sanity (well, Ma used to say she'd lost it, but Elena knew she was just blowing off steam). The fact was that Elena had less than half the number of children to contend with, and unsettling fender-bender or not, she'd manage, too.

Giving up on packaging her now sloppy buttered and jammed English muffin, she shoved it between her teeth, grabbed her coat, and headed out to the car to wait for Jillian, so she could drop her off at her school on the way to work. As she opened the door, the cool, damp air hit her. *More rain.* She'd forgotten her umbrella, so the rain coated her hair with a fine mist as she made her way to Ma and Pa's old car, her heels clacking in the driveway.

She pulled open the driver's side door, squinting through the wet to look back at the house just before she got in. *Probably too late to get a goodbye from Claire.* Anyway, Claire thought her mother was a nerd for wanting to give her a goodbye kiss and hug, and she only tolerated it at home because none of her friends were there to see the embarrassing display of affection.

No, even if Claire came out at the same time as Jillian, the most she'd get would be a wave from her on her way to Max's car. And chances were Claire was late (again). Max would have to call upstairs to tell her to hurry, while she dawdled in getting her makeup on just right and her hair to a state of perfection.

Teenage self-absorption. It was part of the package, Elena knew. But she hadn't been a typical teenager herself, so it was difficult to relate. She supposed she just had to accept these changes in Claire—the changes happening in all three of her girls—but it wasn't easy.

As she slid into the driver's seat, she glanced up into the rearview mirror, wishing that it was a little bit bigger so she could check to see how many new gray hairs she had.

The Homestead
Moose Junction, Upstate New York
August 13, 1974
Elena is five years old

Every (storm) cloud has a silver lining. . . .

After all these years Ma knew she ought to be good and used to the idea that life was unpredictable and that there was more to do than there was time to get it done, but sometimes it got the best of her. With so many people in the house, it was a challenge to stay on top of everything and still be the kind of mother she wanted to be to her daughters—one who could sit down and have heart-to-hearts with the older girls or play another game of Who Broke the Ice? or Mouse Trap with the little ones.

Today, though, things had been progressing as they usually did; lunch was over and the dishes were put away. There was one load of laundry in the washer, two waiting to be folded and ironed, another waiting to dry, and she'd just taken two large pans of blonde brownies out of the oven for part of tonight's dessert and finally put in a six-pound meatloaf, so it would have time to cook. A thunderstorm was moving through, and it had begun to rain, so she couldn't hang the wet load of laundry out on the line yet.

Compounding everything was the fact that before too much more time passed, she would need to dodge the raindrops and drive down to the Super Duper for some extra provisions because they were having unexpected company for supper. Yes, Pa had invited two "hot-shot" lieutenants from the air force base (where he worked as a civilian) to the house for a visit tonight.

Bringing fine, upstanding, yet also usually pretty full-of-themselves, young officers to the homestead for an evening meal was a favorite pastime of Pa's. It was his opinion that most of them could benefit from a little more humility. What better way to achieve that than through some good-natured grilling, offered by all eight Wright sisters, sitting around the table like an interrogation squad through the entirety of a home-cooked supper, dessert, and coffee?

The girls certainly had a way of playing off each other to bring arrogant young men down a peg or two. All they lacked was a spotlight to shine on their target's expression as it shifted from cocky bravado to deer-in-the-headlights shock by the time the meal was over.

Ma shook her head, half smiling at the thought as she sat at the table to jot down the list of what she'd need at the Super Duper. "Mr. Roger's Neighborhood" was beginning on the TV in the living room behind her, and Zippy and Elena were happy to watch that while Lisa kept an eye on them as she read her latest mystery novel. Jen was in the bedroom she shared with her three younger sisters, working on a macramé purse. Patricia was holed up in the playroom, practicing on their out-of-tune upright piano, and Kat was at a friend's house. Melanie and Anne had been gone since this morning, to register for their fall classes at the community college. Everyone should be set until she could get back.

She'd just written down the first item, ten pounds of potatoes, when a flash of lightning cut through the gloom outside, followed a few seconds later by a rolling rumble of thunder. Gasps and nervous giggles came from the living room, but it went quiet again as the two youngest girls settled back to watching their program. Quickly, Ma finished her list: *whipping cream, 1 gallon of milk, 5 lbs. of flour. . . .*

Suddenly the lightning flashed again with an almost simultaneous boom, rattling the dishes in the china cupboard the same as if one of the dozen or so B-52s or KC-135s that flew over their house daily was roaring on the way to landing down at the base. This time screams and shrieks arose from the living room, but when Ma jumped up and looked in from the doorway, she saw that Lisa had moved to the couch to cuddle her younger sisters, much to her relief.

"It's okay, Ma," Lisa said. "I'll take care of them until you get home."

Zippy wiggled her fingers at Ma with an impish grin, but Ma couldn't see Elena's face, buried as it was in Lisa's side.

She smiled at all three of them. "I'll try to hurry, girls."

As she grabbed her purse, she looked out the kitchen window to see the branches of the two large weeping willows in the backyard swinging around in a wild dance like hundreds of skinny arms flailing in the wind. But she couldn't wait any longer; she'd just have to get wet and hope for the best or the butterscotch pudding she still had to make when she got home would never set in time.

"'Bye, girls! I'll be right back!" she called out, and a chorus of answers rang out from the various rooms. Pulling on her rain bonnet, Ma ran outside, feeling the rain soak through her coat as she hurried along the walkway toward the ancient family van.

Before she'd gone five steps, she heard the muffled sound of the phone beginning to ring inside the house; then the playroom window rattled upward, and Patricia pressed her face up to the screen.

"Ma, phone's for you!"

Ma stopped in her tracks, getting even more soaked with rain. She put her purse over her head for some added protection and pressed her lips together to rein in her temper before calling back to be heard over the storm, "Can't you take a message?"

"It's the college. They need to talk to you before they'll let Melanie register!"

Groaning, Ma turned around and ran back to the house, her irritation increasing with every step. Of course. Even getting out the door to go to the grocery store couldn't be simple. Wasn't it always the way, and that—

Before she was fully back in the house again, Ma heard the loudest cracking sound she'd ever heard, followed by a long whoosh, scrape, and giant thudding noise. The house seemed preternaturally quiet in the moments afterward. Even the television had blinked to a sudden, silent black.

It didn't take long to realize why.

Pulling the door shut and taking a few dripping steps into the kitchen, Ma looked out the row of kitchen windows to her left. To her shock, her normal view of the back yard was completely blocked by a tangled mass of wet leaves and branches.

One of the weeping willows had blown over.

In its descent, it had knocked the antennae off the roof . . . and the bulk of its twenty-foot long trunk and hundreds of whippy branches had landed smack-dab where Ma would have been standing on the path leading to the driveway if she hadn't gone inside for the phone call.

Somehow, she made her way to the table and sat, her legs suddenly feeling as wobbly as the pudding she'd hoped to make for tonight's dessert. The girls had come running in from their various places, and they all gathered around her, asking questions, hugging her, and exclaiming about the sight of the tree outside the window. Ma couldn't really speak much yet. Her keys clattered to the table, and she instinctively pulled her girls into her soggy embrace, sending up a silent prayer of thanksgiving.

Embedded in that offering was a fervent promise, never to complain about an irritating interruption again for as long as she lived.

(Willow tree down)

WGRR FM 103.9, THE BEAR

"Give a Growl for the Adirondacks'
Most Trusted Radio Station"
December 1, 1974

Welcome back, Adirondack listeners. It's Willard T. Boggs here with you on a night so warm the kiddies might need to add "please send snow" to their Christmas lists. Speaking of that, there are only twenty-three more shopping days to go, so hope you got out for some of the holiday sales. The missus and I had a nice bowl of split pea with ham at the Woolworth's counter during a break from the hustle and bustle. Boy, was it good. As my granddad used to say, "That'll sell!"

As for progress, on This Day in History, Henry Ford installed the first moving assembly line for mass production of a complete automobile. Thanks to him, we can all run around easier at the holidays, going hither and yon like chickens with our heads cut off.

Locally, many Moose Junction families came out to support the talent show at the American Legion last night. All monies raised will provide Christmas toys for needy kids in the community. Legion Post Leader Hank Steiner was thrilled to announce a total of $686 was raised—a tribute to the generosity of our town and its citizens. Winning the show this year were the Singing Wright Sisters—all eight of them—harmonizing to "Edelweiss" and sounding just as nice as the kids in The Sound of Music. *Hank is the Wrights' neighbor, and he tells me all those girls have been real good to him and Gladys. They're a breath of fresh air, the kind of big family that reminds us of simpler days gone by. Don't tell her I said it, but Marge even had a tear in her eye at the end of their number.*

Next door to the Homestead
Moose Junction, Upstate New York
August 28, 2005
Elena is thirty-six years old

Change is the only constant in life. . . .

Hank Steiner, the Wright family's much-loved next-door-neighbor, took one hesitant step out his back door. Then he took another, tipping a little and leaning on his cane as he paused to regain his balance on his brand-new artificial leg. Dave stood next to him in silent support, just as they'd stood by each other in their days long ago as young and invincible United States Marines. Dave knew Hank wouldn't want or accept any help; he'd have felt the same in Hank's place, and so he just waited, holding on to the suitcase.

There was no rush.

In fact, Dave wished he was helping Hank with just about anything other than this. Moving to Towers Community Assisted Living and Long-Term Care Facility had been Hank's idea, and he'd stubbornly held on to it these past weeks, no matter what Dave, Elizabeth, or any of the girls had said.

It was the only time that Dave could remember any real disagreement between them. For decades Hank and his wife, Gladys, had lived next door, not only as good friends but also as a kind of second set of loving, reliable parents looking out for the girls. They all used to joke about how great they got along, none of them realizing how much they took for granted that easy connection over the years.

But when Gladys had gotten sick and passed away, Hank had changed almost overnight. It was like the flame inside Hank—the one that had flickered and guttered for a while after their boy, Jim, died in Vietnam in '73—had extinguished at last. Then the trouble came with his leg, and . . . well, it hadn't been long before he'd made up his mind that he couldn't live alone in that house anymore. It was too hard, when every corner and room reminded him of Gladys and the empty hallways whispered with memories of happier times.

As the youngest (and perhaps most sensitive) of the Wright sisters,

Elena had taken Hank's decision hardest of all.

For Elena, Pa would always be her original hero, and the man who'd set the moon and the stars in the sky as far as she was concerned, but Hank was still *Pops*. He'd been Pa's best friend since the day they'd met on their way to boot camp as teenagers just after World War II, and in some ways that had ended up being better than an actual blood connection.

She was broken up about Hank leaving, all right. *Everyone* in the family felt sad by what was transpiring that late August morning, even though all the girls were grown and living within a three-county radius in northern New York State (except for Zippy, who commanded the world at large). But the cold truth was that things like this happened every day. It was simply part of life's journey for some sixteen percent of America's senior citizens. Elena had tried to comfort herself with that statistic, but it hadn't helped much.

Making her feel even worse, she couldn't even be at the homestead on that awful day, since she was still ensconced on the maternity floor of North Country General, cradling the new daughter Max and she had planned to christen Emma but had ended up naming Violet after she'd looked up at them and blinked her big, violet-blue eyes.

In thinking about it after the fact, she'd decided it was probably for the best that she wasn't there. If she had been, she might not have been able to keep up the brave face that she knew Pa and Pops would have needed from her. The emotion would have rivaled the aching, bittersweet feeling she'd fought all through the requisite father-daughter dance on her wedding day when, during the entire song, her beloved Pa had resorted to quietly whispering in her ear the process of gutting a fish so that neither of them would embarrass themselves by crying.

So instead she'd heard secondhand about how Hank had helped Pa put his suitcase in the back of the station wagon, along with a box of his most treasured possessions. Then he'd walked slowly, his gait uneven, to the front of his house, where he'd paused and rested his hand one last time on the "For Sale" sign they'd pounded into his front lawn. No one had said a word. They couldn't; there was nothing to say (at least without crying). After a few minutes, he'd turned and made the slow trek back to the driveway before climbing into the passenger seat of Pa's vehicle.

Balancing himself on the seat, he'd reached both hands beneath his right knee and lifted, moving his artificial leg into place inside the station wagon. Ma had slid into the back next to Hank's suitcase, trying to pretend that her watery eyes were the result of allergies.

When the door slammed shut and the Mercury lurched to uneasy life to roll down the driveway toward the street, Hank had taken one final look at his house. Then he'd turned his face resolutely forward, staring straight ahead as he let his friend drive him to the Towers Community Assisted Living and Long-Term Care Facility downtown, where he planned to live out the rest of his days.

It was the end of an era, almost sixty years of abiding friendship and next-door-neighborhood. A full and colorful half century of family gatherings and Fourth of July barbeques, of holiday celebrations, hard work, shared sorrows, and tragedies endured or averted . . . all woven together by moments of peaceful appreciation and routine that fill out the patchwork of an ordinary life.

'Round about when he'd hit seventy-five, Hank had told everyone he'd aged past the point of new beginnings. But fate had proved a capricious companion on his life's journey, and so on that misty summer morning, crisp with the first hints of autumn, he'd found himself starting over again.

It was the way it had to be. Grief had eaten away at his resolve, and his self-respect and fear of being a burden had forced him to refuse the Wrights' offer to move in with them. He didn't like having to go live elsewhere, any more than Dave, Elizabeth, and the girls did. But none of them had to like it; they just had to endure it.

And so that's just what they all did.

Chapter Five

Maple Creek, Upstate New York
December 7, 2007

It had been more than five weeks since the accident, and something was definitely wrong. Elena felt like an emotional yo-yo. It was making her and everyone around her crazy. She couldn't explain why she was feeling and acting as she was, but it was bad. She'd always been the complete opposite of Drama Queen Zippy. Now she was flying off the handle at little things—or bursting into tears at sappy coffee commercials or an upcoming Hallmark special. She'd never done that. Not even when she was pregnant.

Claire and Jillian walked on eggshells around her, and even Violet seemed fussier and more demanding than usual. As for Max . . . well, he either peppered her with questions she wasn't ready to answer, or else he avoided her altogether. Today was one of those second types of days.

Friday night or not, he was away again, gone on a weekend business trip this time—his fourth overnight trip in two weeks. Elena knew it had more to do with her moodiness than any burning need to attend the trade show up there, or for the plumbing stores up in Malone to have a new shipment of toilet fill valves, brass faucets, and PEX pipes.

The fact that Christmas was fast approaching only made things worse. It was usually one of Elena's favorite holidays. She loved going all out with the decorations, baking, and present-buying, but this year everything seemed like a chore. She was doing her best for the sake of the kids, even if her heart wasn't in it.

She was trying not to let the accumulation of negative feelings bother her, but that was about as likely as getting the stores to wait until after Thanksgiving to put out the Christmas stuff. She'd seen her first green, red, and glitter-filled Holiday aisle in Target just before Halloween.

As always Pa could sense how she was feeling without her having to say a word. They were on the same wavelength and had been since Elena could remember. It was a special frequency the two of them shared, and their bond had remained close even after she grew up, went to college, married Max, and moved into her own home a half hour away from the homestead.

Pa had been worried about her lately, she knew. Neither of her parents had said much about it, but they both seemed to realize she was having a tough time since the accident. It wasn't anything physical; she'd only ended up with a few bruises and a mild concussion. However, attempting to keep a lid on all the emotions the accident had stirred up had proved more problematic. So tonight Pa and Ma had offered to host the kids for a sleepover to give her a chance to sort through some of her feelings, or just enjoy a little time to herself.

Elena had arranged to meet them over at Towers tomorrow near suppertime for a quick visit with Pops, and after that she'd either go back to Pa and Ma's with them to stay another night with the kids (since Max was gone until Sunday night), or else the kids would come back home with her. They were going to play it by ear.

Pa saw Pops every few days, though the rest of the family couldn't get out there as often because of work and kids and such. Elena was looking forward to the visit; seeing Pops was always good, but seeing Pops, Pa, and Ma all together was even better. It was like fitting back in the missing piece of a puzzle: a throwback to the old days, when Pops and Gladys used to come over to play cards with Pa and Ma on Saturday night and eat peanuts and pretzels while sipping high balls or 7-Up with gin.

In the meantime, though, Elena had tonight and most of tomorrow to herself. At the moment, she was home, completely alone for the first time in ages. She wandered around the house, feeling strange. The peace and quiet was decadent in a way it had never felt in her pre-children days, but at the same time there was an emptiness that the girls' absence left behind. It seemed strange, a little like a school building at night or during summer, when all the kids and teachers had gone home—deserted.

Opening the fridge, she rummaged around for something to eat, the surge of delight in the freedom of that simple choice making her shake her head. She'd become a sad case if hunting up leftovers was enough to give her a thrill. God forbid that she was becoming one of those mothers she'd always pitied in the grocery store or the mall. They were usually a hot mess of untrimmed hair, poorly fitting clothes (with assorted stains from the kids), and often no makeup.

The makeup part brought her up short, suddenly, as she considered the last time *she'd* taken out her foundation or a tube of mascara, even when she was getting ready for work. *Oh, God.* Seeing the mirror hanging over the top of the fireplace, she took a wide berth, so as not to glimpse her reflection. No more self-examination tonight.

Wine. That's what she needed. She'd just poured herself a glass of pinot noir and settled down to eat the salmon burger she'd rescued from the freezer, micro-waved, and then slathered with a mix of mayonnaise and sweet relish, when the phone rang. Sighing, she put down her plate and answered it on the fourth ring, just before the voicemail picked up.

"Hi, Eek. It's me." The sound on the other end of the line was crackly, but Elena knew it was Jen, thanks to the nickname. Elena had earned it from Jen the day when they were kids and she'd lifted the toilet seat cover at the camp's outhouse to find a big, ugly spider lurking there.

Nature had dictated that she and Jen were kindred spirits, even though they were several years apart and there were two sisters born between them. It was just the way it was, and Jen had always been a little protective of baby sister Elena, so the nickname sprang from a kind of loving playfulness.

Zippy, on the other hand, had preferred to call Elena by a similar-sounding nickname, but one that was instead formed by Elena's initials (EEW). Elena supposed it was inevitable as soon as Zippy learned how to spell. Her teasing wasn't malicious; it was just instinctive to Zippy's flair for drama and comedy . . . and that single letter made all the difference. Conversely, Zippy's initials spelled out something much nicer (AWW), a fact she never failed to point out.

"I can't hear you, Jen. Where are you?"

"Oh, sorry."

Elena heard a louder rattling noise, followed by the metallic squeak of a door.

"Damn, it's icy out here! I'm just walking outside now. Must be some kind of interference from the equipment. I stopped to talk to Pam before I called you."

"No problem." Elena bit her lip, keeping back anything else she might be predisposed to blurt without thinking. Pam was the dispatcher for the Maple Creek Police Department. Jen had been a patrol officer for almost two decades, and she and Pam had been friends for at least fifteen of those years.

Pam was a nice enough gal, but Elena wished she'd be a better influence on Jen in the romance department. Pam had terrible taste in men. Her current boyfriend, Steve, was the drummer in a band. He played two gigs a month at most; the rest of the time he spent mooning around in her basement apartment, acting like a tortured artist and working on his music while Pam supported him.

Jen's choices weren't much better. She seemed to be attracted to the easy-going, drifter types. Elena's theory was that her free-spirited sister liked them that way because there was no danger of commitment. Her latest man was on the way out the door (Elena hoped). Larry, the pool-deck-and-house-contractor, was handsome but lazy. Ironically enough, he had a tattoo of Superman emblazoned on his chest. From what she could tell, the only super power he had was the uncanny ability to remain horizontal on the couch for days at a time. In the six months Jen had been dating him, he'd finished only a couple jobs.

"So, what's going on with you tonight?" Elena tried to keep her voice neutral after another pause that had been filled with more rattling sounds on the line, followed by a salty, good-natured shout from one of the other officers to her sister in the parking lot. Jen usually didn't call from work unless there was something important or police-related to tell. The last time there'd been a jailbreak at the medium-security prison on the outskirts of town, and Jen had wanted to warn all the sisters along with Ma and Pa.

"Not much . . . I'm taking Pam to The Hopper later for a quick game of pool after her shift."

"Why? Is she on the outs with Steve again?"

"Yup." Jen paused and then cursed, clearly fiddling with her keys. A few seconds later, an electronic beeping sound told Elena that she'd made it into her squad car.

When she spoke again, it was with the sharp, business-like tone Elena recognized as her way of trying to change the subject, so her sister wouldn't go to the next logical topic of the loser-boyfriend. "I just called because I wanted to give you a heads up that I'm stopping by to drop something off. I won't stay long. Pa said Max was up north for the weekend and that the girls are staying with them so you could have some time alone." Jen's voice lowered a notch and softened. "I know it's been rough for you lately, Eek. That's why Pa asked me to bring this stuff over. If it doesn't help tonight, then maybe it will eventually."

Elena felt a tingle of warning. "Why? What is—"

But before she could finish her question, Jen went back to her business-like tone, saying, "I have to do my radio check-in before I can leave. See you in a few," before hanging up the phone.

Great. What could her tough-as-nails-outside-but-soft-as-a-creampuff-inside sister be bringing over? Her mind ran over the possibilities, from a sappy DVD, to a giant Hershey bar (Jen's favorite choice when hormones got the best of her), to something as crazy as a new puppy (not that Elena disliked animals, but she had no desire to lead another living creature through potty-training at the moment). She just didn't know what Jen was up to, which was pretty apropos. Jen had always been a bit of an enigma.

After taking a healthy gulp of her pinot noir, Elena sat down to try to finish her supper before Jen made it to her house, resolving that she'd just have to wait and see what the mystery gift was going to be.

WGRR FM 103.9, THE BEAR

"Give a Growl for the Adirondacks'
Most Trusted Radio Station"
September 7, 1986

Welcome back, Adirondack listeners. It's Willard T. Boggs here with you on a mild and rainy Saturday. All the kiddies are celebrating their first weekend since school started up again. Yes, the dog days are past and the time of pencils, books, and dirty looks is upon us. Of course, a poll of all the grateful mothers and fathers out there may reveal a different kind of celebration. There is something to be said about keeping kids busy with homework and such.

Speaking of homework, This Day in History features a British lady who had a lot of it. Today in 1533, England's Queen Elizabeth was born. She lived to the ripe old age of sixty-nine, a testament to her smarts since her father was that monarch who had many wives and a fondness for cutting off their heads.

On a slightly less dramatic note, Avery Thompson of Otter Creek won the Labor Day Chili Cook-Off with his entry, "Three-Bean Venison Chili." I was one of the judges, and I can tell you competition was tough. Avery says to send in a self-addressed stamped envelope if you want a copy of the recipe.

And now, all of us at the station offer a congratulatory growl to Moose Junction High's Black Bears, who won their first football game of the season against the Trenton High Spartans. The Bears were led on the field by recent transfer and star quarterback Jesse James Wilder, whose mother, Janie Simms, hailed from Moose Junction. Seems the younger Wilder has inherited his legendary father's football prowess. WGRRReat job, boys!

Chapter Six

Maple Creek, Upstate New York
December 7, 2007

Twenty minutes after Jen called, flashing red lights in the driveway signaled her arrival. Elena smiled, shaking her head as she headed for the door. Hopefully the neighbors wouldn't mind Jen's official police entrance. Elena knew Mrs. Crandall across the street would ask her about it tomorrow, even though Jen's visits usually involved similar theatrics. Mrs. Crandall was an old-fashioned "spinster"—a spry woman in her eighties—but she had a penchant for spying out the windows at her neighbors and then gossiping about what she (thought she) saw.

"Do me a favor and put me out to pasture if I ever get that bored when I'm old," Jen had said, when Elena had mentioned the quizzing Mrs. Crandall gave her the first time Jen had driven up in her squad car. Most of the other neighbors called Mrs. Crandall a busybody, but she was harmless. Since then, though, Jen had made a point of turning on her flashing light bar and sometimes even letting the siren blare for a few seconds whenever she drove in, to give Mrs. Crandall a kick, she said.

It was stuff like that that sometimes made Elena think Jen was a lot more like Zippy than she let on . . . except Jen's flair for attention-getting developed only after she became a police officer, while Zippy had embraced the skill from her first breath. In fact, it was part of oft-repeated family history that not long after her birth, Zippy had been scooped up and taken into another area for further examination because she'd failed the respiration part of her Apgar and wasn't crying (a circumstance she more than made up for once the shock of being born wore off).

Elena swung the door open before Jen could ring the bell. Her sister walked toward the front steps, looking official in her uniform. When Jen was a teenager she'd hated that she was always mistaken for a much younger kid, but now her youthful appearance served her well, taking a decade off her age. The fact that she was tall (five feet, nine inches), lean, and strong helped to reinforce her I-mean-business demeanor when in uniform.

It was impossible not to see the big plastic bin Jen cradled against her chest as she approached. There was no movement from inside it—no barks or yelps either, which Elena considered a good sign. Jen's expression, however, looked slightly grim. Like she was preparing for something difficult.

Elena frowned. What the heck was it? Old winter clothes? Christmas ornaments? *Body parts?* Just then, she caught a glimpse of some crinkled plastic orange and black streamers hanging a few inches down on one side of the bin where they'd been trapped when the lid was snapped on top.

"Those had better be Halloween decorations," Elena muttered as Jen reached the top of the steps and kept coming, forcing her to back up. But even as she said it, she knew they weren't. They were her old high school pom-poms. Elena had been a football cheerleader from seventh grade all the way through junior year of high school. Now, before you jump to any conclusions, rest assured that Elena knew all the stereotypes about cheerleaders. She didn't fit (most of) them.

She'd made the team the first time she tried out in junior high because she was good at jumping and kicking, and she was strong and tall enough to hoist other girls above her head. Plus, it was the only sport around where she could use some of the flexibility she'd earned from more than a decade of dance classes.

The popularity aspect that was supposed to come with cheering never worked out for her, though, and except for a few of the more tolerant girls, she was mostly ignored by the rest of the team, other than when they needed her to choreograph a dance or lift one of the pipsqueak-sized members.

It didn't even matter that she shared a blood connection and family resemblance with Zippy (who was only one year ahead of her in school and popular beyond Elena's wildest dreams, without ever having been a cheerleader). No matter what Elena did, she just wasn't part of the "cool girls" clique. She and Zippy might have been sisters, but style made all the difference in how people perceived them.

Some of that had to do with how Zippy wore her hair and makeup (meaning her hair was styled and she wore some). She also knew how to act like she couldn't care any less about what anyone else thought about her. Elena wore her heart on her sleeve, which definitely was *not* cool. Her hair was all one length, and she favored a natural look. In other words, she couldn't be bothered with blush, eye shadow, and lipstick.

It also helped that Zippy insisted on buying designer clothes. Each girl in their family had the same, limited amount of money to spend on school clothes each year, but Zippy would spend all of hers on two pair of Guess jeans and one or two Calvin Klein tops, while Elena got more than double the number of no-name jeans and shirts, along with a purse, socks, and maybe a skirt from Sears or Montgomery Ward.

It was all about fashion for Zippy and bang-for-the-buck for Elena. For the most part Elena didn't care about the fallout her apparel choices caused her. She'd decided to be herself, even if that came at a cost.

"Aw, come on. It's healthy to sort through things once in a while, Eek. Otherwise, you'll end up like Mrs. Crandall," Jen quipped. "There have got to be *some* good memories in this plastic tub."

"Not from cheerleading."

"That's not all that's in there."

"What else then?"

Jen conveniently sidestepped Elena's question. "Besides, I said it then, and I'll say it again now: It was their loss."

Elena didn't make any comment this time, only making a snorting sound as she headed into the kitchen for a refill on her wine.

"Do you want any?" Elena called over her shoulder, knowing Jen would know what she was talking about when she waved the empty wine glass in her sister's direction.

"Can't. I'm in uniform, and I still have to drive back to the station."

Elena nodded and disappeared through the doorway. She needed a couple minutes anyway to gather her thoughts while refilling her glass (to the brim . . . it was shaping up to be that kind of night). She knew she should try to work up the guts to ask Jen if Pa put together the bin, or if she had. Then she might have an idea of what else was there, without even needing to open it. If it was just a mess of cheerleading stuff and junior high mementoes that would be tolerable, but if it was other stuff, too, from later on, then . . .

Her brain shut off the possibilities like it always did. She took a deep swallow from her newly refilled glass and retreated to the safety of annoyance. Not with Jen (yet), but in remembering the whole cheerleading thing. Over the years it had dwindled to a level that barely registered on the irritation scale, but it was enough to keep her distracted now, so she allowed herself to fan the flames a little.

It had gone like this: She'd been good enough to make the varsity cheerleading team in her junior year. That rarely happened at her large, football-obsessed high school. Varsity was comprised of seniors. Except that she had been *good* at cheering. The jumps, splits, and dance routines had come like second nature to her, thanks to her years of three-times-a-week dance lessons, and because she was tall and strong, she'd made a sturdy base girl for many of the mounts and stunts. So, fresh from that season as a varsity cheerleader, she'd gone to try-outs as usual the summer before she was going to be a senior, run through all the drills and cheers, stronger than ever. . . .

And she was cut from the team entirely. Let go. Passed over.

She still remembered the shock and humiliation of looking at the sheet that listed the new team for the season and realizing that her name wasn't on it. The other girls had noticed, too, some of them whispering, squirming, or trying not to make eye contact with her.

Except for Sharon, another upcoming senior.

Sharon was one of the "preps"—that top level of the school's social ladder. She had cheered for years as well (though like the other juniors, she'd been kept back on JV the year Elena had made varsity). Sharon was expected to be named captain as a senior due to her popularity, but she had never been gracious about it.

By the beginning of middle school, Sharon had mastered the ability to separate girls into groups of "acceptable" and "not good enough" according to her rules of looks, coolness, or even family connections and background. And if you were too nice to the kids in special-help classes, or the ones who wore Salvation Army clothes and could have used a shower, then you might as well forget it. You didn't exist as far as Sharon was concerned. All the lemmings did whatever they could to be part of Sharon's acceptable group and avoid social suicide.

When the list was posted, Sharon had given Elena a smirk (looking up at her to do it, since she was one of the pipsqueaks). Then she made a deliberate show of turning her back on Elena to talk to the other girls comprising the new team, both dismissing and shunning her all at once.

Elena remembered the hot, angry feeling that had spread from her toes all the way up to her ears as she left the building and went home. As she'd walked down the sidewalk, the realization had hit her like a ton of bricks. She'd been cut from the cheerleading team after *five* years, one of them already on varsity. Sharon had always had it out for her; maybe she'd found a way to influence the new cheer coach into cutting her. But Elena had known even then that it had nothing to do with which kids Elena was nice to, her looks, her lack of popularity, or even her ability to cheer, kick, dance, jump, and perform the necessary stunts. No, it had been something else. Something a lot more personal.

The thoughts clicked off again to avoid going any deeper than that, and Elena headed back toward the living room where Jen had set the plastic bin on the coffee table.

Jen had backed up to the door, looking like she was getting ready to escape. *Uh-oh.*

"Making a quick getaway?" Elena leaned against the kitchen doorjamb and raised an eyebrow at her sister.

"I told you I couldn't stay long."

"I'm not going to open that up, you know." Elena didn't need to flick her gaze toward the bin. Jen knew what she meant.

Jen didn't flinch. "It's your choice. But if you want my advice, Eek, you'll open it *and* look through it." She tipped her chin a little, finally acknowledging the proverbial elephant on the coffee table. "You know, sometimes people have to go backwards before they can move forward. You ought to at least think about it." Then she blew Elena a kiss and slipped out the door.

It wasn't until after she'd heard the crunch of her tires pulling out of the driveway that Elena moved from the kitchen doorway into the living room. She walked with measured steps toward the couch, setting down her wineglass on the end table there, and sinking into a seat cushion that had been worn into a concave shape from years of the kids flopping into it (mostly when she wasn't looking so she couldn't scold them).

A jumble of emotions rolled around in her stomach, making her wish she hadn't eaten that salmon burger. The turmoil of the past five weeks bubbled up again, fighting for dominance, while behind it memories and feelings that had been stirred up by the accident brewed beneath, biding time. Just like the big plastic bin. There it sat, mute, silent, but still powerful, waiting for her.

All that remained was finding out if she would have the courage to open it up and look inside.

WGRR FM 103.9, THE BEAR

"Give a Growl for the Adirondacks'
Most Trusted Radio Station"
December 7, 1968

Welcome back, Adirondack listeners. It's Willard T. Boggs here with you on a clear Thursday evening. It reached a balmy thirty degrees in Moose Junction this afternoon, but sorry to tell you, folks, the fine weather won't last long. The first nor'easter of the season is forecast to hit our area on Friday. Elmer over at High Peaks Hardware says they just got a shipment of new shovels in for anyone who needs to spruce up their supply for dealing with Old Man Winter.

We pause to remember that on this date in 1941, Pearl Harbor was attacked. President Roosevelt declared it, "A day that will live in infamy," and it is. Also on this date in 1873, American author Willa Cather was born in Virginia.

Locally, the missus and I were invited to a surprise party for Hank Steiner's big four-oh. It took place at Mohawk Lanes in Moose Junction, where everyone enjoyed birthday cake and sherbet punch for the occasion. Hank's wife, Gladys, was the hostess, assisted by longtime neighbors Dave and Elizabeth Wright and their soon-to-be-increased family. Dave and Hank are close friends, having served in the Marine Corps together just after WWII. Nearly sixty well-wishers attended, and every bowling lane was full. Hank was so surprised he threw a gutter ball. He thought everyone had forgotten his birthday.

Last but not least, listeners, colder temperatures mean it's time to check the survival kit in your car or truck. You don't want to be caught unawares and lacking the necessary items if you break down in a storm.

Chapter Seven

Towers Community Long-Term Care Facility
December 7, 2007

Hank sighed. They were at it again.

Mabel and Helen sat over in the corner of the recreation hall, half hidden by the lopsided Christmas tree, bickering. It had been going on for nearly half an hour, along with some angry gesturing at each other, the tree, and the TV, which happened to be blaring *It's a Wonderful Life* in all its black and white glory. An odd pressure started building up in the back of Hank's skull, and he reminded himself to relax—to take a deep breath in through his nose and out his mouth, just like the doc had told him to do.

It wasn't helping, damn it. The old biddies just kept pecking at each other until a man couldn't think straight. He'd been here over two years, but it was at times like these that he got as close as he ever would to seriously reconsidering Dave's offer to spring him from this geriatric trap. It would mean living with Dave and Elizabeth in the house next door to where Hank had spent most of his adult life—nearly all of his forty-nine years of marriage to Gladys.

That would have been just fine by him, when push came to shove, but it didn't make it right. He couldn't impose on his friends that way. Besides, Dave wasn't getting any younger either . . . he'd faced some health problems himself lately. And the shake up the whole Wright family had been dealt with Elena's fender bender a little more than a month ago had left them all feeling on edge, he could tell, even though they'd tried not to let on whenever they'd called him or visited. It was too much of a reminder of the last time, and everyone was tiptoeing around it, wondering how Elena would manage.

He expected it would be the same thing tomorrow when they'd said they were planning to come by for a little while. No, the last thing Dave and Elizabeth needed was another person in the house to tend to. He'd just make the best of things here for whatever time was left to him.

He glanced at the other captives around him. There were nine of them, aside from him and the two biddies. Gentleman Joe looked like he was getting ready to throw his tapioca pudding on the floor again. Elsie had her face set in that way that told anyone who bothered to look that she wasn't paying any attention to Mabel and Helen, even though the two old women broke off squabbling every now and then to try to draw her into it. Andrew was asleep, slouched in his chair, breathing with his mouth open.

Nora, frail and bird-like to begin with, seemed nervous. Her bony fingers were threaded together, the knuckles white, and Hank couldn't rid himself of the crazy notion that that was the only way she was keeping herself fixed in her chair and that if she opened her hands, she might flap up to the ceiling like a startled pigeon. The others watched the television screen with studious attention, apparently used to the commotion.

Well, he wasn't. And they were ruining the show. The best part was coming up, when Clarence jumps into the water to save George.

The biddies fell silent, and Hank hoped they'd stay that way for another ninety seconds or so. Just long enough to get to the part he wanted to see. . . .

"Help! Help!" shrieks Clarence from the TV in his distinctive, singsong voice. "Heeeelp, George. Help!"

Hank chuckled. The dark of the water was suddenly lit as if the beam of a helicopter spotlight shone down on the struggling Clarence from overhead, the camera making a quick cut to show the bridge keeper, holding nothing more than a simple flashlight.

"I'd love to have me a flashlight like *that* one," Hank couldn't resist murmuring, as he did every year when he watched this particular scene. Gladys used to get a twinkle in her eyes and shake her head with him. That and at the part when the old bald guy tells George to kiss Mary and quit talking her to death. Sweet Gladys. . . .

Well, Toots, I can't say I ever stop missing you, but this very second it's a little more than most. I'm glad you and Jim-bo at least have each other to keep good company until I get there.

After closing his eyes and sending up a little prayer for her and their son, Hank glanced at the two biddies again. Mabel was glowering at Helen, who was giving her back a scowl just as black. Then Helen opened her mouth and Mabel answered in kind, and the verbal deluge started again.

With a sigh, Hank looked down to his right leg. In his mind's eye, he could see the artificial limb that was strapped beneath the fabric of his pants, extending from just below the knee. He shifted his gaze slightly to look at the walker propped beside his chair—the silver monster he both loved and hated for the freedom it gave, even as it reminded him of what he'd lost.

But that was neither here nor there. The way he saw it, he could keep sitting here listening to Mabel and Helen bicker in competition with the TV, or he could get up and go back to his room, calling it a night. It was getting late anyway, and he wanted to take his time navigating the short walk to the elevators. He curled forward a little, readying himself to stand, and gripping the walker to help balance himself once he did.

"Hank!"

Helen's voice pierced his eardrum like a rusty nail, but he tried to pretend he hadn't heard her.

"Hank Steiner, I'm talking to you!"

He sat back and swung his head in her general direction. Before he spoke, he reminded himself that even though she didn't much look like it, Helen Cramer was a member of the gentler sex, and he'd been raised to treat women with respect.

"What can I do for you, Helen?" he managed, though it came out more like a sigh.

"We need you to settle something."

God help us all.

"This old fool says that angels are real, like that, that—"She made a short jerk of her hand toward the television. "That ridiculous *character* on the program there. I say it's hogwash. Angels are in heaven, not here." Her mouth screwed into a tightly pious bow. "You're an educated man. What do *you* say?"

Hank paused, his own thoughts on the matter vivid and clear in his mind. Like crystal, perfect and flashing shards of rainbows when the light hit it, but still sharp and sometimes cold in its beauty. His mouth quirked in a half smile, his mind directed inward for a moment. When he looked back at the women, they still sat there, motionless as statues, hanging on every second of his silence as if each was convinced she'd find vindication in his judgment on the issue.

Shaking his head, he gripped his walker, pulled himself up, and started toward the door to the elevators. "I say that it's time for bed. Good night, ladies."

WGRR FM 103.9, THE BEAR

"Give a Growl for the Adirondacks'
Most Trusted Radio Station"
June 25, 1973

Welcome back, Adirondack listeners. It's Willard T. Boggs here with you on a warm North Country night. First, breaking local news: The robber who has bedeviled area camp owners for the past three years was taken into custody by sheriff's deputies today after an extensive search with sniffing dogs. Moose Junction's own Dave Wright first stumbled upon the robber's trail when he was on his way to his not-so-secret-anymore fishing hole.

It seems Bullhead Joe—real name Joseph Tinker III—had been living the hermit life. Jeb White of the Highway Department said, and I quote, "A lot of camp people and other folks seen him and whatnot, but they just wasn't able to track him." A "WGRReat job!" goes out to everyone involved for their diligence.

In other news, songstress Carly Simon was born this day in 1945. Any of you with high schoolers have probably heard her recent smash hit, "You're So Vain," in your sleep. I know my Louise plays the record every three minutes or so.

Speaking of high school, Moose Junction class of 1973 tossed their caps this past Saturday. Congratulations to the graduates, especially Dave and Elizabeth Wright's oldest girl, Anne, who was valedictorian. We also recall the four young men who didn't cross the dais with their class, having made the ultimate sacrifice for their country in Vietnam: United States Marine Corporals Eric Hutchins, Thomas O'Malley, Jason Dodd, and James Steiner, who earned a purple heart. Semper Fi, *boys.*

Chapter Eight

Maple Creek, Upstate New York
December 8, 2007

The clock on the mantel, which was a gift Pa had made long ago for Elena, complete with a special musical movement, began to chime three as she startled awake, shattering into fragments any lingering images of the dream she'd been having. She looked around, confused for a moment. Lifting her hand up in front of her face, she saw nothing but a shadowy outline of fingers and thumb, splayed widely apart. Low-burning embers provided the only light, crackling softly in the grate from the fire she'd lit just after Jen left.

The fog from too little sleep and too much wine began to lift. She was in her living room. Alone. She coughed and rubbed her eyes, sitting up a little and massaging her stiff neck. Oh, man. She'd fallen asleep on the couch.

Just as she thought that, the pieces of the dream rose up, clicking into place in her conscious memory. *Jesse.* She'd been dreaming about Jesse.

She closed her eyes and tipped forward to balance her forearms on her knees, cradling her head in her hands. His laughter echoed in her ears, his image flooding her mind. He'd come again to haunt her in sleep, as he'd been doing with ever-greater frequency these past weeks. Her continual memories of him felt like a scab she couldn't help but pick at. It was a wound she'd thought had healed, but she knew now that it hadn't, and it never would unless she cleaned it out and bandaged it properly.

She coughed again and swiveled her head to look at the shadowy outlines of the plastic bin Jen had brought over. It hadn't moved (big surprise). Elena felt a surge of anger and desperation that pushed aside everything else for the moment. She was not a coward by nature, but she felt like one at this very moment.

Stubbornly, she lurched to standing, reached over, and threw another log on the fire. It flared to life on the hot coals. With the rise of the flames, the living room took on a brighter hue. She could see the bin in full view where it sat, taunting her.

Ridiculous. It was an inanimate object. Why was she letting it get to her like this?

She took a deep breath and held it for a few seconds before blowing it out, trying to expel all her fears with it. If the box contained what she thought it did, sorting through the stuff would be a wrenching experience. But what was it Jen had said? *Sometimes you have to go backwards to go forward.*

Maybe it was finally time to see what would come of doing that.

"Ok, sis, I'm considering it," Elena murmured, dragging the bin over and setting it on the carpet in front of her.

She stopped in surprise. There was a little note taped on top of the bin that she hadn't seen before: *Give it a try. I'm here to talk when you're ready. Love, Pa.*

Oh, boy. That meant *he* had put together the stuff inside, and he really thought she should go through it (and face whatever emotions the process might instigate). Maybe he was right. As much as it might irk her, Pa tended to be right about things like this, knowing what was best for the person involved. Especially her.

"I guess I'd better get to it, then," she said, as if he was sitting in the room with her right now.

She couldn't help but feel a smile pull at her lips. Pa had a way of getting her to take the plunge into things she didn't want to. Like the time he was taking her out for driving practice, preparing her to take her road test when she was seventeen, and she'd abruptly decided she didn't want to drive anymore because she'd almost cut off his arm against some guardrails; he'd coaxed her to get back behind the wheel. Or the summer more than thirty years ago, when she'd been afraid to put a worm on the hook or take a fish off the line, and he'd talked her through it.

Funny thing was she almost always felt better after she'd accomplished the thing she was avoiding. Pa knew that. They spoke the same language even when they weren't talking out loud, and she trusted his judgment now.

Popping the sides of the bin's plastic lid, Elena lifted it off and set it on the coffee table. The pom-poms went first, though as they were being removed they released a fine coating of dust that threw her into a coughing fit. She treated that like a mini-reprieve.

A few tissues and a glass of water later, she came back into the living room and began in earnest, digging through the pile of high school mementos that had been hidden beneath the crinkly orange and black pom-poms: school ribbons, letters, ticket stubs, her dried-up prom corsage, a bulging white bag underneath everything else . . . and off to the side sat the diary that she'd known would be in there before she even looked.

It was the item she feared most. It contained the whole story, and there would be no further reprieve. She ran her hand over its worn leather surface, once hunter-green, now faded to a mossy color. The trim all around the edges looked good though, the narrow gold design mostly unblemished.

She gripped the book tightly between her hands, closing her eyes and imagining she could feel Jesse there somehow—that she could capture his essence through the smooth covers. She heard his gentle laughter inside her head again, the sound faint, like a music box wound down.

Elena opened her eyes and blinked back the sting. Then, cracking open the cover, she began to read.

(Some items from the plastic bin)

Diary entry #1:
June 30, 1981

This is Elena Elizabeth, and it's my first time writing even though I got this diary five months ago when I turned twelve. I've been feeling a little guilty cuz Ma says I should be using it, so here goes. I met a new kid near Caveman Rock today. He seems like a jerk. . . .

The first time Elena saw Jesse James Wilder she was up to her elbows in dirt and a rotting layer of last autumn's leaves. She was a definite outdoors girl, tall for her age and in the habit of running free all day each summer—sometimes playing with Jen (less often Zippy or Patricia) or maybe the across-the-field-neighbors Lisa and Debbie. But lots of times she just rummaged around in the woods by herself.

She could spend hours looking at plants, collecting feathers, pretending to be a pioneer or an Indian, and finding dead birds and other animals to bury in the little animal graveyard Pa had helped them lay out behind the camp's outhouse. She'd be the first to admit that with only one bathroom at the homestead, the outhouse could be useful in a pinch, even if it was stinky and dark.

She felt safe playing outside by herself all day. Ma had never had to worry about weirdos trolling the streets and byways for kids to pick up. Not in rural areas like Moose Junction, and certainly not out in the acres of woods behind their house.

On the rare occasions when Elena went with her sisters on the ten-minute bike ride down the highway to the lake (from which the nearby town of Lake Pines derived its name), they'd all stuck together. The older girls watched out for the younger ones, and bad drivers were more of a concern than kidnappers.

All in all, Elena relished those summer days of freedom, coming home at dusk and covered in dirt, and, more often than not, with twigs and even burdocks tangled in her hair.

As it was already nearing suppertime on that particular day, she looked quite a sight as she crouched in the dappled light, trying to scoop a half mummified chipmunk carcass into an improvised Maple bark coffin.

She'd been concentrating so hard that she hadn't been paying attention to her surroundings. So when Jesse Wilder surprised her by stepping into her little clearing with his size thirteen feet, snapping twigs like a black bear, she'd lurched to a partial stand and nearly clocked him with the stick she'd been using to dig at the dirt around the dead chipmunk. In fact, she swung her improvised weapon within a few inches of his head at the same time that she pretty much growled at him.

Both of his big hands shot up in front of him in a fist-clenched, defensive pose as he yelled, "Holy shit!" But the terrified look on his face immediately made her feel a little better, considering her temporary lapse of attention to her surroundings.

"What the hell!" he added as his fists slowly came down, but his shock was still apparent by the way his voice cracked on the last word.

Elena's mouth turned down at the double profanities. She gave him a quick onceover, none too impressed. First of all, he was obviously a city slicker, and second of all, he was a *boy* (a.k.a. an alien species). A tall, wiry boy, sporting a shock of honey-colored hair streaked with blond, and staring at her through narrowed blue eyes.

She finally let out her breath, standing up out of her stooped position. "Didn't your mother ever tell you not to use that kind of language?"

"My mother died when I was six."

That kind of set Elena back on her heels. "Oh . . . sorry."

She didn't really know what else to say. The truth was that she didn't know anyone on a personal basis who didn't have a mother. The thought of what it would be like not to have Ma, with her soft hands, sweet smile, and gentle voice (except when Trish, Zippy, and Elena had been squabbling so much that they'd driven her up one wall and down another) took away some of the sting of indignation she'd been feeling.

But the temporary peace lasted only as long as it took for the tall, scrawny blond kid to open his mouth again, right after he returned the favor Elena had given him with a disdainful onceover, his expression having shifted by now from his initial shock to a look of cool mocking.

"What are you, some kind of crazy mountain girl?" His sarcasm was only fair considering the way she looked, she supposed, but she didn't much care for logic at that moment. She snorted, taking in his Jordache jeans, Nike sneakers, and perfectly pressed Ralph Lauren shirt.

"Yeah. Just like you're a walking billboard for name brands."

He did something Elena didn't expect then. He laughed.

(The old outhouse)

Diary entry # 166:
May 6, 1986

My life is over. It's been almost five years—FIVE YEARS!—but Billboard Boy is back, and he's in ALL my classes. Just let me die now and get it over with. . . .

When Elena walked into English 11 Honors on that first Monday of May, she had no reason to expect that it would be any different from any other Monday morning English class of the past eight months. After the bell rang, they'd sit down, pull out their books, and discuss the weekend's reading for forty-two minutes.

It didn't take long for her to realize that something was different today. There was a new student, which by itself wasn't *entirely* unusual, even at this late date in the school year. A lot of military kids came and went every three years or so, depending on their family's transfer orders for the nearby base. The difference this time was that Elena already knew this kid—or at least she thought she did.

It was tough to tell because he was sitting in the middle of a group of girls, most of them snooty preps who never gave her the time of day, trying to act nonchalant as they fluttered around him like some kind of desperate North Country geishas.

Elena tried to get a better look at his profile as she approached to take her seat, which happened to be just one row over and three chairs ahead of him. A flicker of hope burst to life; maybe she was wrong after all. This guy's blond hair was a little darker than the kid Elena remembered.

When she got to within a yard of him, there was an opening in the cluster of girls. At that moment, he turned his head and caught her gaze full on, and she felt like the air had been sucked out of the room. *Oh, man.* It was him, all right. He sat there, staring at her with those eyes that were as startlingly blue as ever. In the next moment, one of his eyebrows cocked up in recognition . . . and he smiled.

The effect was dazzling, and it set the girls around him atwitter all over again, not to mention what it did to the rhythm of Elena's own heartbeat. She tried to ignore that, and the way she could feel her cheeks flaming in response to his handsome grin. The preps unknowingly saved her from further embarrassment when they shifted in a kind of undulating wave as she passed, obscuring him again from Elena's view. She made it to her seat somehow without tripping.

Jesse James Wilder.

It had seemed a lifetime since they'd spent that summer together running around the woods like a couple of natives. Elena had been more tomboy than girl then, and Jesse had been a tall, scrawny kid with big feet, mitt-sized hands, and almost girlishly long-lashed eyes.

To say that five years had changed a few things about Jesse was an understatement. Even though he was sitting down it was clear that he was even taller than he'd been; from that one direct glimpse Elena could tell he still had those amazing blue eyes. But he'd grown into his oversized hands and feet, his frame filling out from wiry to muscular, and his face, which had leaned toward "pretty boy" before, had matured to square-jawed, male model gorgeous.

"Did you hear me, Elena?"

In her shocked misery, Elena had barely noticed that Julia, her physics lab partner and cohort in most of her other classes as well, had taken the seat on Elena's left and was stretching toward her to talk with a stage whisper (in her usual nonstop way).

"What?" Elena managed to mumble. Julia tended to be kind of dramatic anyway, so her having some kind of incredibly important news wasn't all that unusual . . . but this time Elena knew that what she was going to say was going to be about Elena's old summer-buddy-turned-supermodel, and she was too unsettled by seeing him again to want to hear it right now.

"The guy sitting over there is Jesse *Wilder*." Julia's voice verged on a squeal. "You know, *the* Jesse Wilder from that big school near Poughkeepsie? I heard Sharon say his dad made an arrangement with Coach for him to play here because he, like, broke all the football records last year at his old school. He just transferred to Moose Junction because he won states for his team's section last season, and he needed a new challenge to attract scouts during his senior year. Can you believe it?"

Elena made some kind of sound that would approximate interest, but it didn't really matter. Julia kept whispering excitedly, not really noticing anything except the "hot" factor of Jesse Wilder, who was back there, soaking up the girls fawning over him like week-old bread soaking up gravy. Julia's whisper got a little louder as she apparently caught another glimpse of Jesse's face.

"I mean, I know his mother grew up in Moose Junction, so it's not *completely* impossible that he's here, but she's been dead for *years*, and he's, like, the best high school quarterback in the country! Isn't that awesome?"

"Just fantastic," Elena muttered, knowing all too well the great Jesse Wilder's football prowess. Every time he had broken another record it had made the town paper and the local radio station because his late mother and grandma had been from here. At first Elena had had a hard time connecting the football hero of those articles and broadcasts with the kid she'd known. After a while she'd done her best to avoid thinking about him at all.

But now he'd appeared out of nowhere. And he was in her English class.

Elena was thankful when the bell rang and Mr. Fitch called the class to order. She resisted the urge to look back and see if the hole she felt burning into her back was really Jesse staring at her or just her usual, overblown imagination. She wasn't about to look and give all those prep girls the satisfaction of her watching them preen around him. Besides, Elena didn't think she could stand watching him bask in their attention.

Of all the dumb luck.

It wasn't fair that Jesse Wilder had turned out to be a teen god, a star football player on top of that, and, worst of all, a transfer to their football-obsessed community of Moose Junction. This coming fall he would be worshipped if he helped win games for their New York State Section III Championship-chasing high school football team, the Black Bears.

By comparison, Elena felt, as usual, a lot . . . less. In every way.

She was no longer a tomboy, exactly, but she was certainly no beauty queen. The only thing she had going for her was the spot she'd earned last fall on the varsity football cheerleading team, but she was even less popular than she'd been five years ago, if that was possible, thanks to most of the preps. Her hair might not sport burdocks and twigs any more, but it was still the same deep auburn color that had lent itself to unflattering nicknames in middle school. Also, unlike Zippy's lush and layered Lori-Singer-in-*Footloose* hairstyle, Elena's was (still wavy but) all one length.

Zippy. Ah, crap.

Elena barely resisted the urge to thump her forehead on the desk when she realized what would happen as soon as Zippy laid her baby blues on the perfect specimen of masculinity that Jesse Wilder had become. It wouldn't matter that just last month she'd said she needed to have her "space" and finally broken up for good with Drew, her on-and-off boyfriend of two years, or that she was a senior about to graduate and Jesse was still only a junior. She would rationalize that he was almost eighteen, after all (his birthday was in July; he *should* have been a senior this year, but that summer they'd spent together he'd told Elena that he'd had to repeat first grade the year after his mother died).

No. Once Zippy saw him, there'd be no stopping her. She'd forget every derogatory comment she'd ever made about him five years ago, bat her lashes, strut by on her high-heeled long legs, and it would be all over.

Elena didn't allow herself to think past that. Who knew what worse things her mind could conjure? Instead, she just buried her thoughts and her nose in *Jane Eyre* and tuned everything else out.

Diary entry # 168:
May 12, 1986

It's Sunday night, and for the first time since junior high I really *don't want to go to school tomorrow. The preps are making me nauseous! I'm trapped for seven hours, forced to watch the whole hair-sprayed, made-up, Oompa-loompa-tanned pack of them cozy up to and giggle around Jesse James Wilder. Every. Single. Day. And don't get me started on* him. *He acts like I don't exist (big surprise)! Oh, my God, I can't stand the sideshow for another day. Please just let this school year be OVER already. . . .*

"You gonna eat those Ho Hos?"

Elena absently glanced at her best friend, Mindy (her best *school* friend—her absolute best friend was still her sister, Jen, but Jen had just finished her junior year in college, and even though she was home for the summer, she had a job at Stan's Sno-Cones, so Elena didn't see her as often as she wanted to). Mindy was eyeing the little package of chocolate-covered cake rolls Ma had said Elena could pack with the rest of her lunch. Elena had been saving them for that last sugar kick to get her through the afternoon. Before she could tell Mindy that, there was a commotion at the end of the lunchroom and a blond male head came into view.

Rolling her eyes, Elena dragged her gaze away from the fawning gaggle of prep girls that seemed to accompany Jesse Wilder wherever he went (led by her nemesis, Sharon, who was still miffed that Elena had made the varsity cheerleading team this past fall while she remained on JV). Elena's stomach did a funny flip, and she picked up the snacks to hand them to Mindy.

"Nah, I'm not hungry anymore. You can have them."

"Thanks." Mindy took the Ho Ho package, ripped open the cellophane, and bit off half a cake in one bite, all while watching Elena rifle through the stack of notebooks in her backpack. Elena didn't really need anything from the bag, but she wasn't about to sit around watching Jesse play high school stud through most of another lunch period. He'd been at Moose Junction High for almost a week already, and every day in the cafeteria it was the same.

Elena took a quick glance at Mindy who was scarfing down the remainder of the first Ho Ho and then shook her head, biting back a smile. Oh, well. At least the daily, sickening lunchtime display of Jesse and his harem had done wonders for Elena's nutritional goals. That he'd yet to acknowledge her with more than that one smile on the first day had had nothing to do with her loss of appetite. Well, maybe that wasn't entirely true, but she wasn't about to admit it to anyone.

What she *would* admit was that she wasn't going to waste another minute contemplating the subject of Jesse James Wilder. Thank God there were only a few weeks of school left until Regents exams started and she could be free for a little while, at least, from observing the feeding frenzy that surrounded him.

"You don't like him very much now, do you?"

"Who?"

Mindy leveled a "get real" look at Elena, pausing mid-chew with the last of the second Ho Ho bulging in her right cheek.

Elena waved her hand, irritated that she was being forced to answer questions about Jesse. "I only hung out with him for that one summer. It was forever ago. I have no clue what he's like anymore."

"I remember that summer." Mindy had chewed and swallowed the rest of the Ho Ho, and she was being entirely serious now. Sensing that she was building to a full-blown conversation about Jesse, Elena tucked her chin, pretending to study review formulas from the physics notebook she'd taken out and hoping Mindy would take the hint.

"That was the year I spent July and August in New Hampshire with my grandma," Mindy continued, oblivious to, or else deliberately ignoring, Elena's none-too-subtle signals to shut up about this. "But I still remember the letters you wrote me on that cute stationary you had of the clown holding those yellow, pink, and blue balloons."

"Yeah. So?" Elena didn't look up from the page.

"You spent every waking moment with Jesse that summer."

Elena wrinkled her nose. "Hardly."

"Just about." Mindy gave Elena a knowing look. "Come on, El, admit it. You liked him then. *Really* liked him. A lot."

Elena sighed and pulled her attention away from her notebook to look at Mindy. She'd been hoping her friend wouldn't go there. That she *had*, meant Mindy was probably getting fed up with Elena's mood swings. It happened every time Jesse was nearby, which was pretty often, since they had the same lunch period, were in most classes together, and he rode her bus. He and his father had moved into his grandmother's old house while the workers finished renovating it. It was only about a dozen houses up the road and across the woods from Elena's house.

When Elena didn't say anything, Mindy pushed it a little further. "You liked him enough to let him be your first kiss."

Elena glared at her. "If you can call it that."

"*You* did." She smiled, knowing Elena couldn't stay mad at her.

True, though that didn't mean Elena was going to take the bait and confess anything, either. Shrugging, she turned her attention to her notebook, fiddling with a kink in the spiral binding and straightening it before she finally argued, "Look, Min, you're making it sound like it was a big deal, but it wasn't. We were just kids. He was okay back then, once he got over himself."

Without letting her friend get a word in edgewise, she flipped through to another section of her notes and gave an unladylike snort as she finished with emphasis, "It's pretty clear God's gift to quarterbacks reverted to a jerk again as soon as he left Moose Junction, because all I've seen since he came back is an overgrown, stuck up jock who's completely in love with himself."

"Um, El?" Mindy's voice was quiet. "I'm not sure you should—"

"Okay, *please* tell me you're not defending him," Elena broke in, shooting a laser-like glare at her friend. She knew she was being rude, but Mindy's comment was plastering new annoyance over the irritation she was already feeling. "I can't believe *you*, of all people, have fallen for the hype! You couldn't *pay* me to care what the great Jesse James Wilder is like now. Let Golden Boy go feed his massive ego with the harem of airheads who follow him everywhere. I refuse to be part of it."

Elena was sort of surprised that her vehemence wasn't eliciting any kind of response from her bosom buddy. In fact, Mindy had gone completely silent and she wasn't moving a muscle. A shiver went up Elena spine as she realized her friend's expression was blank, and she was staring at a spot behind Elena, above her head.

Way above her head.

Crap. That couldn't be good.

Elena swiveled around slowly, her gaze falling first on the snug, flat contours of Jesse's jeans zipper before she quickly tipped her head up, desperate not to be caught looking *there,* of all places.

The resulting view of his polo-shirt-clad narrow waist, muscular chest, broad shoulders, and perfect face atop all that was hardly less distracting.

He, however, seemed to be enjoying her discomfort, if his expression was any indication. Maybe he hadn't heard what she'd just said about him. Fat chance, but it made her feel better to consider the possibility.

"Anyone sitting here?" He sounded amused as he glanced at the open spot next to Elena. She supposed she should have been grateful he didn't seem ticked, but she couldn't help wondering how he was planning to get back at her for her remarks.

And where were all his yes-girls? A quick glance to either side of him showed that he was alone. For now, anyway. He was holding a full lunch tray, so it looked like he really did intend to sit and eat. But Elena wasn't going to stick around for Sharon or any of the other girls to come back and bump her and Mindy from their usual places—not to mention that she had no idea what Jesse was up to, suddenly acknowledging her after a whole week of ignoring her.

"Nope." Elena shifted back in her seat, swiveling again to grab her notebook and book bag, and standing up. "There's plenty of room. I was just leaving for class."

He plunked his tray on the table, twisting back toward her to use his superior height (which she figured had to be around six-foot-three now that he was standing close enough to measure him against herself) to keep her from getting around him and leaving.

"Already?" he murmured, and Elena couldn't help taking a quick look at his face, devastated and annoyed all over again by her stupid reaction to his gorgeousness.

"Yeah. I, um, have to catch up on some studying before the physics exam."

"Mmhmm. . . ." He didn't sound convinced, but before she could bolt, he pulled a folded piece of white paper from one of the front pockets of those perfectly fit jeans and stuffed it into the flap of her book bag.

"Too bad. See you around, then." He tipped his head down just close enough to add in a whisper, "El-bell."

The warmth of his breath across her ear released a tingling rush of sensation down her neck. Hoping to God her face wasn't as red as it felt, Elena gave him a short, jerky nod and took off, too surprised by their interaction and the fact that he'd remembered his old nickname for her to do anything else. Mindy followed close behind, still speechless herself, until they were completely outside the cafeteria, and Elena slumped against the wall near a bank of lockers.

"Oh, my God. What did he say?" Mindy looked like she was going to burst as her gaze shifted to Elena's book bag. "And what did he give you?"

"I haven't a clue, and I don't care," Elena answered, sidestepping the first question and feigning indifference about the second. But she sounded way too breathless for either one of them to believe what she'd just said.

"Aren't you going to read it?" Mindy seemed ready to bounce out of her shoes with her need to know what Jesse Wilder had written on the note he'd given her.

Elena glanced around the hallway. It was teeming with people getting ready to go to lunch or class, depending on their schedule.

"Not here." Grabbing her arm, Elena steered her toward the girl's room. The stall doors had been removed a few years ago to try to help stem the school's drug and smoking problem, but it still gave a little more privacy than the open hallway. Besides, at this time of day most of the nicotine addicts would be in the student smoking lounge rather than the bathroom, so they might even find it empty.

Once they were inside—there was only one other girl washing her hands—Elena moved toward the windows, set her bag on the broad sill, pulled out the paper, and unfolded it to read it.

Meet me at the spot. 4:30. I have something to ask you. And come alone.

- Billboard Boy

"*Billboard* Boy?" Mindy echoed, scrunching her eyebrows. Elena shrugged. She'd never shared the nickname she'd given Jesse five summers ago with anyone except her diary. Mindy could be trusted to keep it to herself, though.

Elena's lack of response had Mindy adding, "Well, he *does* look like a model, but I'd have gone for 'Cowboy' or 'Outlaw' for a guy with a name like Jesse James Wilder. Not to mention, it would sound more sexily dangerous," she added with a dramatic shiver.

"*Sexily dangerous*? You have *got* to be kidding." Elena jabbed her friend with her elbow, stuffed the note into her pocket and slung her book bag over her shoulder.

Mindy's smile widened. "Well, it would."

Elena shook her head, having a hard time suppressing her own silly grin. "Come on, doofus, before we're late for class."

Diary entry # 169:
May 13, 1986

Beam me up, Scottie, cuz I think I've landed on an alien planet. Billboard Boy started talking to me in school. And he passed me a note at lunch. When Zippy hears about it, she'll fall right off her three-inch spike heels. I'm meeting him in the woods before supper.

Getting out of the house at 4:30 hadn't been easy. Pa would be home from work soon, and he liked supper at 5:30 sharp. Ma had the Shake-N-Bake chicken breasts in the oven, but she'd needed help peeling potatoes. Elena had promised to be back by 4:50—and then she'd done something she'd never done before: she'd lied to Ma. She'd said she needed to go to the woods to see if she could find a fiddlehead fern to bring into science class tomorrow. Shame had filled her as she'd raced out of the house, feeling the weight of Zippy's narrowed-eyed stare from where she sat peeling the potatoes in her place.

Elena had sped through the woods, expertly leaping over stones left from the prehistoric age, when glaciers had scraped through as they'd carved out the Adirondack Mountains in their wake. As she approached the spot she and Jesse had claimed for themselves that summer a half decade ago, she slowed, suddenly feeling less certain.

What was she doing out here? Lying to Ma, running off to meet a guy, and one who happened to be the biggest hunk in the whole school and maybe even the entire northeast. . . . She had to admit that it was one of the first times she'd felt truly connected to Zippy since she'd hit puberty. There was no denying that right now she was feeling dangerous . . . and a little excited. She was definitely acting more like Zippy (who'd been known to sneak to a party or two when Ma and Pa thought she was at her friend Angela's house) than herself.

The sun was starting to ease down toward the horizon, casting shadows that made her have to squint to see clearly as she came within view of their clearing. It only took a second, though, to see Jesse's long, jean-clad legs jutting out from where he sat on their rock, leaning back against one of the pair of trees backing it like some kind of nature-made chair (which was why they'd chosen this spot all those years ago as their hideout). His eyes were closed, his hands tucked behind his head, looking completely comfortable. That took some doing, she knew, since he was a city slicker through and through.

His (probably size fourteen now) feet were encased in Nike sneakers. She slowed to almost a stop, not paying enough attention to realize she was breaking one of the cardinal rules she'd learned long ago for moving around the woods unseen and unheard. As she moved further into the clearing, she stepped onto one of the fallen, dried branches from last season. It snapped loudly as her weight sank in, making Jesse's eyes open and his head swivel in her direction.

Then she had to remind herself to breathe again, because when he smiled at her she could have sworn she'd forgotten how. *Dang!* She had to stop reacting to him like this. She was behaving worse than the preps that swarmed all over him every day at school like flies on a food-smeared picnic table in the sun.

"What's the matter, El-bell? You look like you want to punch somebody." He unfolded his lean, obviously muscular body from its sitting position and stood up before taking a few steps toward her. The smile still hovered on his lips, but he'd lifted his right eyebrow in that way that had always annoyed her, even when they were kids. He looked so cocky, egotistical, full of himself, and—

"You came, though. I didn't know if you would."

Hmmm. Maybe not completely cocky.

She scowled more deeply, trying not to meet his gaze. "Yeah, well, I only have a couple minutes." She looked up at him again, then, instantly regretted it when a warm, melting sensation spilled through her. She clenched her teeth and forced herself to stay in control. That was one thing she was pretty good at if she set her mind to it. It was a skill she'd cultivated back in the midst of junior high, when the teasing and clique-forming had begun in earnest. She nodded at him. "So you'd better ask me whatever it is you called me out here for so I can get back home and help Ma set the table."

"Um, okay. I wasn't going to spring it like this, but—"

As Jesse spoke he took another step closer, the expression in his blue eyes enigmatic. Just then the breeze shifted and the fragrance wafting from him slammed into her.

Body on Tap shampoo.

It swept her back to that last summer afternoon on the side of the lake. The heat from the sun had spilled down on the tops of their heads to blanket their shoulders, the warmed fragrance of his freshly washed hair filling her senses as he'd pressed his mouth against hers in their first fumbling kiss.

The funny feeling in her stomach intensified as the memory stabbed deeper, and she swallowed hard, clueless about what he could want with her here—about why he was paying her any mind at all, after a whole week of ignoring her while he soaked up the worship of the football coaches, his teammates, the entire faculty . . . and the girls (she couldn't forget the girls) at Moose Junction High.

"Okay, here goes." He appeared to gather up his thoughts (or his courage?) and quirked his lip up on one side. "So, it looks like prom is in less than two weeks, El-bell. . . . Will you go with me?"

"What, like, as your *date*?" The words slipped through the airless vacuum in her chest before she had a chance to think about them.

He laughed, his eyes crinkling in the corners, and he suddenly seemed less the conquering football star and more like the tall, scrawny kid she remembered. "Yeah, like, my *date*." He leaned forward a little as he said that, and she took a step back, all sorts of feelings flooding her. "I even have a car to take us," he continued. "My dad says he'll let me borrow his Camaro."

Whoa. This was going way too fast. It didn't make any sense. Elena was not the kind of girl to be asked on a date, let alone to prom. By *anyone*, no less the school's newest, most gorgeous, most popular guy. The same guy who hadn't spoken to her until today in the cafeteria because he was too busy letting every female in the student body at Moose Junction fawn all over him.

And so she did what any sensible, completely confused teenage girl would do. She took another step back, mumbled, "Uh, I don't think so," and then turned tail, crashing through the woodland back home and trying to push from her mind the look of shock her answer had brought to Jesse's perfect, sculpted face.

Diary entry # 173:
May 25, 1986

My world is officially rocked. In two short hours, I'll be going to the prom with Jesse. He keeps trying to hang around me in school, too, when he could have any girl in the whole town. And he asked me to prom THREE times (!) before I finally agreed to go with him. Oh. My. God. . . .

Prom was a disaster.

Prep goddess Sharon (who was so popular that she'd been asked to every Junior Prom since she was in ninth grade, the same as Zippy) had noticed that Elena's dress was a hand-me-down.

Sharon apparently remembered that Zippy had worn that same dress to prom two years ago (when Zippy was a sophomore and Sharon was a freshman). That, combined with the fact that she'd been livid when she'd heard that Jesse had asked Elena to be his date, had meant it was open season. Now she was going for Elena's jugular. The snide comments had begun an hour ago, if not directly from Sharon, then from one of her cronies, uttered under their breath or whispered from behind their hands, and punctuated by sly, spiteful glances.

The worst had been a few minutes ago, when Elena had made the mistake of going over to the refreshment table to get some Pepsi while Jesse was in the restroom. Sharon and her boyfriend, Steven, had been standing nearby, and Sharon had smiled and started singing a version of the old Sesame Street tune, "One of These Things is Not Like the Others," adapting the words to include Elena's name and adding "no matter how hard she tries to be like the rest of us."

The stupidity of it would have been laughable any other time, but the fact that it capped off all the other comments made it too much; it seemed to slice deep into all the insecurities Elena had carried around with her since the middle of seventh grade, when eighth-grader Zippy had already blossomed into an adored social princess, while Elena was clearly a second-best version of her older sister: Uninteresting, plain, and awkward.

Leaving the Pepsi on the table, Elena hadn't responded to Sharon's taunt, instead walking with an unhurried pace out of the main prom room (she knew better than to give the wench the satisfaction of knowing her claws had drawn blood) before fleeing as fast as her feet would take her to the ancient and mostly unused ladies room all the way in the basement of the restaurant.

Now she turned on the creaky faucet and ran cool water over her fingertips, trying to dab beneath her eyes in the hope of reducing the redness from the tears she'd finally indulged once she was safe in the confines of the restroom. It was hopeless. She'd just have to force herself to think of other things (so she wouldn't start crying again) and then let enough time go by that her eyes would look better before heading back upstairs. Jesse was probably wondering where the heck she was, but there was no help for it.

It didn't matter anyway.

The whole night was a disaster.

She'd had such a short time to pull anything together, once she'd told Jesse she'd go with him (not to mention that there was no extra money set aside for such an extravagance at the last minute) that Ma had had to pull out this old dress of Zippy's and change some things around for Elena to wear it. Elena hadn't minded too much; she'd felt pretty in the peach-colored gown.

But it paled in comparison to the brand new, fashionable gown Zippy was wearing this year; Zippy's was much fancier, but Elena didn't really blame her sister for not wanting to give it up, even after Ma had hinted that it might be nice for her to do that, since Zippy had been to three proms before and this was Elena's first. They were the same size, but Zippy had bought this gown herself with her babysitting and chore money, saved up from the whole year. She never used her earnings for anything other than clothes (she didn't need to since she had a line up of boys waiting to take her places, and they always paid her way).

Elena hadn't really worried about anyone realizing she was wearing a hand-me-down gown. It had been two years, after all, since Zippy had worn it. But she should have known better, especially with Sharon in attendance.

Blowing her nose, Elena dabbed her fingers beneath her reddened eyes again, trying whatever she could so they didn't look so puffy. Fat chance. She needed some ice or something. Who to send for it? Mindy, maybe. . . .

But her best friend was dancing the night away beneath the mirror ball hanging over the dance floor. How in heck could she get Mindy's attention from down here? Elena heard the music throbbing above her tawdry bathroom sanctuary: "You're the One that I Want" from the *Grease* album. Her friend was almost certainly in the process of reenacting the dance from that scene in the movie. Mindy was talented like that, and she really belonged on a stage.

But that meant that for now she wouldn't be able to help (not to mention she didn't even know Elena was down here).

She'd just have to get a grip on her own. She'd run the water until it got *really* cold and then—

The door to the almost-never-used ladies room swung in with force enough to be just shy of smacking into the wall opposite it. Zippy came sweeping through in a swirl of lavender puffed sleeves, billowy skirt, and Halston perfume (the real stuff; designer fragrances were as much of a must for Zippy as name brand clothing, and she always seemed to have at least one boy hanging around who was eager to spend a month's pay to buy her a bottle for Christmas or Valentine's Day). She paused after the door swung shut behind her, her gaze meeting Elena's in the mirror's reflection.

"Jesse's ready to punch someone up there. He thinks Steven Fiorella insulted you, and that's why you've made yourself scarce."

"It wasn't Steven. It was his girlfriend," Elena said, sniffing and wiping her nose while still looking at her sister.

"Yeah, well, you and I may know Sharon's the guilty one, but Jesse James Wilder doesn't. And if he clocks Steven, he'll probably kill him like Lancelot killed that knight in the King Arthur story you told me about." Zippy wrinkled her nose, the expression managing to look adorable on her. "You know, that chapter near the end where Lancelot punched the guy in the head to get his armor when he was ambushed with Guinevere in her room."

Zippy's rattled-off description made Elena smile. Zippy had always liked romantic things; she managed to remember those parts of the stories, even though she never read school books if she could help it (not to mention that *King Arthur* was an Honors English text, and Zippy wasn't in any honors classes; her gifts did not include academic ability).

Zippy walked up to the mirror to check her already perfect rose-tinted lips before shifting her stare again to her younger sister. "Besides that, though, if Jesse starts swinging up there, he'll probably get in a lot of trouble and not get to play football. Unofficial practices start in less than a month, right after exams."

Elena's smile shifted to a frown.

"You need to go upstairs and do some damage control with your man while I go do some actual damage to darling Sharon." As she spoke, Zippy's expression shifted into one that was sharp and decidedly feline. It was a dangerous look that Elena knew from experience that she never wanted directed at her.

"What are you going to do?" Elena swallowed hard and hoped she didn't look as deer-in-the-headlights as she felt (since she didn't dare pull her gaze from Zippy's to check in the mirror).

Zippy's pearly teeth showed just a bit as her lips curved in a tight smile. "Don't worry. I won't do anything too bad. I'm just going to make sure the nasty little witch has enough to worry about that she'll be distracted and lay off you."

"You'd do that for me?"

"Of course, you ninny; you're my sister. I've got your back." Zippy's smile deepened to what most would describe as dazzling this time, and it crossed Elena's mind to wonder why her own similar expression never seemed to be that stunning.

Still, Elena felt a rush of gratitude, and her lips edged up in response. "Thanks. I'll do my part with Jesse. But you're wrong about him. He's not my man, he's just my date."

Zippy rolled her eyes. "Okay, keep telling yourself that. He's ga-ga over you." Looping her arm through Elena's, she threw in a characteristic Zippy zinger, "*Why* he is, I have no idea, but he is."

Making a sound that was half laugh and half protest, Elena bumped her hip into Zippy, making them tip against the doorjamb so that both of them were full out grinning as they headed up the stairs on their way out to rejoin the fray.

"Are you all right?"

A thrill slipped up Elena's spine, tingling all the way to her scalp at the leashed power in Jesse's tuxedo-clad form as he strode the rest of the way past the dance floor to get to her; Zippy gave her linked arm a last little squeeze before peeling off toward the refreshment tables (and presumably Sharon's general vicinity), leaving Elena to stand by herself with Jesse. His brows were gathered over those gorgeous blue eyes, his square jaw tight with concern.

Concern for her, she realized with another jolt.

Oh, man, he *did* look how she'd imagined Lancelot would: Tall, handsome, and dangerous in defense of a lady. All he was missing was a broadsword and shield to complete the picture.

Just keeping breathing. . . .

"I'm fine," she managed to say as he took her arm and escorted her out a propped door to the balcony area, leading her past a dozen other couples taking advantage of the balmy, star-filled night. Several turned to stare and some whispered as they strode along the entire length of the balcony to the stone steps. Those led down into gardens filled with winding, flower-lined paths shadowed under a full moon.

He tugged her to a stop beneath one of the maples at the garden's center, and then pivoted to face her. His finger touched beneath her chin, tipping her face up as he examined her, his gaze dark. "You were crying." He cursed under his breath. "I knew I should have cleaned that shithead's clock." When he dropped his hand, she saw it clench into a fist. "What did he say to you? I want to know so I can remind him of it when I'm cramming his teeth down his throat."

Elena reached out, feeling his powerful arm muscles contracting beneath her palm. "It's not something worth getting in trouble over, Jesse. Besides, Steven Fiorelli wasn't the one giving me a hard time." She shrugged one shoulder. "He didn't try to stop it, but it wasn't him."

"Who, then?"

"His girlfriend, Sharon."

"That underdressed pygmy?"

Elena choked back an unladylike sound. "Sharon may be short, but I'm pretty sure the underdressed part is why every guy in school loves to watch her sashay down the hall, flaunting her assets."

"Not every guy."

Elena's heart beat faster, and she saw the muscle in Jesse's jaw twitch again as he glanced back toward the balcony.

Her breath was still stuck like a big bubble above her thudding heart when he slid his gaze back to hers.

"Do you want me to take care of it? I mean, obviously I can't do what I was planning to do to her boyfriend, but I can tell her what I think."

Elena shook her head. "No, it's okay. My sister, Alex, told me she already has a plan in mind, but I'm not sure I even want to know what it is."

Jesse's mood seemed to shift, then, and he smiled. "Oh, yeah. I've heard about your sister from a few of the guys on the team. She sounds like something else. I wouldn't want to get on her bad side."

"Me either."

He paused and looked at her sort of sideways. "You know, for being so close in age, you two aren't very much alike."

Elena took a step back and tried to swallow the sudden rush of hurt. "Yeah, I'm aware of that."

"I didn't say it was a bad thing."

Elena's gaze locked with his again. "Look, I know exactly what she is that I'm not. It's been that way for years, so you don't need to humor me about it."

Jesse sighed and shook his head. "Wow, El-bell. For a smart girl you don't always catch on so well."

"Oh, really?" Her brows shot up.

"Yeah, really." He gave her a half smile. "I didn't ask your sister to prom. I asked *you*—three times, by the way. There's a reason for that."

"Oh."

That took the wind out of her sails. Crossing her arms over her chest, she frowned, wanting to get off this rollercoaster of emotions she seemed to be on lately.

Jesse shook his head again, his blue eyes lit with humor. "Listen, why don't we blow this popsicle stand? We can take a ride to the lake before I have to get you home."

"Why, what time is it?"

He glanced at his watch. "11:50."

"I won't turn into a pumpkin at midnight, you know."

"No, but your father will have my head on a plate if I'm not driving you up your driveway by 1:00 a.m. sharp. I just figured we could take a look at the moon over the water first." He smiled again, sending that liquid warmth spiraling through her. "It's too nice a night to let it end with stupid high school drama."

"All right." Elena glanced away, uncertain what this was going to mean, other than that she was going to be alone with Jesse. Completely alone, like when they were kids. Except they were older now, and they'd be in a romantic setting (because you couldn't get much more romantic than overlooking a lake on a warm, starry night, as far as she was concerned).

The instincts Pa had instilled in her and all of his girls—to be wary of her surroundings, to always have a backup plan, and to not get into any situation with a guy that might turn dangerous—kicked in.

Because of that, she told Zippy exactly where they were going and asked Jesse to drive to Drop Off Point, the little cliff over the palisades, as the place they could look at the lake; it was practically across the road from the homestead, so if something went wrong, she could make a big enough ruckus to alert Pa, the Steiners, or another neighbor.

But her gut feeling told her that this would be okay, that she could trust Jesse to be a gentleman around her.

Fifteen minutes later, they arrived at the palisades. A few insects clicked and fluttered against Jesse's headlights as they pulled up. Once he cut the motor, it was peaceful in the dark, the only sounds coming from the crickets, the rustling of breeze in the trees, and lake water lapping against the shore. She was surprised that no one else had had the idea to come out here tonight. The stars twinkled in the velvet canopy of sky as if they'd been flung up there by the handful. Taking a breath of sweet air, she approached the cliff's edge, her insides filling with that deep well of appreciation that swelled whenever she was near the lake.

Jesse had taken a few steps away from her when they'd left the car, and she watched him now as he walked up to an old white lilac bush that had once been in someone's backyard but had grown wild in the eight decades since the village that had been here before was moved to make way for the dam that had created the lake. Moonlight gilded his hand silver as he reached up and broke off a bloom.

"Here," he murmured, coming back to her. "I like this a lot better than that corsage."

Elena glanced down to her wrist. The cream and peach roses he'd slid over her hand before the prom remained unblemished, cradled in baby's breath and intertwined with a sparkly gold ribbon. "But these are still perfect."

"Yeah, because they're hot-house flowers, probably sprayed with some kind of chemical to keep them from wilting. I'd rather have something a little flawed but straight from Mother Nature." He lifted the lilac bloom to her nose. "See? No one in the world could manufacture a smell as perfect as this, no matter how hard they tried."

Elena breathed in the distinctive fragrance, closing her eyes. When she opened them again, he caught her gaze and her heart skipped another beat. *Oh, wow.* The way he was looking at her was making something funny happen deep in her stomach. It was making her heart flutter and her breath catch.

"Flowers like this remind me of you, El-bell. Honest and real."

Her legs felt wobbly, and she had the sudden urge to slide her hands up his arms to loop them around his neck.

As if he'd read her mind, he threaded his fingers into hers, the lilac pressed between their palms as he tugged her closer, finally letting go of her hands to wrap his arms around her in a warm and protective hug. He held her carefully, as if he was trying to make sure he didn't overpower her. It felt wonderful to be enfolded in his arms like that, but after a while she leaned back a little and tilted her face up to his, wanting more. He hesitated for only a second before tipping his head forward to respond to her invitation.

When his lips grazed hers, a jolt went through her. That touch deepened into a kiss that made the warmth already building inside her spool into heavy, thick heat. Instinctively, she pressed closer to him, recognizing in that instant just how physically powerful he was, even beyond what she'd been able to tell from sharing a few dances at the prom. He felt good—and he tasted good, too, she thought, her hand brushing against the silky blond waves at his nape.

After a few seconds, they both pulled back and looked away from each other, the moment feeling a little awkward now. Still, Elena couldn't stop smiling, and a soft laugh escaped her before she could hold it back.

"Shit. . . . Did I do something wrong?" Jesse looked so stricken for an instant that she reached to link her hand with his again.

"You need to stop swearing . . . but no, you were amazing."

He grinned. "Oh, that's cool. Amazing I can handle." Any tension seeped away as he led her back toward the Camaro, leaning back against the warm hood before turning her to face him and pulling her lightly toward him.

"I can see you're relieved," she countered, only half teasing him.

"Well, yeah. I mean, I'm pretty good at getting the job done on the football field, but this is more complicated. . . ." He trailed off and glanced away with an embarrassed laugh before looking at her again.

"It's just that I haven't had much practice in this department."

You could have knocked Elena over with a feather. She stared at him. "You're kidding, right? *You*? Not have much experience kissing girls? Give me a break! You're a star quarterback who looks like a Polo model."

"You think I look like a Polo model?" He grinned again.

"Don't change the subject."

"What?"

"How many girls have you kissed, really?"

"Counting you?" He suddenly seemed more self-conscious.

"Yes, counting me."

"Well, uhhhh . . . in that case, the answer would be *one*."

A little pain pierced suspiciously near her heart. "Okay, even *I'm* not naïve enough to believe that, Jesse."

"Sorry, but it's the truth."

Elena pulled back, taking a couple steps away and studying him. "You're being *serious*?"

"Yeah." He shrugged, looking almost hurt. "I don't go around locking lips with every girl I see, El."

"But you have girls throwing themselves at you constantly. It had to be the same in Poughkeepsie. And you're telling me that *I'm* the only one you've kissed?"

"Yeah," he repeated. He'd crossed his arms over his chest, seeming more uncomfortable by the second. "It's not much fun being a piece of meat, you know. I'm supposed to be this great championship-maker and maybe fulfill a few fantasies on the side while I'm at it. Unless I want to be an ass, I have to try to stay neutral when girls come on to me. Which is pretty much all the time."

Elena stood in shocked silence for a moment more, not believing what she was hearing. And yet when she thought back to all those times she'd seen Jesse surrounded by the flock of popular girls and other fawning females at the school—in class, the hallway, or the lunchroom—he'd been doing nothing but standing or sitting in their midst. He hadn't participated in anything. He'd been pleasant but noncommittal. All while they viewed him as a stud, a hunk, a teen god . . . a title-winning commodity.

Suddenly she felt like the biggest jerk in the world.

She sucked in her breath. "Oh, geez, Jesse . . . I'm sorry. I didn't realize what it must be like for you." She took a step toward him again, wanting to reach out, but not sure whether he would welcome her touch.

With an easy motion, he caught her hand in his again. "It's not that big of a deal, El; it's just the way it is. But it's one of the reasons I like hanging around with you." Standing now, he pushed himself away from the car, adding, "You're different from them. It's like you see me for *me*, and not for all that other stuff."

"Yeah, I guess I do." A swell of happiness filled her at his admission. "And maybe I was wrong, too. Maybe you're not so different from the nice guy I thought you were five summers ago." She gave him a teasing look. "Except you're probably cockier than you used to be, along with a *little* more intelligent—"

"Hey!" He barked a laugh and swung her around to pull her close again, making her giggle. "Don't forget amazing," he whispered in her ear, and she could hear the smile in his voice. "You said I was amazing."

She breathed in the warm spice of his aftershave, relishing the feel of his arms around her and his breath tickling the hair at her temple. Smiling with him, she murmured, "Oh, all right. I guess amazing works, too."

Diary entry # 189:
July 5, 1986

I could have died last night. Jesse came to pick me up to go see the fireworks with him at Alder Creek, and Pa was sitting at the table in his white t-shirt with his arms crossed, biceps bulging, and that stern look on his face like he does for any of us when the same boy keeps coming to the house. He told Jesse he expected him to remember I was a young lady whenever we're alone together. I love Pa, but I wanted to disappear when he said that! Jesse's never been anything but a gentleman with me! Of course he said, "Yes, sir," and his face turned red, but it must not have bothered him too much because he's taking me to the beach today. I'm wearing my new bathing suit (a bikini—yikes!). . . .

The air shimmered with almost visible heat, and white clouds seemed to hang unmoving in the blue-washed sky above Elena as she sat on a striped towel in the sand just past the grassy part leading to the beach, trying her best to stay cool. She didn't do well in the heat. Other girls tanned, but Elena just got red-faced and sweated. Thank goodness for the breeze. There was enough of one that she hoped it was keeping her from looking too much like a tomato.

Sipping from the icy-cold Pepsi Jesse had brought her from the concession stand a few minutes ago, Elena looked around, watching the activity and people. Coconut oil scented the air, baked into everyone's skin. With every puff of hot breeze, it swirled together with the mouth-watering aroma of hot French fries, the tang of ketchup left out in the sun, and every now and again, a whiff of the burgers sizzling on charcoal grills dotting the picnic areas.

There had to be almost two hundred people here today, either in the water, sunning themselves on big beach towels, or involved in games (usually with Frisbees or balls) at the edge of the sand. Lake Pines Park was *the* place to be in the summer. Elena had always felt out of place and pale here among the masses of sun-kissed bodies (unlike Zippy, who didn't mind being fair-skinned and loved the extra attention she got in her itsy-bitsy bikini), but Jesse loved the outdoors, and so Elena had found herself agreeing to come with him.

The day had been fun so far, to her surprise. About an hour ago, she'd even been invited (along with Jesse, of course) to take part in a beach volleyball game started by some of the popular kids. Her height had given her an advantage, and she'd found herself feeling accepted in a way she'd never known before, with guys, and even girls, talking to her who had barely looked in her direction since elementary school. She knew it was because of Jesse, but she didn't care. It was nice to have even a hint of what Zippy enjoyed everywhere, all the time.

"Heads up!"

The shout came from twenty yards down the beach where a bunch of guys from the Moose Junction football team had started an impromptu game. The football hurtled in her direction, but before it could connect with the ground (or her head) someone came running from behind, leaping up past her to pluck the ball from mid-air and clutching it to his chest before tucking and rolling in the sand with it.

It was Jesse (of course).

For a star quarterback, his skills as a receiver were also surprisingly good.

He got up, laughing, and brushed sand that clung like a dusting of sugar off his bare arms and chest. When he lifted the ball high in the air with one hand, showing that it was still in his possession, another shout went up, this time of victory. He grinned as his "team" came running up to surround him, all of them looking like young gods of war with tanned, hard bodies and flashing white teeth as they shoved each other in mock attacks.

"Not bad, Wilder," called Jay Arseneau, the Moose Junction High Black Bears' best receiver, flicking his gaze from Jesse to Elena and back again. "Not sure I like you taking my spot, though. Pretty soon you'll be catching your own passes." His grin took away any sting the comment might have otherwise had.

"No worries, braw." Jesse fell into the lighthearted exchange without missing a beat. "I've got enough to worry about just getting the ball in the air, praying the O-line keeps me from getting sacked." Jesse tossed him the ball, and Jay caught it easily, almost without looking.

Still grinning, Jay glanced at Elena again. "Hey," he said.

"Hey," she answered, squinting up at him through the sun. At almost the same moment, Jesse shifted closer to her so his body gave her some shade, and she could see Jay without scrunching up her face. She waited, uncertain. Jay had never spoken directly to her before.

"For a second there, I thought you were your sister," Jay continued, clearly appraising her. She sensed more than saw Jesse tense up a little. "Where *is* Alex, anyway? I haven't seen her since graduation. Did she already leave for college?"

"She isn't going to college for now. And she didn't come to the beach today because she's in a play at the community theater next month and they had rehearsals," Elena answered, for a minute having some trouble getting her mind around being mistaken for Zippy. Ever.

"Too bad. Tell her I said hello, will ya?" he asked, just as Lacey Benson, a blonde, air-headed senior Elena had cheered with since eighth grade, came running up to grab Jay's arm. "Later," Jay called as he was led away toward the concessions.

Lacey was what she and Mindy secretly called a "cling-on"—a tongue-in-cheek reference to *Star Trek* (Elena still loved James Tiberius Kirk as the Captain of the Starship Enterprise and had named her very first baby doll James in his honor), but also meaning one of those girls who tried to get their claws into a guy and then wouldn't let go. Lacey was one of the worst, but she'd learned from a master, being a minion of the one and only Sharon.

Glancing a little farther down the beach, Elena saw her nemesis sitting on a bright orange towel with her boyfriend, Steven, having clearly told him to stay on the sand with her rather than go to take part in the pickup game. Sharon continued to ignore Elena every time they'd been in the same place at the same time—just as she had for the past six weeks since prom.

That was fine by her. She'd never liked Sharon anyway, though she'd always done her best to be civil toward her, especially because they had to work together in cheerleading. The coming football season promised to be even more interesting than usual. As seniors, they'd probably have to come up with a few new cheers. With the buzz around school, the community, on local TV, and in the newspapers about their championship prospects with Jesse playing for Moose Junction, the games were bound to be exciting (even if Elena hadn't had a personal connection to the quarterback).

She smiled as Jesse flopped down on the towel next to her, unfolding himself with sinuous ease to lie back, crooking one powerful arm over his eyes to block the sun. Feeling a little devilish, she held her mostly-full-and-very-cold cup of Pepsi a few inches over his bare stomach, trying not to focus too much on the amazing play of muscles in his abdomen as he shifted, reacting subconsciously to the first splash of icy condensation that dripped from the bottom of the cup onto his sun-heated skin.

When another two or three drops fell in quick succession of each other, he lifted his arm a little and did a half sit-up, rolling toward her and tackling her to the blanket with a laughing growl. She made a sound that echoed his as she tried to roll away, managing to keep the drink upright as she set it down next to her. But she couldn't get away. Jesse clamped one big hand on her shoulder and held her in place, grabbing the cup with the other and pressing it against her bare back in playful retaliation.

With a laughing shriek, she jerked away and sat up, finally, before twisting to confront him with taking their "war" so far. In that second or two, he'd managed to stretch out on his side in an exaggerated pose of tranquility, his head propped on one hand. He held the drink in the other, sipping through the straw and blinking at her with an innocent expression. Laughing again, Elena tossed the suntan lotion bottle at him, hitting him in the chest.

"Here. Since cold, wet objects pressed into a person's back don't help to prevent sunburn, why don't you use some of your overbearing energy to put more of this lotion on me before I look like a cooked lobster."

"I like lobster," he drawled, smiling around the straw even as he rolled to sitting and picked up the lotion.

"Trust me when I tell you that sunburn doesn't look good on me. It takes my ugly to a whole new level."

"Anyone who could think you look ugly, with or without sunburn, is crazy."

"It's obvious you haven't been in Moose Junction for very long."

"Ugly comes from the inside, El-bell. That's definitely not you," he said, as he smoothed the lotion over her shoulders.

She closed her eyes, enjoying the sensation before she half turned her head toward him. "Call it what you want . . . plain, homely, whatever. Being sunburned makes it worse. I've never been what my grandfather used to call a 'looker.'"

"Yeah, right. If you don't qualify, then who would?"

"My sister."

"Uh, El? In case you forgot, you have *seven* of those."

She gave an exaggerated sigh. "Okay, I'll narrow it down for you. Anne, Kat, and Lisa are definitely in the looker category, but the one who's got us all beat is Zippy."

Jesse stopped rubbing lotion into her back, but even before she looked to see what was wrong, she heard the smile in his voice. "Come on, El. You're kidding, right? Don't you realize how much you and Alex look alike? You're both tall, and you have the same color hair." He started rubbing some more lotion on her. "And you both have the same really fair skin."

"I know that, doofus." She craned her neck to see him, smiling in spite of herself. "But Zippy has always had a flair for looking amazing. I don't know, it's like a gene that's missing in me or something. What I do know is that Zip is really particular about how she looks, and she always looks . . . *awesome*. No matter when or for what occasion." Elena shrugged. "It's no big deal. I'm used to it."

Jesse shook his head. "Sometimes I don't get your logic. You're a little nuts, you know that?"

Elena grinned. "So I've been told." She tipped her head and gave him a goofy, mock-psycho look, punctuated by a mad scientist voice. "See, Jesse? You could have picked the prettier older sister . . . but you picked the crazy younger one instead."

"I'll take it," he murmured, giving her a good-natured bump to move over on the blanket before settling back with her on the golden sand, both of them propped on their forearms with their feet extended, watching the waves splash against the shore and the sun-drenched world go by.

(At the beach)

Diary entry # 194:
August 25, 1986

I'm so nervous! Jesse is coming over after church to spend the rest of the day. Thank goodness Trish already left for her fall semester, because I'm going to have to bribe Zippy (and Jen, who doesn't leave for her senior year of college until Tuesday) not to tease him like we used to do to the guys Pa brought home from the base. That may be the least of my worries, though. The big City Slicker got the bright idea to help Pa build a raised flower bed today, and then help him plant his new fancy iris bulbs. I kid you not. What is Jesse thinking*?! As far as I know, digging in the dirt is NOT at the top of his skill set! I admit it was cute earlier this summer when he was so interested in Pa's gardens, but I never thought he'd actually want to try it himself. Oh, geez, this has disaster written all over it. . . .*

Elena put the last of the cauliflower cheese puff into the leftover container. She snapped on the lid and used her black marker to write the contents and date on a piece of masking tape that she pressed onto the top. While she did that, she kept glancing out the window at the activity in the backyard.

Everything looked okay out there. There was no yelling, waving of arms, or jumping out of the way, as had happened *before* Sunday dinner when Jesse had almost taken Pa's head off with one of the railroad ties they were using to form the outlines of the raised iris bed they were building. Jesse had lifted one of the heavy ties to his shoulder to carry it from the red shed into position for the rectangular bed—one of the long sides so that each end of the heavy wooden tie stuck out about five feet in front of and behind him. Without thinking, he'd turned to answer something Pa said, and Pa ended up having to duck to avoid the massive swinging chunk of wood.

The minutes following that hadn't been pretty. Pa had never been one to suffer anyone without a brain in gear, especially while engaged in something potentially dangerous. But Jesse had accepted Pa's reprimands with grace, listening, apologizing, and nodding in recognition of what he needed to do in order for them to get the project finished right, using the least number of "man hours" (Marine Corps style, which was one of Pa's favorite ways to measure efficiency in any kind of physical work).

After the dust of that near-accident had settled, they'd gotten back to work, with Jesse concentrating and moving a little more cautiously as he'd carried the heavy ties over and helped Pa put them in place, followed by the two of them carting wheelbarrows full of compost and topsoil to fill in the bed.

The heat had caused sweat to run off both of them, and Jesse had taken off his shirt to work bare-chested after the heavy lifting part of the morning was accomplished (almost giving Elena a heart attack, since she'd found it really difficult to breathe when she watched his muscles moving like that). Just before it was time to eat, they'd leveled the rich, dark dirt, readying it for the bulbs. Then they'd come in for a break (with Jesse putting his shirt back on, sadly) to wash up and drink some lemonade before sitting down to the nice meal and dessert Ma had prepared.

Teasing had been kept to a minimum, and Pa had asked Jesse a few more questions about his plans for the future—along with engaging him and the rest of the family in talk about what, if anything, should be placed in the center of the garden: the metal sundial, the birdbath, a small fountain, or a special, larger flowering plant or bush? The fact that he'd included Jesse in that talk meant that all was forgiven from the morning's slip up, and Elena felt Jesse relax more and more as the meal went on.

He and Pa had been outside for about an hour again by the time Elena was putting away the leftovers. They seemed to be working well together now, planting each bulb with care, measuring and spacing them according to the color and height each iris would be when it bloomed, forming a pattern the two of them had ultimately decided upon.

She glanced out into the back yard once more after she'd put the Tupperware in the fridge, catching herself smiling at the happy expression on Jesse's face. He and Pa stood to the side of the almost-finished garden, leaning on a shovel and a spade, respectively, and apparently discussing the pros and cons of what to do with the still-empty center part of it, if the hand gestures and glances back and forth to the spot were any indication.

"Too bad stud muffin doesn't take his shirt off again," Zippy said, leaning in toward Elena to look out the window, too. "That was quite a sight this morning. Almost enough to make me wish I'd tried a little harder to nab him myself this past spring."

Elena gave an exasperated laugh and elbowed her sister. "Jerk!"

Zippy laughed, too, the sound light and sparkling as fine crystal.

"Oh, don't get bent out of shape. I'm just kidding. I'm not going to be around here long enough to have a relationship with anyone, anyway. I knew that back when lover boy first showed up again in Moose Junction." Zippy shot a glance in Ma's direction, still stinging a little from the safety and money requirements Ma and Pa had told her she needed in place before they'd give their blessing for her to head for Los Angeles. "And I know it now. It won't be long before I'll be in sunny California, auditioning for roles. No time for romance, baby sis."

"Good thing," Jen drawled from over near the sink, continuing to dry a glass while she walked over toward the window to join them, "because Jesse is obviously head over heels for Eek. He wouldn't give *you* a second glance."

Zippy made a huffing sound, while Elena tried to hide the blush she felt creeping up her face. She wasn't used to feeling so . . . good. So warm and happy inside. Zippy was the one who got all the guys and all the attention; she always had. This was new territory for Elena. It was like she was finally coming into her own a little bit and gaining a sense of her own worth and power, thanks to Jesse and their friendship-changed-into-something-deeper relationship.

"Oh, look, Eew." Zippy had reverted to Elena's old nickname in apparent retaliation for having to acknowledge she'd come in second place with Jesse. "Your football god is waving to try to get your attention. How sweetly annoying."

"What's he want?" Jen asked.

"I don't know." Elena squinted, trying to decipher the hand gestures. In the next second, it dawned on her. "He wants a camera!" She turned to Ma. "Do you know where Pa's camera is, Ma?"

"Oh, dear." Ma dried her hands and hurried back toward her and Pa's bedroom. "Your father had it on top of his dresser the last time I looked, but I don't know how to work it. I'm not sure it's even got film in it."

Elena followed her in, taking the camera when Ma found it and held it out to her, and then turning to head back through the kitchen to get outside. "If something is missing, Pa will tell me and I can come back in," she said as she made her way to the back door. "Thanks, Ma!"

"Wait a minute. He's making motions for all of us to come out!" Jen called back from the window.

Zippy snorted and laughed. "Look at the way he's flapping his arms! Maybe he's been in the sun too long and thinks he's signaling a game." She proceeded to do a (pretty good) imitation of a football jock, saying, "Okay, coach! Yup, yup, I'll get them to come over here, coach. Whatever you say, coach!"

"That's enough, Alexandra." Ma took off her apron and folded it before putting it on the kitchen counter. "Now let's go look at the garden and see what those two have been working on."

Elena gave Zippy a dirty look as they shoved each other through the back door to the yard. Jen got between them once they were on the grass, holding her arms out to keep them apart, and laughing as they walked toward the garden.

In a few seconds they'd crossed the entire yard to the back corner and stood in front of the new, raised iris bed. The late-day sun had warmed the freshly turned soil and filled the air around them with the moist, earthy scent of all the recent planting, blended with the sharper smell of the wood ties. The garden was about eight by twelve feet in dimension, with the weathered railroad ties giving it just enough height and style to set off what Elena could already envision as a miniature field of colorful iris blooms, bobbing in the early summer sun next year. And they'd placed Pa's antiqued sundial in the center of it, which gave it the perfect final touch.

"It's beautiful, Dave." Ma beamed at them.

"Awesome," Jen added.

Even Zippy couldn't help but acknowledge it, her eyes widening with appreciation as she uttered a single, "Wow!"

"What do you think, El?" Jesse's expression was hopeful, and he looked so handsome standing there. He seemed to glow with vitality from the work they'd been doing all day, his hair glinting golden in the sun, and his blue eyes crinkling in the corners when he smiled.

"It looks amazing." She smiled back at him, and he broke into a deeper grin. Looking to Pa, she added, "It's perfect."

"I think it turned out pretty good." Pa was clearly pleased with the results. He glanced at Jesse and nodded. "Nice job, once we got past the rough start. I'm glad to see you're not afraid of a little work. You showed some natural talent out here."

Jesse grinned at the unexpected praise. "Thanks, Mr. Wright."

"Let's commemorate it . . . what do you say?" Pa gestured to the camera and took his spade to stand at the corner of the raised bed.

"Yes, sir!" Jesse grabbed his shovel and moved into position next to him, laughing and switching sides when Pa indicated that he would be blocking the front of the flowerbed otherwise.

Pa looked at Elena. "Go ahead, Ellie."

"You want *me* to take the picture?" Pa's camera was one of the few (very expensive) remnants from his bachelor days, and the idea of it made Elena nervous.

Pa nodded. "You can handle it. Just crank the lever to advance the film, look through the viewfinder, twist the lens a little if you need focus it, and then click the button on top to take the picture. Do one of the garden first, then one with us in it."

"Okay, I'll give it a try." Pa might challenge her to try new things, but he never asked her to do something unless he knew she could handle it. "Here goes."

She went through the processes he had directed for the first shot and got it ready for the second. It took a while to readjust the focus . . . and then there Pa and Jesse were, captured perfectly in the little rectangle of the frame, with the sunlight spilling over them as they stood next to each other and the graceful garden they'd created behind them.

"Smile!"

Then, smiling herself, she pressed down on the button, hearing it click as they preserved the moment forever.

(The raised bed garden before planting)

Diary entry # 208:
October 18, 1986

Oh, man, I think I'm in love. . . .

It was Friday night, and just before the start of the big homecoming game. Elena sat in the stands with Mindy and a big group of other Moose Junction students—mostly nerds and theater-types—to cheer on the team for what would hopefully be their seventh win of a so far undefeated season. Mindy sat next to her, almost jumping out of her seat with excitement as the marching band finished their entrance and made their way into the stands above them, settling there to play bursts of spirit songs throughout the game.

Then the cheerleaders ran out onto the field.

Elena didn't react at all, but Mindy paused in her happy shrieks, shifting to make a big raspberry sound. It made Elena laugh, and she playfully elbowed Mindy, connecting with her fleece vest that was layered over the orange and black school sweatshirt she insisted on wearing to all the games (no matter that it was cold enough tonight to warrant pulling out the winter parkas). The wind picked up, and a few snowflakes swirled by.

"You're such a dork!" Elena said with a laugh, avoiding looking at the cheerleaders doing their "Go, Fight, Win!" routine.

"I told you before . . . I'm going to do that every game. They don't deserve anything else," Mindy said, elbowing her back and making another distinctive raspberry in the direction of the field.

Elena shook her head, and looked around the stands again before fiddling with her jacket and pulling her mittens from her pockets, waiting for the cheer to be over.

The fact that she'd been cut from the cheerleading team at the end of summer still hurt. Elena had always known there could be politics in high school sports, but she'd thought ability was supposed to matter at least a little. She'd been in top form during try-outs, having cheered, kicked, and lifted other girls for the past five years. Being cut as a senior was a huge slap in the face.

But something had gone on behind the scenes—something personal—and Elena knew it had to do with Sharon, who'd been named captain this year and had become sudden buddies with the brand new cheer coach.

Sharon had never liked her, but that dislike apparently had increased by leaps and bounds when Jesse asked her to the prom . . . and then during the prom, when Zippy had managed to knock the entire punch bowl over onto Sharon at just the right time, it had only gotten worse.

Still, she'd never thought Sharon would go to such lengths as to get her cut from the team.

The shock of it had worn off after a couple weeks, leaving behind nothing but dull anger. Pa and Ma had felt bad for her, and Jen had even come home early for a weekend from her senior year at college to try to spend some time to try to make her feel better, but Zippy (who was the only sister of Elena's left at home) didn't seem to get why she was so upset. There had been a lot of tension anyway at the homestead because Zippy was bound and determined to move to California to be an actress, and Pa and Ma were worried about her.

All summer, every minute she wasn't at play rehearsal, Zippy had been working at three jobs trying to save up more money, and the end result was that she was preoccupied with her own issues. Besides, she'd never understood what Elena saw in the activity. She preferred being the center of attention, so Zippy had never even tried cheerleading. Instead, she'd focused on getting lead roles in local stage productions. Ultimately, Zippy had shrugged her shoulders at Elena and said, "It's not like there's nothing else you can do. Why don't you join the band?"

Jesse had been far more understanding. He'd stuck to her side like glue at school, glaring at anyone who dared to stare and whisper in that first, awful week back at classes in September. It was always the same when some social scandal broke in the building, fresh gossip and all that. But the talk had lasted only until the first football game of the season. After that it died off, replaced by the news of a junior girl's pregnancy.

By the beginning of October, Elena had been able to joke a little about being cut, telling Jesse that at least there was a silver lining to the whole thing: she could cheer for him alone now instead of for the whole team.

Jesse's smile in response to that made it all seem less important, and she'd been shocked to realize that she really *could* move on.

It wasn't so bad. She'd been able to watch the games from the stands in a way she'd never been able to from the sidelines during her entire junior high and high school years of cheering.

And she got to watch Jesse.

The opposing team had already been introduced. Suddenly the Moose Junction cheerleaders grabbed an enormous, brown paper "poster," painted with the team's mascot in orange and black school colors, and held it up in front of the entrance to the home team's locker room. A second later, as the announcer began the lead up to the Moose Junction players taking the field, the crowd began to rumble, stamping their feet in the stands and starting a low chant that got louder and louder with every second.

"The time has arrived, ladies and gentlemen. The Moose Junction High's football team is about to enter home stadium, led by Jesse James Wilder, championship-winning quarterback. Let's hear it for the UN-defeated BLACK BEARS!"

The crowd went crazy as the team ripped en masse through the paper sign, running onto the field with Jesse leading the pack. He held his helmet tucked against his side, and as his golden-blond head came into view, the noise and cheering swelled even higher.

The announcer chose that moment to add a final stroke to the masterpiece of excitement he'd created, calling out the trademark phrase, coined right after Jesse had led his then team to its first championship victory in Poughkeepsie, "Aaannnd . . . the . . . crowwwddd . . . goeeesss . . . WILDER!"

Jesse held up his helmet in a salute, his gaze scanning the stands as he always did at the beginning of every game. Elena held her breath, her heart skipping so much she knew she should probably pass out.

But she couldn't. Her attention was riveted on Jesse.

He spotted her. A grin broke on his face, dazzling up to light in his eyes, and he pointed his helmet to her, giving her a wink.

She grinned back and waved the big, foam #1 finger she held, feeling the sounds of the crowd rumbling up through her feet and the swell of her effervescent emotions sweeping down from the top of her head. His gesture of recognition to her—to her *alone*—never got old.

She might not be a cheerleader anymore, but she was the girlfriend to this amazing, sensitive, kind, smart, strong, handsome guy.

And it was enough, she suddenly realized.

More than enough.

Diary entry # 214:
December 7, 1986

Jesse's father invited me to come to the dinner he hosted last night at this fancy restaurant called Table de Bon Goût in Utica; it was for the whole football team and their families to celebrate their winning the Section III Football State Championship last Saturday at the Carrier Dome. Jesse warned me it would probably be pretty stuffy, and that his father isn't anything like Pa. Boy, was he right. I'd heard Pa tell Ma that Jesse's father was a blow-hard, and now I know why. Mr. Wilder likes to show off, and he's sort of a bully. I felt so bad for Jesse. And there was one point when I wanted to crawl under the table because I was so embarrassed for him (and me!). . . .

Elena took a deep breath when the salad course arrived and picked up the fork farthest away from her plate. The salad looked nothing like the ones Ma made. On the plate in front of her rested six shriveled, purple leaves that might have been picked from a bush somewhere, with a slice of carrot and a few curly things tossed on top.

But at least she knew which fork to use.

She thanked her lucky stars that Pa and Ma had taught her proper dinner etiquette. *Work from the outside in.* She'd repeated the mantra a few times already tonight, and she didn't think she'd embarrassed herself yet—though even if she did something wrong, she didn't think anyone would notice. Jesse's father certainly wouldn't have.

Former NFL great Jim Wilder was into his third scotch-on-the-rocks by the time the salads came. He was decked out in full NFL regalia, his dress jacket embroidered with his former team's logo, and he was sporting an enormous NFL ring and a thick, gold-linked watch. With each scotch, he'd gotten a little more talkative. She, Jesse, and Mr. Arseneau (with his son Jay) were sitting closest to Mr. Wilder, though, and no one else seemed to notice or mind. In fact, everyone seemed to be having a good time.

Jesse, however, was on edge and more uptight than Elena had ever seen him. His father was launching into another story from his NFL days, and Elena watched as Jesse fiddled with his fork, tipping a piece of crinkly leaf back and forth on his plate, his jaw set and a polite but miserable half smile glued to his face. She was sitting next to him (he was between her and his father), and she reached under the tablecloth to give his knee a squeeze of support. He shifted his gaze briefly to her, and his smile reached his eyes at least for that moment.

Jay's father seemed to be completely into the story, which was about the groupies and cheerleaders who chased the players. Mr. Arseneau had been divorced twice already and was on the prowl for another girlfriend. Even though he was balding and had a paunch, he clearly thought he was still a catch for the ladies.

"Countless beautiful women, all throwing themselves at you," he echoed, shaking his head when Mr. Wilder had finished the story. "Ah, the good old days." He gave a wink. "Good thing they're not over yet."

"Yeah, it was a trip all right," Jesse's father said, before taking another healthy swallow of his scotch. "Course, once I married Janie I had to forget about that kind of thing for a while." Elena felt Jesse stiffen. "But after she was gone, I still had plenty of offers. I had to handle myself a little differently, though, because by then I was raising this championship-maker."

He punctuated his comment with a grin and a friendly punch on Jesse's arm that might have knocked most people over. Jesse was apparently expecting it because he hardly shifted except to look down, the muscle in his jaw twitching but his expression unchanged.

"We're fielding offers from some pretty big schools, aren't we buddy?" he continued, not even looking at Jesse anymore, but around the table as he settled full swing into his pride-filled announcement. "Ohio State and Alabama are pushing hard, but we're leaning toward the blue and gold of Notre Dame. Can't beat those Fighting Irish, right son?"

"Right," Jesse answered, before swiveling his head toward Elena with a look that read, *Not that I've had much say in it.*

The main courses arrived then, interrupting further conversation. After the plates were served, conversation seemed to shift and spread to various smaller groups all along the long table. But Jay's father wasn't ready to give up talking to their host. After sampling a bite of the Duck *a l'Orange*, which he pronounced "Perfect!" he picked up the college discussion with Mr. Wilder where they had left off.

"Yep, Jim, it's been quite a season," Mr. Arseneau said. "Jay's got a few offers on the table himself. The two best are from Oklahoma State and Southern California. Notre Dame is still on the fence for us, but it sure would be great if it worked out and Jay could go there with Jesse—" Elena saw Jay's head snap up to meet Jesse's gaze from across the table, "because these boys of ours made quite a unit this year. I lost count on how many times I heard the announcer call a 'Wilder-Arseneau Connection.'"

"One hundred and fifty-seven," Jesse said aloud, and Jay nodded. Elena felt the current of something passing between them, undoubtedly an understanding that came from fighting it out on the field every week. She was glad that Jesse could derive some support right now from Jay, even if she knew the guy probably wasn't the most loyal friend in the world.

"What was that, Jesse?"

Jesse shifted his gaze to Mr. Arseneau. "One hundred and fifty-seven. That's how many completions Jay and I had this season. A ninety-one percent success rate."

Mr. Arseneau's brows lifted. "By God, Jim, your son is a statistical genius in addition to being a star quarterback. How in hell did you manage that?"

"He inherited his mother's brains, not mine," Mr. Wilder answered, before boasting, "He got my height, my throwing arm, my love of the game—"

"And your luck with the ladies, if all the screaming and poster waving I've seen from the girls are any indication," Mr. Arseneau broke in with a laugh.

Elena's face felt hot; she wanted to disappear under the table, and Jesse looked just as stricken. She didn't think it could get any worse, until Mr. Wilder spoke again.

"The girls have been throwing themselves at Jesse for years, but this pretty filly is the first to rein him in." He flashed a dazzling smile—a slightly wider version of Jesse's—in Elena's direction before taking another drink of his scotch (his fourth one now).

She felt paralyzed with embarrassment. Jesse had gone still as a stone next to her, and Jay was squirming across the table from them both. A fierce desire to get up and run battled inside Elena with the good manners Pa and Ma had instilled in her. Manners won for the moment, and she remained unmoving, trying not to choke, since her throat felt like it was closing up on her, too.

Mr. Arseneau chuckled in response to Mr. Wilder, seemingly

unaware of the discomfort their conversation was causing.

"Yes, sir, before Elena came along," Mr. Wilder continued, "I was starting to worry a little, if you know what I mean. Jesse's lack of a girlfriend sure as hell wasn't for lack of the girls trying."

"*Dad*," Jesse finally muttered, shooting his father a glare.

"Relax, buddy," he laughed, waving his drink in Jesse's direction. "I'm just kidding around."

"It's not funny."

"Oh, all right." Mr. Wilder glanced at Elena again, still smiling and adding for her benefit, "No harm intended, sweetie. I just like rattling Jesse's cage every once in a while. Keeps him tough."

Elena tried to nod, but she couldn't speak. She was more grateful than ever that most of the others in attendance had started their own conversations and were oblivious to this one. An uneasy silence fell over their end of the table, and Elena saw that muscle in Jesse's jaw twitch again before he jerked his head up.

"This is the restaurant with the desserts displayed in a special room across the hall." Jesse swung his gaze to Elena before his father had time to say anything. "Let's go take a look."

She glanced between Jesse and his father, trying to make sure their leaving wouldn't make anything worse. But Mr. Wilder was already warming up to answering another of Mr. Arseneau's questions, this time about the famed NFL triple sessions, and so she nodded, letting Jesse move her chair back and walking with him into the hall.

Once they were clear of the room, Jesse pulled her a few more feet down the corridor and then stopped, leaning back against the wall with his head tipped back and his eyes closed as he grated, "Oh, my God, I can't believe my father just pulled that shit in there." He cursed a few more explicit words under his breath, before opening his eyes and looking at her. "I'm really sorry, El-bell. I don't know what else to say."

"It's not your fault."

"Yes it is. I shouldn't have brought you here. I knew he'd say or do something stupid, but this is way worse than what I'd thought. *Damn*." He closed his eyes again, strain showing in every rigid muscle of his body.

Elena grabbed one of his hands and held it, trying to calm him down. Even the muscles in his fingers felt tense, and she jiggled them to make him look at her.

"Stop it, Jesse. You can't control your father. It's over, and it's no big deal."

Jesse didn't say anything more for a long moment, but he opened his eyes and she felt some of the tension begin to ease out of him. "I don't know how you can be so easygoing about it, El. I'd be pissed if I were you."

She shrugged. "I feel bad for *you* more than anything. As far as what your dad said . . . being called a 'filly' is a lot better than some of the names I was called in junior high, believe me."

Jesse looked surprised for a second, before his eyes darkened with empathy. "I didn't realize that's what you meant when you said you'd hated junior high."

"It wasn't anything I couldn't handle. It pushed me to be better in school." Elena smiled. "I'll probably end up getting into a better college thanks to it."

He made a sound of disgust. "I can't believe people can be such idiots. I wish I'd gone to school here then, so I could have set them straight."

"I'm glad you didn't. You would have either gotten in trouble or you might have decided the same things about me that they did. I was a pretty dorky kid."

"Um, no you weren't. I met you the summer before seventh grade, and I don't remember you being dorky at all. Just down-to-earth."

"Code words for *boring*."

"Not a chance. You were all natural. Real. You still are. It's one of the things I love about you."

Elena flushed with pleasure, but her mission was to lighten his mood, so she teased, "One of the things I love about *you* is that you like to say nice things about me."

"Oh, I get it. You keep me around because I'm good for your ego."

"Among other reasons." She grinned.

She was relieved to see she'd coaxed a smile from him with that, but his expression shifted swiftly to one that was more pensive again, making her frown a little as he tugged her closer to stand directly opposite him.

He held her gaze, adding more quietly, "But what I'm really glad about is that no matter what, you have a family—and a father—who will support you through thick and thin. That's important, El. I mean, I know my dad loves me and wants what he thinks is best for me, but that doesn't help much at times like this. He can be a prick, but he's my father, and he's all I've got left, you know?"

She couldn't speak so she nodded, her feelings for him rising up to fill her as he pulled her close. She loved the way he held her. Being wrapped in his arms was as safe and wonderful a place as anywhere she could imagine. Resting her cheek on his shoulder, she enjoyed the moment, hugging him back. "It'll be all right, Jesse. Everything will work out like it's supposed to."

"Thanks, El-bell," he whispered against her hair. "I don't know what I'd do without you. I really mean that."

She hugged him tighter. "Well, you'll never need to find out, because I'll always be here for you."

"No matter what?"

"Cross my heart with cherries on top."

She felt him smile against her, and he pressed a kiss to the top of her head before saying, "Right back-atcha, El . . . but speaking of cherries—"

"We'd better pick out our desserts and get back into the war zone," she finished for him, getting him to smile again.

Jesse nodded, looking a lot happier than he had when they'd first come out into the corridor. His blue eyes twinkled with the humor she was used to seeing in them—and after a quick kiss to seal the deal, they made their way across the hall to choose something sweet together.

Diary entry # 225:
February 14, 1987

It's Friday night (Valentine's Day!) and Jesse and I are going to see Youngblood *at the rerun movie theater. I don't think it'll be too romantic, being a hockey movie and all, but at least it's got some handsome guys in it (Rob Lowe + Keanu Reeves = swoon). I can't wait to give Jesse the card and giant Hershey's chocolate bar I bought for him. I'm SO in love!!! He tells me he loves me, too, pretty much every day, BUT (and I'd only tell* you *this, Diary) I've been a little worried about him lately. He's been quieter than usual, like something's on his mind. I'm going to try to surprise him tonight and get all dressed up for our date. I'll borrow Jen's black suede miniskirt (if I can get out of the house without Pa sending me back upstairs to change) and wear some of Zippy's Halston perfume. I'm even putting on a little makeup. Keep your fingers (pages?) crossed that I can cheer him up a little. . . .*

It was frosty outside, but Elena wasn't cold at all, reclining in the front passenger seat of Jesse's new black Mustang (his Christmas present from his father) at the hidden turn off up behind the trees on Dibble Road. Jesse's seat was reclined as well. He'd shifted himself a little across the center console in order to wrap his arm around her, and she'd snuggled against him, her head resting against his shoulder as they talked.

The windows were steamed up from the warmth of their bodies, their conversation, and a few kisses they'd shared in the close confines of the car. Now Jesse turned his head to watch as she wrote on the passenger window and drew a heart below it. The delicate, gold-linked bracelet he'd given her for a Valentine's Day present dangled from her wrist, catching the moonlight as she finished. When he tried to add an arrow to the heart, Elena reached up to tickle his ribs, and he jerked his arm, making the bottom of the arrow look more like a rocket trail.

"Hey, no fair," he said with a low laugh, his voice husky and sounding so sexy that she just about wanted to die, since she felt like she was already in heaven anyway.

"Read it to me," she whispered, turning her head and tipping it up to graze a butterfly caress with her lips along the line of his jaw.

"E loves J."

"Mmhmm." She lifted her hand to brush back a wave of blond hair that had fallen over his forehead, and he sat up a little, catching her hand and pressing a gentle kiss into her palm.

"I love you, too, you know."

It was pretty dark inside the car, the only light coming from the waxing crescent moon, but Elena could still see the flicker of something that looked like hurt (or sadness?) in his eyes. It was gone in an instant, but she knew she'd seen something.

"What's the matter?" She used her fingers to tip his face into the faint light.

"Nothing. Why?"

"You had a funny look for a second," Elena held her breath before plunging in. "And you've seemed really preoccupied for a few weeks. Kind of quiet."

He shrugged and sat up, sliding back fully into the driver's seat and lifting the lever to bring his seat mostly upright. Though he'd had to drop his arm from around her shoulders when he moved, he reached now to take her hand in his as a comforting replacement.

"There's just a lot going on right now, El. Lots of stuff to think about." He glanced over at her. "I'm not too good at making decisions."

"Except on the field," she reminded him.

"Well, yeah, but that's different. My entire life doesn't depend on those decisions. It's the all or nothing ones that stump me." He gave a kind of laugh, and she could tell he was trying hard to sound upbeat.

She nodded, silent. He couldn't be talking about college. Notre Dame was a foregone conclusion for him. His father had done everything but send out glossy announcements that Jesse was soon to be one of the Fighting Irish. His dad had made sure an article appeared in the paper, and he'd even decked out his big, fancy Mercedes with Notre Dame floor mats, seat backs, and steering wheel cover.

"So, what kind of decisions are you talking about?" She only hoped her voice didn't sound as wobbly as her insides were feeling right now.

"It's nothing, El-bell. Just a lot of stuff that's been on my mind."

"Is it about me?"

He looked at her and lifted his brow, teasing, "It's *always* about you."

"That's not what I meant, and you know it."

That same polite-but-miserable smile she'd seen him wear whenever he was being forced to deal with something he'd rather not handle curved his mouth, and she felt her heart fall to her toes. *Oh, no. Oh, no. Oh, no. . . .*

She held back her panic as she reached down to pull the lever that allowed her seat to come up from its reclining position, too, so it was even with his. Twisting as much as she could to face him, she said quietly and more seriously than she'd ever spoken to him before, "I need to ask you something, Jesse, and I want you to answer me honestly. Promise me."

"Shit, El, what is it?" He seemed surprised, and then stricken; if she could have seen more color instead of shadows in the dim light she would have sworn he went pale.

"No, first promise you'll be completely honest with me."

"Okay, I promise." He looked like he was going to be sick.

She swallowed, not sure how she was going to get this out, but knowing that she had to, no matter how embarrassing it was. "Are you rethinking things between us because we haven't . . . because we've never gone beyond—" She broke off and looked down for a second, biting her lip before jerking her head up to look at him and just asking him straight out. "Does this have anything to do with me telling you I want to stay a virgin through high school?"

If an expression existed called 'man-suddenly-evades-execution,' then what came over Jesse's face at that moment would have been a textbook example of it. His breath escaped him in a rush, and he burst out, "Oh, my God, *no*!" He just looked at her, almost dumbfounded for a second, then jabbed his hand through his hair, shaking his head and croaking another laugh at the same time. "Jeez, El-bell. It has nothing to do with that."

"Then you're not having second thoughts about us because we haven't slept together?" She almost couldn't breathe from the combination of fear, embarrassment, and relief that spilled through her.

"*No*, I swear it!" He laughed again more softly, looking sideways at her before brushing back the hair from her face to tuck it behind her ear. "I'm fine with the way things are, trust me." He took her hand in his, tracing a heart in her palm. "You're my best friend, and I love you.

That's what really matters, right?"

She nodded. Her throat felt achy with all the emotions she was holding back, and she leaned into his open embrace with a hitched sound. "I want you to be happy, Jesse, but I just can't do that. Not yet anyway . . . and I was worried that I might be losing you because of it."

He held her close to him. "It's not an issue, El, honest. I *am* happy—and I hate to tell you, but you're stuck with me. I'm pretty sure you'll want to get rid of me way before I'll ever be ready to say goodbye to you."

"It won't happen, I promise." She hugged him tighter.

"Don't promise. Just keep loving me, okay?" His voice was quiet as he pressed a kiss to the top of her head. She nodded, lifting her face to give him a quick kiss in return before he leaned his forehead against hers. His eyes were closed, but she could see the gentle curve of his lips, and she felt his warm breath on her face. She closed her eyes, too, soaking up the sweet rightness of their connection.

They sat like that in companionable silence for a few minutes more. Then Elena shivered a little, and he tipped away to look at her, murmuring, "Come on. We should probably go before you turn into a popsicle."

She nodded and reached up to grab her seatbelt while Jesse turned the key and started the motor. He revved it a few times, encouraging it to warm up and send some much-needed heat spiraling into the now chilly confines of the car. Twisting his head to look behind him, he backed up, then shifted gears and aimed the Mustang at the road. But before he could go, Elena laid her hand on his arm and he put on the brakes, glancing over at her.

Love for him welled inside her. "Thank you, Jesse, for a lot of things, but most of all just for being *you*."

"You, too, El-bell." He grinned, his teeth flashing white in the shadows when he reached out and clasped her hand in his again. "Happy Valentine's Day."

Elena squeezed his hand and murmured the same in return, joy sparkling through her as he took his foot off the brake and they began driving home. She smiled and looked ahead through the windshield at the road unfolding in the beam of their headlights, knowing that it was indeed a happy Valentine's Day.

And that she'd likely never know another as perfect as this one for as long as she lived.

(Valentine's Day, 1987)

Diary entry # 230:
March 28, 1987

Jesse should be coming over soon! His dad said he could have dinner with us tonight, since they didn't have anything planned. Of course I LOVE to see him any time, but it'll be really nice to have another person in the house, too. I still can't get used to it being so quiet here. I told you about Jen getting her own apartment now that she's a college senior and about Zippy moving to California, but until Patricia gets home from school for the summer, it's just me, Pa, and Ma. I guess now I know what it would have been like to be an only child. I would have hated it! It makes me feel bad for Jesse, though, because that's all he's ever known. One of these days I'd love for him to experience "the whole crowd," but that only happens on holidays anymore. At least when he comes over today, he'll get some of Ma's home cooking. . . .

"There's something I want to show you over at our spot."

"Seriously?" Elena twisted her head to look up at Jesse, who sat flush behind her on the rocky ledge of the palisades overlooking the lake. They'd ended up there after going for a quick walk before dinner, lured by the spring breezes and beautiful views after a long, cold winter spent mostly indoors.

"Yeah. We have enough time left before your father said to be back for dinner."

Elena sighed and closed her eyes. She wasn't so sure she wanted to move just yet; it felt so good to be nestled like this in Jesse's arms. Even through their shirts and windbreakers, she could feel his stomach and chest muscles move against her back when he shifted, and tingles swept up her neck from the gentle warmth of his breath along her sensitive skin there.

Opening her eyes and looking at him again, she tried to draw the moment out. "I don't know, Jesse. It's probably not a great idea to go trekking through the woods this early in the season. We're dry here because we're on high ground, but I'm sure there's still some snow out there with all the shade."

"Nah, it's mostly melted." Jesse's blue eyes twinkled down at her, his expression like that of the cat that caught the canary. "I've already been out a few times since the warm spell started last week."

Elena laughed. "Oh, geez, leave it to you! Pa was right; you *are* turning into a country boy. Wasn't it mucky?"

"Yeah, but I didn't think that would be a problem for an outdoor girl like you."

"It's not, you big lug," Elena said, giving him a playful shove as she reluctantly broke free of him and stood up. "You're the one who wears expensive sneakers. If you want to get them all muddy, be my guest. I'm always up for a hike in the woods."

"I thought you might be, Daniel-san," he said in a teasing voice, following her lead and pushing himself to his feet, too, "which is why when I got ready today, I put on an *old* pair of sneakers from last year." He suddenly shifted his weight onto one leg, lifting his other knee to dangle his sneakered foot in front of her and raising his arms in an exaggerated replica of Ralph Macchio's "crane" pose at the end of *The Karate Kid*. As he held the position, he offered another mangled line from the movie. "See? I use head for something other than target."

Elena laughed, slapping at his foot and making him tip sideways. "Okay, first of all, you're way too tall to play Mr. Miyagi *or* Danny Larusso," she joked, "and second of all, how am I supposed to tell what's new and what's old on those size-fourteen clobbers? All your shoes look the same to me!"

Jesse was laughing as he caught himself before he could fall over, shaking his head at her as they both brushed off their jeans from having sat on the ground. "Okay, so I don't have a future in the *Karate Kid* movies and you don't have one in the sneaker business. Come on. Let's go to the spot and see what's there." He grabbed her hand, his grin as handsome and breathtaking as ever as he tugged her along with him. "I think you'll like it."

Grinning, too, she followed him up the lake path away from the palisades. From there it was only twenty feet or so to the highway, and they ran across the double lanes and up over the culvert that led to the part of their road that curved north, nearer to Jesse's house than to the homestead. They cut across his yard and approached their secret spot from his side, entering the woods and picking their way through soggy brush and trickling streams that had sprung up here and there from the rapid snowmelt.

Elena laughed at the squelching sounds their feet made when they got into a particularly swampy section, and Jesse let her take the lead, following her steps as she leaped from stone to stone to get through the worst of it. Picking up speed, they came to the edge of their little clearing, and their familiar boulder "seat" came into view. She scrambled over to it and sat down, out of breath but still smiling and feeling exhilarated with the activity and fresh air.

She tried to talk between gulps of air. "So, what is it you wanted me to see?"

Jesse had come to a stop in front of her, and he was leaning forward to rest with his hands propped on the tops of his thighs. Although he was breathing a little heavier than usual, too, it was a lot less labored than her panting. Clearly, he was in better shape.

"Showoff," she murmured, grinning at him as he made a flourish with his arm and stepped off to the side, gesturing to the far right of the clearing from where she sat. She hadn't paid much attention when she'd run in, but now she looked more closely and saw an oval border formed from about a dozen stones of various sizes. Some of the stones had moss on them, while others looked like they'd been dug out of the ground recently and placed end to end to enclose a little patch of green trefoil vegetation.

"Oh, wow." Surprise rippled through her, and she stood and moved closer to it. "Did you plant a *garden* out here?"

"Well, not exactly. Mother Nature did the planting. I just put the border around it to make it look nice."

He came up behind her where she stood next to the front edge of his creation, and she reached back and took his hand.

"It must have taken some time to dig out these rocks this early in the season," Elena said, squinting at the vegetation inside the border.

"Yeah, it took a while to find enough similar-sized stones."

Elena did a double take as she realized, suddenly, just what it was that was growing inside his rock barrier. *Uh-oh.* Glancing back at Jesse, she saw his obvious pride in his work and did her best to smile back at him.

"It's awesome, really." She squeezed his hand. "I love it. But . . . what made you pick *this* patch of plants to build your border around?"

He shrugged and looked at her. "I guess because they looked

different from the rest of the ground cover. I figured they'd end up being flowers of some kind." He let go of her hand to squat down and point to one of the plants inside the stone boundary. "See? It's early, but each one of these has three pretty good-sized leaves on top of a stem that sticks up a few inches above the ground. I can just see buds forming in the center above the leaves."

"Mmhmm." Elena nodded, this time trying *not* to smile. "I see."

He must have heard something in the tone of her voice, because he twisted his head to look at her, frowning and standing up again to tower over her as usual as he crossed his arms over his chest. "What?"

"Nothing." She shook her head, beginning now to grin like a fool.

"Are they *not* going to be flowers or something?" He stopped short, looking so distraught that it was all she could do not to hug him as he asked in a lower, horrified tone, "Oh, shit. Are these plants poison ivy?"

"No, they're definitely flowers," she managed to get out before she broke down into giggles, unable to keep it back any longer.

He heaved a big sigh, looking skyward and leaning back on his heels with his arms still crossed over his chest. "All right, then, El-bell. How about you enlighten me on why that's so funny?"

"It's because they're trillium, Jesse." She grinned ear to ear. "You remember those dark red flowers I showed you last year? The ones that smell like a wet dog? You made a garden out of *stink pots*!"

Jesse froze for a second before he let go a stream of curses. He'd dropped his head into his hands, groaning and shaking it slowly back and forth before Elena's giggling infected him, and he started to laugh, too. She grabbed his arm and made him lift his head, still smiling as she took his face in her palms and planted a kiss on him.

"What was that for? My big surprise is nothing but a royal screw up."

"It is not. The rock border is still pretty for a garden, and it's something *you* made. I'm glad you wanted to show me."

"Yeah?" He swung her around in front of him, pulling her into a hug. "Well, thanks for that, El-bell." He was grinning now, too, as they began walking together out of the clearing and back to her house, adding as they got closer, "Just don't tell your father about this, or I'll never live it down."

"Your secret's safe with me, Billboard Boy." She was still giggling as they reached the outer edges of the homestead's yard. "You owe me one, though, because it's not going to be easy to keep my mouth shut about you deciding to make a fancy garden out of the grossest-smelling flowers in the whole woods!"

(The trillium garden and a red trillium in bloom)

Diary entry # 237:
April 10, 1987

Jesse's home by himself until late tonight when his father gets back from a business trip. Pa would kill me if he knew I was going to go over there with no adult supervision, but I have to know what's going on. I mean, I know senior year is almost over and a lot of changes are coming up for both of us, but Jesse's been acting like he's never going to see me again. It's not like there aren't telephones when we go away to college. Besides, we haven't even graduated yet! When we're together he acts the same—but the weird thing is we're spending less and less time together outside *of school. He says it's not me, it's him, and that he loves me more than ever. I just don't get it! I'm so confused. I NEED to talk to him. Wish me luck. . . .*

Rather than walk up the road like she'd normally do, Elena decided to keep a low profile and cut through the woods to get to Jesse's house. Jesse's grandmother had lived her whole married life there. After she died, Jesse's father had gutted and updated the inside of the house, but he'd kept most of the grounds and outbuildings the same.

Shivering a little, Elena paused at the edge of Jesse's backyard, looking to see if he was anywhere around, doing some of the outdoor work he'd grown to love so much.

It was too early in the season to be opening up the big, in-ground pool his father had put in last summer, but Jesse might have found some kind of landscaping or gardening to do. Not counting the debacle of the stinkpot garden last month, he was really good at working outdoors. He had a knack for it. A natural, Pa had called him.

She knew Jesse had been planning to put in a little fountain near the rectangular flower bed Pa had come over and helped him dig and plant with iris bulbs last autumn, after Jesse had helped him out at the homestead, but she didn't see any sign of him out there right now. It looked like she'd have to go to the back door of the house and knock.

School had gotten out an hour ago, and she was pretty sure he was home, even without seeing his Mustang. That wasn't unusual, since he tended to keep it in the garage. Taking a step into the yard, she looked toward the driveway and paused again. There *was* a car there, but it was parked behind the garage, where it couldn't be seen from the road. And it wasn't Mr. Wilder's Mercedes or his Corvette, or even Jesse's Mustang. It was an old, blue Ford Escort. A beater car. Like the one Jay Arseneau drove.

Jay Arseneau?

Frowning a little now, Elena stepped more firmly into the yard as she made her way toward the back door. She knew Jesse and Jay spent a lot of time together during football season, working out or practicing their pass combinations. All their hard work had paid off since they'd been named the best high school quarterback-receiver combo in the entire state last season. But she hadn't thought they were great friends outside of football. Jesse rarely talked about Jay off-season, and she hardly ever saw them together, even at school.

Elena had just reached the ten- by fourteen-foot wooden shed—newly painted white—that Jesse's father had fixed up for storing the mower and planting tools when she heard a voice calling from inside the house. Right after, the back door creaked open and Jesse came out, wearing his letterman jacket against the chill and making his way down the steps with that same, easy grace Elena loved so much. She let out her breath and smiled, getting ready to let him know she was there . . . but then Jay came through the doorway, too, bounding down the steps to stand in the yard next to Jesse.

Elena stopped, uncertain, still in the shadows alongside the shed, where she knew she hadn't been seen yet.

So it *was* Jay's car.

Was Jay here to help Jesse with the fountain, then? It seemed unlikely. Jay hated outdoor work; his grandparents had a farm and he always complained about having to help with the dirty, sweaty job of baling hay every summer. So why was he here in the off-season, when Jesse's father was gone—and parked *behind* the garage?

Elena watched as Jay said something to Jesse though she couldn't hear the words, and Jesse leaned in to say something back. . . .

And then Elena's world shattered, the pieces of it tumbling away as if in slow motion.

Jay turned his head and kissed Jesse on the mouth before their arms slid around each other—not hugging in the way most guys did, with a brief, fierce grip and thumping each other's back before stepping quickly away—but a tender embrace. And they held on tightly, with Jesse's golden-blond head leaning into Jay's dark one, both of them closing their eyes. . . .

Like a couple.

Like lovers.

Like two people who never wanted to let go.

Shock washed over Elena in waves, stealing her breath and making her heart pound. She couldn't move. Couldn't speak. Through eyes that suddenly stung and began to fill with tears, she watched Jesse walk Jay to his car. Watched Jay get in, back around the garage, wave, and drive away, all while raging emotions, questions, panic, and hurt battled for precedence and swept through her in a sickening tide.

She kept silent until Jesse reached the back steps of his house again, then she forced herself to call his name, even though the sound came out a husky rasp.

His body went so rigid that he looked like a statue.

Slowly he turned around and saw her; his gaze fixed on hers, his face a shifting mask of shock, guilt, sadness, and shame. In the next breath, he burst into motion, crossing the distance between them until he stood before her. Silent. Either unwilling or unable to explain what she'd just seen.

"*Jesse*?" she repeated again, searching his face and leaving the other questions unspoken. She couldn't put voice to them, had no words to ask him for the truth that she wanted to deny. It hammered through her, and she held herself very still, afraid to move, almost afraid to breathe. She clasped her fingers so tightly in front of her that she thought they might break. But the pain kept her grounded . . . kept her firm when everything seemed to be giving way beneath her.

He reached out as if he wanted to touch her, to offer comfort, but he dropped his arms to his sides when she shifted almost imperceptibly back.

"I'm sorry," he said finally, his voice sounding as hoarse as hers had been. He looked away, and the muscle along the side of his face jumped as he clenched his jaw. "I'm really sorry, El. I tried. I wanted to tell you, but I—"

"How long?" she broke in in a whisper, forcing the words out the best that she could, forcing herself to stay calm, and blinking to try to see him through the wash of tears that kept welling up to cloud her vision.

His face was rigid, his expression anguished. "A few months."

Hurt stabbed her anew, but she refocused, demanding, "No—how long have you *known*?"

He flushed, his eyes darkening as he looked away again before swinging his gaze back to her. "I've known my whole life. I just tried as hard as I could to pretend I wasn't—" His voice cut off, and his jaw clenched. "Believe me, I'd do anything not to be this way, but I can't change it."

"Oh, my God, Jesse. Why didn't you tell me?"

When he remained silent her composure cracked, and her next words tumbled out broken and wild. "I don't understand! This whole time I've loved you—" Her voice failed with the denial and grief tearing through her. She came at him, hitting his chest. "You said you loved me, but you were lying! The whole time, pretending and *lying*!"

"I *do* love you—I swear I do! I never lied about that."

"Oh, God, how can you say that now?"

"Because it's true." His eyes were bright with unshed tears. "I've always loved you, no matter what. You have to believe me!"

"Not the way you love *Jay*," she choked, using the name as a weapon to wound him.

"Don't, El," Jesse said lowly. "Please don't say that. It's not the same thing." He was trying to calm her, to hold her, but she jerked away, unable to bear the pain of his touch. "I love *you*," he continued, his hands dropping in defeat. "The rest is—it's separate. It's something I can't make go away. I wish I could, but I can't."

She backed away, shaking her head, and still the hurt and disbelief continued to bubble up, strangling her. She squeezed her eyes shut against it. More than anything she wanted to crumple into a heap on the grass, but she couldn't. She wouldn't. She would be strong and get through this.

She had to get through this. Had to get away to think.

Opening her eyes, she looked at Jesse again. The depth of what she felt, what she couldn't help *still* feeling for him, lanced through her, stealing her breath. Somehow she found the strength to lift her hands and unfasten the delicate golden chain that he'd given her for Valentine's Day, the bracelet that hadn't left her wrist since that night.

"I don't know what to think anymore, Jesse," she said quietly, just managing to get the words out as she dropped the bracelet onto the grass at his feet. "I don't know how to feel. I—I just need to be by myself right now. I can't be near you. I have to go."

"El, please," he said, his plea husky and filled with self-loathing. "I never wanted to hurt you. You're my best friend. Please come back and talk to me. I'll go to our spot and wait there tonight. If you don't come, I'll wait again tomorrow and the day after that and every day until you'll talk to me again." His voice broke then, and he looked down before lifting his gaze to her again and adding in a hoarse whisper, "I love you, El-bell. You have to believe me."

Elena couldn't speak to respond, and her eyes were filling again with tears she refused to shed. She took in a shallow, shuddering breath and shook her head, half lifting her hand as if to ward him away.

And then even though it was the most difficult thing she had ever had to do, she turned her back on him and took off at a sprint, heading back into the woods toward home.

Diary entry # 238:
April 12, 1987

I have to see him. I have to. Oh, God. . . .

Elena stood in the light green shade of the woods less than thirty feet from their spot—the spot where she knew Jesse was right now, waiting for her as he'd been for the past two days when she hadn't had the courage to show up. As the thought stabbed deep, her breath caught and she squeezed her eyes shut, feeling hot tears seep past her lids anyway. Funny, she hadn't thought she had any left to cry.

Even after she swallowed and sucked in some chilly spring air, the aching in her throat refused to go away. This was so much harder than she'd thought it could be. She might have dealt with things more easily had they been separated because of college, or even if he had just stopped loving her. But she'd never imagined this.

Yet winding through the grief now was something calmer. In spite of everything, *love* underscored the rest. And that realization lit a wick of anger inside of her now, just as it had all weekend.

What kind of idiot was she? Didn't she have any self-respect? How was she supposed to make sense of this? He'd known what he felt—who he was—all along, but he'd made her fall in love with him anyway. It hurt more than anything she'd ever experienced, more than all the social snubs, more than getting cut from the cheerleading team . . . more than years of feeling like the pale and uninteresting shadow of Zippy.

He didn't make you do anything. Be honest. You let it happen. You wanted to believe it as much as he did.

The little voice nagged at her, and she closed her eyes again, wrapping her arms around her middle and bending over almost in half where she leaned against the newly leafed out maple. *Oh, God.* She didn't want to hear that. She wouldn't.

But it was true. This wasn't Jesse's fault. It wasn't anyone's fault. It just . . . was.

Choking back another sob and gasping past that horrible lump in her throat, she pushed away from the tree and took a halting step toward the clearing. The need to be near him overwhelmed her. It had been two days. She had to see him. What she would say—whether or not she could say anything—she didn't know. She wouldn't know until she faced him. But she couldn't avoid him, or these feelings, any longer.

She crashed forward through the brush, not caring for once that she was making enough noise to raise the dead. She slowed only as she reached the entrance to the little clearing, taking the last three steps on the balls of her feet, quiet at last, eyes straining, throat aching.

He sat hunched over, his long legs almost hidden by his powerful chest, his arms wrapped around his knees with his face buried in them. Her heart lurched again with pain and a rush of love and longing so great she thought she might not be able to move again. He looked miserable and lost. So alone.

She took another step closer.

He heard her. His head lifted slowly, his face turning toward her, the anguish palpable in his eyes and the painful set of his mouth. A muscle clenched in his jaw. He stood up, the motion slow and stiff, his breath catching with a harsh sound in his throat as he twisted to face her. Even though his arms remained at his sides, she could feel the yearning spill from him, and she took another few halting steps.

Her movement seemed to release something inside him, and he lurched toward her, reaching out to embrace her as she stumbled the rest of the way to him. Her face crumpled as she buried it in his chest and sobbed, gripping handfuls of his shirt and pulling him closer, as if she could make all of what she'd seen and all of what he'd told her not true.

And then she knew nothing but the bittersweet ache of being enclosed in the safety of his arms again. She felt nothing but the solid wall of his chest with the strong thumping of his heart beneath. She heard nothing but the quaking rasp of his breathing as his pent-up grief found the same release in her arms that she'd found in his.

"Oh, God, El-bell. Thank you," Jesse whispered into her hair, his voice thick with anguish and relief as he cradled her against him a little while later. "Thank you for coming back."

Elena opened her eyes and exhaled, forcing herself to pull away from the comfort of his embrace. The April sun wasn't strong enough in the woods to provide much warmth, so her tear-streaked cheeks felt cold as she swiped her fingers under her eyes. Looking up at him, she struggled to find words to express what was going on inside her—what had brought her back here, even though she probably should have stayed away.

"I still don't know how to . . . how—" She stopped, shaking her head, her voice unsteady. "What I saw makes everything all jumbled up inside of me, Jesse, and it hurts. But these past two days I've realized . . ." She paused again, measuring her words, wanting to get them right. "I've realized that I still love you. No matter what. I know that hasn't changed."

He took a sharp breath and closed his eyes. When he met her gaze again, she saw such tenderness and gratitude there that her heart felt like it was breaking all over again.

"I never wanted to hurt you, El," he said quietly. "I swear I didn't. I love you. I always will. You're part of me in here." He tapped his chest before taking her hand in his, the movement deliberate as he curled his strong fingers over hers, warming them. The caress felt just the same as it always had, sweet and comforting . . . except that nothing would ever be the same again and she knew it.

Still, it helped, somehow, when he added, "No matter what else is true about me, my feelings for you go deeper. You mean everything to me, even if I can't show it exactly the way other guys would."

Her heart lurched, and she bit back a sad smile. "Well, at least I know now why you weren't upset that we hadn't slept together." Frowning and glancing away, she added, "But it must have been totally awkward for you to be kissing me all this time. I feel like an idiot not to have noticed."

"You're not an idiot. There wasn't anything *to* notice." Now it was Jesse's turn to look away self-consciously. "Being . . . what I am doesn't mean I can't like being with you in certain ways. Kissing you is always nice."

"Well, that's something, I guess," she said, shrugging and trying her best to keep from crying again.

This was so hard. Oh, God, why did it have to be like this? It was the same question that had hammered at her heart all weekend, but she knew it was a dead end, with no answer. It was this way—*he* was this way—because . . . it was. That was all.

Letting go of his hand, she walked over to their rock and sat down, pulling her knees to her chin and wrapping her arms around them. "So what happens now?"

"I don't know." He stood next to her, shifting his weight from one foot to the other and looking as uncertain as she felt. "What do you *want* to happen?"

"It doesn't matter because I can't have it." Elena swallowed back the pain and pasted on a watery smile. "I'm stuck loving you, Jesse, the way a girl completely and totally loves a guy, but with nowhere to go with those feelings. I haven't figured out how to handle that yet."

He sat down next to her, his blue eyes solemn. After a long silence he said, "I have to tell you something, El. Even now, I feel the same for you as I've always felt. It might sound over-the-top, but I would protect you with my life. I want to make you laugh, I love talking with you, taking you places, hanging out, and kidding around with you the way I always have." His brows came together, his expression conflicted. "The thing is, I don't know if that's going to be enough for you now . . . well, now that you know everything."

Elena frowned. "Not to mention how, um—" her voice cut out and she had to clear her throat before she could finish, "—how Jay would feel about it." She still had a difficult time saying his name. Stupid, but she couldn't help it.

"Jay's not an issue."

"Why not?"

"Because he's known about you and me all along. And he's dating Lacey. It's way different from what I feel about you, but he'll keep it up anyway. He sure as hell can't broadcast anything else. It would be suicide for both of us if anyone knew the truth." Jesse closed his eyes for a second, blowing out his breath.

For the first time, Elena noticed how exhausted he sounded. Resigned. His voice was gravelly, like he hadn't slept in a long time. That probably wasn't too far from the truth if these past two nights for him had been the same as they'd been for her. But she couldn't decide anything about where she wanted to go in her relationship with him. Not yet. No, right now she needed to shift gears a little, to something she could actually manage without wanting to break down and cry.

"Have you told your dad, Jesse?" she asked softly.

"Hell, no!"

He tensed even more, his hands clenching into fists. "My father would never understand." He tipped his chin down, looking at the muddy ground that was visible between his knees. As he dug at a stone with the toe of his sneaker, a bitter sound escaped him. "He'd probably beat the shit out of me if I even said the word 'gay.' I can't tell him." He swiveled to look at her, panic tightening his mouth. "You haven't told anyone, have you, El?"

She shook her head. "Pa and Ma saw how upset I was when I came home Friday night, but I just told them we'd broken up. I didn't give any details, and they left it alone." She frowned, meeting his gaze. "But they know how close we've been. They'll probably ask questions sooner or later."

"You can't tell them. Promise me. No one can know the truth. My life would be over if anyone knew." He looked away. "Jesus, I don't even want to think about what it would be like." There was a shadow in his eyes that she'd never noticed as he turned back to her. "At the very least, some of the guys around here would think it was their duty to kick my ass. Maybe they'd decide to aim at me instead of the deer come hunting season. 'Former Black Bears Quarterback Shot in the Woods.' That would make a great headline for the newspapers, wouldn't it?"

"Oh, God, Jesse, don't say stuff like that!"

"It's the truth. Most people think being the way I am is about the same as being a mutant or an axe murderer or something. Moose Junction is mountain country, where the men are tough and the shotguns outnumber people."

"No one could say you're not tough. You're strong enough to bench press two of *me*. Besides you're a football hero. That counts for a lot around here."

He raised his brow at her. "Yeah, and you don't think that would change in a heartbeat if anyone found out?"

"It would probably be a shock to a lot of people," she said quietly, looking sideways at him. "It was to me, too, but I'm getting over it. Anyone who knows you would get over it, Jesse. Maybe you just need to give them that chance."

He took her hand again when she said that, and she let him, realizing it felt good to be near him like this, finding this sense of connection like they used to, even with what had come between them.

"I wish I could see the world the way you do, El, but I don't. There are plenty of people who wouldn't want anything to do with me if they knew the truth. My dad . . . he's one of them. He thinks any guy being with another guy is a freak." He picked at the moss covering the rock where they were sitting. "Maybe he's right. Either way, he sure as hell isn't going to accept his only son being like that."

"I don't think you're a freak, Jesse."

His expression after she said that was the same mix of adorable, vulnerable, and tough-as-nails she'd seen from the very first day she'd met him. And he was so incredibly handsome. It made her want to cry again, but she kept her composure as he lifted his arm, asking her to come closer to him. With a sigh, she slipped her hand under the edge of his open jacket to circle around behind his back, snuggling against him and resting her head on his shoulder as he tucked his arm over her. Warm and safe, as always.

They sat there together in companionable silence on their rock for a few seconds more before he pressed a kiss on the top of her head, murmuring, "You're special, El. You always have been. But you're probably in the minority on my freak status. Like I said, I'm not even so sure how I feel about it myself." She tilted her head up to look at him, and he gave her a half smile. "I can tell you I've wished for as long as I can remember that I *wasn't* this way. Everything would be a whole lot easier if I wasn't."

"Maybe easy isn't better," she answered. "I did a lot of thinking this weekend, and I kept coming back to the fact that sometimes things just *are* and we can't change them. God made you the way you are, Jesse, and I don't think that's a mistake."

He glanced at her again, his voice lower as he asked, "I know your family goes to church and all, El, but do you really believe in God?"

She thought about it for a second, weighing her feelings. Finally she nodded. "I question things sometimes, and it's hard to explain some of the feelings I've had about death and that kind of stuff since I was little, but, yes, I believe in God. Do you?"

Jesse shrugged. "When I was a kid, yeah, I had this whole picture in my head of a giant old man in white robes, sitting in the clouds on a throne somewhere and directing all the traffic." He laughed, tossing away a twig he'd been spinning between his fingers. "Typical, huh?"

Elena smiled and nodded again. "Yeah, I guess. What about now?"

"I don't know. After my mom died, I stopped believing in everything. I was pretty messed up."

"But you were really young. I remember you telling me about your mom that first day we met each other in the woods." She rubbed her finger over the design on his t-shirt. "I felt awful for you."

"I was in first grade when she died." His voice was matter-of-fact.

"I couldn't figure out why God would take her from me. I was pissed at everyone. Then my dad got me into football, and it helped. I could get it all out on the field. I learned to push myself—run faster, throw harder, ram the training sled toward the end zone, anything to drive out the demons, you know?"

She nodded, hugging her arm around his waist a little tighter.

"I guess I haven't thought about the whole concept of *God* as much since then. I sort of pushed it to the back of my mind. But a few things have made me think that maybe I believe in something bigger after all."

"Like what?"

"Nature, for one." He nodded to indicate their little clearing. It was laced in shades of green, and though the afternoon sun might not be warm this early in the season, it was still pretty, slanting through the branches in shifting golden patterns. Newly leafed trees ringed the clearing, and the brown debris from last year mixed with fresh ground cover coming to life, with the heads of a few pale-pink Spring Beauties beginning to peek through.

"You had a lot to do with me noticing this kind of stuff," he continued, still looking around them. "Ever since that first summer with you, I've paid more attention to plants and animals and stuff like that. It's pretty amazing how it all works. Even the seasons and the way they change. Makes me think maybe it's not chance. That maybe someone arranged all of it."

"I know what you mean." She sighed, feeling the gentle rise and fall of his breath and his steady heartbeat under her cheek. "I've always loved being in the woods or near the lake. It's kind of magic."

"Not surprising, considering you're the original Mountain Girl," he said, and she heard the smile in his voice.

"Yeah, Billboard Boy, that's me, burdocks and all."

He smoothed her hair back over her shoulder, his touch rhythmic, soothing. "But you're also another reason why I've been thinking that maybe God is out there after all."

Elena pulled back a little, giving him a look.

"No, listen. You don't get how important you are to me. You're the one who saw me for *me* right from the start, not just the flash and external stuff, you know? From day one we connected on that level. That's never happened with anyone else my whole life."

"I didn't see all of you, Jesse, or we wouldn't be here right now."

"That part's my fault, El, not yours."

"Not really. I understand why it would be a tough thing to tell someone."

He shook his head. "I still screwed it up big-time. But that's what I mean. Even with all the shit I've put you through, you still care about me."

"Oh, believe me, I've tried not to, but I can't help it." She raised her brow at him. "Even though I'd feel a lot better if I could get you to stop swearing all the time."

"Yeah, well . . . I'm still working on that," he drawled.

She smiled again, feeling grateful for the easy affection of these moments. Maybe there *would* be a way to move past this point together. Maybe there was still enough left, even without the part that had been forced to fall away once she knew the truth.

Swallowing hard against the lump in her throat, she looked at him with a steady gaze, wanting him to understand. "You were there for me, too, you know, Jesse. Even before—" she forced herself to go on "—even before I thought of you as my boyfriend. Just being with you helped me feel different. I felt stronger somehow. It's nice to know that someone other than my parents gets who I am and likes me anyway."

"*Loves* you anyway," he corrected gently, kissing her forehead.

Her heart skipped a beat, and she pulled away from him a little again. "Yeah, well, *I'm* still working on how to handle all *that* now, okay?"

"Okay."

Her throat felt achy, like it did every time she contemplated how to redefine her feelings for him. How to love him again in the old way, like she had before they'd dated. After all this time, it seemed brand new and almost impossible, but the thought of losing him completely hurt far worse. She didn't think she could survive that.

"I seriously don't deserve you, El." He tugged her closer again. "Most girls would have told me to go to hell and hung me out to dry. That's what I mean about maybe there being something out there, like God or whatever. You've been like this unbelievable gift who sticks by me no matter what else happens."

"I feel the same about you, Jesse."

"And I think maybe we found each other for a reason."

"Yeah?"

"Yeah."

Before Elena could say anything else, her stomach made a loud gurgling noise; she hadn't eaten more than a couple of bites all day, and it was rebelling. Thankfully, Jesse didn't seem to have heard it.

"How will we ever know, though?" She tried to ignore her hunger pangs. "If there's a reason for all this, I mean?"

He shrugged. "I don't think we can. Not while we're here at least. I guess we'd have to die to find out." He wiggled his eyebrows, looking mischievous. "So, if I bite the dust first and get the inside scoop, I'll try to let you know, okay?"

"Hey! I told you I don't like it when you talk like that!" She gave him a playful shove, and he laughed.

Just then her stomach made another loud gurgle, and he looked askance at her. "That *is* you, isn't it?"

"Yeah . . . I guess the last couple days are finally catching up with me."

"You and me both. Want to come with me to get something to eat?"

"Not if we have to go to one of our houses to do it." She stood up, shivering now that he wasn't close enough to keep her warm. She'd run out in such a hurry to get to the woods earlier that she'd left her windbreaker behind. "I don't really want to have to talk to anyone or explain anything."

"Me either." He'd been watching her, and now he took off his jacket, holding it out for her to put on. "Here. You're cold, and I'm not right now." When she protested, he slid it over her arms anyway, insisting, and so she let him ease it on her the rest of the way, snuggling inside its woolen warmth and relishing the way his scent surrounded her . . . until she remembered that she really shouldn't be allowing herself to feel attracted to him that way anymore.

Oh, God. This is hard.

She took a couple breaths and closed her eyes, her heart lurching with need and longing for him anyway. Blinking, she gritted her teeth and tried to focus on walking with him out of the clearing.

"I was thinking of going someplace like the Sweet Thyme Diner up near Boonville," he said over his shoulder. "It's far enough away that we probably won't see anyone we know, but they make some awesome soups and homemade bread."

"Sounds good, but I can't stay out too long. I told Ma I was coming to talk to you, but I said I'd be back before it got dark."

"That gives us more than an hour. I've already got my car keys." He reached into his jeans pocket for them. "I just need to poke my head in at home, grab another jacket, and tell Dad I'm going out for a few."

Elena nodded as they continued through the woods toward Jesse's house. "I'm going to go into the garage and wait for you in the car, okay?"

"Yeah, that would probably be best." He looked back over his shoulder again, his blue eyes twinkling. "I'm thinking about a big bowl of beef and barley. Or maybe chicken noodle. But I also had their clam chowder once, and it was amazing. What are you going to get?"

"Yes." She smiled, thinking she was so hungry she probably *could* eat all three.

He grinned back at her, taking her hand in his as they jumped over the ditch into his yard and covered the remaining distance to the house.

The sun was just starting to make its way toward the horizon as Jesse and Elena drove toward Moose Junction again. They'd be home in plenty of time. The diner hadn't been busy, so they'd gotten their food without a wait. If anything, it had come so quickly that Elena had eaten too much.

Now she leaned her head back in the passenger seat of Jesse's Mustang and pulled his jacket closer around her, feeling content and even a little sleepy. A huge bowl of corn chowder and three buttermilk biscuits would do that to a person, she decided. "Forever Young" by Alphaville was playing on the radio as she looked over at Jesse, wanting to make sure he wasn't feeling the same effects of food overdose that she was.

"You tired?"

"Nah, I'm good." He was alert as always behind the wheel, and he smiled at her for a second before looking back at the road. "Much better than earlier."

"Ma always says a good meal makes all the difference."

"Yeah, but this time it's not just that, even though I was starving and it *was* good." As he spoke he reached over the console for her hand and squeezed. "It's mostly you, El-bell. Just being with you. It's like I've been empty for the past two days and now I'm finally filling up again with what matters most."

She gripped his hand, too, brimming with the conflicting emotions of it all, but with love outweighing the rest. It was the same as always whenever she was with him. "I missed you, too, Jesse," she said quietly. "I hated being apart. You're the reason—"

But her words were cut off when he cursed and stiffened suddenly, pulling his hand out of hers to grip the wheel. "Shit," he said almost to himself. "What the hell is that guy doing?"

Elena's gaze snapped to the road ahead, and her heart skipped a beat, then began to pound. A silver SUV had come around a bend in the road and was weaving across the lanes about fifty yards away, heading toward them.

Disbelief numbed her mind for an instant before everything seemed to shift into slow, agonizing motion. She swung her gaze to the right and then the left, realizing in silent desperation that there was nowhere to go, nowhere to pull off to safety. Guardrails hemmed the curvy, mountain road on both sides.

She looked at Jesse again, feeling like she was moving under water, seeing his face register the same shock, fear, and horror that were rocking through her.

"Oh, God, oh, God, oh, God," she breathed, her body going rigid and her voice rising in slowly building hysteria as her head swiveled forward again and she saw the SUV coming closer. "Jesse!"

"Jesus, I can't get out of the way," he said, his entire body tensing. "Oh, God. Oh, my God. El, hang on!"

He threw his arm over her as the SUV crossed the center line just in front of them, barreling at them head on.

At the last moment, Jesse slammed on the brakes, jerking the steering wheel hard to the right, protecting her, shielding her as he spun the Mustang to take the brunt of the impact on his side.

There was a blinding flash, the sickening sensation of grinding metal, and a sudden explosion of shattering glass. Sound seemed to vanish into a vacuum, coming down a tunnel toward Elena before it enveloped her in a roar. With it a wall of pain slammed into her, stealing her breath, eliminating her sight, cutting off her awareness. . . .

And then there was nothing left but blackness.

Maple Creek Dispatch
April 13, 1987

MOOSE JUNCTION MAN DIES IN AUTOMOBILE CRASH

A two-car crash Sunday evening claimed the life of Jesse James Wilder, 18, of Moose Junction and left his passenger, Elena Wright, 18, also of Moose Junction, seriously injured. The Boonville and Remsen Fire Departments responded, using the Jaws of Life to free the victims. Wilder was pronounced dead on the scene by Oneida County Coroner Stephen Jones. Wright was airlifted to Adirondack Medical Center in Syracuse, where she is listed in critical condition. Both attended their local high school as seniors.

Wilder's car was struck by a 1981 Chevy Blazer driven by Joseph Tibbett, 54, of Turin. Tibbett's vehicle swerved across the center line of Route 46 north of Lake Pines Park, striking Mr. Wilder's vehicle at a high rate of speed. Mr. Tibbett was taken to North Country General Hospital, where he was treated overnight and released.

According to reports, Tibbett had spent several hours at the Tip-Top Tavern in Floyd prior to the crash. State Police continue to investigate and are awaiting full results of toxicology tests before determining whether to charge Mr. Tibbett with reckless homicide for driving while impaired by alcohol or drugs, a police spokesperson said.

Mr. Wilder, the son of former New York Giant's standout Jim Wilder, was a star quarterback for both the Poughkeepsie Pioneers and the Moose Junction Black Bears, having led both teams to recent state-level championships. He had been accepted on a full scholarship to the University of Notre Dame in South Bend, Indiana, beginning in the fall.

Arrangements are being handled by Boyd & Hawkins Funeral Home. Service dates and times are pending and will be announced later, at the family's discretion.

Chapter Nine

Maple Creek, Upstate New York
December 8, 2007

Elena held the old newspaper clipping, blinded by tears that wouldn't fall and not really paying attention to the way her fingers rhythmically smoothed the jagged, worn edges from where someone (Pa or Ma, probably) had cut it out of the Dispatch all those years ago and tucked it into the diary.

Oh, God, it still hurt.

Even after all this time, the feelings rushed through her like it was happening all over again, sucking her back down into that agonizing well of loss. She had almost drowned in it after the accident, had wished with every fiber of her being that she had died with Jesse. Forcing herself to keep breathing without him had been the most difficult thing she'd ever had to do.

But the world had kept turning. Hours, days, weeks, and months had trickled by. Eventually, her body had healed and the bruises had faded. The part deep inside, though...that part had stayed raw and aching, and she'd known that she'd never be fully whole again.

After the accident she'd realized that trying to navigate any kind of grieving process was out of the question, because to remember Jesse, to think about *any* of it, hurt more than she could bear. Except for breaking down at the moment she'd learned he was dead, when she was lying in her hospital bed hooked up to all kinds of tubes and monitors, she'd refused to let herself cry or confront the gnawing pain inside. She'd focused on the physical pain instead and used her ultimate recovery from it to manage her emotions.

Yes, she had done everything she could to prevent her feelings from getting close enough to the surface again to wound her. So she just kept pushing them down, cramming them deeper inside, until finally she was able to shut the lid on them, sealing them in and hiding the key in the part of her heart that had died with Jesse.

Because of her injuries, she hadn't been able to graduate high school in June; she'd gotten through by August instead and headed to college as planned. But she'd never really coped with Jesse's death or her guilt in knowing he'd died saving her. Over time, she'd fooled herself into thinking she'd really moved on. It had been her only choice if she was going to win the struggle to keep functioning after losing him.

That purposeful oblivion had become a habit and one that had served her well for just over 20 years, until the car accident this October. Being in that fender-bender had breached her emotion-tight vault, creating cracks that had widened so much that she couldn't glue them shut anymore. Her repressed feelings had seeped out and affected her life and the lives of those she loved here and now, filling her with unexplained anxieties, sadness, and distraction.

Elena knew that once and for all she had to come to some kind of terms with the pain of Jesse's loss and the sacrifice he'd made for her. She needed to face her emotions head-on and try to continue on to the other side of grief with hopefully some peace to carry her through.

Carefully, she tucked the clipping back into the page after the diary's last entry and turned to the bin, rifling through the contents, looking for the white plastic bag she'd seen tucked underneath everything else. She knew exactly what it was, and she wanted – she *needed* – to see it and hold it again.

There it was, under some papers: A white bag with Adirondack Medical Center's green logo printed on it. Pulling it out, Elena set it on the floor and unsnapped the hard plastic handles that kept it closed. The edges of the bag gaped open enough to see some black woolen fabric and a black collar with two bands of orange ribbing. The waistband and the cuffs at the bottom of the leather sleeves had the same orange stripes, she knew, even though she hadn't looked, hadn't let herself even think about this for more than two decades.

Reaching into the bag, Elena pulled out Jesse's varsity letterman's jacket, bracing herself for what she knew was coming next.

She had been wearing his jacket that night. The emergency personnel had cut away most of her clothing when she was airlifted to Syracuse, but the jacket had been mostly intact, except for the left sleeve where glass and metal had sliced into her during the impact that had killed Jesse.

There were bloodstains on that ravaged sleeve, almost invisible on the leather that was left, but looking like rusty smears across the cuff stripes. Jesse's blood or hers? She didn't know. Maybe both.

Elena's hands were shaking as she lifted the coat and brought the inside of the collar up to her face. Closing her eyes, she breathed in.

It was faint, but the spicy-sweet musk of Jesse's cologne clung to the material there. It filled her senses, rocking her back in time to other memories. To senior year again, immersed in all the laughter, yearning, fun, and tenderness. The pure joy of being young and together.

Always together.

Elena swallowed hard against the pain that was intensifying in earnest now, trying her best to concentrate on breathing in those lingering hints of Jesse's scent. She realized that she couldn't open her eyes even if she wanted to. They were squeezed shut against the pressure, the need to release that she couldn't trigger. Not yet.

Blindly, she tugged the jacket on, pulling it up her arms and around herself, needing to feel it wrapped close around her again. Even now, with her figure matured by time and the birth of children, his jacket was too big on her. Jesse had been tall, broad-shouldered, and so strong.

He had seemed invincible.

Oh, God.

Elena slipped her hands into the pockets, wanting to hug the sides tighter around her body...and it was then that she felt it. Down deep, at the very bottom of the right pocket.

Something cool and delicate. A chain made of tiny links...gold, she knew even before she pulled it out and cracked open her aching eyes to look at it.

It was her bracelet. The one Jesse had given her that Valentine's Day. The same one she had tossed at his feet when he'd broken her heart just two days before he died.

He must have picked it up after she'd dropped it. She hadn't felt it when she'd worn his jacket on that last day, because she hadn't put her hands inside the pockets. She rarely did whenever she'd worn any of his coats; the sleeves were always so long on her that if she got cold, she just needed to pull her hands back inside the cuffs to warm them.

The hot fullness in her eyes blurred her vision of the chain resting in her palm. It was so fine and delicate. Fragile. But it had survived, enduring despite the brutality of the accident, the tragedy of Jesse's death, and the burden of decades, waiting quietly in the secret dark.

Just like love: invisible but real nonetheless.

Choking back sobs now, Elena sank down to the floor, closing her fingers around the bracelet and holding it close. Protecting it in a way she hadn't been able to protect Jesse. Not physically anyway. But she'd accepted him and loved him with a full and honest heart, in a way that had mattered to him. And she knew he had loved her too – truly loved her in a way that had gone deeper than sexuality, deeper than passion or physical desire. It had been real, and he'd sacrificed himself because of it to save her.

The feelings overwhelmed her then, waves of loss, grief, love, gratitude and what seemed a thousand other emotions filling up and spilling over inside her. She gave vent to it all at last, curling up on her side on the floor, wrapped in Jesse's jacket as she cried for what had been...for all they'd known and lived through with each other, for all they'd learned and all they'd lost, with her diary and the bracelet he'd given her clutched to her chest.

And after a long time, she slept.

WGRR FM 103.9, THE BEAR

"Give a Growl for the Adirondacks'
Most Trusted Radio Station"
April 12, 1988

Welcome back, Adirondack listeners. It's Willard T. Boggs here with you on a quiet Tuesday. I'm not feeling too chipper, but Marge says it's my own fault. I ate all my Easter candy then bought more at the after-sales. I didn't think I'd been bad, but Marge said my expanded waist must be affecting my mind, since there were five pounds in the basket alone. I say it looks like she snitched a few chocolate bunnies herself, but don't tell her I said so. If you're listening, Marge, then carrot sticks will be just fine for supper, and you can put my pillow and blanket on the couch.

Speaking of cosmic isolation, on This Day in History in 1961, Soviet Yuri Alekseyevich Gagarin became the first man in space aboard the Vostok I.

And now we have some solemn local news. This evening many members of the community gathered at the high school stadium to unveil a memorial honoring Jesse James Wilder, the Moose Junction senior tragically killed in an automobile crash one year ago today. A marble bench with an engraved plaque was placed at the entrance to the football field in tribute to the star quarterback, a fine young man who lost his life due to the callous actions of a drunk driver.

We at WGRR reported for several years on Jesse Wilder's football prowess both in Poughkeepsie and locally, and our radio station adds our sincerest condolences to those of the rest of the community as we join his family and loved ones in remembering a vibrant and promising life cut so needlessly short.

Chapter Ten

Maple Creek, Upstate New York
December 8, 2007

Elena awakened to the phone ringing. The sound disoriented her, shaking her as it did from a deep and dreamless sleep. Her eyes felt swollen as she pushed herself up to sitting and reached for the phone, groaning from the stiffness in her joints, and swiping the back of her hand across her mouth.

"Hello?" she mumbled, hoping she didn't sound too out of it. She didn't want anyone to think she'd been on a bender or something.

"Hi, Ellie. It's Pa."

Pa was using the nickname he'd given her in childhood, but that never bothered Elena; at times like this, in fact, it was more comforting than anything else.

"Don't worry," he continued. "Everything's fine. Your mother and I just called to see how you're doing."

"Oh, hi, Pa. I'm . . ." Elena hesitated, not sure exactly how she was, but she wasn't going to worry him. "I'm fine. Did the kids cooperate last night?" As she spoke she squinted, trying to see the clock. No dice.

"We had a good time. Claire was a big help with her sisters and we played some cards before bed. We had lunch a little while ago and thought we'd check in on you before we went out to run a few errands."

Elena's vision finally cleared enough to see the time. 1:32 p.m.. *Oh, geez. . . .*

"Wow, I didn't realize it was—uh, so late," she said, stumbling to her feet and sucking in her breath as she stubbed her toe on the edge of the couch. "Sorry, about that. I just hit my foot."

"I guess you saw my note, then." It was a question, but Pa said it like a statement, being gentle but persistent like he always was when he thought the subject was important.

"Ummm . . . yes, I did. Thanks. I looked through the bin

last night."

"How'd it go?"

Elena paused again, everything swirling in her brain. Too much to process into any kind of coherent answer on the spot. She settled for saying, "Maybe we can talk about it tonight. I'd like to come over to the house, if that's okay, after we see Pops." She rubbed her forehead, closing her eyes. She needed to wake *up* out of this fog.

"Whenever works for you is great for us. You know your mother and I always love seeing you. We're planning to go see Hank after Violet's nap. We should get to the Towers around five o'clock if you want to meet us there."

"That sounds good. Right now I'm going to take a shower, put a few things away, and try to get my head on straight so I'll be able to keep up with everyone." She tried a laugh, but it came out sounding pretty strained.

"Just give yourself some time, Ellie. Don't push it. And be careful driving, especially on these roads."

Elena smiled. Pa (and Ma) always said a version of that to each of their kids whenever they said goodbye, like some kind of verbal charm that would protect them. Of course it wouldn't, but it made them feel better to do it . . . and as Pa always said, a reminder to slow down never hurt. "Ok, Pa. Thanks again for everything," she answered, adding as she always did, "I love you."

"I love you, too. Your mother says the same. See you in a few hours."

Elena murmured goodbye and then clicked off the phone, setting it aside.

Leaning her forearms onto her thighs, she paused, realizing that she was still wearing Jesse's jacket. It had kept her warm through the night and into the morning as she'd slept on the floor. Sitting back, she assessed her emotions and was surprised to realize that (except for the stiffness) she felt . . . okay. Steady inside, with a calm, sane ticking that let her know she'd come out on the other side of last night's grief intact and maybe even stronger. She *was* fine, just as she'd told Pa.

She still mourned Jesse; she knew that would never change. She'd always carry the ache of his loss somewhere deep inside. But the realization she'd come to after confronting the anguish of the past meant that now there was a sense of bittersweet acceptance, too, edging out some of those darker emotions that had haunted her for more than two decades.

After taking a final moment to close her eyes and send out a few last thoughts of gratitude and peace to him and the universe, Elena got up, took off Jesse's jacket, folded it, and placed it carefully back into its bag in the bin, along with the diary and everything else she'd taken out. Everything except for the bracelet. That, she intended to keep in a special box on the top of her dresser, where she could take it out and look at it whenever she needed a reminder of what was important and real in this world (and maybe in the next one, too).

She grabbed a banana from the kitchen on her way to the bedroom, driven by the need to move forward in other ways, too—showering and getting dressed would be a good start, she decided—but as she pulled some jeans and a sweatshirt from the drawer, she saw her cellphone hooked up to its charger on the nightstand. She usually kept it there when she was at home, so that she knew where it was and to make or take a call if there was an emergency or the power went out after she'd gone to bed. Except that last night, of course, she hadn't slept in her bed.

Picking up the phone, she hit the power button and looked at the screen. One missed call and a voicemail. *Crap.* A quick glance at the missed call record showed it was Max. He always called when he was away overnight, to check in and make sure everything was okay at home. But they'd had another argument just before he'd left; because of that, Elena hadn't been sure he'd make the effort to call, since he knew the kids were going to be at Pa and Ma's.

She looked at the time of the missed call: 9:37 a.m. Pretty late compared to when he usually checked in when he was away on a Saturday. Elena had always been an early riser, regularly waking up to her own internal alarm clock by half past seven most mornings, even before the kids were born, so she knew Max would be wondering why she hadn't picked up. He was probably irritated, thinking she was ignoring him on purpose.

She debated whether or not to listen to the message right now. She was feeling peaceful for the first time in quite a while, but the feeling was still wobbly, and she really didn't want anything negative to set her back.

Don't be ridiculous, the little voice inside her nagged. *You're in charge of your own emotions. Besides, it's a voicemail, not a declaration of war.*

With a sigh, Elena picked up the phone and dialed in her code to hear the message. From Max's first words, she was set back on her heels all right, but not for the reason she'd thought.

Hey, Babe, you've been on my mind all night. Pa told me what was going on this weekend, and I wanted to give you your space, but I've been worried about you, too. I'll be working the trade show all day, so I can't really answer a call. Text me when you get this, okay? I need to know you're all right. I know I haven't always been as . . . understanding as I could have been about the way you need to deal with all the stuff that happened to you before I met you, but I love you, angel eyes, just remember that. I'll see you tomorrow.

Elena sat on the edge of the bed, having a hard time believing her ears. Max was offering the proverbial olive branch . . . and (even more surprising) he'd been *in* on Pa's plan?

Max had known about Jesse from the beginning. Once Max and Elena had become a real couple, a little more had come out (and because Jesse had been so well known in high school football, Max had even remembered reading something about the car accident when it had happened). But any of the details about Jesse and Elena together or the emotional fallout she'd experienced after his death, Max had been forced to learn from other people in her life. She just couldn't talk about it.

Over time they'd agreed to leave the topic alone, but Elena knew it had always bothered him. He'd hated that she couldn't confide in him with her feelings. It had ended up becoming one of those "issues" in their relationship, but she just hadn't been able to go there, no matter how much she loved him.

Eventually they'd gotten married, the kids came along, and life shifted focus, allowing that tension between them to ease even more. But just as something would occasionally jar Elena into thinking about Jesse, every now and then Max would get sulky and allude to the emotional wall that her choice (which is what he called it) had built between them.

So, the fact that he was acknowledging it and trying to make up to her in a recorded message, instead of waiting until he got home to try to kiss her into surrender, was a shocker. Surprised didn't cover how she was feeling.

She smiled. Max had been surprising her in one way or the other since the day they'd met. She knew she probably should have been prepared for these moments out of left field by now, but somehow he still managed to rock her world just a little when he pulled them on her.

Stubborn, annoying, persistent, handsome, loving, protective Max.

His timing was perfect, considering that lately she'd been wondering if he'd finally turned that corner she'd heard about from other friends who'd been married even longer than she and Max had been; that sinking of a relationship into something worn and comfortable, like a favorite pair of once awesome but now pretty ratty jeans. Safe familiarity with no spark.

Max had just fanned the embers again, at least in Elena. The finishing touch had been that he'd resurrected his old college endearment for her (taken from the song by the same title that they'd danced together to for the first time). He'd had to know that would soften her up toward him even more.

Grinning now, she typed a quick text, letting him know she was all right. Then she scooped up her clothes and headed to the shower. But before she got far she stopped, grabbed the cellphone again, and typed another message to him, adding that she missed him and telling him she'd feel even better once he was home so she could show him in person just how much. . . .

And knowing that for the first time in ages she really meant it.

Darby Dining Hall
Holbrook University, Rochester, New York
October 4, 1990
Elena is twenty-one years old

Except for the night, we could never know the stars. . . .

The dining hall was packed for a Thursday.

That was good, Elena decided, since it would be easier to disappear in a crowd. She was a college senior, working hard to keep her 3.8 GPA on track; she shouldn't have had to play hide-and-seek with an idiot, but that's exactly what she was doing.

She tried to duck behind one of the large pillars that separated the eating area from the food stations, and then shifted toward the cereal bar in her efforts to evade the guy following her. It was Joe Jeverone, a junior from the campus newspaper, the *Holbrook Herald.*

Joe was a journalism major at Holbrook, who also happened to be a tall, handsome, image-obsessed hockey player. He'd been hounding her for a "date" since the school year started—only she'd realized from their first conversation that his interest had almost nothing to do with her; what he really wanted was an exclusive on Zippy (who had moved to Hollywood a few months after graduating high school and her dream came true when she'd landed an agent and then a role in an A-list movie in quick succession).

Elena hadn't been able to do anything to back Joe off; the university couldn't help her in the same way they'd stopped the reporters who'd started crawling out of the woodwork about eighteen months ago when Zippy first appeared on movie screens everywhere. There had been dozens, all trying to get the scoop on new starlet Alexandra Wright from her younger sister. But as a fellow student at Holbrook, Joe had every right to be on campus.

Even worse, when she'd gone to campus security to complain about him dogging her, she'd been forced to admit that he hadn't done anything technically wrong. He hadn't touched her, tried to get into her dorm room, or said anything inappropriate. The fact that he wouldn't leave her alone made him a pest, but there really wasn't anything official they could do to stop him.

It was becoming an issue for her. Elena had done her best in the past three years to become a face in the crowd—a college kid that no one noticed, with her head in her books and a work ethic that helped to keep her demons underground where they belonged. Joe's continual pursuit was pushing buttons she didn't want pushed, and she was starting to feel edgy.

But right now she was also feeling hungry.

Joe or not, she had to eat, so she grabbed a bowl of Cocoa Puffs with chocolate milk (a vice she indulged in once a week) and then retreated to sit with her back to the wall at one of the tables near the door so she could make a quick getaway if necessary. For the moment she seemed safe, having lost sight of Joe near the salad bar. It crossed her mind that maybe he hadn't been following her, and she'd just been unlucky enough to be in the dining hall at the same time he was. If that was the case, she might be able to slow down and eat like a human being instead of having to wolf down her food tonight.

Pulling her overstuffed bag onto the table and tugging it in front of her as a sort of barrier between her and everyone else in the dining hall, Elena pulled out her copy of *Twelfth Night* and began to read as she took another bite of her cereal. The Shakespeare elective was a lot of work, but it was a nice break from the constant research and technology classes that were required for her major.

She smiled as she read the scene with Sir Toby Belch loudly singing his drunken song with Sir Andrew in the middle of the night. Malvolio was just coming in to scold them for their carousing, when Elena was brought back to the here and now by seeing a movement out of the side of her vision as someone sat down next to her.

"I've always thought you have a pretty smile."

She restrained herself from rolling her eyes at the insincerity in the voice, but her expression shifted to a glare as she put her book down.

"Uh-oh," Joe said in mock concern, shaking his head, "It's gone. How can I bring it back?"

"Leave."

"But if I do that, I won't see when you smile again."

"That's the idea."

"Oh, come on. What's the big deal about grabbing a coffee with me? I just want to ask you a few questions," he said, reaching out to fiddle with the Moose Junction Realty tag (Kat's realty office) dangling from the zipper on her bag.

Sliding her bag away from his hand, Elena said, "We've gone over this before, Joe. I'm not going to give you any information about my sister."

"Why are you so against talking with me?"

"It's what you want to talk *about*."

"Even if I make it worth your while?"

"I'm not interested," she answered, standing up.

Joe got up, too, and shifted closer to her, his expression tightening. "Okay, then maybe you'll be interested in hearing about another piece of information I uncovered last night while I was digging for some of the stuff you keep refusing to share with me."

"Nope, afraid not," Elena said, knowing she was being rude but feeling like she had no other recourse with this guy. He just wouldn't leave her alone.

"Oh, I think you will be," Joe said, and his voice had an edge to it that made Elena pause. "See, with just a little of your help I can run the story spotlighting your sister . . . or I can use what I found last night to write a whole different story—one that will throw *you* into the spotlight at Holbrook and maybe other places, too. It's your choice."

"Okay, now you're really reaching."

"I promise you I'm as serious as a heart attack."

He still didn't touch her, but what he'd said was creepy—not to mention how physically intimidating he was being as he moved a step closer to her. He was at least six feet tall and built like the hockey player he was. To say he was making her uncomfortable was an understatement.

Picking up her bag and slinging it over her shoulder, she turned to leave, trying to pretend she wasn't affected. "Look, Joe, I'm not that exciting. No one at Holbrook or anywhere else is going to want to read a story about me."

"They will once they know you were sitting next to the country's hottest college quarterback prospect the night he died in a car crash."

Elena froze. She felt like someone had punched her in the stomach and sucked all the air from the room at the same time. A strangled sound escaped her, and she dropped her bag, jerking away from him only to find the wall at her back. "I can't believe you just said that," she said in a choked whisper.

"Interested now?"

"No—oh, my God, *no*." The words barely made it past the horrible constriction in her throat. "Get away from me!" But he had her cornered; she couldn't get by him. Tears stung the backs of her eyes, and she shook her head as the waves of raw, painful emotion swept up and pummeled at her, trying to break free from where she kept them locked away. She tried to get around Joe again, moving to the left and then to the right, but he shifted with her, refusing to let her pass.

And then suddenly he was gone, shoved up against the wall by a guy who seemed to have come out of nowhere . . . a guy even taller and more muscular than Joe, with dark hair, dark eyes, and a very pissed-off expression on his face. Elena took a step back, trying to find her breath and feeling almost disappointed that the guy was grasping handfuls of Joe's shirt to pin him to the wall because he looked like he could do some serious damage if he decided to use his fists on him instead.

"Why is it that every time I run into you, you're being an ass, Jeverone?" the stranger grated.

"Lay off, Maguire!" Surprise and maybe even fear made Joe' voice crack. "This is none of your business."

"I've told you before: It becomes my business when you act like a dick in public, especially to a woman." He jerked upward with his hands still twisted in Joe's shirt. Even though he wore long sleeves, Elena could see his arm muscles bunching as he shoved Joe a little higher against the wall.

"Take it easy. It's for the newspaper," Joe grunted. "It was nothing personal."

"That's not what it looked like."

"I'm just doing my job."

"It's a shitty way to do it then."

Keeping Joe pinned, the dark-haired guy shifted his gaze to Elena, his voice quieter as he asked, "Am I over the line here, or was Joe bothering you?"

Elena's heart was pounding and she still felt sick and shaky, but she managed to confirm, "You're not over the line."

He nodded, and looked back at Joe, using the same fistfuls of his shirt to jerk him away from the wall now and bring him almost nose-to-nose. "Let me make it perfectly clear then, Joe, since you seem incapable of picking up the cues on your own: This woman doesn't want you in her space. If you bother her again and I find out about it, you're going to answer to me. Got it?"

Joe cursed. "Get off me, man. Damn, you're wrinkling my shirt!"

Her unknown defender ignored the comment, giving Joe a shake and repeating in a lethal voice, "*Got* it?"

Joe scowled. "Shit, yeah, Max. Whatever. Just let go of the threads."

Max did, releasing Joe with a shove that had Joe stumbling and cursing under his breath. While Joe was still finding his feet, Max swung around and scooped up Elena's bag. She headed toward the door on the opposite side of the dining hall, while he followed behind, positioning himself as a buffer between her and Joe until they got there.

Once they were outside, he walked with her down a set of stone steps to one of the benches outside of the campus bookstore. After gesturing for her to go ahead and sit if she wanted, he looked at her, assessing her.

"Are you okay?"

When she nodded, he put her bag on the ground near the bench and sat down next to her, still looking around to make sure Joe hadn't been stupid enough to follow them.

"Sorry about the scene in there." He glanced toward the dining hall and then back at her again, meeting her gaze. He had really nice eyes, she noticed, now that she was looking at him face-to-face. "I don't usually act like a Neanderthal, but it was Joe and it looked like he was going way overboard with you. Sometimes I have to get physical to back him off when he gets like that."

"No, it's okay. I'm glad you stepped in. Otherwise I might have had to make an even bigger scene myself to get away from him," Elena murmured, glancing up at him. "Max . . . right?

"Yeah." He held out his hand. "Max Maguire."

"Elena Wright." She shook his hand, noticing how firm a grip he had. He was definitely as strong as he looked, and he seemed to be sincere, but she'd been fooled before. "Did you overhear what he was saying to me?"

"No, but Joe being Joe, I figured he was trying to get you to go on a date with him."

"Well, sort of, but only because he wanted information about my sister."

Max laughed. "That's a new one, even for Joe." As he gave her a thorough look of appreciation, he added, "And I'd say he's even more of an idiot than I thought."

Elena felt herself blush. "It's nothing personal. He wanted me to give him an inside scoop so he could write a story about her for the campus paper." She shrugged. "At least he wasn't asking me to set him up on a date with her, the way pretty much every other guy I've met does."

When Max looked at her blankly, she realized he hadn't made the connection yet between her and Zippy. She'd have to tell him, and for some reason she didn't want to, knowing it would probably change how he acted around her, if he even bothered to pretend he cared about anything but Zippy after he knew. But it couldn't be helped; he'd find out sooner or later.

She took a shallow breath and got on with it. "My sister is Alexandra Wright."

He still looked blank.

"You know . . . *the* Alexandra Wright?" She felt like an idiot for repeating herself, but she thought he'd have to clue in any second now. "From *Agency*?" she finished lamely.

It was a no-go. Max continued to look at her with an expression that indicated he thought she might be a sandwich short of a picnic. "Okay." He paused for a second before breaking into a (very attractive) smile. "I'll take your word for why that's important."

A sense of almost giddy surprise swept through her, and she smiled, looking him in the eye. "You're telling me you've never heard of her?"

"Ah . . . no. Should I have?"

"I guess I just figured most people knew about her. She's been pretty visible on the Hollywood scene for the last couple years."

"Like she hangs out with movie stars?"

"Like she *is* one," Elena said dryly. "She's in a movie that's showing over at State Street Cinemas right now. *Force RECON*. Her character is the scientist the Marines are trying to rescue because the Soviets are trying to kill her."

"Oh, yeah. I saw the trailer for that one."

Elena nodded. "It's her latest. But her big breakout role was in *Agency*, the government thriller that was out about a year and a half ago."

"That's cool." Max shrugged. "But I guess that explains why I didn't recognize her name. The whole entertainment world isn't really my thing. If I watch anything, it's mostly reruns on TV or the old movies they show on campus." He leaned forward to prop his forearms on his knees, his body relaxed but his expression intense. "Now *real* military people—or surgeons, police, astronauts, government agents . . . the kind who put it on the line every day—those are the names I tend to remember more."

"Well, that's refreshing."

Max sat up again, looking a little embarrassed. "No offense to you or your sister though. If being in movies floats her boat, that's great."

"No offense taken." Elena cleared her throat, surprised at how much she was enjoying their conversation. She smiled. "Back to Joe, though . . . you mentioned this kind of thing happening before. Have you known him long?"

"Yeah, we were in high school together. I graduated a year ahead of him, though, so I had a little break before he decided to come to Holbrook, too." Max leaned fully back against the bench now, stretching his linked hands behind his head as he settled in, and she found herself admiring the view. *Very nice*. That was followed immediately by, *Oh, my God, I can't believe I just thought that*!

She coughed, hoping he hadn't noticed her staring at him and tried to focus on what he was saying as he continued, "He's decent enough when he's chillin' with the guys, but he can be a real jerk when it comes to women. Sometimes he's more of one than usual, like today. I won't be sorry to leave him behind for good come graduation."

"No kidding," she agreed, hiding her distraction by glancing away. After a second, she tipped her head and looked at him again, deciding his athletic build could prompt another question, at least. "Are you guys on the hockey team together, too, then?"

"Not a chance. That's Joe's gig, not mine. The fights can be entertaining, but you couldn't pay me to spend hours freezing my butt off at an ice rink." Max shook his head as he brought his hands back down to rest on the bench on either side of his (muscular) thighs. "Nope, I'm more a turf-burn and pigskin kind of guy. I've been a starter for Holbrook since sophomore year."

Oh, no. The dark, panicky feeling started to unfurl inside her again. "Football?" The single word came out in a croak.

"Yeah. You been to any of our games?"

Now it was her turn to shake her head, and she was forced to clear her throat again before she could speak. "No, I, uh, I don't really watch football."

"Why not?"

"I . . . it's kind of complicated." She forced herself to use a lighter expression and tone. "I just don't follow sports all that much."

"Well, if you come to one of my games, maybe I can change your mind."

She nodded, making a noncommittal sound and pushing back hard against the nausea that kept rising up to choke her at the thought of watching a football game again. Anytime, anywhere. The sick feeling filled her, along with a gnawing sensation of fear and loss that always seemed to come when anything reminded her of that time. Of *him*.

Gritting her teeth, she forced the feelings down farther, back where they belonged. Max seemed like a nice guy, and she was pretty sure she wouldn't mind getting to know him better. Even so, she knew she had her limits.

"You're not the quarterback are you?"

He laughed. "No. I'm not fast enough. I'm just one of the guys keeping his ass out of trouble. An offensive tackle. Lots of guts but no glory."

"Thank God," she murmured.

Still grinning, Max looked at her sort of sideways. "Yeah, I'd say that's pretty much what he's thinking every time I keep the defense from sacking him." Just then, the university's clock tower began to chime, and Max glanced down at his watch. "And right now I'm late for weight training. *Damn*. That'll mean extra laps."

"That's my fault." Elena grimaced. "Do you want me to come with you and explain it to your coach?"

"Hell, no!" Max laughed again. "I'll be running an extra *ten* miles if you do that, and I'd never hear the end of it from the other guys." Standing up, he winked and patted his already toned middle. "It's no big deal. I can afford a few more laps."

"Then you'd better hurry up before it gets any later." Smiling, she gestured down the hill toward the sports complex. "I'm just going back to my dorm now anyway."

"Yeah, okay." He paused for just a few seconds more. "I'm glad everything worked out all right, but if Joe bugs you again, let me know." A twinkle lit his eyes as he added, "It was really nice meeting you, Elena."

"You too, Max."

"Later," he said, turning and setting off on a jog in the direction of the complex.

As she watched him go, she realized that whatever dark feeling had been brewing inside her had shifted again to something lighter in the last few seconds. Happy. She really liked Max and wished they'd had more time to talk. As an afterthought, she called out to him, "Thanks again for everything, Max! I'll be seeing you around."

He stopped mid-stride partway down the hill, twisting to face her with an enigmatic and utterly charming expression on his face. He really *was* handsome, and right now he was giving her a look that made her want to grin like a fool.

"How about tomorrow?" he called back. "I could meet you at the commons, after practice. Maybe we could grab a sandwich or something. You know, hang out and see what's happening on campus."

That made her heart flip-flop. She nodded. "I think I'd like that." Pausing, she shook her head, and the grin she'd been holding back broke free. "No, wait, let me rephrase . . . I'd definitely like that."

"Yeah?" He grinned now, too.

"Yeah."

"See you at six o'clock tomorrow, then."

Laughing, she nodded and then waved him off before leaning over to pick up her bag and head back to her dorm, still wearing that same, goofy smile . . . a smile that kept that coming back all night long, every time the thought of Max crossed her mind.

WGRR FM 103.9, THE BEAR

"Give a Growl for the Adirondacks'
Most Trusted Radio Station"
June 30, 1992

Welcome back, Adirondack listeners. It's Willard T. Boggs here with you on a damp North Country evening, with fog outside our studio window. I guess we can handle one night of cool drizzle after the beautiful day yesterday. Look on the bright side: You may need your sweater tonight, but at least the black flies won't be eating you alive.

I recommend staying inside with a good book, like that old classic, Gone with the Wind. *Yes, folks, it was on this day in 1936 that Margaret Mitchell's Civil War tale was first published. Some of you may know already that the author originally conceived her heroine with a different name. I think it's a good thing she changed it to "Scarlett." Somehow watching Rhett Butler saying, "Tell me, Pansy, do you never shrink from marrying men you don't love?" in the film wouldn't have had quite the same ring to it.*

Speaking of the silver screen and marriage . . . yesterday, the younger sister of Moose Junction's own famed starlet, Alexandra Wright, married a man from out Corning way. Miss Elena Wright and her new husband, Mr. Maxwell Maguire, met while both were attending Holbrook University in Rochester. Congratulations to the happy couple from all of us at WGRR!

And now, a word from our sponsor, St. Gregory's Farm, in Mexico, New York, where the missus and I pick apples every fall, and where you can get many delicious items, including the best sweet onion relish this side of Canada. . . .

Chapter Eleven

Towers Community Long-Term Care Facility
December 8, 2007

"What do you say, Hank? The fresh air would be good for both of us."

"I don't know Dave. . . ."

Pa pushed a little harder. "If you're worried about the timing, don't be. We'll work around it."

Elena felt a jolt of surprise as she settled into her chair. She'd come in a few seconds ago and given him, Ma, and Pops her normal kiss and hug of greeting, but she'd missed the first part of their conversation because she'd stopped by the family lounge room down the hall to see the girls. Claire had taken her younger sisters there to keep them entertained, and she and Jillian were involved in playing a game of plastic blocks with Violet so that the grownups could have some time to talk.

Now Elena looked from Pa to Pops; she wondered what the "it" Pa had mentioned was that might affect their timing. Was it the impending winter weather, or something else that might affect whatever plans he was trying to persuade Pops to consider?

Pops didn't respond right away. He looked away from Pa to glance at Ma and then at Elena, who tried to look supportive. She might be in the dark about all the details, but she knew that for more than a year, Pa had been trying to get Pops to leave the Towers facility with him on his visits so they could walk and maybe get some lunch either at the homestead or one of the nearby diners. Pops had shot down the idea with various excuses in the past, but this time she sensed something might be different.

At last Pops broke into a smile, exhaling as he shook his head. "No one can say you're not persistent, Dave, and I appreciate it. I suppose it's time. As long as it doesn't disrupt your life too much, maybe it'd be a good idea to get out and walk at the lake again. I do my laps up and down the hallways, but it's not the same as being near the trees and water."

"I knew you'd come around." Pa was clearly pleased as he slapped Hank on the shoulder and shook his hand.

"And I'll be glad to make you both lunch," Ma offered.

Elena smiled, too. This was a breakthrough in more ways than one. Since he'd arrived here, Pops had gone on the occasional bus trip the Towers sponsored for its residents to the mall or movies, but he'd refused to go to anything that would bring him near the lake, since that would involve getting close to the home he and Gladys had shared for so many decades (which of course was right next to the homestead).

Shortly after he'd moved here, his house had been sold to a young couple that had a three-year-old and a new baby, and Pops had been glad for that. But the memories had been too fresh for him to venture back himself.

"Just be careful, okay? When I drove by on my way here this morning, the lake already looked pretty frozen," Elena said. "Those paths can get icy."

"What do you know, Dave, here she is all grown up and worrying about *us*, now."

"That's all I hear from these girls lately. They think we're old and feeble." Pa laughed.

"You are *not* old, Pa." Elena smiled.

"I'm pushing eighty and Hank's even closer, so if we don't qualify for 'old' yet, I don't know when we will."

Elena gave him the look that conveyed how much she loved him. "All I know is that you and Pops are two of the youngest men over seventy-five that I know."

Pops made a whooping sound and grinned.

"It's because you're both young at heart," she teased, "And that counts for a lot." But when she said that, a frisson of something swept through the room. "Besides," she added evenly, watching them all now to see if she could figure out why the atmosphere had become charged. "You've always told me how important a positive attitude is, Pa."

He nodded. "And keeping the blood moving." He raised his hand to forestall her from cautioning him, as she was about to do. "Within reason, I know. I can't do everything I used to do anymore. That's the kicker. Lots of times I still feel eighteen on the inside, and when I get up and look in the mirror, I wonder how that old man got there."

"Age is just a number. You still snow-blow, rake the leaves, mow, do all the gardening, and change the oil in the cars," Elena reminded him. "And you're still as handsome as ever." She grinned. "That waitress at the coffee shop tells you every time she sees you."

His blue eyes twinkled. "I've got some kick left in me. I'll do what I can to stick around." That subtle tension swept through the room again. She saw Pops glance at him quickly and then shift his gaze away, while Ma nodded and looked at the floor for a second before pasting her smile back on and looking at Elena with encouragement. Or as if she was trying to prepare her for something.

"Okay, I'm getting the feeling that everyone here knows something I don't," Elena said, looking from one beloved face to the next. "What's going on?"

Pops shifted and Ma looked a little anxious. When Pa finally spoke, it was in the calm, matter-of-fact way he handled anything serious. "It's just some news we were discussing before you came in, Ellie. Last week I went to see that specialist I told you about."

"Dr. Zeidner?"

Pa nodded. "After he went over my latest scans, he recommended I schedule a procedure with him at the hospital next month."

"A *procedure*? What kind? And why didn't you tell me earlier? Oh, geez, that's all you needed, having the kids with you last night—"

Laughing, Pa broke into her stream of comments. "That's exactly why I didn't say anything right off the bat; I knew you'd get all worked up about it." He got more serious again and patted her knee. "Come on, Ellie. You know I like to stay on top of things health-wise. It's nothing unexpected, and I'm not going to stop living my life because of it. It's all going to be fine."

He must have seen that his assurance didn't help her much, because he added, "I've always been upfront with you about anything that's happening medically with me or your mother, and that's not going to change now. If there was a real problem I'd let you know."

Elena swallowed the fear that inevitably rose when she thought of anyone she loved being hurt, sick, or in danger. She had to try to keep everything in perspective the way Pa had taught her to do, or she was going to lose it. "Okay, so what's the procedure?"

"It's to take care of that pulmonary aneurysm that showed up on those scans a few years ago. Apparently, it's gotten bigger, and Dr. Zeidner said it's time to repair it."

Elena's heart was beating faster, even with her efforts not to blow anything out of proportion. The pulmonary aneurysm? She remembered Pa telling her about it back when Jillian was a baby, but it had been so small back then that no one had worried. Now apparently there was reason to be concerned, not only because it had gotten bigger, but also because of the toll she knew surgery could take on a man of Pa's age, regardless of how active and positive he was.

She tried to slow her racing pulse and the worried thoughts that came with it to ask, "Can they fix it laparoscopically?"

"I wondered the same thing, but Dr. Zeidner said no. It'll be a full-blown operation, so it's going to be done at Adirondack Medical Center in the regular operating room, instead of through outpatient surgery."

She swallowed, breathing in slowly to keep herself composed. "Do you trust this doctor?"

"He's a good guy. I like him."

Elena let out her breath fully. "All right, then. I'll try not to worry too much. It just caught me off guard, I guess."

Pa patted her knee once more. "That's my girl." Then with a sort of hitched sound that revealed the ache in his stiff joints, he pushed himself up from his chair to stretch his legs. "I know the whole thing is causing a lot of hullaballoo, but I'm trying to be realistic. It's got to be repaired, and that's that. I'd rather get the surgery out of the way and know I'm in the clear, than feel like a sitting duck, waiting around for the thing to burst."

"Oh, wow . . . *that* doesn't sound promising," she said, trying to keep her voice from rising again in pitch. "Is there any reason Dr. Zeidner is waiting until next month to do the surgery then, instead of, like, *today*?"

"It's not at crisis size right yet," Pa soothed. "It's just headed that way unless I do something about it. I need a few weeks to get all the pre-surgery check ups and stress tests out of the way before anything else can move forward."

"Okay."

Elena couldn't say anything more, she realized, without bursting into tears. That familiar, fluttery shadow of panic had settled deep in her chest again, and no matter how hard she tried, she couldn't seem to shift her thoughts and feelings to a better place. Standing up, she walked over to the window to look out at the winter-glazed parking lot as she tried to stay calm.

Pa came up next to her. "Look, Ellie, I know this surgery may be a little more serious than routine, but it's nothing to get too concerned about."

"I can't help it, Pa," she finally managed to say, her voice cracking a little as she leaned in to hug him tight. "I worry about you no matter what, and this kind of thing makes me worry more than usual."

"Your father's a tough one." Hank had been behind her, and now he moved over to stand on her other side. "He'll be raring to go again in no time. Meantime, I'll help him get shaped up for the surgery with a few walks along the lake."

"As long you don't go too fast, or when it's too icy," she said, offering them both a half smile.

Pa chuckled. "I promise we'll only go quick enough to get warmed up. We can talk some more about it after supper, after I hear about how you've been doing since last night."

She nodded, remembering now that she'd promised to fill him in about what had happened to her during yesterday's long evening alone, coming to terms with her thoughts and memories of Jesse. There was a lot to share. So many changes on this rollercoaster that comprised her life lately.

"Right now, let's go get the girls so your mother doesn't have a fit. Just before you came in, she was setting the stage for why supper's going to be late again, blaming it on the lasagna not getting in the oven on time or some such thing," Pa teased while Ma, who had been so quiet while he'd filled Elena in on all the medical issues, sputtered back at him in good-natured argument.

Chuckling and calling her an "old biddy" under his breath, he put out his arm for Elena to link hers through it, following Ma and Pops as they made their way out of Hank's room toward the family lounge. They talked as they walked.

"Are you sure it's not going to be too much for you to have me and the girls again at the house tonight, Pa?"

"I'd be disappointed if you didn't stay. I'm counting on you and Claire to help me bring the boxes of Christmas decorations up from the cellar after supper so we can do a little decorating."

That stopped Elena literally in her tracks, and she was pretty sure she gaped at him. "Wait a minute . . . you haven't pulled out the Christmas decorations before the third week of December since I lived at home and used to force you to do it."

Pa chuckled again. "Well, the apple doesn't fall too far from the tree. Your oldest daughter got very specific last night when she told me I needed to stop being a Scrooge and get on the stick for Christmas."

"Oh. Sorry about that." Elena grimaced. "If it makes you feel any better, you're not the only one she's after. She complained to me about the same thing at our house on Wednesday."

Pa nodded. "Claire mentioned that she was trying to instigate the holiday spirit at home, too. I told her she was old enough now to get the ball rolling and help you out a little. So she decided to practice her technique with your mother and me—"

"By talking us into getting our tree last night," Ma broke in from ahead of them, not missing a beat as they made their way down the hall.

Elena choked back laughter. That was another first. She knew she shouldn't be surprised, though. Claire was a typical teenager in many ways, growing up too fast for her own good, already tall and beautiful (though she was convinced she was hideous), with Max's dark, wavy hair. Personality-wise, she was shaping up into quite a spitfire, oscillating between bossy or loving, moody or sensitive, all of it wrapped up in the sparkling garments of a social butterfly. The truth was that right now Claire tended to act a lot more like Kat or Zippy than she did Elena, and sometimes Elena didn't know how to handle her.

"Claire has the right idea," Pops said, teasing. "Maybe she'll get some Holly Jolly to rub off on you too, Elena."

"Maybe . . . just like I'm told watching *It's a Wonderful Life* last night in the lounge did for you, Pops," Elena shot back with a grin.

They had reached the lounge, and she let Hank and Ma go in ahead of them, tugging Pa to a stop for a second, just outside the door to whisper, "You *really* got your tree already?"

"Well, we bought one from that tree stand at the side of the road downtown." His blue eyes twinkled. "When we got it home, I dragged it out of the car and stuck it in the snow bank next to the garage. So I suppose the answer to your question is yes."

Elena laughed out loud at that.

"I think I must really be getting into the Christmas spirit." Pa's voice took on a mischievous pitch as they pushed open the door to join the others. "Because I just can hardly wait to haul it into the house and gussy up the place."

(Christmas at the homestead)

The Homestead
Moose Junction, Upstate New York
December 24, 1975
Elena is nearly seven years old

Peace on earth, good will to men. . . .

The house was quiet.

All Elena could hear as she lay in her bed was the steady breathing of three of her sisters (Jen, Zippy, and Patricia), who were in the bunk above her and occupying the bottom and top of the second bunk bed across the room. Her other four sisters were in the bedroom next to hers in a similar arrangement, though she couldn't hear them at all. Every now and again, the blower for the furnace came on with a click and a hum, sending an invisible plume of warmth into the room to offset the creaking winter cold outside the windows. But everything else was still.

Not a creature was stirring, not even a mouse. . . .

Those words from "The Night Before Christmas" by Clement C. Moore rang through Elena's memory, fitting and perfect. Like he did every year, Pa had read that poem aloud to them a few hours ago, while they'd all gathered around him on the couch after they'd had their cups of hot chocolate with a candy cane stick for stirring. And now everyone was asleep, waiting for Santa.

Elena knew that Christmas was really about Jesus' birthday. They'd gone to church right after supper because of it—the only time they ever went to Mass at nighttime. She loved how pretty the church looked in the candlelight, with all the green branches and ribbons, the beautiful music, and the way the story of Bethlehem was acted out in costume on the altar, with teens from the congregation playing the innkeeper, Joseph, Mary, the angels, shepherds and wise men, and a real baby for Jesus.

But once bedtime came, her focus shifted to jolly Saint Nicholas. She couldn't help it; it was too exciting. When Pa read the poem aloud to them, she knew Christmas morning was almost here.

However, "The Night Before Christmas" came with a strict rule attached to it for the Wright girls: it could only be recited once each year on Christmas Eve, and then only by Pa. The beautiful picture book was put away shortly after he'd read the last line, only to re-emerge again like magic the following year on December 24th.

They were certain that reading or even hearing the poem at any other time was too terrible to contemplate—so much so that if anyone around them started reciting or singing it (once the song of the poem became popular, thanks to that new cartoon Christmas special on television), the girls would preoccupy themselves with something else, walk away, or stick their fingers in their ears, saying, "la-la-la-la," over and over until the person stopped or the channel broadcasting the poem could be changed on the TV.

Elena didn't realize it at the time, but Pa and Ma had created their rule about the story to add to the mysterious, magical feeling that Christmas evoked for the Wright girls. Their once-per-year glimpses of the gorgeous artwork in the special Christmas book made an impression on them, and they often would occupy themselves in the weeks leading up to the holiday by trying to describe favorite pages or remember details that would be confirmed (or disproved) during the next reading.

Tonight had been no different. As always, Elena's favorite page was the one that showed the inside of the storybook family's living room just before Santa Claus came down the chimney. The book's illustrator had painted such a detailed scene. Everything in that family's fancy, old-fashioned living room looked so pretty, with overstuffed chairs wearing lacy doilies, dark wooden furniture with curved legs, vivid, rich fabrics, and elegant draperies. Best of all, next to the pine-trimmed fireplace there was a huge, decorated Christmas tree lit with real candles.

Elena liked to imagine herself in that room, which was so different from their own sturdy, cozy homestead. The Wrights' home was an efficient little Cape Cod-style house that managed to shelter ten people regularly, with two more during the summer months when the same Fresh Air Fund sisters, Cheryl and Jenny, came up to stay each year from New York City to experience life "in the country," courtesy of the not-for-profit agency. The whole house was only seven rooms (with the biggest one being the kitchen) and one bathroom, and it was nothing fancy, but it was *home*. Still, Elena always thought it was fun to imagine other places and people.

Tonight she'd been dreaming of the events from a few pages earlier in the poem, when the children had "visions of sugarplums" dancing in their heads, while the mother and father had "just settled down for a long winter's nap." Something must have awakened her, interrupting the good part, but she couldn't tell what.

She was just about to drift back to sleep when she heard a rattling noise outside. A few seconds later, it was followed by several stamping thumps all in a row. To her they sounded like . . . like hooves. With a start, she realized that what she was hearing might very well qualify as a *clatter*. The same kind of sounds Pa had read about when the reindeer were landing Santa's sleigh!

Elena clutched her blankets to her chin. Oh, if only her very special prayer of the past three years was coming true! Could Santa Claus be in the act of visiting *her* house *right now*?

"Jen!" she called out in a hissed whisper, terrified that she might be too loud and alert Santa that someone was awake, sending him flying off into the night without leaving any presents behind.

No answer.

She tried a little louder. "*Jen*!" There was still no movement from the bunk above. In desperation, she whispered, "Zippy? Trish? Are you awake?"

Nothing.

Suddenly, the sound of jingle bells shivered through the frosty stillness, ringing merrily once, twice, then three times. Still clutching her blankets, Elena felt her eyes widen. She *definitely* wasn't imagining this, and she couldn't wait any longer for someone else to wake up and give an opinion about it.

Moving slowly, she eased her covers down and slid out of bed. Chilly air enveloped her, and the wooden floor felt cold against her bare feet. Wincing in an effort to be quiet, she pulled her flannel nightgown tight around her and ran on her tiptoes to the window as gently as she could so that the creaking floorboards wouldn't alert Santa. She had heard him outside; she knew it. If she could just move the shade in time, she might catch sight of him, one of his reindeer, or at least some tracks in the snow to let her know he was real.

Elena carefully pulled back the shade (not daring to raise it all the way up), peeked out, and gasped at what she saw.

The moon on the breast of the new-fallen snow gave the lustre of mid-day to objects below. . . .

As her gaze swept over the snowy side yard bathed in pale blue moonlight, she caught with the side of her vision the very back end of a sleigh whipping around the corner of the house and out of sight. It was only a glimpse, but it was enough to tell that the sleigh was dark green with silver runners jutting out the back. And it had seemed to be in the process of either landing or taking off, gliding several feet above the ground.

That meant it *was* Santa's sleigh!

Another tinkling of jingle bells, this time sounding a little farther off, sealed her belief in what she'd just seen.

Overwhelmed with joy, Elena ran back to her bed, jumped in, and pulled the covers over her face, trying not to shriek her utter happiness aloud and wake everyone else. She would tell Pa all about it in the morning because he never made her feel silly about anything. She already knew that none of her sisters would believe her.

It didn't matter; she had seen what she had seen. And she *believed.* Santa Claus had come to her house. He was real, and he'd allowed her a glimpse of his enchanting powers so that she would know.

Still beaming, Elena closed her eyes and willed herself to go back to sleep in hopes that morning would come quicker. No matter what else happened to her in her life, she knew that one thing was certain: She would never, ever forget what she'd seen on this magical Christmas Eve night.

Dave smiled to himself where he stood behind the garage, unloading the pile of firewood from the toboggan and then carefully rolling the long, leather strap of jingle bells he'd been holding onto while he ran around the house. When the strap was in a tight ball that would prevent the bells from jingling any more, he stuffed the whole thing into the big pocket of his winter work coat, picked up the now-empty toboggan, and headed toward the old red shed in the back yard.

He felt lighthearted as he walked, and as if in harmony with his feelings, a gust of wind lifted the loose snow and swirled it up in front of him, sparkling like flecks of diamonds in the moonlight. With his free hand, he tugged his jacket a little closer and slowed down, taking in the natural splendor all around him—the deep quiet of the woods, the moon-gilded snow, and the black, empty branches of the trees that ringed the yard of the homestead, reaching silent and strong into the velvety sky.

Logical thinking had always been the guiding force of Dave's existence, but recognizing beauty of all kinds was just as important to him. He might not go to church very often (though he supported Elizabeth in encouraging the girls to go since he knew it was important to reinforce the awareness that there was something out there greater than themselves), but appreciating nature in all its forms was a little bit like religion to him and being outdoors was his kind of church. He sent up a prayer of thanks now that the moon shone so brightly tonight. Its light had helped his efforts to hopefully provide a little magic for the girls.

He'd taken three running trips around the house with the jingle bells, moving pretty quickly and sticking close to the walls to keep from being seen, in case anyone decided to be daring and peek outside. The snow was trampled now as if a whole fleet of reindeer had landed, and on the last time around he'd also pulled behind him the old toboggan with steel runners. Loading it with firewood all tucked in with his big, green tarp had made it heavy enough to make the "sleigh" tracks that the kids might notice in the morning.

Pulling that loaded sled had reminded him of some of the drills they used to run in the Marines back when he was young and indestructible. He was older now, by more than thirty years, but he didn't feel too far removed from those days in mind or body. He was grateful that he was still strong from all the physical labor needed to keep up the homestead and its property, cutting trees, building the garage and outbuildings, and hauling and chopping wood for the furnace. Physical stamina was useful, especially when it came to engineering and executing ideas like this one.

Undertaking his plan had been a calculated risk, but he'd waited a half hour after everyone had gone to bed, hoping the girls would have fallen asleep—just not deep enough so that the bells couldn't wake them. Especially little Elena. She wanted to believe so badly, and he knew she was getting old enough that that wouldn't last forever. He wouldn't know if he'd been successful until tomorrow, but he could at least point out the tracks if nothing else.

Grinning now, he slid the empty toboggan into the shed and leaned it up against the wall. Next came the jingle bells. Taking them from his pocket, he stashed them in an old coffee can he kept on the shelf. They had done their job, but he didn't want any "evidence" found that would ruin it for anyone.

With everything back in its place, it was time to get going on the rest of what needed to be accomplished tonight. There were bikes to put together, games to set up, and dozens of presents to wrap and put under the tree. It was going to be hours until he and Elizabeth would get to bed.

But as he pulled the shed door shut behind him and made his way back to the house to get started, he was still smiling, filled with a sense of rightness in his world. He knew that even if he had the chance to do it all over again—to be a single man with boatloads of money, fancy cars, trips, job opportunities, and excitement—he would turn it all down.

He was living the life he wanted to live. The life he had *chosen*. Before anything else, he was a husband and father, responsible for loving, guiding, protecting, and providing a good and stable life for his family. No matter how much effort it took or worry it caused him, it was a gift beyond anything else the world could offer.

And he was a happy man.

(The red shed and backyard after snow)

Chapter Twelve

The Homestead
Moose Junction, Upstate New York
December 9, 2007

Everyone but Pa and Elena had gone to bed hours ago.

Midnight had come and gone and still they sat in companionable silence in the homestead's cozy, dimly lit living room as they'd done countless times before over the years. Pa rocked in his recliner and Elena sat curled on the end of the couch nearest him, just enjoying each other's company or else talking quietly and sometimes pondering questions of the universe. It had been a favorite pastime for the two of them since Elena was a teenager, and even after she'd moved away to college and gotten married they'd continued to carve out these conversations together whenever they could.

Time had passed quickly tonight, beginning to drift into what most would consider the wee hours, but neither of them felt too sleepy.

The graceful carved mantel clock on the shelf above the television began to sing out a single portion of its Westminster chime. It rang in concert with several of the other clocks on the shelves, indicating the quarter hour (which, in this case, was 1:15 a.m.). Elena knew the tone of this particular clock's chime well, even though it was one of more than forty timepieces of all shapes and sizes that Pa had in several rooms of the house.

He had collected clocks for years, and there were usually at least a dozen running at any given time (because if they were *all* going, no one would be able to hear anything every quarter hour). The tick-tocking and ringing of chimes was a gentle and comforting cadence that had played in the background of life at the homestead for as long as Elena could remember. Pa had always felt an affinity for clocks, and all the Wright girls treasured those he'd given them—sometimes making them himself—over the years.

Glancing over at the mantel clock's face, Elena smiled to see the colorful Christmas tree lights reflected in the glass door covering it (since, as promised, she and the girls had helped Pa and Ma put up their tree and decorate it after supper). She settled back with a contented sigh; the quiet and contemplative mood she was in right now felt good after the emotional weeks that had preceded it.

Earlier tonight, while Ma was still awake, she'd recounted for her and Pa the basics of what had happened last night and how she'd felt when she'd finally faced her feelings and memories about Jesse. Then, after Ma had gone to bed, Elena and Pa had kept talking. Their conversation kept coming back to elements of the past and Jesse, but they also delved into "deeper" subjects in between, as they liked to do.

So far tonight they'd talked about where animals fit into the matter of eternity, whether it was possible for human beings to comprehend "infinity," quantum physics, the idea that everything in the universe might be connected, and a few assorted philosophers, like Spinoza, who had offered their thoughts on many of those same issues in earlier centuries.

They'd taken a break about fifteen minutes ago to refill the modestly sized highballs they'd been drinking as they talked, and after they'd sat down again, their conversation had wended its way back to Jesse and the revelation that had changed everything so completely for Elena.

"I never told anyone his secret," Elena said quietly, before taking a sip. The sweetness of the ginger ale was cool on her tongue, balancing out the sharper flavor of the whisky. "Not until tonight, anyway."

"He knew he could count on you. But I wonder how many others suspected the truth anyway."

"I can't imagine why anyone would have."

"I did." Pa set his drink down.

She didn't think there was much Pa could have said that would have floored her, but this did. Her brow furrowed. "What could have made you think that about Jesse? He didn't fit any of the stereotypes from back then."

"No, but I watched how he acted when he was with you. And I saw him with the Arseneau boy, too, that winter and spring."

"Wow. I had no idea."

Pa rocked lightly in his recliner. "I didn't know for certain, of course, but it seemed like a real possibility."

"I guess I shouldn't be too surprised," she said. "You were always a good read on human nature."

"I did my best to try to protect you girls."

"You did a good job of it." After a minute, Elena smiled, reminding him, "I'm thinking of that 'river test' you set up all those years ago. You always knew which boyfriends would fail it."

He laughed. "That wasn't too difficult to figure out. Any of your sisters who agreed to take that canoe ride were so blinded by love that they needed something to help them see what was obvious to the rest of us."

"Good thing, or else Anne might have ended up with . . . what was his name? Daryl . . . Denny?"

"Darren. He was a doozy." Pa's expression shifted again, a little more somber. "Jesse, though . . . he was harder to read. I knew he was a good boy, but the other part was more complicated to figure out."

"He was good at covering that up to pretty much everyone, including me. At least until the very end."

Pa kept rocking gently, using his finger to make a trail in the condensation on his glass. "The night you two broke up I wondered if he'd told you something. I was planning to see if you wanted to talk after things settled down. Then the accident happened and I thought it best to leave it alone."

Elena's throat tightened. "I just couldn't talk about it back then, even with you. It hurt too much."

He stopped rocking and nodded. "That accident was a terrible and senseless thing. I've been angry at the other driver's selfishness many times since then." He met her gaze, his steady and loving. "But I've been grateful to Jesse, too."

Elena stiffened. "What do you mean?"

"I know what he did to try to protect you, Ellie. It was pretty clear once I read the police report and saw both vehicles."

Elena's breath caught in her throat, and tears stung the backs of her eyes. She swiped her fingers across them before she exhaled as she looked at Pa. "Oh, boy. I guess I should have known you'd put two and two together." She shook her head. "Until last night, I'd never really made peace with it. Maybe I never would have, if it hadn't been for that fender-bender I was in."

"Too close of a reminder?"

She nodded. "It threw me for a loop. I thought I was in control of all those emotions, but I was wrong." The clock chimed again, and she paused, thinking over it all. "And then when Jen brought over that bin of stuff you put together and I looked through it all and read the diary . . . well, everything broke through. I had to own up and deal with it."

"I'm sorry to have blindsided you like that, Ellie. I just couldn't see any other way to help you get the ball rolling in the right direction."

"No, I needed the push." Elena tucked her legs beneath her on the couch. "It was a blessing in disguise, even if I wasn't too happy when I first saw it."

She gave Pa another gentle smile, struck again by his wisdom and patience. Confronting the past in a healthy way was almost always easier said than done, and yet he'd found a way to help her to it without badgering or nitpicking at her, a way that was peaceful and even healing. Then he and Ma had put on the finishing touches by taking the kids and giving her the time alone to do the emotional work she'd needed to do to get to this better place.

"I'm really glad you did it," she admitted. "It helped me let go of some of the stuff that's been weighing me down for more than twenty years."

He smiled, too. "Sometimes things have a way of working themselves out if you let them."

Elena nodded. It felt good to let go of the darkness, grief, and guilt after all this time . . . like some of the thick scar tissue covering her heart had been cut away, making it easier for it to beat freely and for her to breathe.

Still, she wasn't entirely in the clear yet. She had something else she really wanted to talk to Pa about, but it was getting late, not to mention she was afraid she'd sound like a complete fruitcake when she brought it up. She wasn't even sure how to do it.

The furnace came on with a low and steady hum, blowing warm air through the living room, and Pa rocked back in his chair with a contented sigh, clearly happy to just enjoy this peaceful time together. Elena looked out the picture window that took up a big portion of the wall across the living room from her, trying to think about the best way to broach the subject with him. Stars winked in the dark sky over the lake while the even blacker bare branches of the trees in the yard stood in elegant contrast. It was beautiful. *Serene.*

She looked back at Pa. He, too, seemed lost in thought, and she knew she should just delve in; he was always open-minded about anything she wanted to discuss, no matter how strange other people might think it was. That was how they ended up in so many stimulating and long discussions.

Well, here goes. . . .

"So . . . there's something else that happened during the accident in October that I'd like to run by you."

"Sure. Go ahead."

She swallowed and took a deep breath. "I, um . . . well, I saw Jesse. I turned my head, and he was just . . . there, sitting in the car with me."

Pa didn't respond right away, and Elena went on. "I know it sounds crazy. I'm not sure I believe it myself."

"I didn't say I didn't believe you. I was just thinking I'd like to know a few more specifics."

Elena sat back, remembering. "It was right after the accident. I was disoriented and thinking how much easier it would be just to fall asleep. I tried to fight against it and opened my eyes, and that's when I saw him. He was in the passenger seat, looking exactly the same as he did when we were in high school, with his big, happy smile. And he talked—I mean I could hear what he said in my mind, but his mouth didn't move." Elena shrugged and looked at Pa again. "That's it."

"What did he say?"

"Just that I should keep calm. That everything would be all right." She felt that stinging sensation at the backs of her eyes again, and her throat ached a little.

"That's a nice message."

"Yes, but was it *real*, or did I just imagine it?"

Pa's expression seemed thoughtful, like he was considering what she'd told him. He remained silent until the clock's chimes finished sounding three quarters past the hour; then he spoke. "I don't think there's any way to know that for sure, Ellie."

Elena half smiled, remembering how Jesse had said almost the same thing to her on that last day when they'd talked about knowing for certain if there'd been a reason they'd come into each other's lives.

Pa broke into her thoughts with a question. "Do *you* think he was real?"

"I don't know. Seeing him felt real. At the time I knew in my bones that he was there and that he was talking to me. But when I look back on it or say what happened out loud, it seems kind of crazy."

"Just because something is out of the ordinary doesn't make it crazy."

"This seems pretty out there, though."

"Not really. Someday, someone may find a way to prove or disprove life after death. Until then it's up for discussion, and there are going to be people on both sides with pretty strong opinions about it. History is filled with similar stories."

"Like what?"

"The discovery of electricity, sound waves, even magnetic fields, for a few examples." Pa tipped his head and gestured for emphasis. "And it wasn't all that long ago humans learned to harness nuclear energy. None of those were thought to be real until they were able to be measured somehow."

Elena shrugged. "I guess I never thought of it that way."

"The world is full of wonderful mysteries." Rocking back in his chair again, Pa paused before adding, "I often think that's one of the sad things about having to die: There's so much to see, listen to, think, and learn about, and we run out of time to experience it all."

Elena nodded, agreeing with him, but at the same time having to push down the twist of panic that had always threatened whenever she contemplated him (or Ma) dying.

After draining the rest of his drink, he finished his thought. "But what it all comes down to, Ellie, is that I don't know the answer to what happened in your car that afternoon. Whether it was real or your subconscious created it under the stress of the accident, no one can tell for sure. Maybe we're not meant to know."

"That's the part that drives me nuts."

"You have a lot of time to mull it over." He set his empty glass down. "In the meantime, there are some good effects from it all. If nothing else, you're able to think about Jesse now without shutting down like before."

She picked at a loose thread in the couch fabric. "That's true. I guess I'll just have to let the rest of it brew until I figure out how I feel about it all."

Pa smiled again. "We can't solve all the mysteries of the universe in one night, much as we usually try to." He stretched, laughing when Elena yawned. "Those are catchy, you know. I think it might be time to hit the sack."

She stood. "That's probably a good idea. I'll just take the glasses in the kitchen and—"

"Wait a second before you do that," Pa broke in, getting up also and walking over to adjust the hands on one of the clocks. "There's one last thing I want to ask you before you head off to bed."

"What is it?" She couldn't help feeling a little surprised. Pa never brought up something if it wasn't important. Especially not this late in one of their conversations.

"Have you thought about going back to your spot . . . that clearing in the woods where you and Jesse used to meet?"

"Oh." Elena felt a fluttering sensation in her chest that shifted to a deeper, bittersweet ache at the memories of all the easy, funny, happy times she'd spent with Jesse there that flooded her, unbidden. "I didn't realize you knew about *that*, too."

"It's a father's business to know where his daughters are at the age you were then. I never intruded, but I knew you went there."

"Hold on to that thought while I get these in the sink." She brought the glasses into the kitchen, using the time to let this new information sink in before she came back in and continued. "I know I've already said it, but I'm going to say it again. I guess I shouldn't be surprised that you were one step ahead of me during those years. I try to do the same thing with Claire, and I'm sure I will with Jillian and Violet, too, when they're a little older. The world can be a scary place."

"Yes, it can. That kind of worry through all eight of you girls helped make my hair gray," Pa joked, before he added pointedly, "But you still haven't answered my question."

Elena felt herself flush and then blanch, her heart pounding the way it used to before whenever anything threatened to crack the vault of her feelings about Jesse. She shouldn't be having that reaction now; she'd faced her demons last night. But even considering a visit back to the place that had been so much a part of her and Jesse was new territory for her emotionally, and she wasn't sure how to handle it yet.

She settled on being matter-of-fact when she answered Pa. "I haven't been there since that last day, and I honestly never really considered going back. I blocked it out like I did everything else involving Jesse."

He nodded. "It's just a suggestion, but it might be worthwhile and even give you a sense of closure, now that you're making peace with his memory."

"Okay, I'll think about it," Elena said with another smile, leaning in to hug him tight. When she pulled back, she could see that though his eyes looked tired, he was smiling, too.

Afterward he walked into the kitchen to turn out the light. That left only the glow of a nightlight in an outlet on the wall near the bathroom; it was a design of a black metal tree against a blue and green stained glass background of a lake, hills, and sky. Pa made sure it was plugged in tightly and then came back to the living room for their quick goodnight kiss on the cheek.

"I hope you sleep good, Pa . . . thanks for another great talk tonight."

"I always enjoy the ground we cover together," he said, patting her on the shoulder and holding open the door to the upstairs bedrooms for her. "Sweet dreams, Ellie. See you in the morning."

(The nightlight)

Letter from Pa to Elena
September 20, 2003

Dear Elena,

Enclosed are the two giant allium bulbs I told you I was sending you for your garden. They are supposed to be fancy ones. We'll see in the springtime, after the irises are about done if not all done flowering. There is no hurry to plant the bulbs, but they need a little while to let the roots develop before the freeze of winter. That way they are ready to grow in the spring.

It's a cool but really beautiful morning, and I am in sort of a peaceful mood, listening to a tape of music that you recorded almost twenty years ago while playing the piano. When I started today I was in a pretty black mood and I had to make an attitude adjustment or I was going to make trouble. Up until now I have been in a black mood for a few days. My mind has been sort of boggled up with a lot of thoughts that I don't know how to get out in any meaningful order, some of them about people and their connections to each other (or more often their lack of connections).

Well, anyway, you know what I'm talking about. I'm sure glad we can talk, mostly just whenever we have a chance, but sometimes even like this, when I can take a little more time in telling you how I feel.

You know, Ellie, I don't think you are perfect. I would sure hope not! I wouldn't want you to think that I was perfect either (once you got past eight or ten years old anyway). We are just a couple of regular human beings who understand each other. I don't mean in an informative way, like understanding a book or an equation, but more in a sensitivity of other peoples' feelings and thoughts. It is really nice knowing that I can tell you something and know that you understand where I am coming from. No, it doesn't require either agreement or disagreement, just understanding. I'm not sure if you know how rare it may be that two people can have that awareness and mutually know it. I don't mean to scare you, Elena, because there may be many people out there with some degree of that sensitivity waiting for a connection. Well, not waiting really, because it is hard to anticipate and could lead to disappointment, especially if your expectations are too high.

I've told you before about some past connections for me that were pretty good. Not that I was aware of it, or maybe *conscious* of it is a better word. Sometimes life goes on without a second chance or by not having enough time to let things develop. That's okay though, because it all becomes part of the sum of who you are. Some seemingly small things contribute more to who I am than many seemingly bigger things in my life.

I am happy that we understand each other. What we have does not require reinforcement or affirmation. It just is, and that will last the rest of my life. I hope after I'm gone you will develop (or maybe have already developed) a similar sensitivity with someone else, as it can be lonely to go through life feeling never truly understood. I am glad you are who you are, and I love you very much. Words can never describe the actual sentiments, but you know what I am saying. We have a pretty good connection!

Love,

Pa

Moose River Boat Landing
Moose Junction, Upstate New York
August 5, 1975
Elena is six years old

All that glitters is not gold. . . .

The sun sparkled on the river, lighting the riffling water with shiny spots that reminded Anne of the diamond ring she hoped Darren would be giving her before the year was out.

Of course it was still summer, and the most romantic time for Darren to pop to question would be Christmas. But he might choose her birthday, which was in a little less than two months. It was possible, anyway. Especially if everything went the way she hoped it would today.

"So, this is it, then."

Kat's voice cut through Anne's fantasizing, forcing her back to the reality of the "test" that was about to take place. Anne didn't look at her fifteen-year-old sister, instead squinting and using her hand to shade her eyes from the sun as she watched Darren readying the canoe for their impending journey down the rippling currents of Moose River.

Soon, her gaze shifted to the rest of the family, milling around near the parking area. Cheryl and Jenny would be headed back home to New York City next week, now that their seventh summer spent as Fresh Air Fund girls with the Wright family was wrapping up, but they'd been eager to witness today's ritual. At the moment, they looked like they were trying to cheer up eighteen-year-old Melanie, who stood off to the side of the lot scowling because she was missing a beach day with her boyfriend. Fourteen-year-old Lisa leaned artfully against the front of the van, trying to attract the attention of a couple teenage boys who were fishing from the little bridge a few feet away, and the four youngest sisters were giggling and chasing each other around as Ma tried to hush them and get them into the van.

It only took one look and a barked command from Pa, still down here by the riverbank with her and Darren, for all the girls to immediately comply with Ma's request. Without another word, Lisa, Jen, Patricia, Zippy, and Elena ducked into the shadowy recesses of the old green Volkswagen van.

It wouldn't be long now.

"Are you nervous?"

This time Anne caught Kat's gaze. Tipping her chin up, she said without hesitation, "No."

She tried to weight that single syllable with contempt. What did she have to be nervous about? She was almost twenty years old, Darren twenty-one, and they'd been together for more than a year.

No matter what Pa said about holding off until they were both more mature, she knew they were ready to show everyone what a good couple they made . . . and what a good marriage they'd have, based on love, respect, and their phenomenal ability to work together. Darren was a modern man. He would work *with* her, not try to take over and make all the decisions. He'd agreed to take this boat trip, hadn't he? He'd even thought it was funny and a groovy idea. She knew she could count on him, and he could count on her.

"Maybe you'd better wear the waterproof jacket, Anne. Just in case. You remember what Pa said to do if the canoe tips. If you're near rapids, just let it go and don't get—"

Anne scowled and broke in, "I'm not going to need a waterproof jacket. The only getting wet I'll have to worry about will be from what splashes off the oars while Darren and I are paddling our way to the pick-up point, using the teamwork that no one in this family seems to think we have."

Kat shrugged. "Whatever you say." She put her arm around Anne's shoulder and gave a quick squeeze. "Good luck. See you at the pick-up point."

Anne didn't trust herself to say anything more as Kat turned to make her way up to the van, so she just nodded, trying to look more confident than she was suddenly feeling. She pasted a smile on her face and started to walk down to the riverbank to join Darren, where Pa was giving him some last minute advice about the canoe and its quirks.

More than forty-five minutes later, at the pick-up point ten miles down the river, the entire family was gathered, talking quietly or watching the littlest ones trying to catch minnows at the river's edge. Pa and Ma stood about ten feet apart, each of them keeping an eye on Elena and Zippy. Pa turned his head upstream every now and again while he held Elena as she leaned in toward the deeper part to see a river clam. It was taking a long time for Anne and Darren to ride the current downstream.

The sounds reached everyone first, echoing through the woods that flanked both sides of the river. They heard shouts and the rise and fall of two separate voices. They were the shrill sounds of an argument, with a male's lower, growling comments intersected by a higher-pitched female tone. Pretty soon, the canoe came into view with both Anne and Darren on board, both of them dripping wet as they battled the currents—and each other's efforts, by the looks of it—with the single oar each held.

Just then, the back of the canoe spun forward around a jetty formed by a tree stump. Anne shrieked one command, Darren did the opposite, and the canoe tipped over for what had to have been at least the second time, but was probably the fourth or fifth time. The couple's arguing rose in pitch, once they both stopped sputtering, and Pa took off his watch in preparation for wading in and helping drag them and the canoe to shore.

Elena looked solemnly up at him as he started to enter the water, his shoes making a squishing sound with each step.

"There's not going to be a wedding now, is there, Pa?"

She could have sworn she saw the hint of smile—and she knew she saw the twinkle in his eyes when he glanced back over his shoulder at her just long enough to say, "No, Elena Elizabeth, I think it's safe to say there won't be a wedding anytime soon."

Chapter Thirteen

Maple Creek, Upstate New York
January 10, 2008

"Happy birthday, angel eyes." Max came up behind Elena where she stood washing the girls' after-school snack dishes at the kitchen sink. Wrapping his arms around her waist, he tugged her against him and kissed her neck.

"Thank you . . . and wow, you're home early this afternoon," she said, relaxing against him and feeling some of the tension of the day slip away.

Things had been really good between them ever since that weekend in December that she'd spent at Pa and Ma's. It was like they'd found a new lease on their marriage; not that it had ever been bad, but getting over that emotional bump had pulled them closer in a way that felt really nice. It was nicer in other ways, too. Almost like it had been when they were first married, only better because they knew each other so well now.

"Mmhmm," Max murmured against her ear. "I had to get home early. It's a special day, and I was hoping I could convince the most beautiful woman I know to go with me to the movies tonight. You won't even have to cook."

"What? *You're* going to make dinner?" she said with a laugh, turning in his arms to face him.

"Well, I'm not exactly making dinner; I'm arranging it. Claire is calling King Buffet to order your favorite takeout along with some stuff for the rest of us, and Jillian says she'll set the table while they both entertain Violet. Pretty good, huh?" He wiggled his eyebrows, giving her that little half smile that always made her heart skip a beat or three.

"Ah, now I see the method to your madness." She smiled, looping her arms around his neck. "Very clever."

"You could use a break, El. I know you've had a rough couple of months and there's still that surgery coming up for your father." His warm hands rested on her waist. "You deserve a night with nothing to think about but you. And me a little I suppose, since we're going to be on a date." Max pressed a gentle kiss to her forehead before making a trail of soft kisses down to her mouth.

He took his time kissing her then, and she felt herself melting into him, wishing she *could* just push every nagging thought aside for this one night—including Claire's volatile teenage attitudes, Jillian's tendency to emulate everything her older sister did, Violet's persistent ear infections, her worry about Pa's surgery in two weeks, and the fact that she just kept getting older (and grayer) every time she looked. It seemed the list could go on and on.

"The night is young, even if we aren't so much anymore," he murmured, pulling her closer and rocking side to side with her in a sort of slow dance, though there was no music playing. She could feel him smiling against her lips. "What do you say, El?"

"Mmmm . . . that's a loaded question," she said, smiling now, too. She was enjoying being pressed up against him. He felt good. Really good. "What do I say about *what*?"

"Vixen," he said, with a low and sexy laugh that would have sent a pleasurable little shiver up her spine on its own, even without the added incentive of him tipping his head to nibble kisses along the sensitive area under her ear at the same time. "That part will come later tonight, *after* our date. What do you say about having dinner together now with the girls and then taking in a movie with me? You know, a little fun and diversion. It's been a while since we went out, just the two of us."

Elena leaned back a little to look at him. "I'd say that sounds amazingly good. What's playing?"

"I'll have to look it up. It can be your choice."

"Even if I pick a chick flick?"

Max grimaced, trying to cover it up by shifting into a brilliant smile. "Tonight, my love, your wish is my command. I'll sit through anything if it makes you happy."

"Ahhh, such power," Elena laughed as she shifted away to pull out some glasses from the cupboard. "I wonder if Claire will mind watching Jillian and Violet, though. Does she have homework to do or anything?"

"I'm good!" Claire called in from the dining room, and Elena and Max looked at each other in surprise.

Elena sighed and folded her arms, leaning back against the counter while Max shook his head. That Claire was being generous in offering to babysit her sisters made getting upset with her for snooping a little more difficult . . . but they still needed to call her on it.

"Were you eavesdropping, young—" Max started to say before he was cut off by the phone ringing and Claire's equally loud answer that she would get it.

Shaking her head now, too, Elena started filling the dinner glasses with water. "I don't know what to do with her. She's so different from what I was like at her age. She tests the rules constantly and seems to think she can do whatever she wants."

"She's definitely a full-blown teenager," Max said, rummaging in the fridge before leaning back against the counter himself and popping a handful of grapes into his mouth, followed by a rolled up piece of deli turkey he'd just taken out.

When Elena gave him a pointed look, he shrugged and mumbled around the food. "What? I'm too hungry to wait for the Chinese to get here."

"Honestly, Max, you're worse than the kids sometimes," she said, raising her eyebrows at him.

"Well, at least I picked something healthy," he added after swallowing, making her laugh again.

"Yeah, and I can see where Claire gets her tendency to do what she wants at the moment she wants it," Elena said. "It's a good thing Violet and Jillian didn't just see you doing that, or they'd be asking for bowls of grapes, too, no matter how close to supper we are."

She didn't get any further in her teasing; suddenly they heard Claire squeal in the other room, and the tail end of her conversation became audible as her voice raised in excitement. "Really? That's *so cool*! Okay. I'll tell them. Love you. 'Bye!"

In the next second she came bounding into the kitchen, wreathed in smiles, looking like she'd just been granted a wish by her fairy godmother.

"Who was that?" Max asked.

"It was Aunt Alex," Claire answered, her voice still bubbling over with enthusiasm.

Elena frowned. *Uh-oh.* Zippy hardly ever called here, especially when she was on a film set, which she was right now—in London, according to the last Ma had heard from her at Christmas.

"She said I'm supposed to tell you four things," Claire went on, holding out four fingers on her right hand and tapping each off one at a time as she went through her list. "The first is to wish you a happy birthday, Mom. The second is to make sure to tell everyone she loves them, the third is that her movie will wrap filming this week . . . but the fourth one is the best one of all!" Claire paused, her drama of milking this moment worthy of any of Zippy's movie performances to date.

"What is it, honey? Don't keep us all waiting," Elena said, though a part of her already sensed what Claire's news was, leaving her with feelings of both anticipation and dread.

Jillian and Violet had wandered in from the dining room now, too, to hear what was going on, and a round of happy, ear-splitting shrieking ensued when their sister finally announced, "Aunt Alex is coming home to be here in time for Grandpa's surgery, and she's planning to stay in Moose Junction for at least a whole *month*!"

WGRR FM 103.9, THE BEAR

"Give a Growl for the Adirondacks'
Most Trusted Radio Station"
May 9, 1993

Welcome back, Adirondack listeners. It's Willard T. Boggs here with you on a finally comfortable Sunday evening in the North Country. It was hotter than usual today for this time of year, hitting eighty-one degrees by 3:00 p.m. By the way, Happy Mother's Day to all the mothers out there. Our son, Delbert, took Marge out for lunch after church to the Boonville Hotel. He let me tag along, and I had my favorite: a Reuben with sweet potato fries and coleslaw. Boy, was it good.

Fittingly, on this day in 1914, President Woodrow Wilson proclaimed the first Mother's Day holiday. Also on this day in history, back in 1671, Irish adventurer Thomas "Captain" Blood tried to steal the Crown Jewels from London Tower. He hammered the crown flat while his accomplice shoved the Royal Orb down his breeches. They were caught, but the king was so taken with Blood's daring that he made him a member of court. That led to celebrity status, with the pubic clamoring for glimpses of him. Not a bad gig if you can get it.

Speaking of celebrity sightings, as everyone who isn't living in a cave knows already, Moose Junction was treated to a visit by homegrown movie star Alexandra Wright yesterday. You would have thought all five living presidents were in town the way traffic was backed up. I don't know about you, but Marge and I decided to stay away from all the screaming crowds and security. The entire top half of the state was in a tither. I guess this means I'd better not pursue my dreams of the stage, as I clearly wasn't meant for a life of fame. . . .

Chapter Fourteen

Adirondack Medical Center
January 25, 2008

Elena sat in the cardiac and vascular surgery wing's waiting room at exactly 10:57 a.m., gritting her teeth and trying to think about anything except the incredibly slow passing of time. Each tick of the clock grated her nerves. It was nothing like the soothing sounds of Pa's clocks at home, and it only added to her misery as she sat worrying about him lying there in the operating room while Dr. Zeidner tried to repair his aneurysm.

She coughed, and the sound ricocheted off the decaled green walls, even with all the people there to buffer it (there were sixteen from her family alone camping out, and another smaller family for another patient at the other end of the room). The place was quiet as a graveyard. Elena shuddered and tried to push that thought from her mind.

It wasn't fair that this had happened to Pa, not that fairness had anything to do with it. Pa had quit smoking more than forty years ago, but she'd learned from Dr. Zeidner that it didn't matter—the damage done in the twenty years prior to that had left its mark.

So ready or not, here they all were, trying to pull Pa through the surgery by force of sheer will, while keeping their own sanity relatively intact. Everyone else seemed to be handling things all right, but Elena felt like she was about to snap. She wanted—no she *needed*—a distraction.

Over the past hour she'd tried to start a conversation with three of her sisters, a brother-in-law, and each of the nieces and nephews that had come to support their grandpa through surgery and Grandma while she waited for him. No luck. No one was in a talking mood.

Max and the kids weren't here to enlist in the effort because Claire was sick at home, Jillian was in school, and Violet was too young to keep entertained here for the long hours of surgery (not to mention the germs she'd be exposed to in the hospital). Max had taken the day off from work to stay home with Claire and Violet so Elena could come to the hospital.

Hank had planned to be here with the family, but when Elena had called to make the arrangements to pick him up from the Towers, he'd said he'd come down with a bug (probably the same one Claire had). He'd felt lousy and didn't want to take the chance of spreading the illness. She couldn't blame him, even if she would have loved to have the diversion of talking about old times with him while they waited.

Then there was Ma. Ma usually got real quiet and distracted herself by playing solitaire when she was worried or upset about anything, and the cards had been flapping onto the waiting room's coffee table for going on an hour already. Elena knew Ma would go out of her way to do anything for any of her daughters if she sensed a need, but Elena didn't want to risk causing her any more strain today of all days.

They were all putting on a good front, but *everyone* was too worried to talk much. It was a bad situation any way you sliced it, but there was nothing to be done. Elena knew she'd just have to sit here and wait with Ma and the rest of her sisters (except for Zippy, who was late, of course) for any scrap of news about Pa's progress. In the unbroken silence. Reduced to staring at the muted TV.

She popped a beat-up mint from her purse into her mouth and clicked it against her teeth. No one seemed to notice. The silence hummed on, broken by nothing but the infrequent whispers of the others in the room.

By dint of sheer will, Elena resisted the urge to stand up, wave her hands, and shout out something inappropriate.

Just to break things up a little.

She knew it was a weird compulsion, but at least she also knew she wasn't the only one in the family afflicted with it. For her the urge was brought on by too much artificial quiet, striking most often when she was in the midst of a larger group of people (though it could happen in smaller groups, too, like the time she was visiting her in-laws and ducked into the spare room to indulge in the feeling . . . forgetting that the baby monitor was still turned on and piping every sound she made into the living room).

Unfortunately, that meant she felt that way at church some Sundays, or at funerals, graduation ceremonies, and the like. She controlled it, of course, but it could be awkward. As a child she'd been worried that there was something wrong with her, but when she'd learned that most of her sisters felt similar inclinations (squelched for the most part, with a few notable failures), she didn't feel so bad.

Right now Elena was shocked that none of her siblings were combating the same feelings. Or at least if they were, they were hiding it really well.

Suddenly, a terrifying thought struck her, almost making her suck the half-dissolved mint into her throat (which might have been a good distraction, except that choking to death wasn't exactly high on her list of ways to achieve that goal). What if all of her sisters had outgrown it, and *she* was the only remaining freak in the family?

It had been a long time since she'd talked to any of them about that kind of thing, but she'd have to ask Jen about it. She was Elena's usual partner in such crime in the past; if she no longer felt that way, Elena would know she was the lone, abnormal holdout with the family quirk.

And that would really stink.

This day was going to be more awful than she'd anticipated if she couldn't count on even *one* of her sisters to distract her from this endless worry and silence. Out of all six of them that were here at the moment, *someone* should be able to offer a small outburst—or at least a look of empathy. Maybe they were keeping themselves under control because of the other family on the other side of the waiting room, also hoping for news of their loved one's surgical progress.

That fact didn't help Elena at all, she had to admit. The need to bust out and sing or do something crazy was building with every tick of that cursed clock, and she felt helpless to stop it. Anxiety rolled through the space like noxious fumes. Everyone was trying to act unconcerned, sometimes glancing at each other with half smiles, exchanging brief, whispered comments, or pretending to read or play cards, but it was feeble.

Elena coughed again—louder, deeper, and more raggedly than she really needed to—and then looked around with wide, innocent eyes. Nothing. No one budged or seemed to notice in any way. Man, oh, man . . . what were they all? Heartless? Well, Ma looked up, but she hadn't been Elena's intended target.

Instantly Elena felt a flood of guilt at the worry she saw in Ma's gentle blue eyes. Mouthing the word "sorry," Elena smiled, feeling as contrite as she had all those times when Ma had climbed the stairs from the cellar hauling up yet another load of laundry only to catch Elena and Zippy making tracks in the Blue Bonnet margarine with their finger tips and then dipping them in the sugar bowl.

Looking at Ma settled Elena down for a second, like always. Ma was still lots of fun (when they were younger Ma had been known to march around the kitchen with a pot perched on her head like a hat, tapping a wooden spoon against it and singing, "Yes, indeed, I'm Johnny Appleseed!"), but she was a lady, first and foremost. She knew when to let loose and when to be proper.

After blowing a kiss, Ma eventually went back to her ninth game of solitaire, and Elena's resolve to be good wore off pretty quickly. The next thing she knew she was trying to catch Jen's gaze. But Jen was all the way across the room, rummaging around at the table that held coffeepots, stained mugs, sugar packets, and powdered creamer. *Good luck*, Elena thought with a twinge of sympathy. Jen and caffeine went hand-in-hand, but even when they'd all first gotten here early this morning, the coffee in those pots had looked like sludge.

It looked like Elena was going to be on her own. She clenched her fingers, closed her eyes, and did the best she could do under the circumstances. She started humming the "Battle Hymn of the Republic" in her head. With any luck it would stay right up there, locked in the gray matter of her cranium where it belonged.

St. Paul's Catholic Church
Moose Junction, Upstate New York
April 2, 1972
Elena is three years old

The spirit is willing but the flesh is weak. . . .

The place was packed.

This rare occurrence was thanks to the fact that it was Easter Sunday, and the typically full church was good and truly crammed with all the "Holiday Catholics" who only came twice a year.

As usual, the Wright family took up a whole pew, with Ma at one end and the eight girls spread down the row by age. Pa didn't attend Mass. He did his worshipping in God's great outdoors in the woods behind the house, though he never failed to set out a dollar for each girl on the kitchen table to put in the collections basket for them to help him "buy some graces to heaven."

Most of the time, Ma arranged it so that Anne went in first and was at the far end of the pew, followed by Melanie, then Kat, Lisa, Jen, and Patricia, so that Elena and Zippy would be nearest to Ma, who brought up the rear of the group. This was especially helpful when one of the younger ones invariably needed a tissue, or got a little distracted and needed a reminder to be good. But with the extra confusion and crowds of this Easter Mass, things had gotten all messed up, and Elena found herself flanked by Melanie and Patricia, while Jen was wedged right next to Kat, who was next to Anne, and Zippy had Lisa in between her and Ma.

Compounding the problem was Anne and the fact that she was rather distracted this particular Sunday. At sixteen and a half, she was intelligent, serious, and had a tendency to be a little bossy. But like the old saying, she'd never been kissed (which she thought was completely square), and she'd recently developed a crush on a slightly older boy named Jonathan Lambert, who happened to be sitting with his family two pews in front of the Wrights. Jon lived on a farm about a dozen houses up the road from the Wright homestead; he rode the school bus with the older girls everyday to Moose Junction High, but Anne hadn't seen him in almost a week because school had been on recess for Easter.

As a farm boy, Jon took his calling in life seriously. He got up before dawn to help milk the fifty head of cows on the family dairy farm, and then milked them again in the evening before finishing his chores; he did the haying every summer with his pop, and drove the tractor up and down their neat and trim twenty acres, pulling the plow to ready the soil for planting every spring. It was a lot of work to keep a farm going, and Jon had the muscles to prove it. He was a hunk, all right—tall, ruddy-cheeked, and strong.

The sight of him again was like rain on parched earth for Anne. She was almost giddy to have the chance to soak up Jon's groovy good looks after the long drought of absence (the fact that she was in church and supposed to be praying against just such sinful thoughts notwithstanding). And this fine Easter morning, Jon was looking more groovy than usual, wearing what appeared to be a new, light blue polyester suit and a white shirt with a fashionably long, pointed collar. Totally hip with his curly brown hair.

Anne was in love, and all her sisters knew it.

Anne's crush didn't mean too much to Elena and Zippy, who were only three and four years old, respectively; all that interested Elena was Jonathan's connection to cows, which happened to be her most favorite animal in the world (Zippy couldn't care less about anything unless princesses were involved). Patricia was obsessed with horses, so none of this fazed her either. But from Jen on up, the teasing of the "lovebirds" had been going on something fierce for a few weeks now, having ebbed a bit during the span of Easter vacation. The time was ripe to start it up again.

Kat took on the challenge.

It was during the empty silence between the second reading and the Gospel, when everyone was supposed to be sitting quietly and thinking about God. It was just too quiet—so much so that Kat couldn't stand it any more. A minor disturbance was in order, and Anne would be the perfect target. The priest was standing near the podium, readying himself to read from John 20, verses 1-9, and then give the Homily, when, low enough for only Anne, Jen, and Melanie to hear, Kat let go a soft "moo-ooo-oo" in Jon's direction, followed by a little kissy-sound with her already puckered lips.

Anne glared at her twelve-and-a-half-year-old sister, her hands clenching the pew seat until her knuckles turned white.

Delighted with the fun of this distraction, Kat did it again, and this time Anne's elbow came out with ninja-like swiftness, catching her sister on her funny bone, which would have normally elicited a yowl and laughter from Kat, but considering where they were and needing some outlet for the pain, it caused her instead to lurch forward onto the kneeler as if she were overcome with a desire to pray.

Ma was alerted by the commotion by this time (it was at a point in the Mass where no one was supposed to be kneeling), but by then it was too late.

Anne's shoulders had started the quake with suppressed laughter, matching Kat's, who had her head buried in her steepled palms for a moment before she shrank back into her seat, still trying desperately not to laugh out loud. And then it spread down the line, to Jen, Melanie, Elena, Patricia, Zippy, and Lisa, so that the whole row was jiggling like the fruited lime Jell-O at home waiting in the refrigerator to be topped with fresh whipped cream as part of their Easter dessert.

By the time they could get themselves completely back under control (Ma's warning looks only made it worse and started them up all over again), it was time to stand for the Profession of Faith. The rest of the Mass passed by pretty uneventfully.

The Jell-O was left in the fridge for another time, however, as, thanks to their antics at church, there was no dessert served to the Wright girls that day, Easter or not.

Chapter Fifteen

Adirondack Medical Center
January 25, 2008

The time was now 11:09 a.m. "The Battle Hymn of the Republic" had come to an end in Elena's head, and she'd just started on the "US Marine Corps Hymn" (in honor of Pa), when a bellow split the silence, making her actually inhale the last sliver of mint, though luckily it was now small enough that no real damage was done.

"Hey, Aunt Elena, would you pass me that magazine?"

At last. Nothing earth shattering, but at least it was an interruption, offered by sixteen-year-old Ben, Melanie's youngest son.

Like a precision drill team, everyone's head snapped up to look at the culprit while Jen swiveled around from her futile search at the coffee table to see what the excitement was all about.

As a tenth grader, Ben was the youngest of any of the nieces and nephews here at the hospital today. He, like the rest of the grandkids in high school, only had to report to school this week if he was scheduled for an exam. Elena knew he probably wasn't too thrilled to be spending one of his few days off sitting in a waiting room of the hospital, especially without Claire to commiserate with, but he loved his grandpa, so that had been that.

Elena worked with kids his age all the time at the library. The iPod wires dangling from his ears solved the mystery of his bellowing pretty quickly, and Melanie reached over and tugged them out, scowling and snapping at him to adjust his voice—and tell him that not everyone was plugged into deafening music.

He looked embarrassed, poor kid, but Elena winked at him as she handed him the issue of *Car and Driver* he'd asked for, and he gave her a little grin before hunching down in his seat, tucking his earbuds in again, and pulling up his hoodie so that it almost covered his eyes.

Having left the coffee table to retake her position leaning up against the doorway, Jen glanced now at Elena, raising her brow and quirking her lip.

Ah, yes, Elena thought, relief sweeping through her; they were finally connecting, which meant the possibility of some better distractions from the constant worry about Pa. While Elena rarely managed to rock the boat much (her failed attempt to gain sympathy by coughing was a perfect example), Jen was more of a wildcard. Jen might be more than three years older, but they were what Ma had always called "compatible" sisters. Elena knew it went deeper than compatibility, and that they would have been bosom friends even if they hadn't been related by blood.

Just as she had since they were little girls together, whispering from the dark confines of their bunk bed, Jen seemed to possess an uncanny ability to click into Elena's renegade thoughts, whether or not they were saying anything aloud. Now, Elena made a goofy, eye-rolling face at her, and Jen's half smile shifted to a full-blown grin.

Her sister was out of uniform for the moment, her dark, shoulder-length hair loose from the usual clipped-up knot that was necessary for police protocol, and both her arms and her jean-clad legs crossed casually as she leaned against the doorjamb. She had long legs, strong and toned like a dancer's, though Elena knew that even now Jen didn't consider herself attractive in a physical sense. Too many years of more popular classmates taunting her with names like "Granny Oakley" and "spaghetti legs" had prevented that.

But Jen had grown into those legs eventually. By the time she was out of high school and the eighties were in full swing, braces had straightened her buckteeth and she'd cut her thick hair into a spiky, punk-style, *a la* Prince and the Revolution. She'd been a force to contend with then, tough as nails (especially to any guy who tried to get a little too cozy with Elena when they'd go out together on college breaks) but still the same funny, irreverent, insecure-on-the-inside Jen that she'd always been.

Elena couldn't help wondering, sometimes, how Jen might have been different if she'd been gorgeous from birth, the way Zippy had been. Zippy, who'd earned her nickname for the way she wheeled around corners in her baby walker at Mach thirty, was (as has already been mentioned) a piece of work. You know how people talk about how funny it is that multiple kids from the same parents, raised in the same household, can turn out so differently? Yeah, well, Zippy would have won the award for that one, and not just in personality.

None of the Wright sisters were Quasimodos or anything in the looks department, but compared to Zippy . . . well, there really was no comparison. She was the tallest girl in the family by a half an inch (which put her at about five-foot-ten), and her slender-but-curved-in-all-the-right-places shape meant she could wear any style. And while she put a fair amount of time into "keeping up" her appearance, she really didn't need to. Even in her natural state she looked incredible.

Yes, all the best of the family's beauty genes seemed to have concentrated in her. Zippy had had one pimple at the onset of puberty, but because of the trauma that single blemish had unleashed, everyone joked that none other had ever dared emerge from her perfect skin again.

If the Ivory-girl complexion, knockout body, and perfect, silky hair weren't enough, Zippy had also been blessed with a straight nose, full lips, and violet-blue eyes. Not hazel or brown or even regular blue. Oh, no, those would be too mundane for Zippy. Hers were true, gorgeous purpley-blue like Elizabeth Taylor's.

People sometimes thought she had tinted contacts or that she'd had plastic surgery to look like she did. But it was all natural. And it was annoying as all get out when you were related to that kind of perfection, especially when her personality was such that she saw no need to be especially gracious about it with anyone, including the members of her own family.

Jen's movement as she pushed away from the doorjamb brought Elena back to the here and now. Her sister had been leaning in the doorway closer to the other family who was sharing the waiting room, and it took her a few extra seconds to make her way back toward Ma and the rest of the extended Wright family. Elena waited with baited breath, her senses leaping to full alert; from the look on her sister's face, Jen had clearly decided it was time to shake things up a little around here, and she could be unpredictable in how she chose to accomplish that.

Elena didn't have to wait too long to find out.

"So," Jen drawled once she'd walked up and swept her gaze around their gathered family. She took an obvious glance at her watch, cocked her eyebrows and then slid into the open chair near Elena. "Where the hell is Zippy?"

Dead silence and Ma's disapproving look at her use of a curse word greeted her question.

"*En route*, I'd guess."

It was Anne who had spoken, taking charge and trying to keep things on an even keel like she always did. "Her train was due in around nine, and she was supposed to rent a car at the station and drive here."

"She's taking the *train* and *renting* a *car*? What happened to her limo . . . or her private helicopter? I figured she'd be touching down on the hospital's landing pad any minute." Jen's tone was dry, but her smile took the sting out of her comment. It earned her a chuckle from Kat and Patricia, and a smothered grin from Elena. Melanie and Lisa were trying to stay out of it for the most part, but their kids and husbands were beginning to loosen up and relax a little in response to Jen's kidding around.

Jen wasn't being mean or anything. Even though she kept in touch other ways, Zippy had only been home a dozen times or so in the past two decades—the last time almost two full years ago. Whenever she arrived, it was usually with an effort at a big splash. She'd seemed disappointed that the locals' reactions to sightings of her had settled down considerably the past few times, with no crowds gathering any more, and so she'd tried all different ways of regaining their attention.

The last time she'd come home, Jen had tried to (gently) remind her that the public was a fickle beast. They clamored for the latest, hot thing on the screen, not for the tried and true. Especially when it came to women (unless you were Meryl Streep, Dame Judi Dench, Helen Mirren, or Emma Thompson, but three of them were Brits anyway, and as for Meryl, well, she was in a category all by herself). Tinseltown was notorious for gobbling up and spitting out its share of starlets, and she should be proud that she still worked regularly twenty years later.

It hadn't helped.

Zippy had pursed her lips, made a sharp comment, and clicked off in her high heels to make a call to her agent. She'd flown out two days later with the same kind of glint in her eyes that she'd had the very first time she'd set off for California a few months after graduation.

Still, over the years, the family wondered if she'd taken the adage, *Absence makes the heart grow fonder*, a little too seriously, although she periodically called, texted, or sent expensive gifts. In general, her focus seemed to be on clinging to the limelight at all costs. That had included when and how she came home.

The dark side of it all was that fame had infringed on her personal happiness; she'd never managed to stay in one place or maintain her privacy long enough to cultivate any lasting romantic relationship. *All* her relationships seemed to suffer under the strain of her career. It felt to her family like she'd forgotten that though the rest of the world saw her as Alexandra Wright, movie star, the people who had loved her all her life still thought of her as Zippy first, and they missed her.

Ma hadn't said anything yet in response to Jen's comment about Zippy's mode of arrival, only shaking her head at her. Elena knew she wouldn't scold Jen unless she crossed the line, which she rarely did. She just pushed it a little for the sake of everyone's amusement.

Anne hadn't reacted much either by this point (another tactic she'd learned years ago as a way of managing any rebellious younger sisters in her charge). She kept her gaze even and shrugged. "All I know is that she texted last night saying she was taking the train. Maybe it was late."

"Or maybe she was late getting to it." One of Jen's eyebrow's arched again. "Zip's never been what anyone would call an early riser."

No one could argue with that, even Anne. The room went quiet again, the tension that had built up waiting for word on Pa's surgery still not entirely broken. But Jen wasn't done yet.

Giving an exaggerated sigh, her sister leaned back in her chair. "Well, I'll bet that even *without* a limo or a plane, Zip is going to make a grand entrance today. She's just setting the stage by being fashionably late." Patting her own pockets as if looking for something, she mumbled, "And . . . I seem to be fresh out." Then she lifted her gaze to her "audience" with the kind of wide-eyed innocence worthy of an Academy Award. "Anyone have a camera, so we can capture the moment?"

That did it.

Ma gave Jen a long-suffering look while the rest of the family snickered. Even Melanie, Lisa, and Anne got caught up in her humor, and the last of the accumulated tension deflated like a cartoon balloon popped with a pin. Giving a little shrug now herself, Jen leaned her forearms on her knees and looked impishly at Ma. "What?"

"Really, Jennifer," Ma fussed at her.

"I'm just trying to lighten things up a little until Zippy gets here to take over the theatrics." She gave Elena a half smile, making the unspoken connection for support. "I mean we're all sitting around here like we're expecting the worst, and everyone knows that Zippy and flashbulbs have always been a perfect combination."

Elena couldn't help but snort a laugh at that.

"Elena Elizabeth, your sister doesn't need any encouragement."

Jen's grin flashed in full again, pulling Ma's attention back. "It's the truth. If Zip were here, I'd tell her myself."

There was a half beat of silence—the calm before the storm, Elena couldn't help thinking—and then the atmosphere seemed to pull into itself, an electric undercurrent shivering to life as a voice came, clear as a bell, from outside in the corridor.

"Tell me what?"

With a waft of air scented by expensive perfume, Alexandra Wallis "Zippy" Wright clicked into the waiting room on her matte leather, high-heeled boots. As she walked in, she pulled off a stylish, slouchy hat, releasing her trademark dark auburn hair so that it fell over her shoulders like silk. Her whole entrance looked like something you'd see on a television commercial, minus the slow-motion camera work and background music. She managed to look at once casually elegant, bored, and maybe a slight bit worried if you took into account the stiff set of her (still plump-lipped) mouth and (sag-free) jaw.

Elena tried not to roll her eyes.

Zippy was wearing a pair of jeans that must have cost at least four hundred dollars, a cream-colored cashmere turtleneck worth three times that, with what was likely an even more expensive soft-as-butter cinnamon-hued leather jacket belted expertly over it. No one had a right to look that good one month shy of forty years old.

None of them could see her famous violet-blue eyes, though. The sunglasses that she seemed to wear everywhere shaded them, a habit from her years of being hounded by paparazzi.

"I was just reiterating how much the camera loves you, sis," Jen clipped, giving her a wave as Zippy made her way to Ma.

"Oh. Right."

Elena frowned. Zippy seemed distracted. It had never been like her *not* to deliver a razor sharp comeback to one of Jen's teasing remarks. The leather and perfume scents surrounding her blended in an artful mix as she leaned over to kiss Ma on the cheek while everyone else was in the process of getting up to offer their hug and greeting. "Sorry I'm late. I missed the first train."

When she faced Elena for their greeting, Elena murmured a welcome and hugged her, feeling the same push and pull of complicated emotions as always. She used to wonder if it would ever get easier, but it hadn't, really. It had changed in some ways with time and the distance caused by Zippy's fame, but it still always felt like there was a brewing undercurrent of misunderstanding just waiting to blow up.

"It's strange to see you by yourself. Where's the entourage?" Jen asked with another grin, still trying to get a rise out of her when it was her turn to embrace her sister.

Zippy made a huffing sound. "None of the ingrates would come." She looked toward Ma. "How's Pa?"

As she asked that, she finally pulled off her shades. Elena was startled at how tired her eyes looked, with shadows under them and no trace of artfully applied liner or mascara. This wasn't like Zippy. Not at all.

"We haven't had any updates yet." Ma motioned for Zip to sit next to her on the long pleather couch.

"It's probably too soon to expect anything, though. They didn't take him into surgery until around ten thirty," Lisa said, leaning forward a little as her husband, Mike, absently rubbed the spot between her shoulders.

Zippy looked confused. "I thought he was scheduled at nine o'clock?"

"A hold up with the patient ahead of him," Kat answered. Then she gave a rueful smile. "And you know Pa . . . he likes to be on time, so the delay drove him crazy. The fact that he'd been fasting since suppertime last night didn't help his mood, either. We could have used one of your stories or a little performance or something to keep him distracted, Zip."

It might have been her imagination working overtime, but Elena could have sworn that Zippy's mouth tightened a little more at that. She didn't have a chance to say anything in response, though. At that moment, there was the sound of another person approaching from the hallway, and then a woman wearing green surgical scrubs appeared.

Elena craned her neck and saw that a similarly garbed man lingered just behind her, standing in the hallway. Jen also twisted around to look, and the atmosphere in the waiting room crackled again as everyone in the family seemed to lean forward a little, recognizing that this might just be the update they'd all been looking for.

"The Joseph Horton family?" the woman called out.

Everyone on Elena's side of the room seemed to exhale together in disappointment, even as the half a dozen or so people sitting closer to the door lurched to their feet. A woman who was probably younger than Ma by about a decade led the way out into the hall and the conference with the medical people (doctors? nurses?) followed by a man who appeared to be related to her. By the looks of him, he was probably her son.

It wasn't more than ten seconds later that the muted, panicked sounds of the woman's voice and the raised cadences of questions interspersed with lower-pitched replies, drifted in from the hallway. Then there was a sharp cry. Several of the others who were still in the waiting room rushed forward and out the door, even as the man came back in with his mother, who leaned heavily on him with her hand pressed to her lips, choking back sobs and closing her eyes as she shook her head.

From the now filled hallway, a jumble of sounds ensued as the other family members peppered the hospital staff with questions. Bits of the conversation, "tried to resuscitate," "no brain function," and "organ donation," came through the open doorway into the once again deathly pall that seemed to have been cast over the waiting room.

The man had by this time led his mother over to the couch again, embracing her as she rocked and cried softly. Elena could see his face now. He looked like he was in his thirties, probably only a few years younger than Elena. She saw the tight set of his spine and the feelings he was struggling to hold back, and the heat in her own eyes rose up. Strange and awful emotions spilled outward from inside her; she felt a painful empathy for this family and the horrible news they'd clearly just received, but to her shame she felt a sense of relief, too . . . relief that it hadn't been Pa the surgeons had come to give a hopeless report on.

Elena couldn't seem to pull her gaze away from the mother and son. From her peripheral vision, she saw her own family was reacting in a way similar to her. Everyone had gone still, their expressions tight, and their eyes filled with combined sympathy and dread.

Here it was, another hammering home of the message.

Some things just *were*, and there was nothing you could do about it. Time was precious. And finite. Elena had known this pretty much from birth and then had it brought more firmly into her focus through her two childhood brushes with death. And she'd kept learning; her experience with Jesse had taught her a whole different angle on that excruciating lesson . . . and that as difficult as awareness of one's own mortality was, it was often worse facing it in light of someone you loved.

She looked down at her hands, which were clasped on her knees, she realized, as if in prayer.

All that was left to do was hope that when Dr. Zeidner showed up at the waiting room door with news about Pa, the unforgiving reminder they'd all just witnessed through the Joseph Horton family's pain wouldn't be repeated in a more personal way. Closing her eyes, Elena prayed for that happier outcome, her mind pushing away the other possibility as inconceivable and something for which she was absolutely not ready.

But she knew better than most that that didn't mean it wouldn't happen anyway. Life was precarious, and you never knew when your number—or the number of someone you loved—was going to be up.

Adirondack Medical Center
Syracuse, New York
April 15, 1987
Elena is eighteen years old

Grief is a solitary journey. . . .

The door to Elena's hospital room creaked open.

She didn't look, instead feigning the sleep that had eluded her all night. The only benefit to being awake was her awareness that it was barely dawn and too early for this intrusion to be anyone other than another doctor or nurse. They came in on regular rotations to check her vitals, inspect her bandages or the wounds beneath, or to assess her pain level.

To ensure her heart was still beating, whether she wanted it to or not.

To try to fix what could never be fixed again.

The pile of tubes, wires, and medical equipment attached to her beeped in steady rhythm, but the person who came into the room didn't complete the usual flipping of charts or checking of monitors and dressings. With a grimace, Elena mentally cursed and roused herself as much as she could. If they were here to pump her full of more narcotics, she had to put on a good show to prevent it.

Of course she was in pain, and it was relentless. Her entire body ached or burned or throbbed, with her left arm, ribs, and pelvis leading the way in their own special agony. But she needed to pretend it was manageable because whenever she allowed herself to drift too far on that cloud of dulled, medication-induced relief, crippling memories unleashed in her mind that were worse. She *needed* to feel physical pain, needed to concentrate on it so she could avoid confronting that deeper hurt and loss that no medicine in the world would ever be able to touch.

Elena cracked open her eyes and struggled to focus them in the dim light. If she'd been able to vocalize more than a croaking sound of surprise, she would have, because the person who'd come into the room wasn't part of the medical staff. In fact it was one of the last people she would have expected to see—someone who *should* have been 2,600 miles away, hard at work on the set of her first big movie. It was her sister, Alexandra, the fresh-faced star of a big budget action-thriller that had started filming last month.

Zippy took several more hesitant steps into the dusky interior of Elena's room, and Elena squinted at her, making sure her blurry vision wasn't playing tricks on her.

It was Zippy, all right, and she looked like hell. At least for Zippy. Her hair was pulled into a messy ponytail, and she was wearing sweatpants, a flannel shirt, and ratty-looking sneakers. Not a drop of concealer had been applied to the dark circles blooming under her eyes, and for the first time that Elena could remember, Zip wasn't wearing any gloss on her perfect mouth.

"Oh, my God, El. . . ."

Zippy's voice trailed off, and Elena realized that her headstrong, glamorous, poised sister was near tears at the sight of her. And if Zippy broke down, Elena didn't know if she could hold it together herself.

"No crying," Elena managed to rasp, waving her right hand (since her left arm was completely immobilized).

But moving made her wince, and so Zippy rushed forward, putting her cool, manicured fingers on Elena's arm. Then she just stood there looking down at Elena in silence, her expressive gaze shimmering with all the emotions she was clearly doing her best to hold back.

Elena swallowed, feeling the sting in her own eyes but refusing to give in to it as her gaze connected with Zippy's across the awful, aching gulf of what had happened. There were no words to bridge it, nothing that could take away the pain of the truth. It just *was*. That horrible lesson again. . . .

Grasping at straws to keep her composure, Elena edged away from the danger zone. She gave voice instead to what she'd thought when her sister came in. "You look awful."

Zippy laughed then and swiped a hand under her eyes. "Yeah, well, you don't look so great yourself. I didn't get much sleep on the plane. And I forgot my makeup bag in the rush to get to the airport. I took the red eye after filming ended for the day yesterday, but Ridley made me promise to be back to Los Angeles before four o'clock."

"*Today*?"

Zippy nodded.

"Who's Ridley?" Elena coughed and then grimaced at the pain that shot through her. She tipped her head, grateful to take a sip of water through the straw of the cup Zippy tilted toward her mouth.

"The director of *Agency*, the movie I'm in." Zippy helped Elena take a drink. "I'm not scheduled to shoot another scene until tonight. That's how I was able to sneak away, but it only gives me an hour or so here." She set the water cup down and made a dramatic flourish. "Then it's back to the airport for a return flight so I don't get myself in trouble. I'm too new to push it too far."

"That's crazy. You shouldn't have done it, Zip. Pa and Ma could have kept you up to date over the phone." Elena had to force herself to get out that many words in a row, and the effort exhausted her.

"They did. They were great about it." Zippy's gaze took on a warmer, penetrating intensity, and her hand tightened on Elena's arm. "That's one of the reasons I had to come. I had to see you myself, El. Pa told me the doctors said you'll heal in time. But it's *all* the healing that I'm worried about."

Elena couldn't muster the energy to say anything in response, but her expression must have shown her confusion, because Zippy shrugged.

"I might not be book-smart, but I'm good at reading emotions. How cool is it that it's my actual job for my roles to pay attention to that kind of stuff now?"

She had flashed her megawatt smile during that last part, but the smile faded and her voice fell to a softer pitch as she continued. "I know about feelings, El. I was there from the beginning, and I saw how you were." Her eyes welled again. "I saw how much you loved Jesse, and how much he lov—"

"No!" Elena choked, cutting her off and stiffening with panic. "No. *Don't.*"

Her strangled plea stopped her sister from saying more, but not the flood of memories her words had unlocked. Elena closed her eyes and sucked in her breath, but they kept coming: images of Jesse flashing through her mind, stabbing, aching, burning, overwhelming.

"Don't," Elena begged again in a whisper, shaking her head and looking at Zippy. "Please . . . I can't. I can't talk about it."

"Okay, okay. . . . Oh, honey, I'm so sorry." Zippy's face was a mask of hurt, guilt, and empathy, and she looked like she was about to burst into tears again as she fumbled for a tissue on the bedside stand, dabbing it under her eyes before looking back at Elena. "My God, El, I just feel so *bad* about it all, and I want to help you." She blinked, her expression filled with the kind of sincerity even the best actor in the world couldn't fake. "I know I haven't always shown it, but I love you, little sister. I just wish I could do something for you to make it better. *Something. . . .*"

"You already have," Elena said in desperation. She called on every ounce of energy to patch the invisible raw wounds, pushing everything back beneath the surface, retreating to the safety zone of childhood banter. "You flew across the entire country to see me for one measly hour."

Zippy looked startled for a second, and then seemed to realize what Elena was doing; she played along without missing another beat. "Hey, don't knock it." She arched her brow and gave a wicked smile. "A whole hour of *me* is worth *mucho* bucks nowadays."

Elena tried to smile in return, closing her eyes again as the quiet stretched out between them, not uncomfortable, but weighed down with all they knew couldn't be spoken of now. Maybe not ever.

After a while she felt Zippy's hand on her arm again, reassuring. "Isn't there something I can do? Bring you a magazine? Get you some ginger ale?"

"Yes." Elena looked at her sister. "Distract me." Clearing her throat, she tried to get the rest of the words past the lump still lodged there. "Tell me what it's like. Hollywood."

Zippy put on a good show, her tone playful. "Wow, I'm shocked. I never pegged you for being interested in gossip and drama."

"Beggars can't be choosers," Elena murmured, taking another sip of the water Zippy offered. "Just don't get mad if I fall asleep."

"I won't." Zippy laughed. "It's probably safer if you sleep through some of what I'm going to dish about for the next half hour, anyway. If you're still asleep I promise I'll just kiss you quietly goodbye when I leave, so don't worry if I'm gone when you wake up. I'll call tomorrow to check on you."

Zippy kept smiling as she said that, and Elena realized that with or without makeup, tired or well rested, her sister was truly gorgeous . . . and she was glowing, too, lit up from the inside from living her dream. At that thought, a tiny surge of happiness poked its way through the shrouding weight of grief that had become Elena's constant companion.

Tapping her finger to her lips, Zippy looked up as she considered where she wanted to start and then launched into the first description. "Okay, I'll start by telling you about the endless hours I have to sit in hair and makeup, and all the juicy stuff I get to hear while I'm trapped there. If you thought I took a long time to get ready for stuff when I was living at home, I'll tell you it's *nothing* like what I have to do on a set." Zippy giggled. "But it's so much fun, too, because I don't have to do any of it myself. *Other* people fuss over me and make sure I look just so."

Elena nodded, feeling her face, chest, and the back of her neck begin to relax just a little as Zippy's melodic voice washed over her. She let herself sink into her sister's stories and colorful descriptions, imagining a life so different from the dark reality of her own world right now.

And with a sigh she closed her eyes once more, for a few minutes, at last finding some peace.

Chapter Sixteen

Adirondack Medical Center
January 25, 2008

The clamor around here could wake the dead.

Dave struggled to open his eyes. Prying even one open would be acceptable, but he couldn't do it. His mind went still for an instant as he considered why that might be. Maybe he was in a coma. Or worse. Wouldn't it be a kicker if he'd bought the farm during surgery? He'd known from the get-go that it was a real possibility. Especially at his age.

When the doctors had pointed it out to him during their matter-of-fact discussions prior to the procedure, he'd kept his instinctive response to himself. It did no good to try to explain to them that no matter how old his body became, who he was on the inside hadn't changed an awful lot since he could conquer the world at eighteen. For decades, he'd felt invincible. Even at almost seventy-eight years old he found it difficult sometimes to accept the things he could no longer do. And like he'd told Elena last month, every so often looking in the mirror in the morning gave him a shock.

All that aside, logic told him he couldn't be dead right now. If he was, he would either be floating above all the action on his way to speeding down some tunnel of light, or else his other theory would have come to pass, and the lights would have simply gone out permanently, with him none the wiser. Since he was able to think and could feel sensation (he was lying on his back, and his middle felt strangely heavy at the moment), it stood to reason that he had made it through the surgery alive.

Still trying to open his eyes, he listened to what was happening around him, hoping to get a fix at least on *where* he was. A clattering sound, like someone had dropped a basin or bedpan or something, rattled nearby, followed by a string of under-the-breath curses.

Almost certainly still in the hospital. Probably in the recovery room.

His eyelids finally edged up a crack. A splinter of light pierced his brain at the same moment that a deep, aching pain lanced through his gut and brought forth an involuntary groan.

And definitely still trapped in his body.

"Mr. Wright? Can you hear me, Mr. Wright?"

His eyes had finally obeyed him, and now he tried to make his head comply with the command he was giving it to look to his left, toward the young woman who was calling his name. Nothing.

"Are you in pain, Mr. Wright?"

He tried again and slowly managed to accomplish the motion. No words of answer would come out, though, only another sound that echoed that first groan. Damn, he hated having to chew his cabbage twice, but when he couldn't get his body to cooperate the first time around, it was that or give up. And he hadn't gotten this far in life by waving a white flag when the going got tough. Forcing his eyes to focus, he saw the owner of the persistent voice; she was nurse, and a pretty one, too.

"Let's adjust your pain meds, then." The nurse worked efficiently as she spoke, not looking at him anymore, just chattering away in the manner of nurses who are used to talking to patients who never really respond to them.

Through the fog in his brain, Pa tried to shake his head. It wasn't that he didn't hurt. He did, though not so bad that he couldn't take it. It was that pain medication did funny things to him, to his awareness first of all, which usually led to a crushing headache, and then to a sluggish digestive system later on, which threw everything off for him. He didn't want more drugs right now. What he wanted was something that would help him more than any medicine they could pump into him.

He wanted his family.

The doctor had promised him they could come to see him in recovery, once he was out of surgery—well, maybe not all of them, and not all at once, but at least his wife and the girls. He needed to see them, to let them know he'd come through all right.

He squinted to see if any of them were coming into the room, trying to figure out if they'd even been told he was out of surgery. He wanted to ask the nurse, but his throat was so dry that the only word he could muster sounded like a croak.

She didn't notice. She just kept working busily at his IV tubes, changing his saline bag and getting ready to spill more drugs into his system. He couldn't seem to get her attention.

This was ridiculous. He might be an old man, but he wasn't dead yet.

Concentrating all his energy, he lifted his left arm, tubes and all, and tried to grip the nurse's hand to make her look at him.

She wasn't expecting his sudden motion; with a sound of surprise, she jerked back. Her fingers were tangled in the tubes dangling from the IV rack, and her movement made it topple with a crash that was much louder than the one he'd heard before he could open his eyes. At almost the same time, something tugged sharply against the crook of his arm. He felt a splash of warmth and had a brief vision of something red spraying into the air.

Without warning, his vision blurred around the edges. *Just ducky*. People started to scramble around, and he heard voices, raised in alarm, and he felt an urge (one he'd carried with him since his Marine Corps days) to take charge . . . to line people up and make them calm down and get organized in their response to the situation. A tipped-over IV rack was nothing to get so riled up about, even if it had made the needle pop out of his arm.

But then his thoughts started to fragment, somehow, and the sounds in his ears built to a strange crescendo at the same time that the light dimmed. Just before he lapsed into complete unconsciousness, he imagined that he heard the beautiful sound of a little girl's laughter, followed by the trill of a voice calling his name—not his given name, but the one that meant so much more to him, earned when he'd become a father for the very first time. He answered for her to wait, that Pa was coming. . . .

And with a smile, he slept.

The Homestead
Moose Junction, Upstate New York
January 10, 1969
Elena is born

A joy that's shared is a joy made double. . . .

The old green Volkswagen van rumbled up the driveway just as dusk began to settle over the sloping front yard that led to the highway and on to the shores of Lake Pines beyond that. Pa sat in the driver's seat, waving toward the house as he drove by, up to the rickety lean-to that served as the family's garage. He couldn't see who was standing in the window. The snow banks were high already, and there were still two and half months of winter weather to go.

But he knew that framed in the double panes were his girls—seven of them, aged just under a year to almost fourteen—and behind them the Wrights' good neighbors, Hank and Gladys Steiner, with their son, Jim. They'd been keeping an eye on things while Pa was at the hospital with Ma.

Before Pa could turn off the engine, the back door slammed and everyone in the house spilled out into the yard and down the stone and dirt path that served as a sidewalk. They'd pulled on coats, scarves, mittens, and hats, and their breath made frosty puffs in the air as the older girls helped the younger ones, with Anne carrying eleven-month-old Alex, who couldn't walk very well yet.

No one could tell when Pa was going to give them the news or how he was going to do it—and no one wanted to ask. He'd tell them when he was ready, making the moment special like he did so many others, whether the occasion was big or little, happy or sad.

So everyone waited, stamping their feet, though they were shivering more in anticipation than from the cold as Pa got out of the van and with a wink in their direction turned to step deeper into the black shadows of the lean-to garage. Three-year-old Jen looked up to the second-oldest, Melanie (who was almost twelve), and opened her mouth as if she would demand the answer to the question that had been simmering in everyone's minds since Ma and Pa left for the hospital early this morning. But Melanie put her finger to her lips and whispered, "Hush, now. Be patient," before turning her face back toward the driveway and the lean-to from which a few rattling sounds could now be heard.

"But—"

"Shhhhh!" Kat interrupted, not looking right at anyone in particular; at almost nine, she was only third oldest, but she could always be counted on for cutting straight through to the business of what needed to be done. No fuss, just do it. She held the hand of two-year-old Patricia, who was being quiet and obedient, just as Kat liked.

Anne, who would be fourteen in August, just waited in silence, holding baby Alex in one arm and clutching hands with seven-year-old Lisa on the other side. Anne's fingers were crossed so that they felt like knots in Lisa's grip. For good measure, she also had her toes crossed so tightly that she was sure they were probably tinged blue by now. She'd thought about crossing her eyes, too, but decided that would be going too far. The little ones might get scared, and besides, if her eyes were crossed, she wouldn't be able to see what Pa was about to do to relieve them all of their suspense.

At last Pa emerged from the shadows of the makeshift garage, holding a footstool in one hand, and in the other a rectangular wooden sign that he'd sanded smooth a month earlier, using black paint to write in bold letters the word "HOME" on one side of it.

Twine loops strung through the drilled holes in the corners seemed raw and pale compared to the gray wood of the sign—which matched the sturdy, hand-hewn fence Pa had set up, post by post, years ago. The fence stretched fifteen feet on either side of the walkway, joined over the path by a wooden arch faintly reminiscent of ranch gates from the old Wild West movies that sometimes played on their old rabbit-eared TV in the living room.

With a twinkle in his eyes, Pa opened up the footstool and stepped up on it, just beneath the summit of the arch. Then he reached up with gloved hands and slipped the loops onto the hooks he'd twisted into the wooden beam earlier. But his head blocked the sign itself, obscuring what they were all waiting to see.

Not the side that said "HOME." The other side.

It wasn't until he stepped down from the stool and turned to face them, with the tips of his ears red from cold and flashing that smile that could have charmed any leading lady in Hollywood, that they read the words applied in fresh, black paint.

"For Girls."

Gladys Steiner got teary and pressed her fingers to her lips as a whoop went up all around her, followed by giggling, whispered excitement that let Jen and Patricia, who were both too little to read yet, know the result. Baby Alex just stared and sucked her thumb, watching everyone with her big, beautiful eyes. Young Jim crossed his arms over his chest, shook his head and sighed, while Hank pulled Gladys close for a quick hug then lurched forward to grip Pa by the hand, shaking it furiously as they both grinned at each other.

The baby was a girl, just as Pa had predicted. Ma was cuddling a new little sister down at the hospital in town.

In years to come, people on the outside most often would take one look at the pile of sisters all together and shake their heads, some with bemusement and others with a kind of aghast disbelief. It didn't matter. They were never much worried about what other people thought.

"Elena Elizabeth," Anne breathed. She'd long ago memorized the name Ma and Pa had said they'd chosen if the baby was a girl. Pa had been so certain she'd be a girl that he and Ma hadn't picked out any other name, insisting he'd call the baby "Hickory" if it turned out to be a boy.

"Now let's get some hot chocolate and get you girls warmed up," Pa said, grinning again at the swell of cheers that rose at the suggestion.

He followed his brood into the house, thinking back to the cozy scene he'd left behind at the hospital. He added it in his mind to the one he'd just come home to as well, and felt a sense of satisfaction and happiness he thought he'd never know. After so many empty years of wishing, he was responsible for this large and lively family—*his* family, complete at last—and he knew without a doubt that this was exactly where he wanted to be.

(The homestead, January, 1969)

Chapter Seventeen

Adirondack Medical Center
January 25, 2008

"The David Wright family?"

Elena startled, lurching to her feet. It was 3:52 p.m. The waiting room had emptied of everyone except for them several hours ago, but now they all shifted *en masse*, clustering around and behind Ma (having her back, literally), moving toward the same door through which the Horton family had received their horrible summons. *Please God, please let him be all right*, Elena prayed silently, struggling to suppress the fear that kept welling up inside her.

"Your husband is beginning to wake up from the anesthesia," the doctor said to Ma once everyone settled. "There were a few complications during the surgery that took more time to resolve than we'd anticipated, but it worked out fine, and I expect a full recovery."

Through a wash of relief, Elena noticed how sweaty and tired the doctor looked. His surgical cap was still on his head, but it was a little off-kilter, and a few, sparse curls of silvery-black hair peeped from beneath the green edge of it.

"Can we see him?"

It was Zippy who had spoken from her position near the back. Elena suppressed another little twinge of surprise; normally Zippy liked to be front and center. The doctor looked over the size of the group, the shadow of refusal clear in his expression.

"We can go in a few at a time, if that would be better," Anne said before he could tell them no, offering up a logical solution the way she tended to do.

Finally the doctor nodded, murmuring something to the other green-scrubs-clad person behind him (another doctor? Or maybe one of the nurses who'd assisted in the surgery?). "No more than three visitors at a time and for no more than a few minutes."

"I'll stay back with the kids for now," Anne volunteered.

"I'll wait, too, but Elena ought to go in the first round," Jen offered. "She's got the longest drive home."

Everyone else made quick decisions about who would go in what order of pairs (since Ma would stay there with Pa the whole time), while Elena threw Jen a grateful glance. Jen smiled and blew her a kiss before slipping back into the waiting room with everyone else. In the end Elena and Kat were first in, following Ma and the recovery room nurse, who led them on soft-soled shoes through the hallway and into the surgical area to see Pa.

He was resting in the sturdy white bed with his eyes closed and lots of tubes coming out of both arms. He looked good, considering. He had good color and he was breathing steadily. He opened his eyes and saw them, giving them the barest smile as Ma fussed over him a bit, using the cool washcloth the nurse had handed her as they walked in to smooth over his forehead. When he managed to let them know he was thirsty, she tipped the straw to his mouth for a little sip of water.

Elena got to approach for just a minute, taking hold of his hand. She squeezed, whispering, "Hi, Pa. The doctor said everything went great."

"That's good." His voice was low and croaky, but it was Pa. "Where are your sisters? What time is it?"

"They're out in the waiting room. We can only come in a few at a time. And right now it's four o'clock."

"Lasted all day." He sounded groggily surprised. He tried to move and winced a little with the effort, which brought the nurse over to check his bandages and remind him to keep as still as possible for a while. After she left, another faint smile lifted his expression. "Pretty nurse."

"Oh, Dave." Ma laughed softly. "She already told us what a charmer you are."

"Not too charming right now," he murmured, wincing again.

"Do you want me to have them get you more pain medication, Pa?" Kat asked.

"No, no more." He couldn't seem to talk much at once. He took a couple of hitched breaths and let Kat give him another sip of water before closing his eyes again.

They sat quietly with him for a minute when he suddenly seemed to rouse himself, opening his eyes again to look at them and say, "You've got to drive home in the snow, El. Shouldn't be hanging here too long."

She smiled. "Don't worry, Pa. I won't stay too long. I'm heading out soon so everyone else will have a chance to see you, too," she said, carefully putting her hand on his shoulder where there were no tubes or monitors hooked to him. This was typical Pa: Even half out of it from the anesthesia and pain medication after what ended up being a five-hour surgery, he felt responsible for his family. "I'm really glad everything went so good, though. I'll come back to see you soon, okay?" Leaning down, she gave him a kiss on the cheek. "I love you, Pa."

"Love you, too, Ellie," he said, mustering a smile, though his nod seemed stiff thanks to what he'd been through. "Drive careful."

Letter from Pa to Elena
January 7, 1990

Dear Elena,

Here it is, about eight PM Tuesday night and a broadcast of *Gone with the Wind* is coming on soon. After talking to you on the phone earlier, your mother and I went over to Mr. C's Restaurant across the lake and had a fish fry for supper. The bill was $24, but it was real good food.

We still feel bad about not coming to see you, even though we know that it wouldn't be too smart with the weather the way it is outside. Anyways, that's why I'm writing this, so that we can get something out to you in time for your birthday.

First is the membership in AAA, now that you have your first car. You have to read the stuff, but what it really is is road service (up to six road calls a year). If you have a flat or can't get started, or run out of gas, or any other reason, you can call either the number in Rochester or the 800 number and they will get help for you.

The second is the enclosed check (as you can plainly see) for the car radio we talked about. If you'd rather, you can use the money toward that computer you wanted and then get your radio sometime within the next two months (maybe three and that's it!). In one way I think it's more important for you to have the computer for your writing and work, and in another way I think that for the good of your soul you need a radio. I'm neutral, and your mother says that it should be your choice.

What was it that Scarlett O'Hara said? Tomorrow is another day!? Here are some thoughts about that: You can relive the past but you cannot relive the future. We dumb humans (there is no other kind) get ourselves all screwed up with more than one time base. We are forced to live in the present with minutes and hours and days and years.

Everything is pretty linear, and if we stayed in the present, our lives would pass linearly.

When you are young, you have a little past, the present, and a lot of future. When you are middle-aged, you have a lot of past, the present, and a lot of future. When you get old, you have a real lot of past, the present, and a little future. Notice that the only thing that doesn't change is the present.

When you are young, you waste time looking forward to the future. When you are middle-aged, you waste time looking both to the past and to the future. When you get old, you waste time looking to the past. The problem is that you can look back more than once. There are some moments in my life from many years ago that I probably have spent hours reliving. But those hours were lost to my present, never to be given back to me. It's up to me that any reliving of my past is worth the price of time in the present. Just like I told your mother about Alexandra. It seems that the happier she is, the less she calls home. I hope she is never perfectly happy or we would not hear from her anymore. That's all.

I've come to realize that you can only live ***now***. Don't get hung up on the past or wait for the future.

Living is only for now!

The more that can be true, then the *longer* you live. Think about it awhile.

Running out of room! Happy birthday from your mother and me. I love you, and your mother loves you, and we both love you. That makes four.

Love,

Pa

WGRR FM 103.9, THE BEAR

"Give a Growl for the Adirondacks'
Most Trusted Radio Station"
August 17, 1970

Welcome back, Adirondack listeners. It's Willard T. Boggs here with you on a more comfortable Monday evening in the North Country. After yesterday's heat, it's a relief. The humidity would have done me in without this air conditioning unit the station manager was convinced to put in two summers ago. Marge was jealous until I reminded her of how much satisfaction she took in ripping up my Hawaiian shorts that year. Then she felt a little better.

This Day in History features both an outlaw and a hero. Billy the Kid, who was a teenager at the time, killed his first man in Arizona on this date in 1877, setting off a brief life of crime. The more nobly regarded man in American history today, Davy Crockett, was born in Tennessee on this date in 1786. Our son, Delbert, wore out his coonskin cap, made popular by folktales of Davy's exploits as "King of the Wild Frontier" and of course for sacrificing himself at the Alamo.

Speaking of sacrifice, Moose Junction's Dave Wright saved two swimmers from drowning yesterday at Lake Pines. Mr. Wright was keeping an eye on four of his daughters as they swam with others seeking relief from the heat. He told police he kept counting heads and saw two bob up a few times before vanishing beneath the surface. He dove in without even removing his wallet or his shoes, rescuing both young people who had pulled each other under in a panic after going out too deep. A "WGRReat!" job for his keen attention and selfless actions! It's nice to know there are still some among us willing to risk all to save others.

Chapter Eighteen

The Homestead
Moose Junction, Upstate New York
March 23, 2008

"I'm going to change Violet into her snowsuit and take her outside to run around for a while, El. Want to come?" Max asked, poking his head into the old playroom-turned-office at the back of the house where at the moment Elena was rummaging through coats piled on a chair there.

Even though they'd had a few days in the forties and even one in the fifties this month, in typical late March fashion there were still patches of snow on the ground, and it was cold enough for winter clothing. Elena looked longingly out the window, wishing she could say yes.

She'd always liked the cold, especially the snow. She really wanted to take the girls out snowshoeing, like Pa had done with her when she was young—and she knew Pa would like to come along, too, as another guide for them and to enjoy the woods. But even though he was getting stronger every day since his surgery and he'd begun walking near the lake with Hank on warmer days, he wasn't up to the physical strain of snowshoeing.

Not yet, anyway.

It was just as well. She was too busy to do anything but stay put. The homestead was bursting at the seams with most of her sisters and their families, who had come to Easter dinner (all but Kat and Patricia, who were visiting their spouses' families for the holiday), and she'd been digging through the enormous pile of coats trying to find Jillian's, since she'd left Grandma's present—a ceramic Easter egg she'd painted in Art class—in the pocket. Jillian was thick in the middle of a game of Life upstairs with her cousins, so Elena had volunteered to go look. After that she had to go help with the massive after-dinner cleanup already underway in the kitchen.

So reluctantly Elena told Max to take Violet himself, helping him unearth Violet's snow pants before she got back to her own search. With the puffy purple pants in hand, Max gave her a wink and a quick kiss on the cheek and then headed back into the throng of sisters, brothers-in-law, nieces, and nephews to find Anne, who had been keeping Violet occupied until he could find her snow pants by playing "farm" with the old Fisher Price barn, chickens, fences, and cows the Wright girls had used when they were young.

Smiling to herself, Elena dug through the last layer of coats, finding Jillian's at last. Then, ceramic egg in hand, she headed to the door upstairs, passing through the kitchen as she did. Ma was already at the sink with Jen stacking the dishwasher and drying pans, while Zippy, Lisa, and Melanie (who was visiting the homestead by herself, her kids having gone to spend the holiday with her ex-husband's family) were occupied in putting away leftovers, clearing dishes, removing used linens, and returning cleaned pots to the cupboards.

There had been eighteen at dinner this afternoon, with twelve sitting around the old family table in the kitchen and the remaining six at another smaller "kids'" table set up in the adjoining living room. They'd had the usual abundance of food, too, including an enormous honey-baked ham, candied sweet potatoes, mashed white potatoes, green peas with sautéed mushrooms, butternut squash, string beans, buttered corn, a big casserole dish of cauliflower cheese puff, homemade applesauce, Irish bread, pickles and olives, and cottage cheese rolls.

There was plenty of clean up to do.

Anne was just coming into the kitchen as Max carried Violet out, and Elena called, "Be right there!" to her mother and sisters, as she delivered the ceramic egg to Jillian.

Zippy gave her a glare from where she sat at the table, putting leftover mashed potatoes in a Tupperware container, but Elena didn't think much of it; Zippy seemed to have been in a prickly mood all day. They'd all wondered what was up with her during these last few weeks. Since moving to California when she was eighteen, she'd rarely come home for more than ten days at a time, and no one had expected that she would stay for so long this time, even though she'd been a help during Pa's recuperation.

Jen had caught the look Zippy gave Elena. She raised her brows as if to say, "I have *no* idea," when Elena met her gaze upon her return to the kitchen, having delivered the ceramic egg. Now Elena walked over near the sink to pick up a dishtowel.

"Why don't you let me take over these while you finish stacking?" she said to Jen.

Ma looked up with a smile from scrubbing the roasting pan. "Are you girls going to sing while you clean up, like in the old days?"

"Not likely."

The comment had come from Zippy, who was wearing a pinched expression where she still sat putting away leftovers at the kitchen table. Everyone looked at her.

She seemed to realize how snippy she'd sounded, because she shrugged, looked back down to the lid she was putting on the potatoes, and added, "Well, Kat and Patricia aren't here, so we can't do it like the old days."

Jen's mouth curved into one of her wicked smiles. "It's not like we sang eight part harmony, Zip. We can adjust." She laughed. "Besides, Ma doesn't get the chance to hear our stellar performances very often anymore. Only on holidays, pretty much."

"Then you can adjust to *three* less voices, because my throat is sore," Zipped piped in.

There was a beat of silence, ripe with rising tension that was quintessential of one of Zippy's unexpected snits, but as usual Jen found a way to deflate it a little. She nodded and said (sweetly), "Well, I guess it's important to save your voice for your next big role. You get a pass this time around, sis."

Her teasing earned her another look from Zippy that was sharp enough to draw blood, but Jen went on as if nothing had happened, closing the now full dishwasher and grabbing the soggy dishtowel from Elena. She waved it with a flourish, like a conductor warming up the choir. "Okay, everyone else ready? What should we sing? How about 'On Top of Spaghetti'?"

A few groans and laughs later, and with Ma egging them on, they began singing about the poor, lost meatball that rolled down the hill when somebody sneezed. After that they shifted in a rousing rendition of the gastrically challenged "Harlan Goat."

Zippy kept her lips obstinately clamped shut during both of the songs, continuing to put away leftovers, but not looking quite as sour as she'd been.

That song ended and they were getting ready to begin the crazy mash up of "The Billboard Song" when the back door opened and Max came swinging in with Violet in his arms, both of them red-cheeked from the cold.

"Violet needs the bathroom, Mama." He wore a hopeful expression and smiled, holding her out to Elena. "Will you help me get all the layers off?"

Elena shook her head and laughed, making quick work of undressing Violet, and telling her to scoot off to the bathroom and call Mama or Daddy if she needed any help.

"Thanks, hon," Max murmured, putting one arm around Elena's waist to tug her closer and give her a quick kiss.

"Aw, how sweet," Jen said, patting Max on the shoulder. "So romantic even after all these years. Looks like you took my advice from way back when you were just a college pipsqueak."

"Hey, I had plenty of smooth moves of my own even before you coached me," Max said, laughing softly. He flicked a glance to Elena. "Right, El?"

"Oh, yeah, you were smooth." Elena grinned. "*Very* charming that first time we met." Going up on her tiptoes, she returned the favor with a quick kiss on his cheek, ruffling her fingers through his hair. "And then I made you late for practice so you had to run laps."

The rest of the family had been paying enough attention to smile or chuckle at the easygoing and affectionate banter between the three of them. Everyone except Zippy.

She suddenly stood up, with her back ramrod stiff and her hands in fists at her side as a sound of exasperation burst from her. "Oh, my God, I can't stand another second of this!" With a glare at them all, she took off down the hall toward the little office where the coats were stacked.

They all stood frozen in the wake of her outburst, and Max just looked at Elena in surprise.

Anne shook her head.

"Whoa," Lisa murmured.

"Okaaaay," Melanie said, her brows raised.

"Goodness gracious." Ma dried her hands on a dishtowel and turned from the sink. "What in the world was that all about?"

"Beats me," Jen added with a shrug. "I wasn't even talking to her."

"Maybe your father ought to go in after her. He always knows what to say to help you girls figure things out."

"I don't think Pa's ready to take on Zippy in one of her moods just yet." Elena gave Max's hand a little squeeze. "Besides, he was resting in his chair a little while ago, and that's a good thing for him to do. I'll go."

"Wait a minute." Max tugged her back as she tried to start for the office. "You sure it's a good idea for you to go alone?"

Elena shrugged. "The worse that can happen is that she won't talk to me. I guess then we'll have to come up with plan B."

"I could go in with you, if you think it would help," Jen offered. "You know, to try to even things out in there a little."

Everyone looked at her, confused.

"Oh, come on, everyone knows that when Zippy's upset, she's a force of nature equal to at *least* two regular people." In the resounding silence that followed, Jen lifted her eyebrows and made a funny face. "All right, then. I guess that's only my opinion."

Elena shook her head and smiled. Although decades had come between, when they were younger the effect of Jen's joking on Zippy's moods had always been disastrous. It probably wasn't a great idea to try to mix them together now. Still she nodded acknowledgement of the offer. "Thanks anyway, sis, but I think I'm set."

"All right, Eek." Jen grinned and gave a playful thumbs up for luck as Elena started across the kitchen toward the office. "Then, 'May the force be with you,' because I think you're going to need it!"

(Dinner at the homestead)

The Homestead
Moose Junction, Upstate New York
July 18, 1983
Elena is fourteen years old

Cleanliness is next to Godliness. . . .

Zippy hated them all.

At least that's what she'd just told Elena, Jen, and Patricia before she'd stomped over to the sink to wash the dishes. She'd lost the straw-draw and gotten stuck with the job, which was her least favorite of all the housework because it ruined her manicures and made her hands wrinkly. Now she was bent over a roasting pan, scrubbing and muttering about how stupid it was that any modern family didn't have a dishwasher.

"But we *do*," Elena quipped, reaching the broom under the table to sweep up some crumbs there. "It's the four of us."

"The one of me, you mean." Zippy shot a glare over her shoulder. "You three never do *anything* with the dishes."

"Hey, I resemble that statement," Jen drawled from where she sat at the table, leaning back against the wall with a college brochure propped in front of her before she reached up and stretched with an exaggerated yawn.

"Smartass," Zippy hissed.

"Watch your language." Patricia scowled at her. "You're not old enough to be talking like that!"

"Oh, give me a break! I'm getting my driver's permit in seven months."

"It's not very mature to swear anyway," Elena said, shooting a hot glare back at her.

"Nobody asked you, Miss Goodie Two-Shoes!" Zippy swiveled her head to glower at Elena. "Besides, what do you know? You're just a baby."

"She's only eleven months younger than you," Patricia said.

"Oh, yeah?" Zippy tossed her hair. "Well *you* might be two years *older* than me, Trish, but everyone thinks *I'm* older than *you*!"

"Hardly, pipsqueak," Jen said dryly, with the authority of being the oldest sister present as she curled forward to stand in one fluid movement.

"Don't bother, Jen. It's pointless to talk to her." Patricia opened a drawer in the china cupboard to tuck in a few freshly folded tablecloths and napkins.

Jen shrugged. "I know she's just pouting at losing luck of the draw—" She paused, taking a couple steps forward so that she was directly behind Zippy at the sink, then leaned forward a little, to put her mouth right next to Zippy's ear. "And since that's something only babies do, I'd say that for all her protesting, Zip just proved that she's the *biggest baby* of us all."

Elena cringed.

Even if Jen had just defended her against Zippy's taunt, her comment had been an outright challenge, and they all knew Zippy wouldn't just let it go. Gripping the handle of the broom, Elena held her breath and waited.

It didn't take long.

Rage rippled up Zippy's back, making her stiffen with its progress. And then she exploded.

With a howl of rage, she whirled around from the sink, clutching the retractable sprayer in her right hand; the nozzle's lever was depressed so hard that her fingers had gone bloodless white as she aimed a jet of cold water right into Jen's face.

Jen's shock lasted only a second. With a bellow she launched herself at the now shrieking Zippy, grabbing at her right arm and succeeding in not only getting sprayed again, but also managing to get Patricia and Elena sprayed in the process as well. It was a miracle that the grayish rubber hose of the sprayer didn't rip away from the sink base, the way they struggled over it. Water spurted everywhere, making the floor slippery as Patricia and Elena tried to get a piece of the action, doing what they could to get Zippy to release her death-grip on the nozzle.

When it seemed likely that she was going to be overcome at any second, Zippy made a break for it, abruptly letting go and scrambling past them all down the short hall to barricade herself in the bathroom. Jen was left standing in front of the kitchen sink in shock, holding the dangling sprayer by the hose. Her chest was heaving, and she swiped the back of her hand across her eyes to get her dripping hair out of them, while Elena brushed futilely at her own wet shorts and t-shirt and an equally soaked

Patricia sidestepped a puddle to head toward the cellar door.

"I've had it." Patricia yanked open the door to grab a bucket from where it hung on the wall going down the cellar stairs.

"What's the plan?" Jen's teeth were clenched, the set of her mouth grim.

Elena tamped down her own rekindled fury and fidgeted, struggling to keep her head like she knew she should. "I don't know, you guys. Pa and Ma are going to be home soon. Maybe we'd better—"

"Look, Eek . . . the drama queen has gone too far this time," Jen broke in, taking the bucket from Patricia and jamming it under the faucet to start filling it with cold water. "She's not getting away with it."

Suddenly, they all paused. They could hear the sound of the tub running from inside the bathroom.

"That little shit!" Jen glanced to Elena. "Oh, sorry, Eek. That wasn't too mature."

Elena nodded and pursed her lips. Jen didn't need to say anything else for them all to realize that Zippy was doing the same thing they were: she was filling something—probably the small plastic bin Ma had in the bathroom to store all the shampoo—with water to use in a return attack, likely to facilitate her escape by fleeing either out of the house or upstairs.

Patricia scowled as Jen met her gaze and pointed silently, indicating that Patricia should go into the cupboard to get the big, plastic Kool-Aid pitcher Ma stored up there. As quietly as she could, Patricia got it down and filled it before the two of them moved silently to position themselves, one on either side of the open doorway that connected the kitchen to the little hall where the bathroom was.

Jen motioned for the unarmed Elena to move over toward the kitchen windows, out of the line of fire to act as the lookout. And then they waited in silence, knowing that after a while the quiet would prove too much for Zippy and draw her out of her place of refuge.

It took four minutes and thirty-five seconds to be exact.

The bathroom door creaked open, so slowly none of them were certain they'd heard it opening at all. They remained frozen in their spots, barely breathing.

Another creak, and Zippy took a single step out of the bathroom.

Jen closed her eyes, obviously to listen more closely and count the steps. Four more and Zippy would reach the threshold where Jen and Patricia were hiding. Opening her eyes, she locked her gaze with

Patricia's, both of them mouthing the numbers silently as they readied themselves for the attack.

Two . . . three . . . four!

The kitchen erupted in shouts and great gouts of water flying through the air as Jen and Patricia leapt from their places at the sides of the door and flung the contents of their bucket and pitcher at Zippy at the same time that she retaliated, tossing her water at them (container and all, thanks to her shock at their attack). Zippy was almost knocked onto her backside by the dual waves from either side that caught her square in the face, blinding her and slicking her long hair back so she looked like a seal.

She stood dripping, her mouth open, blinking and trying to see the damage she'd inflicted on Jen and Patricia (which was pretty significant since they were already wet from before, and Zippy's latest missile had caught each of them at least partially). The sound of her Tupperware container clattering to the floor, along with the dripping of the water down the walls, was all that broke the silence after this second battle. That and Patricia's soggy cough.

In the next instant Jen started to laugh, followed by Patricia, who got going so badly she started coughing again at the same time she was laughing and couldn't breathe. When she doubled over and slipped, falling on her side, Zippy finally cracked a smile and started to giggle, too. Pretty soon all three of them were on the floor, laughing so hard they were crying and splashing water from the puddles at each other like they were playing around in a pool.

Elena stood near the window, mouth agape. She didn't know whether to laugh or cry as she looked at the mess all through the kitchen and up the hall.

And then she heard the rumble of tires on the driveway.

She gasped, and her heart dropped to her knees. "Oh, no!"

Craning her neck, she looked out the kitchen window toward the garage, where the automatic door was slowly rising to let in the family station wagon. "Knock it off, you guys! It's Pa and Ma—they're home!"

Jen muttered another (very immature) curse and scrambled to her knees. As the oldest here she was supposed to be in charge, and so she would be the one to catch it most when Pa and Ma walked in to see this kind of disaster. Something had to be done and fast.

Her brain waves must have collided with Patricia's; they both shouted similar commands at the same time.

"Take these, Zippy, and start wiping down the walls!" Jen shouted, rummaging in the cupboard for some rags and shoving a pile of them at her.

"Get over to the sink, Elena!" Patricia ordered. "You're the least soaked. Finish up the dishes and act like you've been doing it the whole time."

Patricia grabbed one of the mops while Jen took the other and the bucket, and they both started mopping up the puddles on the floor as if their lives depended on it.

Zippy seemed suddenly cooperative as the four of them started working together double-time to avoid Pa lowering the boom and grounding them all for being so childish as to physically fight with each other.

"This was intentional, got it?" Jen called in a stage whisper, beginning to mop down the hall furiously as they heard the screen door swing open and the back doorknob turn. "We wanted to—*surprise* them by cleaning the whole kitchen, even the floors and walls!"

The door opened. Pa walked in, carrying a box of paper towels he'd bought in bulk at the store, followed by Ma, who had several bags in her arms.

They stopped just inside the door, taking in the state of the kitchen, with water still pooled on the floor and dripping down the knotty pine wall where Zippy hadn't gotten to it yet, watching their four youngest (waterlogged) daughters exuding more energy than a class of kindergarteners on Halloween.

Pa cleared his throat. "Hello, girls."

A chorus of sunny "Oh, hi, Pa!" and "Hello, Ma!" greetings rang back at him.

Jen leaned on the handle of her mop and paused, flashing them a smile that Elena was sure rivaled the best performance Zippy had ever played at the North Country Community Theater stage. "We didn't know you'd be home so early! We were going to surprise you, since we—um—decided to do a complete cleaning of the whole kitchen *and* hallway, instead of just our normal chores after lunch. But we'll be done in a few minutes, don't worry."

The moment would have been perfect, except for the fact that Patricia managed at that very second to slip again and almost went down (since her feet were bare and it was still really slick behind the kitchen table). Her snafu made Zippy break into another peal of laughter where she stood nearby, still wiping down the walls. She stopped only when Patricia surreptitiously elbowed her and kept mopping, swinging her wet hair out of her eyes and smiling innocently at Pa and Ma after she did.

Elena glanced at Pa since she was standing right next to him, and her heart sank. Oh, no. He knew. She could tell by the look on his face.

But wait a minute. . . .

She caught his gaze, and his blue eyes had a twinkle in them. She saw Ma glance at him, too, and raise her brows, a smile teasing at her lips. It was clear that she was trying to look stern, but she was losing the battle, and in the next moment she scurried with her bags through the kitchen, going into the living room and beyond that to the door of their first floor bedroom, making some kind of muffled noises as she went.

Pa cleared his throat again, gazing at the four of them. "I'm glad to see the four of you working so well together."

He set down the box of paper towels on the counter. "I'm going in the other room to organize today's receipts with your mother, but I'll come out and inspect your work in here later." His eyes twinkled again, the lilting undertone in his voice betraying him just a little. "Be sure to wax and buff the walls after you mop, so the water you've been cleaning with doesn't leach into the wood and ruin it. The wax is under the sink."

Then he nodded at them and flashed one of his handsome smiles, before shaking his head and following Ma on her path of retreat, leaving them all to sigh in relief.

As they got back to work, they didn't have to speak; each was thanking her lucky stars that waxing the kitchen floor and polishing the walls were the only consequences after the crazy fighting—and fun—they'd just enjoyed. Elena looked around at her sisters, busy with their tasks. Only Jen had stopped mopping to come over and pick up the box of paper towels to carry it to the cellar, and as she went by Elena, she gave her a wink and a grin.

Smiling, too, Elena reached into the dishpan to finish scrubbing the pot Zippy had abandoned, rinsing it and putting it in the drainer to dry before leaning over and opening the doors under the sink in search of the wax, humming a happy little tune all the while.

Chapter Nineteen

The Homestead
Moose Junction, Upstate New York
March 23, 2008

When Elena walked into the playroom-turned-office to try to see what had made Zippy storm out of the kitchen a few minutes ago, she found her huddled on the loveseat in the corner, her arms wrapped around her knees and her face hidden. There were no sounds coming from her, however—no crying or sniffling.

Elena closed the door behind her. It seemed strange to see her glamorous older sister curled up in a ball like this. While it was true that they hadn't seen each other often in the past two decades, the last time Elena could remember Zippy acting so upset was just after high school graduation, when Pa and Ma had told her she couldn't leave for California until she had two thousand dollars saved, a reliable roommate to travel with, and contact information in hand for a job agency in Los Angeles.

"What are you doing in here?" Zippy's voice was muffled but still sharp and hard as an ice pick. "Just leave me alone."

"I came in to see if you're all right, Alex." Elena maintained a neutral tone, knowing better than to use her sister's nickname right now. She walked a few steps closer. "Ma's concerned. We all are. None of us has any clue what upset you out there."

"Oh, give me a break!" Zippy lifted her head from her arms, her beautiful eyes red-rimmed and her expression uncharacteristically pinched. "Perfect Elena sent in to comfort the drama queen, right? I know what everyone out there thinks of me. Admit it! You just came in here to gloat."

"What the heck are you talking about?"

Zippy made a sound of exasperation, mixed with a bitter laugh, and jerked her hands in the air. "See that? You *still* won't use a curse word! Goodie Two-Shoes until the end."

Elena scowled. "Are you really going to resort to throwing stupid insults around?"

"I don't know! Are you going to stop flaunting how perfect you are in front of me all the time?"

Elena's temper spiked, then, and she snapped. "Oh, get off it, Alex! *You're* the movie star everyone fawns over. If anyone's in danger of thinking they're perfect, it's not me—it's you!"

When Zippy refused to meet her gaze, Elena forced herself to pause, trying to rein in her annoyance. She wasn't a little kid anymore. She needed to remember what was really important here and not let herself get sidetracked by childish hurts and rivalries.

Clenching her jaw, she breathed in through her nose and let it out through her mouth. Then she tried one last time. "You know, Alex, once a long time ago you helped me out when I was in a really bad place in my life. You went out on a limb to be there for me."

Zippy finally shifted her gaze to Elena.

"I've never forgotten it." Elena crossed her arms over her chest. "So I'm going to go out on a limb with you now. I don't know what I, or any of us, did to upset you out there, but I'm sorry. No one meant to make you feel bad. If you tell me what it is, I'll do what I can to make sure it doesn't happen again."

Something seemed to deflate in Zippy, then; she lowered her feet to the floor and leaned her head back against the top of the loveseat, her hands coming down to rest on the seat cushion. "Oh, my God, this is so *stupid*! I don't know what the hell is wrong with me."

"If you'll just tell me what's going on, maybe I can—"

"Look, Elena, there's nothing you can do unless you can somehow stop being . . . *you*." Zippy gritted her teeth, releasing her breath in a kind of hissing growl before thumping her fist on the cushion. Rolling her head to the side, she looked at Elena. "Shit, I *am* a prima donna pain in the ass, aren't I?"

Elena gave her a wry smile. "You really want me to answer that?"

Shaking her head and sighing, Zippy patted the cushion and Elena came over to sit. After a few seconds, during which they both had a chance to get their emotions in check a little better, Elena asked gently, "So?"

"Yeah, well, like I said, the possibility of you helping me is pretty remote unless you have some kind of magic wand—" Zippy interrupted herself with a bitter laugh, "or you can find some way to trade lives with me."

"Trade *lives* with you?" Elena leaned back against the loveseat, too, a half smile teasing her lips. "Hmm . . . that's an idea. Riding around in limos, visiting exotic locales, going to fancy parties, having enough money to buy designer clothes, and get my hair and makeup done by experts . . . yeah, I could probably rough that out for a while."

Zippy smiled a little, too, before her expression turned more serious again. "It's not all it's cracked up to be."

"I believe you." Elena looked at her sister. "But the bigger question is why you'd even be thinking about giving up everything you've worked so hard for after all these years?"

Zippy's mouth tightened. "Maybe I wish I could just be . . . normal for a while."

"*Normal*?"

"You know, living the perfect life like you, with three great kids and a man who adores you."

Elena laughed, then. "I hate to break it to you, but as much as I love my life, the perfect part is way off—and also probably way different from what you're used to these days. Most of the time I feel like a combination of short-order cook, taxi service, cleaning lady, argument negotiator, and life coach. And somehow I don't see you enjoying Bargain Trims Hair Salon, or buying your clothes from stores with names that end in the word 'mart.' That's just the tip of the iceberg, but you get the idea."

Zippy mustered a weak smile. "Well, when you put it that way . . ." But as her voice faded, her façade broke, and she looked away, pinching the bridge of her nose. "Oh, hell, I don't know who I'm trying to kid. Even with all that, it's been looking pretty good to me these past few weeks."

Elena paused. *Wow*. This was the last thing she would have imagined Zippy feeling. Ever.

"Look, you've been home for a lot longer of a time than usual this trip," Elena began gently, reaching out to take her sister's hand. "It's a big lifestyle change, and you've been helping out here 24/7 while Pa's been recovering. You're probably just tired. It's like the old saying: 'The grass is always greener.' Nothing is ever all good or bad."

Zippy shrugged.

Elena pressed her lips together, wanting to find a way to reach her.

"You know, I remember when you first left for California. I used to worry that the Hollywood machine would chew you up and spit you out. But the opposite happened. You went out there, reached for the brass ring, and got it with both hands."

"Maybe."

"You were never one to settle for what was conventional, Alex. You've always thrived on excitement and travel and the public eye. The spotlight loves you, and you've always loved it. So what gives now?"

Zippy gave a kind of hopeless laugh before squeezing Elena's hand and letting go, rolling off the loveseat to walk over and look out to the yard through the single window in the room. "What gives, little sister, is that I'm forty years old."

Elena frowned. "What does that have to do with anything?"

"I'm not a hot young thing anymore. The roles are drying up."

"But didn't you finish a movie right before Pa's surgery?"

"That was just a cameo. A spoof Miramax is making on *Agency*, which was my first starring role if you want to talk about irony." She glanced at Elena, her expressive face showing uncharacteristic weariness and maybe even worry. "Except for that job, though, it's been a whole year of nothing but low budget stuff. I've *never* gone this long without at least one decent offer."

"Have you talked to your agent? What does he have to say?"

"Larry said there's nothing out there right now." Zippy's jaw tightened. "He's trying to be supportive, but yesterday he reminded me that it's a lot harder for women actors of a certain age to sell tickets at the box office."

"Tell that to Sandra Bullock or Jodie Foster."

"They're A-listers—and Jodie is a director, too. It's a little different."

"You're an A-lister!"

"I haven't been in an A-list movie in five years. Hell, it's getting to the point where I'm going to be lucky to get a job in a film that goes straight to DVD." Zippy's beautiful eyes sparked again with the kind of fire Elena was more accustomed to seeing from her. "I have to face it; my career is going down the tubes faster than a bobsled team in the Winter Olympics."

Elena didn't know what to say, and so she stayed quiet. But her stomach dropped to think of how anyone, especially someone like Zippy, who tended to be emotionally volatile, could handle such a capricious change of fortune.

Sighing again, Zippy tipped her chin up, breathing in and closing her eyes as if trying to ground herself. "Before I came home, I could see the writing on the wall. Larry convinced me that taking a break to be with the family would be a good idea, especially since Ma and Pa needed the help. And I thought a little space would be good, and that I was keeping it all in perspective." Flopping down on the loveseat again, she gave Elena a sardonic smile. "Clearly, I need to spend a little more time in my therapist's chair."

Elena handed her one of the decorative pillows from both sides of the loveseat. "Here, hug on this while we talk. I don't know why it helps in serious conversations, but it just does."

"Uh, thanks." Zippy gave her a funny look, squeezing the pillow. "I guess it's cheaper than the $250 an hour I pay my shrink."

Elena hugged the other pillow and nodded.

"It looks like I'm just going to have to accept that I'm a has-been," Zippy said. "I never thought I'd say that, but there it is."

"Oh, come on." Elena hit her lightly with her pillow. "Now you really *are* sounding like a drama queen."

Zippy made a huffy sound, but Elena kept going. "You can at least consider your options until you sort the rest of this out. Do you have enough money to take a hiatus?"

"I might be spoiled in some ways, especially compared to how most *normal* people live," Zippy gave Elena a pointed look, "but I'm not an idiot. I listened to Pa and Ma about saving for a rainy day, and I have enough to get by for now."

"Good." Elena really meant it, too. "It gives you room to maneuver. So what else do you think you'd want to try for a while instead of movies?"

Zippy gave a rueful half laugh. "Um . . . the *normal* life thing, remember? I'm just a couple decades late in trying to start it." Her eyes glittered with sadness and humor. "Not to mention that I don't have a man in my life to even start working on the kids part."

Elena tried to be encouraging. "That's only *one* option. Try to think about some other possibilities, too."

"That's the problem. I've never wanted to do anything *except* act." Zippy kept clutching her pillow.

"Maybe it's time for a new goal."

Zippy shook her head. "There's just a big blank when I try to think of doing anything else. I was always an actress first, and everything else was second, third, or fourth." Her eyes welled, and she swallowed hard, adding in a whisper, "Oh, my God, I can't believe I just said that in the past tense."

Elena sat in silence for a minute, mulling over everything her sister had said. She might not be as experienced or well traveled as Zippy, but she still knew something about the world and how limiting artificial boundaries could be. It just seemed so unfair to her that they were being applied now to her fiery, spectacular, talented sister. Zippy was a born actress. Anyone who had ever met her, even when she was a kid, had recognized that right off the bat.

Hugging her own pillow tighter, she focused her gaze on Zippy again. "Look, I don't know what the right answers are going to be, Alex, but I'm just going to put something out there. Maybe you *shouldn't* stop acting if that's what you love. But maybe you can try to do a different kind of acting for a while, like on stage or something. You're talented, and you're still as gorgeous as ever. Age is just a stupid number. If Hollywood wants to push you aside for something so stupid," Elena cocked her chin at a defiant angle, "well, then, I hope you'll tell them where they can go."

Zippy actually laughed. "Hell, if I'd realized what an ego-booster you could be, I'd have worked harder to piss you off earlier."

"Yeah, well, I'd be more than happy to tell anyone out in Tinseltown what I think."

"I'm not so sure they could handle you." She gave Elena a grateful look. "But I'm really glad to know you'd do that for me."

"I've got your back, sis. We all do. It's one of the things our family does pretty well, when we're not at each other's throats."

Zippy laughed and held out her arms to Elena, who leaned in as they gripped each other in a fierce, warm hug.

But they were interrupted by a knock at the door, followed by a muffled voice from behind it that was clearly Jen's, calling out in her usual, teasing way, "White flag alert! I have an important message to deliver, but I don't want to risk my life to do it."

Zippy and Elena looked at each other at the same time; Elena saw the mischievous glint in her sister's eyes and grinned back at her.

The door began to open, but they didn't answer, instead nodding at each other in silent agreement as they slowly lifted their pillows high above their heads. . . .

Jen's voice sounded louder as she kept talking, while the door began to swing away from her and into the room. "Zippy's cell phone is driving everyone crazy! It's been ringing off the—"

Just as she came into view, Elena and Zippy shouted a laughing war cry and hurled their overstuffed weapons like they were kids again, their perfect aim catching poor, unsuspecting Jen square in the head.

WGRR FM 103.9, THE BEAR

"Give a Growl for the Adirondacks'
Most Trusted Radio Station"
April 1, 1960

Welcome back, Adirondack listeners. It's Willard T. Boggs here with you on a downright cold Tuesday afternoon in the North Country. March went out like a lamb, but you'd never know it today. The outdoor thermometer barely climbed above freezing. Marge had already put away my long johns for the season or I'd be wearing them. I'm not one to say, 'I told you so,' Marge, but it appears I won our bet. A slice of your famous banana cream pie sure would be a nice prize.

I'll have plenty of time to eat it because this is my last day at the station. I'm on to greener pastures, having tendered my resignation to the manager this morning. . . . April Fool's! Oh, yes, On This Day in History back in 1700, a group of pranksters across the pond decided to play some tricks on each other. The practice stuck, and here we are today. Make sure no one puts salt instead of sugar in your coffee like our receptionist, Doris, did to me a few minutes ago.

One place I can assure you there were no tricks this morning was at the top end of Black River, where eighteen men tossed in lines, braving the chill to open trout season. Placing first and second respectively in nabbing the biggest rainbow trout were longtime friends Dave Wright and Hank Steiner, who hail from Moose Junction. Mr. Wright said he's been fishing since he could hold a pole, but he usually tries his hand in remoter creeks or lakes farther north. Today, he made an exception since Hank had a good feeling about it. Looks like he was right and they'll be enjoying their prize trout while I'm enjoying my pie!

Salmon River
Upstate New York
April 1, 1995
Elena is twenty-six years old

Don't judge a book by its cover. . . .

As the sun climbed higher, it cast pleasant warmth on the rocks all along the edge of the secluded length of river where Pa and Elena stood fishing in companionable silence. It had been warmer than usual this past week, with temperatures climbing near seventy degrees. The surge of nice weather had melted the remnants of snow from the riverbanks and set the stage for a perfect opening day for trout anglers everywhere upstate.

She was just glad no one else seemed to know about *this* spot.

Elena studied the place where her line dipped under the surface of the water and tested the pull, judging the difference between the tension caused by river flow and that of a potential bite. Although they'd started later in the morning, when fish were warmed a little by the sun and more active, those in these waters had been sluggish and apparently not interested in feeding. In the first hour, Pa had snagged a nine-inch brownie, but other than that, neither of them had had any luck.

It didn't matter. Elena loved these times of quiet and peacefulness with Pa, whether or not they caught any fish. On family trips up to camp, he'd taught his girls his best techniques, from baiting the line to safely removing a hooked fish, but Elena's affinity for it had lasted well beyond childhood.

She and Pa had gone together to lakes, streams, rivers, or ponds at least once every year since, setting off from the homestead together when she still lived there, and then after she'd gotten married, meeting at a selected spot to spend the morning together with their lines in the water and nature all around them.

Today was one of those days.

Max had volunteered to take over with eighteen-month-old Claire for the day. That gave Elena plenty of time to meet up with Pa, stop by the homestead for a visit with Ma afterward, and then head home in time to make supper. She and Pa usually sat together and fished for the first few hours without saying much. As the time wore on, they might talk over whatever was on their minds. It didn't matter; it all was restorative for her.

The breeze lifted through the branches, setting off a fluttering chorus of fresh new leaves to back the rising hum of insects and gentle gurgles of the river. The sun glinted off the water, warming everything it touched, and Elena breathed in the damp, earthy fragrance, exhaling and letting out all the anxiety and buildup of stress accumulated in a life spent hurrying from one task to the next.

"Sounds like it's been a long week."

"More like a long *month*." Elena kept her voice soft, just as Pa had. He had taught her long ago that every living thing has its own natural tendencies, and fish were sensitive to the vibrations set off by movement or even the timbre of human voices. "It feels good to get outside again and spend some time with you. Thanks for suggesting it on the phone the other night."

"I'm glad we were able to do it." Pa smiled. "Besides, there aren't too many old men who can say their twenty-something-year-old daughters are still willing to go places and do things with them."

Elena smiled back. They didn't need to say anything more. She knew some thought she was strange for enjoying this kind of time with Pa or similar times (only baking or cooking) with Ma, but she didn't care. When you understood another person at that elemental level, it made perfect sense. Besides, as far as she was concerned, too many people worried about how things *looked* more than how they really *were*; she'd chosen to live life according to reality as she saw it. That wasn't about to change, no matter how old she got.

She took another deep breath, soaking in the beautiful surroundings and the sense of peace that filled her. She didn't think the moment could be any more perfect, but then Pa took a step back and began reeling in his line with the smooth motion that let her know there was no catch on the other end.

He turned his head to look at her. "It's just about noon. What do you say we take a break for lunch?"

"That sounds good." Elena began to reel in her line as well, reaching to take her worm off the hook before tossing it into the water. "We could go to the Kayuta Drive-In for a hamburger and milkshake if you want. My treat."

"No need." Pa's eyes twinkled as he went through the same process with his worm and then clipped the empty hook onto a threading ring of his left-handed "Shakespeare" fishing pole. "It's warm enough today that I thought it might be nice to have lunch outside, right here on the riverbank."

Elena looked at him, not sure where he was going with this. Did he mean get takeout and come back here, or what?

In the next second she got her answer.

He walked over to the cooler he'd carried down to the water. It had held their sealed containers of earthworms to keep them cool, but she hadn't really paid attention to what else was in it. Pa reached in to retrieve a plastic sack, then opened it and started taking out the items: a couple of cellophane-wrapped but obviously homemade submarine sandwiches, a bag of potato chips, two apples, and two bottles of orange soda. He followed it up by taking out a few napkins and two plastic cups (because he'd been raised to believe it was more polite for everyone, especially ladies, to drink from a glass instead of from a bottle).

"Wow!" Elena came over to sit by him on the rocks. "Did Ma put all this together for us?"

"No." Pa had that same twinkle in his blue eyes that he always got when he was enjoying something—or had a little surprise. "*I* did." He handed her one of the sandwiches; it looked delicious, with layers of ham, salami, provolone cheese, lettuce, and a little mustard.

"Oh, my . . . thanks, Pa." In all her life growing up, she'd never known Pa to cook or prepare any food, with the exception of grilling steaks or chicken or putting some frozen vegetables in the microwave. She was bowled over. Just when she'd thought she knew him, he went and did something totally unpredictable.

"Go ahead." He gestured for her to start eating as he poured their drinks and set them on the flat rock in front of them. "I'll have mine in a minute."

She took a bite of the sandwich. It was even more delicious than it had looked. Unbelievably good, in fact; better than any sandwich *she* had ever made. She chewed and swallowed before gazing at him, flabbergasted. "This is amazing!"

"You sound surprised." He'd taken a bite of his sandwich, too, washing it down with a swig of his soda.

"Well, yeah. I didn't know you knew how to do this kind of thing."

Pa smiled. "I haven't needed to do much cooking with your mother around, but I can be pretty self-sufficient." He handed her the bag of chips and one of the apples. "Even back when I was a kid, my brothers and I would catch a few fish over at Bill Hill's pond, roast them over an open fire, and then snitch a melon or two from the farmer's field up the road to make a meal of it. It was during the Depression, and that farmer was nice enough to look the other way once in a while to let us kids have a treat. Then I went into the Marines and they gave me a few more skills, and now here we are."

Elena nodded. "I remember you telling me some of those stories from when you were a kid, but I don't remember you *ever* making sandwiches like this when I was growing up. This is probably the best one I've ever had!"

Pa laughed aloud at that, the sound warm as it rumbled from his chest. "I can't take all the credit. Eating outdoors makes everything taste better." His eyes crinkled in the corners with that twinkle still shining in them. "Your father managing to surprise you might have something to do with it, too."

She grinned. "You sure did. This is a perfect lunch on a perfect day."

"Every day has something beautiful in it, but I agree. This one is especially nice. Spending it together makes it even nicer."

"Thanks, Pa."

"No, Ellie, thank *you*."

They fell silent again, wrapped in good feelings and the warm springtime sunlight. They continued to eat their simple picnic lunch together, looking up at the blue sky and wispy white clouds, hearing the river burbling along and the robins and chickadees singing in the trees as the breeze fluttered and swished through the new leaves . . . knowing that this was one of those perfect moments in life that would linger in their memories forever.

(Fishing spot along the river)

Letter from Pa to Elena
June 20, 1995

Dear Elena,

Here's a little story for you, since you wanted to hear more about when I joined the Marines. It's also about how I met Hank, about perfect moments, and about beautiful music, so you have to be patient to get there from here!

I left my home in Western Massachusetts when I reached the age of seventeen. I had been working in my father's bowling alley setting pins, almost in slave labor. I had never been to a dance or a sports event in high school and as you can imagine, I had a very limited view of the world. I joined the Marine Corps.

I met my lifelong friend on a train between New York City and Washington, DC, the last day of January in 1947. We were both on the train, going to the Marine Corps Recruit Depot for basic training at Paris Island, South Carolina. Hank Steiner was coming in from Saginaw, Michigan, and I was coming in from upstate New York.

We were both assigned to Recruit Platoon 24 for training. After boot camp, as luck would have it, Hank and I were two of only four privates out of our entire platoon who were assigned to report to Camp Del Mar, California, for training as communications specialists. Hank and I were assigned to radio school and the other two guys were assigned to telephone wire communications school.

After we learned to set up and use various tactical radios and Teletype equipment and became qualified Morse code operators, we had to go into the mountains and implement actual operational use of the radio equipment. The entire radio school class spent two weeks operating all the equipment, sometimes communicating between mountains or other tactical locations. Sometimes we went out with portable radios and set them up for reporting various battle scenarios. Of course all of this was with each team carrying the equipment from position to position on our backs. If we got back to the base camp at night, we'd get a hot meal cooked from an open mess tent, but most days we ate C-rations on the move.

After a week of trudging around in the California hills, they gave us a Sunday off to rest and recuperate. Hank and I wanted to show them that they couldn't beat us, so the two of us climbed a nearby mountain that Sunday!

All of the above is just background to set the stage for you to get the feeling for the real reason for this story!

On that Sunday, we got back to base camp in time for evening chow, and as usual, we just sat on some makeshift tables and ate out in the wide open spaces. Somebody mentioned that they were going to show a movie after dark, and later they set up a large screen on one hillside where the Marines could sit on an opposing hillside for a great view of the movie. You also have to understand that after having gone through boot camp and radio school side by side, Hank and I were true brothers in arms.

We walked up the hillside and found a great location to watch the movie just before dusk. It was one of those clear, warm evenings with a cool breeze coming in from the coast. We laid back and looked up at a blue sky in the fading light of the day. Soon, a few stars were visible, and even though the movie hadn't started, we had a movie just looking up into the unfolding picture in the sky. It was as if you could just reach up and pick any one of the million stars. Just take your choice. I didn't know much about Hank's background, but we both seemed to sense the perfection of just being there after climbing that mountain and having a hot meal and the feeling of complete freedom out there in the middle of nowhere.

It got a little darker and they started the movie. It was a musical and right from the beginning was most enjoyable.

Well into the movie, which until then had very good piano music, the title song started playing, and I'll never forget the moment.

It was dark by now. The sound came across the hillside and seemed to just fill the air. The stars were just glittering in the crystal-clear night air and the music playing was a piano composition. There is no way to describe the freedom and beauty and the camaraderie of those minutes of perfection, when everything in the world was as good as life could ever be! I have never heard a more perfect song in a more perfect setting with better friends than I did that night. The movie was the story of George Gershwin, and the song was "Rhapsody in Blue."

Love,

Pa

Chapter Twenty

Lake Pines' Palisades Path
Moose Junction, Upstate New York
April 1, 2008

By ten o'clock in the morning on the first day of trout season, Dave and Hank had already been fishing, gone back to the homestead, and come back out again. The weather was finer than usual for this time of year, warm and sunny, so Elizabeth and the girls hadn't even made a fuss about their plans to head out at dawn today.

It had been just like the old days, the two of them sitting on the side of the stream, their poles propped beside them, sharing a thermos of coffee and enjoying the pink and gold rays of dawn reaching over the horizon. The peace had been broken only by birdsong, the chirruping of insects, and the swishing of their lines whenever they cast into the stream in front of them.

The beauty of fishing had never gotten old for Dave; he could still remember the sense of wonder he'd felt as a kid when he realized the bounty of nature. It was like magic. Using nothing more than a string with a hook, a worm, and some skill, he could cast in a line and bring out food, free of charge. During the Great Depression, that was no small thing. It had felt like a kind of miracle to him, and it remained one of the ways he'd enjoyed connecting with God's creation ever since.

This morning he and Hank had caught three rainbow trout. After bringing them back to the homestead to clean and refrigerate, they'd had some breakfast and another cup of coffee before Hank had suggested taking a walk along the palisades to enjoy the beautiful weather before he had to head back to Towers after lunch.

Dave had been glad to go back out; he'd been feeling stronger every week since the surgery, and Hank, too, while a little tired lately, had seemed to be happier and enjoying himself more than any of them had seen since before Gladys died.

They'd meandered along the palisades path until they'd nearly reached the dam that contained the southern edge of Lake Pines and fed into the river below. As they walked, they'd stopped here and there to look at some of the new growth sprouting after the long, harsh upstate winter.

Spring was Dave's favorite time of year. It could be muddy and a little gray sometimes, but it was also a fresh start filled with possibilities. Nature was on her way back in, stretching out, waking up, unfurling leaves and flowers, and coming back to life with color, moist scents of rain-dampened earth, and sounds of birds, animals, and insects.

Today it was punctuated by the noise of people as well.

The mild weather had drawn other walkers to the path, most of them coming up from the dam where there was a parking area for convenience. He and Hank had already passed a few groups of teens, one older couple, and three families. For the past few minutes, though, they'd enjoyed an open, empty stretch of the trail. Dave realized that was about to end when he heard the sound of laughter up ahead.

"Sounds like more kids." Hank gestured toward the sounds, even though they couldn't see anyone yet.

"It's that kind of day." Dave usually enjoyed solitude and quiet more than crowds, but on a spring morning like this, he'd known what to expect and just rolled with it. "I guess everyone has spring fever."

Pretty soon the source of the laughter came into view far down the trail. A woman with two young children, a boy and a girl, was coming their way. The woman was talking on her cell phone, and it was the kids who were making the noise, shouting and giggling as the girl skipped ahead of the boy, who was trying to catch her. The two were no more than five years old, and they were darting back and forth on the path like kids tend to do when they have a little freedom. They weren't really paying attention to their surroundings, and Dave's instincts snapped into place, making him glance around to gauge potential danger.

In the next instant, though, the woman had pulled the phone away from her ear at the same time that she said something sharp to the kids. Although they were too far away to hear anything distinct, Dave could tell from her tone of voice and the gestures she was making that she was cautioning them away from the path's edge.

On the lake side the path was flanked by an embankment that fell off at a pretty steep incline, especially the nearer you got to the dam. For most of the path's entire distance, trees provided a natural barrier, but this far along, the growth was sparser. He'd always thought the city should put in a fence or low wall up along this particular stretch, but he supposed that would have marred the view.

Dave let out his breath the rest of the way as the woman took both kids by the hand and tugged them next to her. At least there were still some adults out there with their brains in gear.

He'd always taken his job as a father seriously, even though the way he accomplished that had required adjustment through different stages of life. Being responsible meant you did whatever was necessary to keep your children safe, whether that was teaching them to be wary of their surroundings and respond to his issued command without question, or when they were older, to value and use money wisely and try to choose friends and boyfriends who could be counted on and trusted.

When the kids were small, he'd even taken up the practice of counting heads as they played outside or went swimming, checking that everyone was accounted for. It was that force of habit that had helped him spot and save those teens at the lake all those years ago when they'd nearly drowned after getting caught by the sudden drop off ten yards from shore.

"Good golly, will you take a look at that?"

Hank had stopped walking when he spoke, and Dave stopped, too, swiveling his attention to his friend. Hank looked through the sparser trees on their right at the clear view they now had of the gushing water flowing over the dam. "That's the fastest I've seen the water run in a long time."

"It's moving pretty good. It was an old-fashioned winter. All that snow melt had to go somewhere."

"Makes quite a show." Hank shook his head. "It's loud, too. I'll bet there's some hungry fish down where the water's all stirred up." Hank pointed to a smaller dirt path below them. "What's that? I don't remember there ever being a way to get that close to the base." The trail led from the parking area toward the churning pool created by the water spilling over and down the smooth, sloping gray structure of the dam.

"They put that in the fall before last. I walked down there a couple times with Elizabeth and Elena to get a better look after it was first opened. Never saw any fish, though, even in the eddy. "

Hank took another look, tilting his head. “Maybe we should throw a line in and give it a try, after the ground dries out a little more.”

“I don’t know. If the past two springs hold true, every Joe Blow in town will be piling up on that same spot. It’s an advertised, public fishing hole.”

“What a shame.”

“I think we’d have better luck going to our old spot up on Cincinnati Creek. It’s been a few years since I was there, though it may be posted now.”

“Seems like all the good spots are either overcrowded or private.”

Dave nodded, taking a breath of the sweet spring air. “I guess that’s one of the constants in life. That nothing stays the—”

Their conversation was interrupted by a terrified shriek from the woman up the path, and they turned to see what was wrong. Her little boy had freed himself from her grip and was scrambling after a chipmunk on the trail . . . but the chipmunk had skittered over the steep edge on the lake side of the path, and the boy looked like he was too focused on it to notice. The little girl screamed, too, and then started crying as the boy tried to stop but instead slid and tumbled headlong over the edge, disappearing from sight.

By the time Dave and Hank covered the distance to get to them, the woman was already kneeling at the side of the path, trying to keep the little girl back as she reached toward the boy with one hand, with her phone still in the other, holding it to her ear. From what they could hear, it sounded like she was calling emergency services. A couple steps more and Dave could see the boy lying on his stomach some ten feet down the muddy, rocky bank.

The incline at that point was probably the steepest on the whole trail, but somehow the kid had managed to skid to a stop. His forehead was bleeding pretty bad, and he and some smeared dirt mixing with the blood on his face and all over his light-colored jacket. He cried as he stretched up toward his mother, but every time he tried to get his feet under him, the mud acted like grease, causing him to slide a little farther down.

“Stay still, Tommy!” The woman sounded frantic as she crammed the phone into her pocket. She swiveled her head toward Dave and Hank as they approached, her expression anguished. “I don’t know what to do! I called 9-1-1, but they said it’s going to take them a few minutes to—”

“It’s all right, ma’am,” Hank broke in, patting her arm, “We’ll try to help you until then." He sounded a little breathless, but he managed to get down on one knee at the edge of the trail, keeping his artificial leg propped up as he waited for Dave, who got down to business on the other side of the trail looking for anything they could use to help Tommy get up the embankment again.

"Just try to stay still," Dave called down to the boy as he moved into position in front of Hank. He'd used his pocketknife to cut a long branch of green oak, deciding it was better to have something live and flexible rather than a dried out stick that might snap at the wrong time.

The little girl and the woman had gone quiet as Dave put his right foot over the trail edge and dug it sideways into the dirt and rocks for leverage. Hank reached from behind to hold onto him and provide stability, while Dave leaned over as far as he could and dangled the branch down to the boy, urging him to take hold of it.

Tommy's cries quieted in response to Dave's calm, authoritative voice. "Grab onto it and then put your foot sideways like mine," he coaxed, nodding and pulling backward with Hank as a counterbalance to the boy's weight, as he began to do what Dave was asking of him. Tommy gripped the branch and slowly placed his feet, trying to make his way up the incline.

"That's it. Smooth and steady."

Sweat broke out on Dave's face after the first minute. His back and legs ached, and his arms felt tight from the unusual exertion, but it couldn't be helped. He just kept breathing deeply and trying to focus on the boy.

"Just a couple steps more." He kept pulling the branch back with methodical, hand-over-hand movements as Tommy made his way up. His mother, who was standing behind them, offered encouragement and moved nearer to the edge as the boy came closer.

One more step. Then Dave was able to reach out and grab the boy's arms, hauling him up to safety at last, where he collapsed into his mother's welcoming embrace. Both of them were crying and holding each other tight, with the little girl joining in, too, in the way that even the most competitive siblings will if one of them is threatened with danger of some kind.

Letting the branch go now, Dave let out his breath and sank back on his heels. He panted from exertion, but smiled as relief sank in. "All's well that ends well . . . except I'm really feeling my age about now. How about you, Hank?"

But Hank remained silent.

It wasn't like his lifelong friend not to answer a direct question, so Dave twisted his head to look at him. Hank was still on one knee behind him, where he'd been during the rescue, but Dave felt his gut wrench when he saw Hank's pasty complexion.

"Dave. . . ." Hank's voice was low and gravelly. "I—I think something's wrong." He shook his head a little, his breathing shallow and his words sounding thick, like he had cotton in his mouth. "I can't . . ."

"Hold on a second, Hank. Let me get myself turned around," Dave said, thinking his friend might be feeling lightheaded after the adrenaline surge from the rescue. But he had barely maneuvered to face him before Hank made a horrible gasping sound.

"Easy, now," Dave said, as he reached out with both hands to steady him, trying to guide him to a sitting position. "Here, let me help you—"

"Oh, my God, mister, are you all right?"

The woman's question as she scrambled to her feet from where she'd been kneeling and hugging her boy and what happened right after transpired in the blink of an eye but felt like an eternity.

Blindly, Hank reached out and grabbed Dave's forearms as if to balance himself, his fingers knotting in Dave's sleeves and his eyes widening. But his mouth slackened as he let go with one hand to clutch at his chest before suddenly tipping sideways in a violent motion.

There wasn't even time to utter a sound. The only thing Dave could do was suck in his breath as Hank collapsed, deadweight, still holding onto his other arm. The movement was sharp and jerking, pulling him off balance, the momentum causing them both to topple over the edge of the precipice.

Everything blended into a barrage of confusing images and painful sensations as they tumbled down, down, down the embankment, almost twenty feet to the rocky flat below. There seemed to be no sound though, other than the muted thudding in Dave's own ears from the impact of his body hitting the ground in his descent.

When they reached the bottom, they rolled to a hard stop, coming to rest, he sensed, within a few feet of each other.

It was quiet and still.

Dave couldn't move. He couldn't see either. His glasses had flown off and the back of his skull hurt like hell. Even more unsettling was his strange sense of detachment from his limbs. With supreme effort, he tried to lift his head to check on Hank. He couldn't do it. Dark spots were converging on his vision along with a sweep of nauseating dizziness.

Just before he lost consciousness, his sense of hearing came back. It swooshed to life, shifting his awareness from the heavy rushing of his own blood, to registering sounds outside himself again—the rustling of the leaves above them, birds chirping, and the gushing water over the dam—all blending in peculiar harmony with a little girl's cries and the echo of sirens wailing in the distance.

And then it all went dark.

(The dam in springtime)

Chapter Twenty-One

North Country General Hospital
April 1, 2008

Within an hour, everyone had made it to the hospital except for Zippy, who was back in LA to audition for a part in the new crime investigation series her agent had called about on Easter. Melanie had volunteered to keep her abreast of all developments through texts, to avoid a flood of repetitive information from every sister. Zippy could be in Moose Junction within a few hours if word came down that she was needed, but for now she was just waiting to learn more about Pa's condition like the rest of them.

Ma had gotten there first, with Anne driving her, and they'd gone together into the emergency room to speak with the doctors who were treating Pa. Anne could be counted on to write down notes on anything the doctors said, but even more than that, Ma needed her support. According to Kat, who'd arrived just before they were called into the ER, Ma had looked strained and pale and her voice had been shaky when she said how strange it was to have heard the sirens so close and not to have realized it was for Pa and Hank until the call came from the hospital.

Elena learned this all secondhand with her other sisters as they all showed up over the course of the next half hour or so, but soon Ma and Anne came out into the waiting area again. Ma was teary as she sat with her girls around her, gripping Anne's hands while they shared what they knew so far.

Hank was gone.

Since he'd had no other family, the doctor in the ER had told Ma what he would have otherwise conveyed to Hank's next of kin. According to what they could tell from initial examinations, Hank had died almost instantly from a massive heart attack, even before he went over the edge of the steep path.

Pa was drifting into and out of consciousness, but he was breathing on his own and his vitals were stable. He'd suffered some injuries in the fall, though, including a gash on the back of his head. His spine wasn't broken, but tests indicated nerve trauma since he had sensation in his legs, but they were weak and could not support any pressure.

And ever since he'd regained consciousness, he'd been hallucinating.

For the past half hour, he'd thought every medical employee who came in was planning to take him down the hall for experimental surgery. The doctor told Ma that this distressing side effect might be from the head wound or from some of the medications Pa had been given, but it was too early to know.

Pa was also worried about his girls, thinking that they were in some kind of danger. Considering that he and Hank had rescued a little boy just before the accident, that particular delusion didn't surprise the doctors. Elena knew Pa thought along those lines all the time anyway. He'd likely be worrying about his family, regardless, just as he'd done when he'd awoken from his pulmonary aneurysm surgery.

The only difference this time was that he seemed convinced they were all children again, as if the past four decades hadn't happened. The doctors were admitting him and transferring him to a room in the Intensive Care Unit, and Ma told them all to be prepared . . . that Pa might say things that didn't make sense, or that he might not speak at all.

Elena didn't care as long as she got to see him. From the moment she'd gotten the call, fear and worry had risen to knot in her throat, and she'd wavered from feeling weepy, to feeling frantic, to feeling physically sick and back again.

After another hour of waiting, Pa was settled in his ICU room, and before long it was Elena's turn to go in. She and Jen went in together. The room was quiet except for the whooshing and beeping of the equipment. Pa's head was bandaged, but his eyes cracked open when they came in, and he blinked, seeming to recognize them.

"Ellie? Jen?"

"We're right here, Pa. You surprised us! We didn't think you'd be awake."

Jen was the one who'd answered, exuding cheerfulness that Elena knew was forced, but she went along with it, too, knowing it was best for Pa.

"We had to make sure you were all right, you know," she said, trying to smile as she came close to his bed and put her hand on his shoulder.

"I'd be doing a whole lot better if I could get those people to stop dancing up there. There's a lot of hullaballoo with the band playing, and they're loud."

He was staring up at a recessed light in the ceiling above him as he spoke, and Jen met Elena's gaze across the bed. There was no floor above the ICU at this hospital. Elena shook her head, before looking at Pa again, trying not to let her emotions get the best of her as she murmured something about asking the nurses to look into it.

Pa closed his eyes, then opened them again and gazed right at Elena. She saw the glimmer of the real Pa—*her* Pa—in their crystal blue depths.

"I don't think my mind is working too good, Ellie. It seems so real, but even when I say it, I know it can't be right. There's nothing happening in the ceiling, is there?"

"No, Pa, there isn't." Elena squeezed his shoulder and tried to let the love she felt for him seep through her touch. "You hit your head when you fell, and they have you on some pretty strong medicines, so that's probably why you thought that. It should get better in time."

He gave a tired nod then shifted his head on the pillow to look at Jen. "What about Hank? How is he? Is he here?"

Jen was clearly caught off guard by the questions. She started to say something, then cleared her throat and looked away, obviously trying to pull herself together to answer.

The whole family was still reeling from his death themselves; they hadn't intended on telling Pa until later, when he'd had a chance to recover a little. It looked like that plan would have to be scrapped now. Jen broke the news about Pops as gently as she could.

"Damn it all, Hank," Pa murmured after he'd heard about his lifelong friend. He closed his eyes again. "I should have been able to help him."

"It happened too fast, Pa. The doctors said there was nothing anyone could have done," Jen offered, trying to comfort him, but Elena knew from experience that it wouldn't really help. Nothing could ease this kind of loss.

She swallowed hard, blinking back her own tears. At least there was one bit of good news she could give him.

"You and Pops saved that little boy, Pa," she said softly, reaching down to take his hand. "His mother was so grateful. Out in the waiting area, she couldn't say enough to us about what you both did for them."

Pa didn't answer and his eyes were still closed, but she saw him swallow and nod in response. After a few minutes, he took a few deeper breaths, and it seemed as if he might be lapsing into sleep again.

Elena looked at Jen, silently indicating that it was probably time to leave. She saw her sister's eyes had welled with tears, too, as she made her way around the bed closer to Elena, who had been standing on the side nearer the door. This was so hard. It was awful to see Pa like this and to know there was nothing they could do to help him.

Elena cleared her throat as Jen said her goodbye, trying her best to hold it together so she would sound normal when it was her turn to do the same. In another second, it was time. She leaned over to kiss Pa's forehead. "We're going to go for a little while now, Pa, and let you rest. But we'll be back to see you again real soon, okay?"

"All right, El," he mumbled at last, his eyes still closed. "Just do one thing for me first, will you?"

"Sure, Pa. Anything."

Her throat already felt constricted from a crushing weight of sadness and worry, but she thought it might close altogether when her beloved father finally finished his request.

"On your way out, tell those guys up there to tone down their music."

Chapter Twenty-Two

Adirondack Medical Center
April 27, 2008

The past four weeks had been the most difficult, draining, and helpless time in all of Elena's life.

She'd had to manage her grief in laying Pops to rest while also combatting the constant worry and sadness of seeing Pa suffering in the hospital for so long. The doctors at North Country General had had him transferred by ambulance to a larger medical center because of his condition. The hallucinations still plagued him, and he was often in pain from his back down to his legs. It seemed that for every bit of improvement he experienced, he ended up falling back another three steps over and over again.

The entire family had taken shifts from day to day and week to week so that someone would be with him at all times, except for the overnight hours when hospital rules forced them to go home. The goal, of course, was for him to improve enough to be released. By the onset of the fourth week, however, that possibility was beginning to seem out of reach.

Pa still couldn't stand. In fact, he could only sit up all the way for a short time in a chair or even in bed before pain forced a change of position.

Just as troubling, he'd been in and out of ICU two more times since his initial admission to this hospital. None of the doctors, whether on a regular floor or in ICU, seemed to be able to stabilize him for more than five or six days at a time. Elena soon realized that this was at least in part due to the separateness of each department in the medical center; it was almost like each was an island in and of itself.

The regular floor doctor treated Pa for his injuries from the accident, trying to address what was causing the weakness in his limbs. But when some of those medications and treatments led to fluctuations of blood pressure and exacerbated some more serious existing problems with his heart function, fluid retention, and oxygen levels, he was sent back to intensive care. Treatment there shifted to focus on those life-threatening issues until he was stabilized and returned to a regular floor, where the process started up all over again.

It was a vicious cycle that the family had been doing their best to help break by communicating with all the medical staff during each change of circumstance. But with every week that passed, with every transfer back to ICU and every new floor doctor, the task seemed more insurmountable. Life became a roller coaster of emotion, worry, and effort to ensure that Pa's care was consistent and productive, without leading to yet another transfer back and forth from the Intensive Care Unit.

It was smack dab in the middle of this horrible succession of events that one more doctor appeared: a palliative care specialist whose youth belied the depth of her compassion and wisdom.

She stood just over five feet, three inches tall; her strawberry-blonde hair was pulled into an efficient ponytail and she had a wide smile and intense, almost turquoise-blue eyes. From the moment Margaret McMahon, MD, began to work with Pa, she did what no one else had been able to accomplish: She used her professional knowledge and the scope of her position to coordinate Pa's care, get down to the nitty gritty of what *he* wanted to see happen for himself, and then worked with the entire Wright family to ensure it was achieved.

Pa responded to Dr. McMahon immediately. The woman was a minor miracle to them all, and Elena had known she was seeing that in action this morning when the doctor came in for her regular visit. Jen, Elena, and Ma had been sitting with Pa in his room on the regular floor when Dr. McMahon knocked. She wanted to have a private conversation with Pa about his latest test results and talk over his thoughts and goals for the future. All of this would be shared with the family afterward.

They'd done as requested, but as she, Ma, and Jen made their way to the waiting area, Elena had realized what a startling, simple change it was, this act of asserting Pa's autonomy.

Except for Dr. McMahon, it just hadn't happened much during Pa's hospitalizations, including his aneurysm surgery back in January and the months of extensive and painful recovery afterward. Most of the doctors and medical staff Pa worked with treated him as if the terms "senior citizen" and "child" were synonymous, or as if too much information might overwhelm him.

To see him being offered such respect and consideration now was like a breath of fresh air.

Every time Dr. McMahon had met with him, she'd approached Pa as the person he was—a seventy-eight-year-old man in the midst of a health crisis, yes, but also a man of pride, honor, intelligence, and integrity who had been responsible for himself and the care of a large family for more than fifty years. In just over a week, she'd gotten to know him and his circumstances, taking into account the unpredictable nature of his mental state and planning times to speak with him both when he was confused and when his mind was working rationally, so that she could assess him better and maximize their discussions.

It was amazing, the effect this difference of approach made on Pa. It seemed to light a flame inside him, restoring some of his old self; he had a voice once more beyond just what he could convey through his family. He had thoughts and goals he might struggle to articulate in the clear and concise ways he'd known before the accident, but ones that were valued nonetheless.

Dr. McMahon treated Pa as an individual with a history, a meaningful life, and significance in the world, not like just an old man living on borrowed time. And Elena had never felt more grateful.

She was still sitting with Ma and Jen in the waiting area when Dr. McMahon returned from Pa's room after their talk.

"He's resting for now. His lunch should be coming in soon, and I told him you'd be back in to help him eat." Dr. McMahon spoke as she approached them in the otherwise empty waiting room just down the hall from Pa's room and then sat down next to Ma, balancing her charts on her lap. "That will give me a little time to go over with you some of the decisions and information he shared with me."

Ma nodded. "How did he seem to you today?"

"He was tired, but lucid." Dr. McMahon's eyes were kind. "We had a good talk about his goals for the future. About what he envisions for himself, and what he's willing to do or not do to see it happen."

"And what is that?" Elena shifted forward on her seat, her fingers twisting together. She knew they would all support whatever Pa wanted, but she needed to brace herself anyway; the unknown always seemed worse, and her imagination could conjure up some pretty dark possibilities.

"Ultimately, he wants to go home, but he knows he's too weak and physically unstable to do that successfully right now. He's decided he wants to transition first to the kind of care and strengthening regimen available in a nursing home rehabilitation facility."

"Oh. I never thought about that," Ma said.

"Why can't he receive rehabilitation here?" Jen asked.

"What's available here isn't at the therapeutic level he needs. I discussed it with him, and I will tell all of you that the kind of work he'll face in order to regain enough strength and mobility to return home won't be easy. It will require fortitude and patience, but he said if we could find him placement, then he wanted to try to do it. Susan, one of the social workers on my team, can assist you in finding options for appropriate facilities with an open bed if you wish to pursue it."

"Of course." Ma sounded determined. "If that's what Dave wants, then that's what we'll do."

Dr. McMahon nodded in respect. "Your husband is just as unwavering in his focus of protecting all of you. One of his chief worries in all this is the toll his condition has taken on everyone."

"That's Dave." Though she smiled, anyone who looked couldn't help but see the sadness in Ma's eyes. "He's the most responsible, giving man I know. His family means everything to him."

"I can see that. When we were going over options, he's the one who insisted that he didn't want you and your daughters to try to take on the care of him at home yet, even with hospice involved."

"*Hospice*?" Ma's sadness turned to welling tears. "Oh. . . ."

Jen made a little sound in her throat and had to get up and move to the window. Elena sat frozen, so startled to hear that word applied to Pa that she couldn't even take a breath for a few seconds.

Hospice meant the doctors believed Pa had six months or less to live. Deep down she'd known that what was happening to him wasn't something anyone was going to be able to cure. But to hear it said aloud was a whole different experience.

"I'm sorry." Dr. McMahon put her hand over Ma's. "I know it's difficult, but David is very realistic about the seriousness of his prognosis, and he wants all of you to be, too. Hospice is a good resource. What my team and I do here is similar in many ways, only palliative care can be provided simultaneously with curative treatment and hospice care cannot. The goal of both programs, though, is to relieve suffering and to help provide the best quality of life to patients and their families. That covers not only medical issues but also things like coping skills, stress management, spiritual issues, and end of life counseling for everyone involved."

"So Pa definitely wants to stop all his tests and treatments here?" Jen's voice sounded hoarse as she twisted from the window.

"Yes. He's frustrated, as you all have been, with what he called 'spinning his wheels.' He knows he's not getting better in any usual sense of the word. Unfortunately, hospital imperatives require that we persist in efforts to provide curative treatments." Dr. McMahon paused and looked at her charts before looking up at Ma again. "Your husband believes and I concur that the benefit of his being here is no longer as constructive as it once was."

Elena shook her head. "I think it's actually hurting him," she murmured, finding her voice at last. Waves of grief lapped at the edges of her awareness, but she didn't allow them to capsize her. She couldn't afford that luxury yet. "He gets exhausted moving back and forth from ICU, and all the tests and medication changes disorient him. Sometimes they make him feel worse."

Dr. McMahon nodded with a serious but compassionate expression. "It seems to be a case of diminishing returns, and he made it clear that he wants to make the most of whatever time he has left."

Elena closed her eyes as that horrible statement sank in, and Ma's lips trembled from the emotion she was holding back.

"Your husband and father is a strong man." Dr. McMahon looked at each of them in turn. "He knows what he wants and is realistic about his limitations. His loss of mental acuity distresses him even more than his physical pain or lack of mobility. He said he would like to take action to initiate a transfer from here as soon as possible, to maximize any benefit he might gain from rehabilitation therapy before it becomes too difficult for him to do so."

Ma frowned. "I don't understand. We were told his hallucinations and memory loss could improve once his doctors stabilize him and fine tune his medications."

For the first time, Elena saw Dr. McMahon's usual composure slip a little. She paused and cleared her throat, looking down at her papers before lifting her gaze to the three of them again. "I was under the impression that Dr. Warren had spoken with you about this earlier this week."

"No. Another hospitalist has been on this floor since Thursday,"

Elena said. "Dr. Warren doesn't like to discuss much with us anyway, but he had some vacation days to use, so Dr. Tahid has been filling in."

At that, Dr. McMahon's jaw tightened, her eyes darkening. "I see."

"What was Dr. Warren supposed to tell us?" Jen asked.

Dr. McMahon paused for a moment, fiddling with her papers and folders before taking a breath and sitting up straight. She began to say something, stopped, and then began again.

"There's no easy way to share this kind of news, so I'll just say it. David's latest scans indicate that the head injury he sustained set off a form of vascular dementia. It, and not medication or other issues, is what has been causing his hallucinations and memory loss." She pulled out a sheet of paper that looked like a CT scan report, pointing to it as she spoke. "These tests show that the beginning stages of the condition may have been dormant in his brain for some time prior, but the injury is causing it to progress quite rapidly."

"Causing it to progress. . . ." Jen repeated the words as if she hadn't heard them right, shaking her head. "So you're saying that not only is it not going to get better, but that it might get *worse*?"

"I'm afraid it's a medical certainty. The hallucinations and other mental issues may ease or intensify on a day-to-day basis, but the condition is progressive."

"Oh, my God," Jen murmured.

Ma pressed her fingers to her lips, clearly struggling not to cry, and Elena felt like someone had punched her.

It was too horrible to comprehend. Pa had been suffering almost daily from the hallucinations. In his lucid times he was aware that something wasn't right, but it had gotten to the point that he never really knew what was real anymore; sometimes he had to ask the people nearby to be sure. For a man whose powerful mind had always been an unfailing source of logic, intelligence, and strength for him and everyone around him, it had been agonizing for him to endure and heartbreaking for them all to see. Now to hear this news atop it all was a devastating blow.

"Does he *know* it's going to get worse?" Elena whispered.

Dr. McMahon nodded. "Your father and I have built our discussions on honesty and plain talk. He seems to value that, and I have tried to respect his wishes in our conversations."

"Dave doesn't like to sugar coat anything," Ma made an obvious effort to pull herself together. "I know he appreciates what you're doing for him, Dr. McMahon, and so do I. We all do." Then she shook her head, her eyes still glistening. "But he's already suffered so much. I don't know how he can stay strong in the face of even more."

"He's shown a great deal of courage, Mrs. Wright," Dr. McMahon said, and her gaze was filled with empathy. "After watching all of you with him and through our own conversations, I feel privileged to have been given a chance to know firsthand some of what makes him the man he is. I promise to do everything in my power to help him and all of you to see his wishes fulfilled."

"Thank you." Ma blinked back any lingering tears and stood, with Elena and Jen on either side of her, supporting her. "I think I'll go in to see him now. Would you please arrange a meeting with that social worker you mentioned, so we can discuss placement options to a rehabilitation facility? I'll call all the girls together later tonight for a family meeting, so that we can plan out what needs doing."

"I'll get on that right away, Mrs. Wright." Dr. McMahon reached out and touched Ma's arm. "You have my number if you want to talk over anything. Call any time, even after hours. I'll check in with you soon about that meeting."

The Homestead
Moose Junction, Upstate New York
July 13, 1973
Elena is four years old

Half a loaf is better than none. . . .

"Can't we barter for some bologna?"

"I'm afraid not. I can only give you what you girls planned for, and that's all that's left from your list."

Twelve-year-old Kat stood outside the open kitchen window trying to bargain with Ma, who was answering from inside the house.

"Just a jar of mustard?" Kat scratched her knee and heaved a big sigh.

"And half a jar of maraschino cherries." Ma smiled.

"Oh, boy," Kat said, taking the two bagged items Ma passed through the open window to her. "There's gonna be a mutiny when I show up with this."

"Talk it over as a group. I know you'll figure something out. By tomorrow this time you'll be back in the house having hot baths, a home-cooked meal—"

"And the usual rules to follow and chores to do."

Ma smiled. "They *are* part and parcel of living at home."

"After this week, I think I'm actually going to look forward to them."

Ma waved, trying not to laugh at the forlorn look on Kat's face as she shook her head and turned away with her pitiful sack of "food" to walk back across the yard and toward the one-room camp Pa had built years earlier in the woods behind the garage.

Ma was the keeper of the provisions; she doled out the supplies and food from the list the six oldest girls had organized together before their adventure in self-sufficiency had begun. They'd begged Pa and Ma for a chance to "rough it" on their own for one week this summer, thinking that not only would it be fun (no rules or chores!) but it would also be easy because they could eat and do what they wanted, when and how they wanted.

And they'd readily agreed with the single rule Pa gave them (which he'd engineered in order to help teach them about planning and working together): The list of provisions they decided upon at the beginning of the week had to be followed without any additions until the end of the week and their return to the house. That meant thinking ahead to consider all the food, drinks, and other necessities (like soap to wash up with or toilet paper for the outhouse) that they would need to get through those seven days.

Ma had purchased everything on their list, keeping it separate for them, and it was she who kept track and dispensed the items through the kitchen window. If they ran out, they ran out, and then they had to make due.

It was now Saturday, their seventh and last day. The milk had been gone since Wednesday, and the Kool-Aid packets were finished by Thursday afternoon. They had unlimited gallons of drinking water, though, since Pa and Ma had considered that a "free" resource, pumped from their well. By the end of the week, they'd eaten their fill of marshmallows and black olives, but since they'd put precious little in the way of substantial food on their list (because no one wanted to cook over the grated fire pit between the camp and the outhouse), they were less than satisfied most of the time. They'd managed at first with assorted sandwiches of peanut butter and jelly or bologna and cheese, but those fillings had run out, too, even before the milk.

Still, they'd stuck it out together. Except for a few fights over whose sleeping bag was going where on the one-room camp's floor at night (and an incident of bloodcurdling screams when Lisa went to use the outhouse and found a spider lurking there), the week had been free of major problems. They didn't know it, but Pa often looked in on them, and he and Ma knew the girls still had a half a loaf of Wonder Bread hoarded in the breadbox of the camp.

Anne, as the oldest, had placed herself in charge of guarding that important provision. Hopefully it would come in handy tonight. If someone had already gotten to it, though, there would be six hungry, grumpy girls settling down to sleep for their last night of almost complete autonomy.

The experiment would end tomorrow morning with (hopefully) a few important lessons learned.

"Why are most of my sisters *still* living out in the camp, Ma?"

Elena had wandered into the kitchen, and she looked longingly out the window at Kat's retreating back. She and Zippy had been left behind for the week, being deemed "too young" by the other girls (Ma and Pa had agreed) to participate in the experiment.

"Your Pa is helping them learn a lesson about working together, Elena, along with the importance of good planning."

"Is that why they got to eat all those marshmallows and olives this week?"

Ma laughed. "Yes, though I'm pretty sure by now they're wishing they'd thought more about what was *necessary*, instead of just what they *wanted*."

"Why?"

"Because they used up most of their real food early on, and now there isn't much of anything left." She looked down at Elena, apparently seeing the disappointment on her face, because she asked, "Are you still wishing you were out there with them?"

Sticking her lip out, Elena nodded before looking out the window again.

"Well, maybe you and Alexandra can stay out there for part of the week next year if they decide to try it again. But for now, I think you're going to like what I'm making for supper much more than what they're having."

"Why, what are you making?"

"Spaghetti and meatballs."

Elena grinned. "My favorite!"

Ma nodded. "And I'm making a chocolate mayonnaise cake after I get this sauce to simmering."

"Yay!" Elena jumped up and down and clapped before remembering that her sisters were making their *own* supper again . . . and that maybe Ma had said supper at home would be better to help Elena forget that, like parents sometimes did. If her sisters were going to feast on more bags of puffy marshmallows, it just wouldn't be fair, and she wanted to know about it.

She glanced toward the camp again and then back at Ma. "So what are they having out *there*?"

Ma's mouth tipped into a smile as she turned to the counter to finish mixing up the meatballs. "Well, from the looks of it, Elena, I'd say they're going to be having mustard sandwiches for supper—"

Elena scrunched her nose at the idea of eating nothing but mustard on bread . . . but her eyes widened and she thanked her lucky stars as Ma finished in a lilting voice, "With a maraschino cherry for dessert!"

(Inside the little camp that Pa built)

Chapter Twenty-Three

Hawthorn Haven Rehabilitation
Center and Nursing Home
Upstate New York
May 12, 2008

Ma, Elena, and the rest of her sisters sat around the large table in the conference room of Hawthorn Haven Rehabilitation Center and Nursing Home. With them sat the facility's directors of healthcare, nursing, and social services, for a "care plan" meeting about Pa. He'd moved here from the hospital nine days ago and had undertaken the rehabilitation program as he'd told Dr. McMahon he wanted to do. However, the transition from the hospital had been grueling for him on many levels, and it had aggravated his vascular dementia and increased his hallucinations.

He'd had a few decent days, but it had rapidly become clear that he could not sustain the physical regimen long enough for it to make a difference. Neither his mind nor his body would allow him to continue further.

This meeting had been called to plan out next steps.

It had been a sad twenty minutes already. The idea of changing his status from rehabilitation to comfort care seemed so final. It meant that there was no hope of his improving in any meaningful way; there would be only the effort to keep him comfortable for as long as he had left. As that reality sank in, Elena felt like there was a pile of bricks on her chest, and the feeling hadn't been helped by how on-edge the three staff members in attendance had seemed to be, as if they'd expected the family meeting to break out into a war at any second. When everyone had discussed the options calmly, with each sister and Ma offering opinions, the expression on the staffs' faces had shifted from surprise to cautious relief.

The health director looked around the table now, her brows lifted. "So you're *all* in agreement about shifting David's status from active rehabilitation to comfort care?"

"Girls?" Ma sounded subdued, but she glanced at everyone and saw each nod before she met the woman's gaze again and nodded herself.

Elena cleared her throat. "Before we finalize it all, though, I'd like to clarify one thing about Pa's living arrangements."

"Of course." It was the social worker that had responded.

"He's been in a private room since his arrival here, but will he be forced to move into a shared room now that he's shifting to comfort care status?"

"That requires discussion."

Elena's sisters murmured amongst themselves around the table. They all knew how much Pa valued his privacy and how difficult it had been for him at the hospital with someone else living on the other side of a curtain. It wasn't that he couldn't be sociable, but he had some hearing loss stemming back to his days in the Marines, and all the people coming and going through the room seemed to exacerbate his confusion. Pa also valued consideration of others far more than most people did, and he worried that his own visitors might infringe on any roommate's peace. Half of his time at Adirondack Medical Center had been spent sleepless because of it.

If he was going to be forced to share a room now here at Hawthorn Haven, they might have to consider some other options, like moving him to a hospice-based facility where he would be guaranteed a private room for his last months.

Of course they'd already discussed bringing him home and caring for him themselves, but two things had stopped them from that choice: Ma had been drained by all these weeks of traveling back and forth and spending every day at the hospital, not to mention months of worry over Pa's health going back to his aneurysm surgery.

And then there were the very real medical issues Pa still faced. In addition to his mental decline, he was suffering from slowly progressing congestive heart failure, and being bedridden only added to his symptoms and instability. Even with each daughter taking turns at the homestead and a few hours a day of hospice help, it would be too physically precarious for Pa and too much for Ma's health to handle, too.

The social worker pressed her lips together and shuffled her papers. "Technically, at this point we *are* supposed to move your father into a shared room."

"Because he's no longer in rehabilitation?" Anne asked.

"Yes. Also, health insurance and Medicare payments are directly affected by a patient's classification." She glanced through her papers again and looked at the Nursing Director. "We're required to document the date a patient is no longer compliant in the rehabilitation program, and your father has not been able to actively participate in exercises since last Thursday. However, since the meeting to change his status did not take place until today, I intend to use today's date in the paperwork so the cost to you will not increase until Tuesday, if you choose to have David continue on at this facility."

"Thank you." Ma's voice sounded tired, but she was a lady through and through, and she lived by the idea that manners mattered.

The nursing director spoke now, adding, "We can offer one other benefit that we hope will be useful in making your decision about leaving David here or moving him elsewhere. There is no other patient on the waiting list for the room David occupies. We also have a second, empty room that serves in a similar capacity in the event that someone needs it. Because of that, I will be glad to manage the paperwork so that he can stay in his private room for the duration of his stay here, even though he's no longer on active rehabilitation status."

"And even if it's for several months?" Kat asked.

"Yes. There is a small daily up-charge for any resident staying in a private room, but for as long as he stays here, we won't ask him to move."

The murmurings started up again, but this time with a more positive undertone. This could be the best choice for Pa, Elena was certain. Moving him again, whether to another room, to home, or to another facility, would be devastating if his transfer from the medical center to the nursing home was any indication. His damaged mind couldn't make sense of the change, and it had caused him a great deal of stress and confusion. At least he would be able to remain in surroundings that had become somewhat familiar in the last week and a half, and the nursing home was only twenty minutes from the homestead, as opposed to the hour-long trip it had taken Ma to get to Adirondack Medical Center every day to see him.

"Can we also look into getting that rolling recliner you mentioned a few days ago, so that we can take him outside for a little while?"

Elena's question quieted the hubbub a little; everyone waited for the answer. Pa couldn't sit comfortably for any length of time in a regular wheel chair. But he'd been cooped up indoors for almost two months now, and they'd discussed amongst themselves how feeling the sun and breeze on his face and seeing grass, trees, and flowers again might benefit him more now than anything else.

"We've got that request in the works. The chair should be available in a day or two," the healthcare director answered.

"I think we should vote on this, then," Anne said, taking the lead on this opportunity. "The proposition is that Pa stay here under comfort care, with us continuing to come in every day, on rotation, so everyone gets a turn to see him and help support Ma." Anne looked around at her mother and all her sisters. "Everyone in agreement say, 'aye.'"

All "ayes" rang out softly from around the table, and Anne turned to Ma. "Is that all right with you, Ma?"

Ma's eyes were thick with the tears she kept blinking back, but she nodded and finally swallowed before answering, "I think it's what your father would want."

"All right, then. Thank you all for your participation," the nursing director said, effectively calling the meeting to an end.

Everyone started to get up, but as they began to disperse to the waiting area, the nursing director glanced at Elena, Ma, and the others who were nearest to her, speaking just to them. "This has to be the quickest meeting of its kind I've ever been part of. In the decade I've held this position, I've never seen a family work together so well."

The healthcare director nodded. "We usually see anything from squabbles and shouting matches to physical conflicts. It's nice to see the process go so smoothly."

Elena smiled for the first time in what felt like weeks, acknowledging the compliment. "I'd have to say the credit for that goes to our mother," she put her arm around Ma for a quick hug, "and our father. They're the ones who taught us how to work together."

The nursing director smiled, too. "Well, then, thank you, Mrs. Wright. I will stop in to see your husband later, but I think you've done a wonderful job in raising a family that so clearly loves and respects each other and you. It's a pleasure to work with you all."

Elena ducked into Pa's room before she had to get on the road for the forty-minute drive home to pick up the girls from school and get supper started. She'd spent a few hours with him earlier and then attended the meeting, but she hated to leave without at least popping in to say goodbye until next time.

When she came to his door, the aide who had been helping him eat nodded to her, said something to Pa, and then left for a moment to give them some privacy. Elena came closer; she saw that Pa was propped in the large, hospital-style recliner to the side his bed, instead of in his bed as he'd been this morning when she saw him. The regulations at Hawthorn Haven required that every resident, temporary or otherwise, be moved from bed to a chair of some kind each morning, washed, and dressed in at least a few pieces of regular clothing. This wasn't a hospital, they'd been reminded, and so the goals were different.

Because the pain in Pa's back prevented him from sitting straight up, he was half reclined, wearing a regular shirt with his more comfortable pajama bottoms. His left forearm rested across his forehead and he had his eyes closed while he chewed slowly on something.

As she got closer she saw that it was a bite from his lunch, and her heart lurched with sadness and love.

He looked so worn out. Exhausted. But he kept trying. He'd had no appetite for several weeks now, and he had to force himself to choke down half a bottle of a vanilla-flavored nutritional drink when he could. But here he was, still trying to eat regular food because he knew everyone wanted him to try to keep up his strength.

"Hi, Pa. It's Elena," she said as she sat in the chair near him. The rolling bedside tray was in front of him, so she couldn't get too close, but now he opened his eyes and looked at her. Their bright blue color seemed more muted, but his gaze was clear, and she could tell right away that he was lucid and not in the midst of one of his tormenting hallucinations.

"Ellie. . . . "

He couldn't say anything more, but he tried to nod. She smiled at him and fixed the napkin on his tray, but he shook his head when she offered him another bite of food.

"Maybe later, then," she murmured, putting down the utensil. "I just wanted to stop in to tell you I have to head home for now, but I'll be back the day after tomorrow. In between, I have to chaperone Jillian's class up to the waterpark near Glens Falls for their end-of-the-year trip."

Pa nodded and closed his eyes again for a few long seconds before opening them and trying to focus on her again.

Elena blinked back tears, forcing herself to stay upbeat. "We had that meeting this morning that Ma told you about with the nursing director. It's all been worked out. You won't have to do any more exercises, Pa.

You can just rest and try to feel better."

He seemed to register what she was saying, and he nodded again as his gaze took on a sharper focus.

"She also said we can get that wheeled recliner to take you outside so you'll be able to go into the garden. There are lots of flowers already growing out there, and it's really pretty."

"That sounds nice."

His voice was low and gravelly, but he made sense when he spoke. It was her Pa, just so tired and weak that he couldn't say much. Still, he seemed good this afternoon. Far better than he'd been this morning.

"I'll see if they'll let me go outside with you the day after tomorrow, okay?"

He nodded again, and shifted his gaze to look out the window at the vivid blue sky with puffy clouds, fronted by some lacy green trees and a wide-open field just beyond that. After a few quiet moments, Elena stood, forcing herself to get ready to go now before she lost control of her emotions.

Reaching out, she brushed a wave of his silvery hair back from his temple, remembering how she'd combed it and helped him shave in the hospital just a few weeks ago, before he'd gotten so weak that he couldn't direct how he wanted her to do it. He was particular about his grooming habits, and he'd always been fastidious about getting cleaned up in the morning.

She bent over, leaning in to kiss his cheek and lingering to whisper, "I'll be back soon, Pa. I love you."

"I love you, too," he murmured, pulling his gaze away from the window and keeping it fixed on her when she straightened again.

She waved and headed for the door. But when she looked back just before she walked out of his room, his eyes were closed again, and he seemed to have fallen asleep.

The Homestead
Moose Junction, Upstate New York
February 8, 1969
Elena is four weeks old

Happiness opens the arms and closes the eyes. . . .

It was quiet and still inside the house, and almost everyone was asleep. Everyone except Dave, who was holding little Elena and trying to coax her to close her eyes and drift off to dreamland.

The heat clicked on with a low hum, sending warmth spooling through the living room where he sat in his recliner, cradling Elena and rocking. Winter wind howled outside, swirling around the eaves and sending gouts of grainy snowflakes battering against the picture window. It was the beginning of the nor'easter that weather forecasters predicted would hammer New England over the weekend. Moose Junction normally wouldn't be affected, being so far inland, but more often than not being so close to Lake Pines created lake effect snow anyway.

Dave didn't mind. The house was snug and warm, and he'd always liked experiencing nature in her various moods. Winter was no exception.

The way he figured it, he was getting a chance to enjoy it in a way he hadn't in a while, sitting here in the middle of the night. Elizabeth had been fighting a cold, along with caring for a newborn, a one-year-old, and their six other children all week. She was exhausted, and so Dave had gotten up with Elena when she fussed. It wasn't something he normally did; the demands of his job required a decent night's sleep, not to mention that he'd never hear the end of it if the guys at work heard about him getting up like this.

But it was Saturday, and Elizabeth had needed the break.

Besides, there was nothing quite like babies. And daughters . . . well, he couldn't be more grateful that he'd been blessed with eight of them, no matter what the outside world seemed to think. His girls inspired an impulse to love, guide, and protect like nothing he'd ever known. To him, they were magic in the purest, most elemental sense, and he'd realized the very first time he'd cradled one of his daughters in his arms that this was his greatest calling in life.

Trying to be a good father meant more to him than anything he'd ever conceived or accomplished, whether in the Marines, the workplace, or anywhere else. It was the most difficult job he'd ever undertaken but the most important, even if he couldn't go around spouting off about it to everyone. He contented himself with *doing*, and left the saying part for his closest friends.

Elena made a whimpering sound that opened into a wail. Her little face screwed up tight and red, her eyes squeezing shut and her mouth opening so that her tiny tongue vibrated as she cried.

Maybe her stomach didn't feel good. He lifted her to his shoulder to try to pat her back and work out any gas that might be trapped there, but that just made her cry more. So he brought her back down, cradling her in his right arm, tucked up against him, and started rocking again.

She quieted a little, but kept whimpering and looking like she might bust out in tears again any second. She still had her days and her nights mixed up. He knew her diaper was dry, and he'd offered her a bottle she hadn't wanted.

If it wasn't so late, he'd put on some good music for her: a little Gershwin, Glenn Miller, Bing Crosby, or even Mary Hopkins. He couldn't risk waking the rest of the family, though, so he did the next best thing; he started singing as softly as he could with his deep voice that was more accustomed to issuing orders or explaining the results of his latest radar tests at the base. He didn't remember any real lullabies, so he made up the words as he went.

"Go to sleep . . . my lit-tle chick-a-dee. Go to sleep . . . my lit-tle girl. Papa's here now, go to sleep. . . ."

Elena stopped crying and looked at him, blinking her big, wet blue eyes. Then she made a hiccupping sound and gave him a toothless smile . . . and Dave's heart lurched with love so deep it caught his breath.

But in that instant he'd stopped singing, and it registered as soon as her expression began to crumple. He managed to prevent her crying by rocking again, holding her cradled against him and singing his soft, made up song. After a few minutes, her eyes began to flutter shut and her breathing deepened, her little body sagging heavy and relaxed in his arms.

Smiling, he paused to press a kiss to the top of her forehead as he continued to rock her gently. When she started to fuss, he began his song again, his soft crooning settling her down, while peace and contentment filled him long into that blustery, perfect night. She was his little girl, and he'd do anything for her to keep her safe and secure.

"Go to sleep . . . my lit-tle chick-a-dee. Go to sleep . . . my lit-tle girl. Papa's here now, go to sleep. . . ."

Chapter Twenty-Four

Hawthorn Haven Rehabilitation
Center and Nursing Home
Upstate, New York
May 13, 2008

Elena rushed up to the door of the facility, her heart pounding, not knowing if she was in time.

She'd been at the waterpark with Jillian's class for most of the morning when the call had come. She'd been stunned to hear Jen's voice, telling her that Pa had taken a turn for the worse and that the nursing director had advised the family to come as quickly as they could.

Waves of worry and grief had swept over her, and she'd scrambled to call Max and make arrangements with Jillian's teacher and some other parent friends so that she could get here as quickly as possible. Still, it had taken more than three hours, even driving faster than she'd ever gone before, and she'd prayed the entire trip that she wasn't going to be too late.

Jen met her in the hall. Her face was serious, but she put a calming hand on Elena's arm. "It's okay. Nothing's changed."

"Oh, thank God," Elena murmured, hurrying with her to Pa's room.

As a child, Elena could never allow herself to imagine Pa gone forever or she would begin to cry, her mind shutting down and a sense of panic setting in. He was so much a part of her world . . . so vital and present. He was the one they all counted on, the head of this amazing, sprawling, passionate, squabbling, loving family he had built together with Ma.

But now the day she had dreaded her whole life had arrived, and it almost seemed incomprehensible.

Her brave, strong, wonderful Pa was dying.

As awful as it was for her, she knew Pa had never feared death; he'd raised all his girls to accept it as part of the natural progression of life.

If he had worried at all over the actual moment of dying, it was only the concern that he might have to make that transition alone, with no one to care when his time came. But his family was here today to make sure that would never happen.

Elena paused at the threshold to his room for just a second. She tried to brace herself for what she was going to see and what she knew she needed to do, before she pushed open the door and stepped inside.

The air felt hot and close. Jen murmured that the nurses had to keep it like this because Pa could no longer regulate his own body temperature, and the warmth made him more comfortable. Elena was the last to arrive, and when she came in, everyone turned or nodded at her from where they sat or stood; she knew it was a trick of her perception, but their movements seemed slowed down, as if they were all under water.

Then she looked at Pa, and time seemed to stop.

He was lying on the bed, with his head propped up on pillows to help him breathe. There were tubes in his nose, connected to a machine delivering regular puffs of oxygen. His eyes were closed, and other than the labored rise and fall of his chest, he was very still. Some parts of his face and neck were pale while others were flushed.

Swallowing hard, she took another step toward him. The flood of grief she'd suppressed as she'd raced here rushed up through her now and made her legs wobbly. But her desperate need to be near Pa outweighed any weakness. She needed to talk to him, to tell him that she'd made it in time. That she was here for him.

Gradually her senses expanded again to take in what was going on in the room. The sounds around her were muffled, with a few of her sisters crying quietly, while others talked and hugged or sat together. Someone had put a CD of Pa's favorite music in a portable player, and a delicate piano version of "What a Wonderful World" was playing softly in the background. A few of her brothers-in-law were in the room, too, and several of her nieces and nephews.

As her worried gaze found Ma sitting in a chair at the window side of Pa's bed, Elena felt a rush of gratitude. Strong, capable Anne sat just behind their mother, with her arms around Ma's shoulders. Ma was holding Pa's hand, and tears seeped from her eyes as she murmured something to him every now and again. But Anne's body leaned forward toward Ma, and all her energy seemed focused on praying and talking softly to her, supporting her.

Lisa had been sitting opposite them on the other side of Pa's bed, but when Elena came in, she got up, indicating that her sister should exchange places with her. Gratefully, Elena sat down and nodded to Ma, blowing her a kiss. Ma blew a kiss back, but Elena noticed that her hand shook as she did. Her mother seemed so frail. Ma could only mouth the words, "I love you," to Elena before tears welled up again and she looked down at Pa, clearly doing her best to hold onto her self-control.

Elena inched closer to Pa's bedside, taking his left hand in hers. Then she pulled herself together and got ready to do the most important thing she knew she would ever be able to do for her father. It was the only thing left that she *could* do now, and she was determined to do it right, no matter what.

She'd been told that for people in comas, even those in the process of dying, the sense of hearing was the last thing to fade. So now she prayed with every fiber of her being that even though he couldn't answer her, Pa would hear her and find some comfort in it.

"Hi, Pa. It's Elena. I'm here," she said softly, leaning forward and trying to let her love for him seep through her touch. "I came as quick as I could."

His hand felt warm but motionless under hers. It still seemed so strong, with its familiar, broad palm and sturdy fingers—those large, capable hands she'd inherited from him. She wrapped her fingers more snugly around his now, her heart twisting with love and sadness. These same hands had held hers when she was a little girl, had fixed her boo-boos and carried jingle bells to make magic for her. They had strung lines on her fishing pole, guided her through their dance at her wedding, and tenderly held her newborn daughters with their gentle strength.

It seemed impossible to her now that their lifetime of work was finished.

"I won't leave you, Pa," she whispered to him. "None of us are leaving. We're all here, and we all love you very much."

Elena swallowed again, choking back tears, and looked around briefly at the others in the room within the limits of her vision. Most had already been here for hours. Some now were chatting quietly or helping themselves to the cups of water and juice or sandwiches the nursing staff had compassionately wheeled in for them on a cart once they saw how many in the family had gathered here. People quietly moved in and out of the room, the activity seeming a strange contrast of life in this place where death was looming.

Elena looked at Pa again. His breathing had become shallower. She started to pay closer attention. Sometimes she counted four or five light breaths in a row, followed by a spell of nothing, and then it would start up again, with three or four breaths, then nothing. Before long she noticed that the spaces of time between breaths seemed to be stretching out, and panic rose, piercing her to the heart.

The seconds felt like they were slowing down. One song had finished on the music player, and another began. She heard "As Time Goes By" playing now, soft and sweet. And Pa's breathing became even lighter. Four more short breaths and then nothing for a count of six seconds. Then three more breaths and a long space of quiet.

Something was changing. Elena felt the old fear swell up inside her, mixing with bittersweet acceptance. It all seemed unreal, as if she was outside of herself and watching this all unfold before her.

She looked up to see if anyone else noticed anything, but nothing seemed any different from before. Though Ma still held Pa's other hand, she was talking quietly with Anne and Kat who were both behind her, and so her face was turned away from the bed. Everyone else was engaged in conversations or positioned farther away from Pa's bedside.

It was almost time. Elena felt it deeply, unmistakably, although she'd never been present like this at another's passing.

Two more little breaths.

It was here. She couldn't wait any longer.

"Pa," she whispered, leaning close to him and trying not to cry. "Pa, you can rest now and not worry. We'll take good care of each other and Ma, too. You taught us how to do that, better than anyone. You're the best father in the whole world. You are, Pa. You always will be, and I love you so mu—"

Her voice broke off in a sob.

Oh, God. He'd stopped breathing. No more short breaths. Just stillness. Quiet, peaceful, stillness.

"Ma!" she called out brokenly. "Ma, I think something's happening."

"Dave!" Elena heard her mother's cry. She saw Ma turn and half stand, almost collapsing under the intensity of her grief as she realized what it was, with Anne and Kat supporting her as she called out again through sobs, "I love you, Dave . . . I love you!"

All of Elena's sisters rushed forward at the cries. There was a kind of quiet tumult as they embraced Ma and each other, releasing their grief together. Then everyone linked their arms or hands, love filling that small room and tears streaming down their faces as they surrounded Pa in one big, unbroken circle, murmuring a prayer for him, this man who had meant the world to each one of them in his own way . . . saying goodbye as Pa left his beloved family for the very last time.

Letter from Pa to Elena
May 3, 1991

Dear Elena,

The picture enclosed here is of a hibiscus that has been flowering in the parlor window one bloom at a time for what seems like a year or more. It's getting to where I don't remember when there wasn't a bud or two and a flower either out or on the way.

This morning there is a fresh new flower just like the one in the picture, but right next to it is the one that was new yesterday and is already spent. I don't know whether to be happy for the beautiful one or sad for the one that is gone. I guess if I wait until tomorrow I can be sad for the one that is so beautiful now. But how can I anticipate being sad for something that is so pretty?

It's really a good thing that people can only "see" the present because we are on the same train as a hibiscus except that we are on a longer trip.

I've told you before, but it fits in here so I will say it again. Sometimes I get feeling so good that I get afraid to anticipate the loss. If life could be a series of beautiful scenes and beautiful music and pleasant visits with people we love, then life should just go on forever. I suppose that's why people get old and feeble with wandering minds. What *is* can end without too much loss, and what *was* did not stop so will be forever. Right now and as far as I can see, I want to be this morning's flower. I'll be a hibiscus. You be a rose. . . .

The reality of today is that this morning the toilet would not flush all the way. I put some stuff in and tinkered with it, and it seems okay now (I hope). We also have ants under the kitchen sink and they are tenacious little devils. Me, too. I'll get them yet.

I am ready for a new project, but before I start one I have to spend some time on the yard and the gardens. That's good. I need to spend some time outdoors for a while. The first thing I will do is to "summer-ize" the snow blower after I get back from mailing this at the post office.

Well, El, just a little note to put in with the picture. We'll see you soon for graduation. Until then, I hope that all is well with you and that all your days are just nice.

Love,

Pa

PS: Here's a little poem for you that was written many centuries ago. . . .

"If of thy mortal goods thou art bereft,
And from thy slender store two loaves alone to thee are left,
Sell one, and with the dole
Buy hyacinths to feed thy soul."

~ Moslih Eddin Saadi

(Hibiscus bloom in the window)

Chapter Twenty-Five

Maple Creek, Upstate New York
May 17, 2008

The last three days had passed in a blur.

Elena was sitting at the dining room table of her own house a half hour before dawn. She'd come home yesterday after two nights away at the homestead, doing her part to help in the preparations for Pa's funeral. She was up early today, savoring the unusual quiet. Soon enough the girls and Max would wake and come downstairs, but in the meantime Elena decided to take advantage of her morning energy.

Deep down she hoped that some meaningful work would help her to shake free of the sense of detachment that had filled her waking hours since Pa's passing. Oh, she still moved and ate and breathed and thought, sometimes too much in fact. But nothing fully penetrated the wall of sadness that had shrouded her.

It seemed strange how life continued to march on as if nothing had happened. Logically she knew that what had happened *was* pretty ordinary in the scheme of things; almost seven thousand people died every single day in the United States. But when one of those people had been so much a part of your own world, it felt entirely different.

She hadn't fully accepted yet that she would never hear Pa's voice or the timbre of his laugh again, or that she would never get to hug him or talk with him about all those important things no one else seemed to understand. The homestead had felt empty in the days since his death, even with her and Zippy staying there with Ma, and with all her other sisters coming and going.

The hard truth was that the anchor of their family was gone, and it was going to be a long, slow process to readjust the sails, pull the ship out of the storm, and continue on some kind of modified course.

Pa's wake wouldn't be for another two days, with the funeral the day after that. Ma had talked it over with all the whole family and decided to delay everything by a few days in order to give some of their out-of-state-relatives a chance to attend Pa's services.

And so, as painful as waiting was, it was necessary. Elena had decided that some good could come from it, at least, because it meant they would all have more time to pull together a proper tribute for Pa. Ma had asked her to be the one to read something on behalf of the family at the funeral Mass, and though she was honored to do it, she'd felt overwhelmed, too, trying to put into words what Pa had meant to them all.

So she'd been going through photographs, papers, and letters for almost an hour already, sifting through everything to see if something turned up that she could use in her talk. She kept getting distracted, though, and so a few minutes ago, she'd finally just sat and stared out the window into the pearl-gray light, listening to the birds chirp as they flitted around the feeder she kept filled for them year-round.

Keeping focused was a constant struggle. Thoughts, memories, a few regrets and lots of questions kept assailing her, as she'd known they would. She'd experienced it once before after the violent loss of Jesse. Pa's death was different because of the circumstances, but she'd discovered that the specifics didn't matter.

When it came right down to it, losing someone you loved hurt more than you'd ever imagined it could.

That was the impersonal brutality of death. Whether prepared for it or taken by surprise, whether a peaceful passing or through violence, disease, or old age, in the end the reality for those left behind was the same: In the blink of an eye a bridge was crossed, and the one you loved slipped away from you to somewhere unknown.

It was that unknown that had haunted Elena from her earliest memories, sparking that uneasy wariness and acknowledgement of death she had carried around with her from childhood.

The people who were part of her world in the here and now loved her, she knew, and she loved them back, but she'd always realized that not many understood the way her mind worked, especially when it came to subjects like this. Pa had been one of the few who did. With him gone she felt more lost than ever and tormented by the kinds of questions they had wrestled with in their late night conversations. The kinds of questions that even with her faith and connection to church had plagued her from long before Jesse's death. Was there something after this life, or just nothingness, as she knew Pa had sometimes wondered himself?

Worry and doubt rose up, exhausting her with the twisting and turning of her mind. She shook her head, knowing she was letting her grief get the best of her, leading her wounded thoughts onto paths that probably weren't the healthiest to go down.

Determined to make the most of this time alone before Max and the girls woke and came downstairs, Elena directed her attention back to the gathered papers and photos in front of her. Ma had found many of these things as she was sorting through paperwork and the like for what was needed by the funeral home, putting them in a bag for Elena; now Elena pushed herself out of her chair and stood next to the table, gently pouring out the rest of the bag's contents to make a new pile next to the original heap.

Sifting through these new additions, she smiled at the old black and white photos of Pa in his Marine uniform, but she couldn't bring herself to look at the color shots from later years—pictures from when she was just a baby or a little girl, with others from later on, all the way up to the birth of Violet. She'd wait a while for those, after she'd looked through the rest of the papers and perhaps found something to use in her remembrance talk. She supposed she could come up with the speech for church all on her own, but there was so much to say she didn't really know where to begin.

Pa hadn't been a regular churchgoer, and his beliefs weren't what anyone would have termed traditional. Because of all of their talks, Elena knew he had believed in something greater than himself; he'd recognized the majesty of creation, loved his family, and tried to do good for others in a way that no religion on earth would have criticized as wrong. But it still would feel false to speak about him with the kind of platitudes that often seemed part of formal religious ceremonies. Even though they were having a Catholic Mass for him, she wanted Pa's speech to reflect *him* and what he believed.

As she shuffled through the new pile, a single piece of paper slid partially out, and she pulled it free to look at it more closely. It was worn at the edges, and the print was typed in the old-fashioned letters of Pa's typewriter from before he'd even had a computer. Elena had never seen this piece before.

He had titled it "The Last Day" and had composed it, according to the signature near the end, upon the death of his sister, Lenora, years ago. Elena read it, awareness and appreciation dawning as she realized it was a narrative describing Pa's memories of those moments just after his sister's death. He wrote of the emotions filling that room and his realization that her passing was, "not a sad death or the result of a lost battle, but rather a complete scene of fulfillment, peace, and love."

Elena paused when she was done reading, closing her eyes to keep back the tears that threatened to well up. This was just what she had been looking for. She could use Pa's narrative in her talk to give an insight into the depth and complexity with which he'd viewed life, family, and the natural cycles of this world.

It was both perfect and surprising to Elena.

Pa had always been philosophical about life and death. Their talks and his letters to her over the years often touched on his musings in the matter. But this was the first time she'd seen him address a *specific* person's death, and so eloquently. It was clear from reading this that Pa had had a real gift of conveying feeling and images in words that went far beyond what his letters and emails to her over the years had revealed.

Acknowledging that was bittersweet. She'd learned this new fact about him when the ability to talk to him about it, to learn more about what drove him to write as he did, was gone forever. She couldn't help but wonder how many other talents, thoughts, abilities, and truths existed in her father that she had never known about, close as they'd been.

Now she would never know.

He was gone, just as the child she'd been had dreaded happening to him from the moment she'd understood the permanence of death; all that was left were her memories and the uncertainty of what, if anything, had become of him after his body had finished its physical journey.

Closing her eyes for a moment, Elena tried to put that distressing thought out of her mind. She'd think about it later, not now; she had a task to complete and her emotions were balancing on a fine edge.

Taking a deep breath, she opened her eyes and directed her attention back to the narrative Pa had written, looking at it more closely. She noticed that it began in the third person, using "he," and then about halfway through switched to first person, using "I" as if Pa, in writing it, had at first distanced himself from the event, then embraced his part in what proved to be a moving and affirming moment.

She frowned, worrying about how to best handle this situation. Pa was usually very precise in what he said or wrote. One of his more common refrains when she was growing up was, "Say what you mean, and mean what you say." Should she leave this narrative exactly as Pa wrote it, or change it so that it was all one way or the other?

Part of her thought she should leave it alone, so as not to disrespect Pa's original format. What if he'd had a specific reason for writing it that way? But another part of her wanted to be sure everyone who heard her read this aloud at the funeral could follow along without confusion.

That's when it struck out of the blue . . . something completely unlike anything she'd ever experienced before caused her to drop the paper and stiffen with disbelief.

An effervescent sensation began bubbling around her feet before sweeping up through her body and flooding her with a sense of irresistible exhilaration. The unexpected phenomenon slowed and hovered near the top of her head . . . at the same time that she heard Pa's voice, unmistakable, familiar, and clear as a bell in her mind, saying, "Fix it up for me, will you?"

Before she even realized she was doing it, she broke into a grin and laughed out loud, filled with a sense of light and peace she hadn't felt since before his accident. It overwhelmed her in the most wonderful way, startling her with the speed of its onset and the engulfing, blissful elation it sent coursing through her. She didn't know how, but at a gut level she knew it really *was* Pa who had just answered her unspoken question—only a Pa different from the way he'd been at the end. This Pa was young, healthy, and strong, radiating pure joy.

Too soon the bubbly sensation faded, and Elena began to settle back to reality. Taking another deep breath, she shifted on wobbly legs to sit in the dining room chair nearest her. Then she just gazed around at her mundane, homey surroundings without registering what she was seeing, baffled in a strange and somehow splendid way.

It was difficult to focus again on the task before her; she yearned to bask in the lingering, wonderful impression of what she'd just experienced, but she couldn't help trying to logically process it at the same time. Her thoughts kept churning and working, wanting to make sense of it all, and with that, the euphoria continued to slip away as surely as the tangible sensations that had accompanied it.

She shook her head. This was *crazy*. What the heck was she thinking? She knew she was still deep in the early stages of loss. Maybe her emotions were playing tricks on her. And maybe she wasn't adjusting to Pa's death as well as she'd thought she was.

What had just happened *couldn't* have been real.

She must have conjured it up out of some elemental desire to have Pa back with her, alive and well.

Slowly, methodically, Elena lifted her hands from her lap and rested them on the table next to the pictures and papers in front of her. She shut down her thoughts and forced herself to get back to work, sorting and stacking, even though it seemed harder than before to focus and concentrate. But as the minutes ticked by, she felt more in control and her balance returned. She decided to shrug off what had happened. It had been a fluke. An invention of her grief, that was all. Nothing to get too worked up over. She engrossed herself in her sorting, stopping to put on a pot of coffee and throw in a load of laundry before settling down at the table again to finish.

About a half hour later, Jillian's cat, Socks, came up and rubbed against Elena's legs, purring and winding around her ankles. The cat was saying good morning, Elena knew, as she did most mornings, almost like a signal that Jillian was about to awaken for the day. As if on cue, Elena heard a bumping on the floor upstairs (Jillian's room was right above the dining room) and then the creaking of a door and the sound of bare feet thumping out of the bedroom toward the upstairs bathroom.

She smiled and turned to scoop up the rest of the pictures and papers in their respective piles to put them back in the bag before Jillian came downstairs. Claire liked to sleep in, but Violet would be awake soon, too. It was time to get moving for the day, make breakfast for the girls and Max, and think about when she would go back to the homestead to show Ma what she'd found to use for Pa's funeral.

Pa's funeral.

That little flare of panic and loss swelled again as it did any time she was reminded of her new reality. It was like nodding off for a bit only to jerk awake again, startled and flustered, aware all over again of just how much everything had changed in the scope of her life.

It was normal to feel this, Elena knew, but it still unsettled her and hurt at a fundamental level . . . a deep and aching bruise that you knew would take a long time to heal. So she indulged herself, closing her eyes and clenching her jaw. In the short time she'd have before Jillian came downstairs, she'd let herself sink into the depths of grief and allow a flare of self-pity, giving those emotions room to stretch and breath for a few minutes. It was like releasing a pressure valve: after freeing some of that emotional steam, it would be easier to tuck the feelings back away and better manage them in order to go on with the necessities of her day.

So she opened the door to them now, allowing herself to unleash the question that had been twisting beneath the surface from the very first time she'd ever contemplated losing her father: How was she going to face each day for the rest of her life without Pa to talk to, without him to understand her—to simply *be* with her, connected through the sense of profound understanding of each other that they'd shared?

She had Max of course; she loved him deeply, and she knew he loved her, too. She had her friends, her children, her sisters, and Ma. But with Pa she had shared a special bond that couldn't be replicated with anyone else, and she felt bereft without him.

She let it all come to the surface, wanting to confront it so she could deal with it and shift it into perspective. Dragging in a hitched breath, she let it out in a broken whisper. "Oh, Pa, what am I going to do without you?"

And that's when it happened again, like a bolt out of the blue. Powerful and all encompassing. Undeniable this time. It was as real as if someone had taken her by the shoulders and given her a shake (though not nearly as unpleasant), clearly in response to what she had just felt and spoken.

The same effervescent sensation as before bubbled near her feet, sweeping up even more swiftly through her body this time, with that familiar flood of elation rising to the top of her head as she heard Pa's voice, clear and kind, but with an extra little kick of command that was quintessential Pa.

"Visit the spot."

As before, Elena felt stunned as the same waves of peace, joy, and light washed over her, but this time her brow wrinkled in confusion.

Spot? What *spot? That makes no sense. I don't know any—*

Her hand flew to her mouth, and she sucked in her breath and started to laugh again, only this time through the sting of happy tears.

He means the spot in the woods I found as a little girl and then shared with Jesse so many years later.

Squeezing her eyes shut, she let herself relax into the wonderful feelings, reveling in the sensations and mellow warmth that came in their wake.

Oh, my God. This was real. What she'd experienced twice this morning was *real*.

There was no doubting it this time. She hadn't been thinking about anything even remotely connected to Jesse or the place in the woods where they'd used to meet all those years ago. But Pa had told her during one of the their late-night talks that he thought she should go back there again, hoping it would help bring to full circle what she'd struggled with for the past twenty years.

Now that message had come through loud and clear once more, even though Pa was gone in every sense she'd thought was possible.

"Mama?"

Elena opened her eyes and saw Jillian standing in the dining room entrance. Jillian was rapidly heading toward the hormonal upheaval of being a teenager, but for now she was still mostly little girl, and her face looked soft and sleepy, her hair tousled, with her brows knitted in worry over warm brown eyes that were so like Max's.

"Good morning, sweetheart." Elena held out her arms to her daughter.

Jillian stumbled forward into her embrace, hugging her tight and murmuring against her side, "Why were you crying and smiling at the same time, Mama? It is because of Grandpa? Are you feeling sad and trying to pretend you're not?"

Elena stroked Jillian's long, brown hair, using her other hand to swipe beneath her own eyes. "I was crying because of Grandpa, yes, and I miss him, but I was smiling because I'm not as sad anymore as I was."

"Why not?" Jillian tipped her head up and Elena smiled more deeply as she bent to press a kiss on Jillian's forehead.

"I guess because even though I can't see him anymore the way I used to, I think he's doing just fine where he is."

"Because he's in heaven, right?"

"Mmhmm," Elena answered, nodding, unable to formulate any more words at the moment.

Jillian untangled herself from Elena's embrace and took a step back, cocking her arm and putting her hand on her hip in a way that reminded Elena all too much of Claire. Or Jen when she was feeling feisty. Or maybe even Zippy. "Mama, I have to ask you something. I know we get to have chocolate on Easter morning . . . but can Grandpa have chocolate for breakfast whenever he wants in heaven? Like *real* chocolate and not just Cocoa Puffs or something?"

Elena tried not to laugh, instead raising one brow and looking skyward as if to consider the question. She cleared her throat and looked back at Jillian before answering, "Grandpa liked chocolate a lot, but I'm not so sure he'd want it for breakfast. He tended to like oatmeal with brown sugar and raisins. Or Grandma's homemade waffles with maple syrup and a side of scrambled eggs and bacon."

"That sounds good." Jillian unconsciously rubbed her stomach. "But what about never needing to sleep, or jumping on clouds, or flying? Can Grandpa do anything he wants there?"

The questions made Elena smile again, even as they sent a little prick of pain into her heart. What she'd experienced today was still too new and fragile to help her control those aching emotions yet; she needed time to process it all. Contemplating Pa's existence in a way she couldn't define—thinking of him in a place that felt so separated from her—was difficult. In the meantime she would do her best to keep it all in perspective like he'd taught her to do.

"I can't tell you for sure what heaven is like for Grandpa, Chicken Little." Elena paused as she remembered again the rush of joy she'd felt twice this morning. "But I think the universe is a pretty magical place, and maybe what comes next is bigger than our minds can understand."

Jillian nodded as she wrapped her arms around her mother again and looking up at her, her eyes sincere. "That's cool, Mom, but I have one more question."

"What is it, honey?"

"If I want to tell Grandpa something and I just say it in my head, do you think he can he hear me, now that he's up in heaven?"

"Oh, yes, sweetheart." Elena laughed with a sense of relief and joy as she pulled her daughter close in a hug, knowing that she was telling her the absolute truth. "I think he hears you loud and clear."

(Pa's writing)

Epilogue

Father's Day
June 15

Unable are the loved to die . . . for Love is Immortality.

- Emily Dickinson

The yard and the house were filled with people, dozens of them, all related by either blood or marriage.

Elena scanned the hubbub and festivities from where she stood at the kitchen window, taking in the organized chaos that was happening in the back yard—of cleaning and heating the gas grills over near the red shed, teens and pre-teens trying to master croquet off to the side where the willows once stood, and general horsing around on the rest of the lawn as the younger kids played tag and the adults who were outside worked to set up three long picnic tables for the meal to come.

Inside, food preparations were well underway. A big bowl of Ma's famous macaroni salad was already tucked on the main shelf of the fridge, while Anne, Jen, and Kat were trying to figure out how to fit the potato salad, antipasto, and fruit salad in there as well, since most of the available space was already taken up by the tray of raw burger patties and hotdogs, and another of marinated chicken breasts waiting to be grilled. Zippy had even come home again for the weekend and was busy in the yard, entertaining a group of the grandkids with a game of charades.

It might have been an ordinary Father's Day gathering, the same in so many ways (aside from the ever-changing number of people attending) as all the others held here on this day for more than forty years.

Except it wasn't the same, and it never would be again.

This was a last hurrah . . . the final Father's Day celebration to be held at the homestead, in honor of Pa.

During the dinner the family hosted at the American Legion after Pa's funeral, Jen had brought up the idea, suggesting it as a way to honor

Pa that would be uplifting instead of sad. It was more suited to him than the wake and funeral services, which had been beautiful but somber by necessity. From the personal readings Elena and her sisters had offered, to the Marine Corps honor guard and trumpet playing "Taps" for Pa, the services had been poignant, moving . . . and agonizing. No one wanted that feeling to be the family's last memory of Pa in their lives. And there had been nothing Pa had enjoyed more than his family gathering together.

So here they all were, enjoying the day, the beautiful outdoors, and each other. All day long, Elena had fought back tears. It had been more difficult than she had anticipated, coming together for this day. Not because of what was happening, but because, as fitting as it was, it brought into sharper focus again all they were missing.

Just then she felt a tap on her shoulder.

"Ellie, I need to give you something."

It was Ma. She'd been doing all right, everything considered, though she, too, had weeping sessions most days (often when she was alone in her room). After the funeral and Zippy's departure back to LA, Anne had stayed with her for a week, then Melanie, and then Kat. Jen was staying this week, and Elena was looking forward to her turn soon. For the first couple of months at least, no one wanted to leave Ma alone. She was slowly coming to terms with Pa's death, but it would be a long, slow process to find a new normal after building her world around the man who was the love of her life.

"What is it, Ma?"

Ma's eyes looked a little moist, but she smiled and motioned Elena to follow her back to the bedroom she and Pa had shared for so many decades. Ma had taken to sleeping upstairs in one of the girls' old rooms, finding it too painful to occupy this room right now.

As they walked in, it looked the same as it always had to Elena, with its gleaming wooden dressers, neatly made bed, and crisp curtains. All of Pa's things were still here, too: his shoes and sneakers lined along the floor of the open closet, and his sweaters, shirts, pants folded over hangers, with a selection of the suspenders he'd take to wearing in later years, all still hanging where he'd left them.

Ma walked over to Pa's dresser and opened the top drawer. She'd been doing some cleaning and organizing of documents and papers and Elena saw them stacked in piles on the top of the dresser and bed.

Reaching in, Ma pulled out a regular business-sized envelope, then turned and handed it to Elena.

"I found this with some of your father's other things in a file I sorted this week. He must have put it in there knowing I would see it and give to you.

Elena's heart gave a bittersweet twist as she took the envelope and saw her father's handwriting scrawled across it.

Elena, open after trip to Peaceful Glen.

She looked at her mother in confusion.

"What is it?"

"I don't know, Ellie. I just know your father wanted you to have it." She smiled again and touched Elena's arm, gripping her warmly. Elena put her hand over Ma's, relishing the comfort but realizing that her mother's hand was older now, too, with threading blue veins showing under skin that was still soft but thinner and brushed with age spots.

Time kept marching on and none of them could do anything but try to keep up with the beat.

"I suppose I should open it up." Elena felt stinging behind her eyes as she held the envelope tight. It was a last message from Pa. His final gift to her.

"Do you want to just stay here in the bedroom? I can close the door on my way out to give you a little privacy."

Elena almost said yes, but then another thought popped into her mind, unbidden but clear and perfect. *I should go to the spot like Pa wanted me to and read it there.*

She looked at Ma, blinking back her tears and swallowing before she answered, "If you don't mind, I'll just head out into the woods for a bit. I won't be gone long. But I think that would be the best place to read this."

Ma's eyes widened just a little as she seemed to realize what Elena meant, and she nodded. "Go ahead, honey. We'll be fine here until you get back. There's still another hour or so until we'll be eating."

"Thanks, Ma."

Elena gave her a quick kiss on the cheek and then slipped through the kitchen and out the back door. She cut across the front yard and ducked into the side woods, making her way around and behind the little camp and into the main woods that way, to avoid the full back yard where she might have had to explain where she was going.

Her heart pounded slow and steady and then more swiftly as she made her way through the lush woodland, crunching over last year's dead leaves and branches mixed with new undergrowth. It looked much the same as it had the last time she'd been out here over twenty years ago.

In a few moments, she lost sight of the house and the people in the yard, going deeper into the woods at a leftward angle. Her heart rose in her throat as she approached the spot that had been almost centered between the homestead and Jesse's house, trying to prepare herself to see it again after all this time and all that had happened.

Clutching the letter tight against her, she took the last few steps and entered their little clearing between two of the tall, thicker trees that had lined the spot and made it such a private haven.

And then she gasped.

The glade was transformed.

Instead of a bare, sun-dappled clearing, it had become a colorful garden, interspersed with the dark greens and earthy browns of the woods. There were iris beds in a variety of hues, including Pa's favorite blue and whites with their ruffled edges. She saw puff balls of giant lavender allium, creamy lily of the valley with a few late wild violets tucked nearby, spiky, hot pink and dark purple asters with sunny centers, feathery white astilbe, and low-growing carpets of blue phlox, moss pink, and golden-yellow alyssum rolling gently over the rocks that formed borders and groupings all around.

And the stone-lined garden of stinkpots that Jesse had made. Although the blooms had already gone by for the season, his little garden was still right there where he had created it.

Elena felt happiness bubble up in her chest, mixing with tears now so that she was both crying and laughing as she made her way to their old rock seat off to the right of the clearing. Dropping down onto it, she gazed around her, awestruck at the splendor Pa had created here. He must have worked on it for years, and she'd never known. But it seemed so fitting: a grand but entirely natural way to commemorate someone special.

For her, now, it memorialized *two* special people who would live in her heart for as long as she drew breath.

The breeze whispered over leafy branches high above her around the edge of the clearing, causing sunlight and shadows to shift across her face. After another few moments of quiet spent taking in the verdant scents and hearing a cardinal's trilling song punctuated by the raucous caws of a crow, Elena looked down at her lap. Pa's letter rested there, and she ran her fingers over its smooth contours before finally opening it up to read.

January 10, 2008

Dear Elena,

Today's date is only important in that it is your birthday. So happy birthday, my darling daughter. I decided to write this now, since I don't know what the outcome of my aneurysm surgery will be in a couple weeks. Just in case it doesn't work out, I want you to have these words (and maybe give you something to think about me) when I'm gone. I'll try to see if there is any other way to touch base with you like we talked about before during some of our late night discussions, but if all else fails, you'll have this. Whether you're reading this letter soon or years from now, the feelings and thoughts I want to convey are still the same.

I want you to know that life is to be lived and experienced in all its good and not-so-good. Notice I didn't say "bad." There can be bad things that happen and even bad people, but it's how we manage those things and people that makes us or maybe even reveals who we really are. Even if you're lonely sometimes after I'm gone, don't let the black cloud win. It will blow away sooner or later, and the sun will shine again.

I hope that you decide to take my advice and visit the old spot you and Jesse had in the woods. It may look a little different now, but I think you will understand why when you see it. Sometimes the best way to remember people is to live your life—to *do* something and move forward to show what you feel about them.

Don't spend too much time grieving for me, Elena. I know you're probably a little sad as you're reading this, since that means I'm dead and you're having to learn how to go on in a new way. I would be sad if you didn't miss me, so I won't tell you not to, but I will tell you to keep on living. The world is full of beautiful music, flowers, places, and experiences. Enjoy it all as much as you can. Just remember it's the people in your life that make it worthwhile.

You know, having a big family was a choice your mother and I made. It wasn't always easy, but nothing truly worthwhile is. That decision has provided the real meaning in my life. You have your own family and your connections still with your mother and (if she goes before me) your sisters to help you through the days to come. If you had none of those, you would still have friends you could cultivate love and shared understanding with. People and memories, not things, are what's important in the end. Nothing else matters as much as that.

And remember this: If there is one constant in my life, Elena, it is that I love you.

Love,

Pa

Elena read the letter over again, two more times, still crying but unable to stop smiling, too. It was so like Pa not to leave her hanging in any way. To make sure she was covered, emotionally and otherwise, when the time came to face the world without him to talk to anymore.

She leaned back against the tree flanking her rock with the letter in her lap, just soaking in the beauty around her. The tears dried on her cheeks, but she kept smiling. Pa was here, in the flowers he'd planted for Jesse and for her. He was in the breeze and the sunshine, in the memories that bloomed inside of her and in the bustling tumble of family back at the homestead eating, drinking, playing, and remembering together.

A kind of peace settled over her then, the deep and unshakeable realization that Pa was part of something far bigger now than he'd ever been able to be when he was confined in his physical body. And it was the same for everyone who left this life. Part of the mystery and miracle of creation was in that alteration of self from containment to complete freedom. Energy didn't just disappear. It could change, but the laws of science indicated that it was impossible for it to vanish.

Her time to make that transition would come, too, the secret of its arrival as hidden to her as it was to everyone. In the meantime, she needed to live her life and make the most of it, filling her seconds, hours, and days not with regrets and the bitterness of grief, but with the people she loved, honoring what was past and making new memories.

Pushing up off the rock to stand again, Elena smiled and looked around her one last time. She took in a full breath, exhaled, and blew a kiss, sending it through the breeze and into the rippling waves of the universe.

Then turning her face toward the faint sounds of laughter and life still happening in the yard beyond the woods, she took a bold step out of the clearing and headed for home.

THE END

(Pa's favorite iris)

(The "real" Pa, 2005)

(The "real" Pa and Ma, together over the years)

Author's Note

As I wrote it, this novel turned into a kind of love letter to my own family. It's true. But it's also a love letter to all families . . . to friendships, to connections, and to the enduring grace of love.

It is entirely a work of fiction, even though some of the events, especially those depicted in the "past" scenes, are based upon real events or situations that happened to me or members of my family. The only two characters who bear any strong resemblance to the "real" people who inspired them are Pa and Ma . . . and they remain fictional composites that couldn't possibly do justice to the real versions!

I invented the radio broadcasts after being inspired by some old Adirondack radio programs one of my sisters told me about hearing, when she and her family rented a rustic camp up in Forestport, NY. She talked about the homey, old-fashioned tenor of the broadcasts, and so I tried to replicate that in my novel, adding in some of the personality and style of the North Country as I knew it growing up. By the way, I researched all of the "This Day in History" segments, so to the best of my knowledge, all of those entries are accurate.

There really is a family homestead, and I still visit as often as I can. The photos in the book are all mine (which the exception of the red trillium, credited to a friend of the same sister who camped in Forestport, Robert Johnstone), and all reflect actual places that inspired various scenes and fictional locations in the novel. I added them into the text because I like the personal touch they give the narrative, and I hope you enjoyed them, too.

Also, I want you to know that with the exception of the very last letter (which I crafted in about twenty minutes in what seemed to be a flow of words inspired by something beyond myself), all the letters in this novel were written to me in real life by my late father, David L. Reed. I changed minor things like the date or a few names, but they are his words. He was indeed a man of deep insight, intelligence, humor, kindness, and love . . . a man of many talents, some of which, like his writing ability, remained mostly undercover during his lifetime. We girls and Ma used to tell him once in a while that he really ought to write a book, with all the interesting stories he had and the way he could tell them, but he would always just sort of chuckle and shift the conversation to something else. He never was one for the spotlight. It is my pleasure in this book, therefore, to share some of his thoughts and writing with the world at last in published form.

And lastly but not least, I have to affirm that the interplay of family members, the emotions, squabbling, and loving backdrop the fictional "Wright" girls experienced, is based entirely in reality. The values we learned, the insights we gained, and the love shared between parents, daughters, and sisters really happened. The world may be a different place now than it was in decades past, but there is always room for truth, hope, and of course, love. I hope this book has offered some meaning in that regard and perhaps provided you with some moments of pleasure along the way.

As always, thanks for coming along on the journey.

—MRM